EMBRACE
THE SERPENT

EMBRACE
THE SERPENT

Marilyn T. Quayle
and
Nancy T. Northcott

CROWN PUBLISHERS, INC.

NEW YORK

Published by Crown Publishers, Inc., 201 East 50th Street, New York, New
York 10022. Member of the Crown Publishing Group.

CROWN is a trademark of Crown Publishers, Inc.

Manufactured in the United States of America

Library of Congress Cataloging-in-Publication Data
Quayle, Marilyn T.
Embrace the serpent / Marilyn T. Quayle and Nancy T. Northcott.
p.   cm.
I. Northcott, Nancy T.   II. Title.
PS3567.U24E4   1991
811'.54—dc20   91-34804
CIP

ISBN 0-517-58822-6

10   9   8   7   6   5   4   3   2   1

First Edition

In honor of our parents, Warren Samuel Tucker and the late Mary Alice Craig Tucker.

Family is the wellspring from which flows faith, integrity, compassion, confidence, industry, selflessness, spirit—the strength of the soul and the basis of national strength. When family fails, the nation falls.

We gratefully acknowledge the kindness and assistance of Chris Auditore, our computer genius; Bob Barnett; Dick Darman; Rae Evans; Mary Lee Hoge; Lynn Reese; John and Reba Shipp; José Sorzano; and our siblings and their families: Jim and Sherry Tucker, Janet and Bob Hoard, Sally Tucker and Bill and DeeDee Tucker.

Our special gratitude is to our families: Tom and Dan; Melissa, Craig, Tucker, Amy, Ben, Tommy and Corinne, who put up with much, not stoically, but with understanding and good humor.

EMBRACE
THE SERPENT

Fidel Castro raised his arms high and threw back his head, a god basking in the adoration he so richly deserved. His speech had been superb, as always. His voice might have been low, his topics repetitive, but his presence had been hypnotic and commanding. Thirty years of absolute power had done nothing to dim either his magnetism or his vitality.

Now as the acclaim of the ministers subsided, he strode to the head of the table, where he lit the physician-prohibited cigar he allowed himself only at these meetings. With a contented smile, he examined the glowing tip and, drawing deeply, settled back in his chair. After a glance at his taster, he reached for the tumbler of rum that a servant was presenting him.

As his hand touched the glass, he stiffened and jerked upright. Splashes of amber liquid spread darkly on his uniform. The still-glowing cigar jutted rigidly from between his clenched teeth. His fingers began clawing frantically at his chest.

Then his body went limp. Slowly, agonizingly slowly, it sagged out of the chair and settled on the marble floor. His teeth finally released the cigar, which began a macabre journey, rolling haltingly over his beard, then his chest, finally stopping against a flaccid hand. A fine line of smoke continued to thread its way to the ceiling.

The body became part of a frozen tableau, with only the column of smoke, the spreading pool of rum and a curious fly showing any life. The moment, lasting only a few seconds, vibrated through the air with a grim life of its own.

The servant, his mouth hanging open in horror, pressed the drinks tray to his chest like a shield. The crash of splintering glass and the drunken roll of an unbroken bottle across the floor echoed obscenely through the room.

The paralysis ended.

Chairs scraped, one banging against the floor as it fell over backward. Shouts, commands, mutterings—all collided in the charged air, the noises blending incomprehensibly.

A frantic guard knelt beside the body, ripped back the shirt and Kevlar bulletproof vest and exposed a chest unblemished by any wound. He pressed his lips against the cyanotic ones, forcing air into already cooling lungs.

Though seemingly shrunken now, the body continued its absolute domination. All eyes avoided it but were drawn to it irresistibly, at once both fascinated and repelled. Betrayed by the heart many Cubans doubted it possessed, it controlled every thought and action, somehow as profoundly powerful now as in life. But for the first time it was expendable, an instrument only, to be used to cement another's power.

Fidel Castro had suffered the ultimate and irreversible insult: death. From the fawning praise of sycophants he'd fallen to embrace a dirty floor. The magnetism and vitality had vanished; all that remained was a torn uniform below a scraggly beard littered with fading embers and ashes.

It is true that liberty is precious—so precious that it must be rationed.

LENIN

Day One

Wednesday
January 25

4:08 *P.M.*
The pantry next to the conference room
El Palacio de la Revolución
Havana, Cuba

María Estafa whirled toward the noise, a limp dish towel hanging from her hands. Her eyes huge in her blanched face, she stared at the door to the conference room.

A crash. A shattering crash. Something was wrong, she knew. Something was dreadfully wrong.

She gasped and her hands flew to her mouth as the door slammed open, banging against the wall and propelling a stumbling Edmundo, still clutching the drinks tray, into the stifling room. The air immediately reeked of the rum staining his uniform.

"El Presidente," "cigar," "dead." These words were clear to María, as were the shrill protestations of his innocence, but little else made sense. His eyes were unfocused; his appearance, almost demented. He kept babbling, unaware both of María's questions and of her furious shaking of his shoulders. Finally, with a ragged sigh, he slumped to the floor.

María ran to the conference room door and pressed her ear

3

against it. What was going on? Shouts, commands, confusion. She could distinguish no words, nothing that made sense.

She ran back to Edmundo's side and slid the towel under his head. He cringed at her touch before recognizing her and sagging once again onto the floor. María turned to the sink, grabbed a glass and filled it with water, spilling much of it in her haste. When she bent down, Edmundo struggled onto one elbow and drank greedily. Color slowly returned to his ashen cheeks.

"Edmundo, please, please control yourself," María pleaded, clutching his trembling shoulder. "Answer me. What has happened? Tell me. Now. What has happened?"

Understanding finally returned to his eyes. He grasped her hand. "Castro . . . dead . . . He's dead. The rum . . . He took it, didn't drink, really didn't drink, dropped it. Dead. Embers burned his beard. . . ."

María placed her fingers against his lips, stopping the torrent of words. "Castro's dead? Really dead? Can you be sure?"

Edmundo nodded in affirmation, trying clumsily to stand.

María's heart sang even though her face remained as expressionless as always. Thank God! Her prayers, repeated so often and so fervently, had been answered. Cuba might at last have a chance. Their years of labor, all their years of danger and frustration, might finally be at an end. She had to get the news to Alejandro.

She felt a tentative pressure on her arm. Edmundo was leaning against the counter next to her, a look of entreaty in his eyes. She patted him reassuringly on the shoulder, speaking to him gently, as to a child.

"You mustn't be afraid. You've done no wrong."

They both knew this statement to be absurd. In Castro's Cuba, guilt was seldom considered when punishment was meted. Nonetheless, Edmundo stopped the frantic clutching of his hands, even though his body continued its sporadic waves of trembling.

"Let's go clean ourselves," María said. "Perhaps you can find a fresh uniform."

This prospect was unlikely—extra uniforms had long since vanished—but at least Edmundo would be distracted, allowing time to banish the most immediate horrors from his mind.

María led him into the hall, one hand on his elbow, her small, spare frame helping to support him. Both shuffled in their habitual way, heads lowered, eyes on the floor. No one stopped them. The soldiers were still disorganized, trying to make sense out of the senseless confusion surrounding them, unsure of what was happening, even less sure of what to do.

María noted a slight movement to her right. A seldom used side door to El Palacio was just closing behind one of the guards. The auburn hair curling under his cap made his identity certain: Sergeant Carlos Campos. Why was he leaving? she wondered, continuing down the hall. Where was he going? And why now? Alejandro would be interested.

Leaving Edmundo, she went on to the cramped, fetid cubicle that provided a few minutes of solitude for her. Everyone avoided this room. The plumbing hadn't worked for years, and the odor was worse than foul. Some days she wasn't sure the privacy was worth the stench, but today she blessed the isolation.

Barely opening the cracked and dirty window at the end of the cubicle, she surveyed the sliver of sidewalk below. Surprisingly, she could detect no unusual activity. Only a few people were in view, and they appeared intent on their own business. Apparently word of Castro's death had not yet filtered outside the building.

Wouldn't Castro be furious to know how cavalierly his death was being treated? María thought, smiling involuntarily. He was almost forgotten already, only a peripheral force in the events about to unfold.

She slipped out a small piece of paper, then closed the window against it, pinning it in place. From experience she knew the jagged white square wouldn't be readily visible from the street, but when Alejandro or one of their compatriots made his rounds, he'd be looking for this signal. Although the leaders of La Causa knew her identity, only Alejandro knew how to contact her after the signal was given. With any luck, he'd be waiting for her when she took out the trash. This was one message she wanted to deliver to him personally.

The paper signal had been needed only twice before, once when a military coup had been uncovered by Castro and once when Castro had seemed gravely ill. Today's news was much more valuable, breathtaking in its significance. At the thought, María's breath caught in her throat. The miracle had finally happened. Praise the Lord! Castro was dead!

She longed to see Alejandro, to share her excitement immediately. How wonderful to be able to throw open the window and shout down to him. He'd be as joyful as she. Surely this would mark the beginning of freedom in Cuba. Grinning, she spread her arms wide and twirled in the cramped space. Glorious hopes chased each other through her mind.

After a final exuberant wave of her arms, she stood motionless, her eyes narrowing. How could she be wasting time when so much must be done. Who knew what already might have happened. She must find a way into the conference room, and quickly at that. Only then could she learn just what the ministers were planning. She had no way of knowing when she'd be able to meet with Alejandro, she thought as she opened the door to the corridor, but when she did, she wanted to be able to tell him everything that was happening in El Palacio. She'd spent the last four years waiting for just this moment.

Her head lowered, her heavy black braid almost motionless where it hung down her back, she shuffled to the pantry. Her body quivered under the scrutiny of the soldiers lining the hall. Already security was tightening. When would she be allowed to take out the trash and tell Alejandro her news? Or, sobering thought, would she be allowed to leave at all?

Time enough to deal with that later. Pushing away the fear, she entered the pantry.

A short time later, Edmundo was ordered into the conference room. In less than a minute, he scurried back and broke the seal on a new bottle of rum, putting it and tumblers on his tray.

"I'll take it in," María said.

Relieved, he let her.

As easy as that, she thought, pushing open the door with her shoulder.

Several soldiers standing inside the room glanced at her. However, the ministers were too preoccupied with their problems and strategies even to realize that she, not Edmundo, was serving them. She'd be able to stay, at least for the moment. So far she was safe.

"Never! I'll never agree to that!" one minister screamed, slamming his fist on the table.

"You've no choice," another shouted back. No one else seemed interested in those two, engaged as they were in their own confrontations.

Taking a deep breath to help steady her racing heart, María surreptitiously surveyed the room. Her breath froze in her throat: Castro was laid out neatly on a couch under the windows.

The final proof, María thought, exultant. Castro really was dead.

But why was his body still in the room? The fetor of death was naggingly pervasive, subtly nauseating. Her mouth tingled with bile even as her mind rejoiced. Whom would they order to clean the body? she wondered, repulsed at the thought.

Resolutely conquering the shaking which threatened to engulf her, she turned away and began removing debris from the table. As her hands steadied, she became aware of the tension in the room, its presence almost visible through the cigar smoke.

Arturo Registra, Minister of the Political Police and Vice-Chairman of the Council of Ministers—Raul Castro was Chairman, and where was Raul? María wondered—was slowly taking control of the meeting, using his piercing voice to dominate the inchoate rantings of the others. Even now, while he brought a semblance of order to the chaos, his body remained motionless, as implacable as his mind. An omnipresent unlit cigar bobbed between his lips, his sharp ferret teeth gnawing continuously at the end, shredding good Havana tobacco, which disappeared miraculously, as always leaving his uniform unsoiled. María had decided years before that Registra must have a cast-iron stomach to match his cast-iron heart.

She wasn't surprised that Registra was getting his way with the ministers. He was thoroughly repugnant but dangerously clever, two traits well known to the numerous Cubans he'd abused in his position as head of the Secret Police. María had been fascinated by glimpses of his cunning. He liked to sit back quietly, waiting for the opportune moment to expose an adversary's weakness. Without warning, he'd act, destroying the other ruthlessly. A more blatantly vicious man might exist in this age of vicious men, but María had never heard of one.

Castro had been equally evil, but he'd taken pains to hide his amorality behind a facade of charm. Registra employed no such cosmetics.

María had watched Castro play with Registra, encouraging him to destroy mutual enemies but never allowing Registra enough power to be a threat to Castro himself.

But why was César Valles acquiescing to Registra's leadership? María wondered as she wiped up another spilled drink. Maybe Registra's position as vice-chairman was the reason although she doubted that Valles would have let that stop him, certainly not if that look of loathing she'd thought she'd caught once was indeed true. Early on, she'd recognized Valles's cunning and hadn't been fooled by his pleasant, self-deprecating manner. Another one who knew how to hide behind his public image, she thought.

Hadn't Castro liked Valles as much as he liked anyone, more than most? And hadn't even Castro seemed curiously blind or indifferent to Valles's cunning? Appearances to the contrary, Castro may have had his eye on Valles, biding his time. María wouldn't have been surprised. Castro's survival was testimony to his wily—and wary—manipulation of others. Regardless, Valles had thrived under Castro's scrutiny. The question remained, would he thrive under Raul's? From overheard smatterings of conversation, María realized that everyone was considering Raul and how to survive a Raul Castro presidency.

5:20 P.M.
Russian military base
San Antonio de los Baños, Cuba

"Castro's dead?" asked General Vasily Basilov, supreme commander of Russian troops in Cuba, triumph and incredulity mixed equally in his voice. That egomaniac was finally dead! he thought.

Sergeant Carlos Campos—María had been right in thinking he'd left El Palacio during the confusion following Castro's death—nodded. With rising excitement, Basilov listened to Campos. So much had changed for the Russians in the last few years. Maybe Castro's death signaled a chance for renewed international preeminence.

"One minute he seemed fine," Campos said, "and then he just slid to the floor. I was afraid to stay in the room any longer for fear I wouldn't be able to leave if I waited, but my guess is he had a heart attack. No mark was visible on his body, and he'd had nothing to eat or drink, so he wasn't poisoned."

"The cigar?" Basilov asked.

"Possible but improbable. Since no one immediately seized control, I'd say natural causes."

"So no one was prepared?"

"No," Campos said. "Registra was trying to take advantage of the confusion, but he seemed as stunned as the rest. Valles wasn't doing anything at all, just watching."

"Good," Basilov said. "We'll put our plan in motion as soon as we receive permission from Moscow. I'll inform them immediately. Did anyone see you leave?"

"No. Too much else was happening for anyone to care about me. Besides, no one notices a guard. Getting back inside undetected may not be as easy. They're bound to start questioning everyone's movements. One consideration—events were moving so quickly that I doubt anyone else thought to leave. Nor would they have wanted to."

"Good. I'll order all phone lines on the island disabled so that word doesn't leak out before we're ready. Have our man suggest that everyone remain in El Palacio at least until tomorrow morning. That should give us enough time. Anything else?"

Campos shook his head.

"Then return to your post."

Campos saluted and left.

Even before the door closed, Basilov was on the phone.

"Castro's dead?" his superior in Moscow asked after a considerable pause. He had been roused from a heavy sleep and was only slowly realizing the magnitude of the news. "How providential."

"Then we have your permission to implement our contingency plan?" Basilov asked, wondering even as he spoke how the new order in his own country would have affected even this most sensible plan.

"Now, let's not be hasty. No one's made a move, you say?"

"That's correct," Basilov answered, his head pounding with suppressed anger. "But—"

"No," the officer interrupted. "We mustn't be precipitous. Too much is at stake. I'll get back with you."

What idiots! Basilov fumed while he waited for the return call. His brows were creased in anger; his eyes, hard. Why couldn't they make even the most obvious decisions? Now was the time to move quickly and decisively. Now might be the only time they'd ever have. So much had changed since Eastern Europe had been lured by the West. The USSR had been sadly torn asunder, its power emasculated. Basilov's face lengthened with these dreary thoughts. Trying to appease the West in order to get money . . . selling materiel, secrets, prestige, anything to raise even more money . . . And their unholy alliance with . . .

The phone rang. Moscow. The Executive Council would have to meet, Basilov was told, before any action could be contemplated. Basilov politely agreed to the delays, then slammed down the receiver, a look of disgust distorting his mouth. Stomping on the buzzer under his foot, he summoned his aide, Alexis Tuporov.

"Our leaders were pleased with our report of Castro's death," Basilov began as Tuporov stood at attention before his desk. Only the gruffness in his voice betrayed his anger. "A thorn removed and no blame attached to us. All agree that Castro has provided his greatest service to the motherland by dying." Tuporov nodded appreciatively as Basilov waved him to a chair. "Now our man can easily be placed in power and with no hint of our complicity."

Basilov chose his words carefully. He wasn't about to say anything that could be used against him later; he hadn't reached his present eminence through carelessness. No, Tuporov must be prevented from propounding the wrong ideas to the wrong person, especially now with allegiances in such disarray. Basilov shuddered as he thought of the fate of so many of his contemporaries. These last years had been frighteningly brutal as well as capricious.

"For us, the importance of Cuba has changed dramatically since

Operation Romanov was first proposed. Because of its unexpectedness, Castro's death has forced the leadership to debate the proper course. The President himself must make the final decision."

Basilov paused to control his rising contempt, a contempt fueled by his own vulnerability.

"It's late in Moscow," he resumed more temperately, "and no one wants to be responsible for waking our leader needlessly."

"But surely they want us to go ahead!" Tuporov exclaimed, unable to control his dismay any longer. He was young and had had less practice than Basilov at hiding his feelings. "After all, they approved our plan months ago and for just such a situation. Surely, controlling Cuba is even more important now." Tuporov began to stutter slightly, a sure sign of his agitation. "N-N-Nestotovski's a soldier. He at least must realize the importance of acting swiftly."

"I'm sure he does," Basilov replied, "but the rest remain uncertain."

Both men had expected such a delay, would've been surprised had it been otherwise. No Russian relished making a decision; the penalty for a wrong one didn't bear considering. Even so, they'd hoped that such wouldn't be the case this time. The contingency plan was well conceived, and they'd already approved it, hadn't they! Why was their formerly well-ordered life now so fraught with uncertainty, even timidity, especially now, with such an opportunity before them?

"We should know their decision by midnight Cuban time, that is if the President's informed as soon as he awakens."

Basilov hit the desk with his open hand, rattling pencils and overturning the picture of his wife and daughter which he took with him everywhere. "We must control Cuba. It's our only foothold in this hemisphere as well as the finest aircraft carrier in the Atlantic, a tremendous strategic advantage. With the right backing, we could keep this island and regain some of our power and influence. Certainly, no one could ever get a real carrier so close to the United States. Their people would be appalled at the thought. Fortunately for us, they've closed their eyes to the similarity. They've even balked at developing their defensive capabilities. So much the better."

Snubbing out the bitter-smelling Russian cigarette he habitually smoked, Basilov put his hands behind his head, lacing his fingers into his short, graying-blond hair and stretching his long legs onto the desk. "With that arrogant Cuban dead, we can control the drug and arms traffic. What a magnificent coup for the motherland! And just when we need an influx of money."

For a moment, Basilov felt vague misgivings. Money was such a problem these days. Surely the Russian leadership would continue to receive whatever funds were necessary to secure Cuba irrevocably. After all, Cuba could be the final ingredient to their financial rehabilitation. But what was he thinking! All that would be taken care of. He was getting as paranoid as the old men in Moscow. Even they would realize that control of Cuba was of supreme importance.

Basilov looked into the future, a smile playing at the corners of his mouth. "And think of the United States, even more corrupted by drugs, providing the money for their own destruction. Just the prescription to put us back in a position of world power."

He sat up in his chair, the palms of his hands pressing on the papers in front of him.

"I don't care what they say, we're at least going to disable the Cuban phone lines. We can't let the news get out before we're ready. And have the troops stand by. We may need to move quickly."

5:30 P.M.
The Capitol Building
Washington, D.C.

A trim blond woman strode purposefully down the tunnel that connects the Hart and Dirksen Senate Office buildings with the Senate side of the Capitol. She barely noticed the passing subway train. Instead, Cynthia Novitsky mentally checked that she'd done everything necessary for the coming interview. Her boss, Senator Robert Hawkins Grant from Georgia, was going to be interviewed for an Atlanta television news show via a live satellite feed. All was in place, she decided. She'd done her part. And she certainly needn't worry about the Senator; he was good at these things, a natural communicator. Now, if the Senate would cooperate and give him a big enough window between votes to get him over to the television studio in the Hart Building, all would be fine. He had to be on the air at exactly six-ten. Satellite time waited for no man and certainly for no late vote.

Cynthia ran up the two flights of stairs to the doors leading to the Senate floor. She flipped open her notebook and jotted down a reminder to the Senator that he did indeed have a date with a home state television station, ripped out the sheet, folded it and presented it to a Senate page, who would locate the Senator and hand it to him on the Senate floor.

As she waited, Cynthia looked around at the ornate gilt walls and the portraits of the five former Senators which hung there. Interesting-looking men, all of them, she thought, four of whom— Henry Clay, Daniel Webster, John C. Calhoun and Robert Taft— she recognized easily. Of Robert M. La Follette she remembered little. From Wisconsin, wasn't he? She couldn't be sure. Regardless of any later fame, they'd all found a home outside the Senate chamber, where in life they'd served with distinction. What a grand old place this was, Cynthia thought, smiling. Awe-inspiring. Even after fourteen years on the Hill, she found it humbling to be surrounded daily by these marvelous pieces of history.

She thought back to her first meeting with Senator Grant. This newly elected Senator had called unexpectedly, asking her to interview for a job as his administrative assistant. She'd been flattered that others must have recommended her though she wasn't really in the market for a new position. She enjoyed her job as minority counsel for the Senate Commerce Committee.

When she'd arrived at the Senator's office, he'd been businesslike at first, obviously doing his best to conform to his role as Senator. Equally obvious, he'd been somewhat uncomfortable in that role. She'd answered his questions with matching solemnity.

Suddenly, in the middle of a question, he'd grinned at her, his straight teeth white in his black face. "I'm not much good at this polite dialogue, am I? Instead, let me tell you my real feelings." He'd leaned forward, his eyes intent. "I never planned on running for the Senate, but I realized that I didn't have the right to complain about government if, when given the opportunity to serve, I turned it down. Still, now that I'm here, I'm not at all sure where to start. Kind of like the kid on the merry-go-round stretching for the brass ring, knowing he can never reach it. Only I did. Now I have to figure out what to do with it. And to be honest, I'd like to make that ring gold, not brass."

Cynthia remembered finding herself drawn in by his graciousness and gentle humor. "I followed your campaign," she had said. "The former Senator certainly made it interesting."

The Democratic incumbent had gone into the race the favorite. Then, three weeks before the election, the all-too-typical story of the politician caught with his pants down had been uncovered by the media. The joke on the Hill at the time had been that the Senator was superstitious; he never got involved with anyone under thirteen. Both the joke and the Senator had made Cynthia feel slightly sick.

Actually, Grant had been an effective candidate, despite his modesty. He'd been well liked and well known, especially in central Georgia. After all, he'd been a high school basketball star in Atlanta. Then he'd attended the Naval Academy and served in the Navy for twenty years. Highly respected both in and out of the service, he'd retired and become president of Landsdowne College in Atlanta, where he'd spent the next four years. Not a shabby record by anyone's standards.

Admittedly, he'd been the underdog in the Senate race—the incumbent was a proficient pork barreler for his state—but Senator Grant had been advancing steadily in the polls. He might have won regardless—the numbers were starting to look that way—but the sex scandal coming when it did had sealed the victory.

As all that she'd read about him raced through her mind, Cynthia had suddenly felt thankful she'd come to the job interview. He really was quite likable, a charmer. If talk of his competence had any basis in fact, he'd end up being a force on the Hill.

"My opponent was my best campaign weapon, wasn't he?" Grant had asked with a grin. "Now you know the truth about me as well. It's painful to admit, but I feel out of my element, not incapable of doing a good job, you understand—I wouldn't have run otherwise—but like a stranger in a strange land.

"And so we come to you. I need an administrative assistant who knows the Hill, who knows not only the ins and outs of the processes of government, but also the people who make things happen."

He'd stopped for a moment and looked at her searchingly. "I've been told you're the best. A mutual friend says so, one I respect, and that's why I sought you out. He says you're not only good but nice as well, that you'd lead me by the hand and not be too obvious about it. Even though you might not be looking for a new job, I hope I can entice you over to my staff. What do you say? Are you interested in helping a stranger through the intricacies of Washington?"

Cynthia had been unprepared for his offer, even more unprepared for his candor. Things weren't done like that in Washington.

"I'm afraid I've shocked you," the Senator had said. "My wife tells me I'm too precipitous. Why don't you think about what I've said, ask questions about me, decide—"

"I'm sorry, Senator Grant," Cynthia had interrupted quietly. She could remember how opaque his eyes had become, blotting out his disappointment. "No, no," she'd hastened to reassure him, "I'd like to work for you."

Even then she couldn't believe she was hearing herself say it. She knew none of the specifics of the job, none of the important considerations any fool would expect to know before accepting. But she knew she was committed. He'd known it, too. And impulsive as it'd been on both sides, it had proven a decision neither of them had regretted.

She smiled as she saw him now, a tall, distinguished black man, walking out from behind the leather-covered screen that prevented prying eyes from seeing Senators who were resting in the ornate sitting room off the floor of the Senate chamber. A magnificent Sèvres vase, a gift of the French government, stood like a sentinel in front of the screen.

Yes, Cynthia thought as she watched him, she had indeed been blessed.

"We've got to hurry, Senator," she said as they fell into step, "if we're going to get you miked up in time for your six-ten time slot. If the subway train isn't waiting, we'd better walk."

"I feel sure," she continued, "that most of the questions will have to do with the defense appropriation bill, but there's an outside chance that you might be asked about the Governor's proposal to increase the sales tax to cover the pay raises he authorized for state employees. Obviously, that's another easy one. The poor man has yet to try to streamline any part of his administration."

"Anything else?"

"No," Cynthia told him. "I checked the wires before I came over, and nothing had come in. It looks like it'll be defense appropriations and the tax hike. There's really not much else."

They smiled at each other. Defense and tax hikes were a big "not much."

When they reached the studio, the waiting film crew attached the microphone to Grant's tie and put the remote earpiece in place. With a swipe of his powder puff, the makeup artist blotted out the shine on Grant's face. As the Senator gave a voice check, the voice of the producer in the network studio in Georgia came through his earpiece.

"Senator Grant, can you hear me?"

"Yes, perfectly."

"Good. I'm Morty Levin, the producer of this segment of the news. In one minute you'll be speaking to Lucinda Martin, our six o'clock anchor."

"I'm looking forward to it." Grant pulled his shoulders back and stared directly into the lens of the studio camera. He knew he'd better look alert and interested because they could cut to him at any moment. Looking disengaged was forbidden in modern politics. Disengaged, indeed! Omnipresent television had become a stern dictator, even affecting language. How nice to be able to disengage himself occasionally from the camera or at least not feel as if it were his master so much of the time.

"We're fortunate this evening to have our junior Senator joining us from Washington, D.C.," Grant heard through his earpiece. "Senator Grant, you've been debating the defense appropriation bill on the Senate floor all day. In this age of budget deficits, how can you in good conscience be pushing for an increase in spending on defensive weapon systems such as the SDI?"

"Lucinda, when we talk about the SDI, we're talking about the protection of our country, about preserving our very freedom. It's imperative that we be able to protect ourselves from incoming ballistic missiles. Consider Cuba, which, I might remind you, is only ninety miles off our shores and which, not too many years ago, was the recipient of Russian missiles. If Fidel Castro—or some other madman who might control Cuba in the future—should launch an attack against the United States, it's far better for us to be able to destroy those missiles as they leave their source, allowing the fallout to cover the country of origin. We can't allow even one to enter our airspace and have the fallout land in our own country. This is especially important when we're dealing with the type of terrorist who'd use either chemical or nuclear weapons."

Grant spoke with confidence. His concern with the security of the United States and his obvious expertise in that area made his statements persuasive.

"Senator, aren't you forgetting the tremendous changes that have occurred these last few years? Obviously, the Soviet Union is no longer a threat. Peace is the order of the day."

"The rebirth of freedom in the Soviet Union is indeed a cause for rejoicing, but we mustn't confuse their good fortune with a universal move toward peace. China, India, Pakistan, maybe even Iraq have nuclear capabilities. Libya, Iran, Iraq, in addition to innumerable Middle Eastern splinter groups, have frightening terrorist tendencies as well as the money to bankroll them. The world order is changing, true. But not all countries share our view of peace and freedom. Our duty is to protect ourselves against any possible threat."

"But, Senator, your concerns are hypothetical at best. With the chances of any country attacking the United States so slim, is the cost of the SDI really justified? Wouldn't we be better served using that money in more constructive ways, for social programs that benefit more people more directly?"

"I take seriously, Lucinda, the trust that's been given to me by the people of Georgia. I was elected to protect my nation from the unthinkable, from any potential threat to its people or its security. A strategic defense will do just that. Yes, it's expensive. Yes, it's unpleasant to think of an attack against our country. But that's reality. We can't sacrifice our defense just because no threat appears imminent. We must be prepared. Our country devastated by missiles, our people trying to pick up broken lives . . . I'll fight to keep that from happening. We *must* be able to protect ourselves."

"Thank you, Senator Grant, for taking time to speak with us."

"It's been my pleasure, Lucinda."

"And now . . ." Bob Grant heard just the beginning of Lucinda Martin's next story as he unhooked his mike and removed his earpiece.

"Senator, the bells have already rung for the yeas and nays on the Lugar amendment," Cynthia told him. "You'll have to race to the floor if you're going to make it." She hurried him out the door of the studio even as he was thanking the technical crew.

"I'll come on back to the office if no more votes are expected for a while," Grant told her. "We need to go over tomorrow's schedule and discuss next week's trip back home. Even if we have another vote, we shouldn't be in session too much longer."

8:30 P.M.
El Brujo Prison
Havana, Cuba

General José Moya had been imprisoned for nine years. At present he was sharing a cell with eight others. Located on the fifth floor of a massive stone building, one of three such buildings in the complex, the cell was small, barely ten feet by ten, with no room for exercise and little room for sleeping. Crude hammocks were hung in tiers from floor to ceiling on two sides.

Such a tidy description in no way conveys the horror of the reality. Conditions in Cuban prisons are wretched—a powerful deterrent to rebellion.

Cubans have suffered for years from severe food shortages, with meat rationed to three-quarters of a pound per person every ten days and coffee to two ounces twice a month, with even sugar an almost unheard-of luxury; therefore, prison food is limited to murky water with shreds of cabbage and fragments of spoiled meat floating in it. Years ago, prisoners derisively named this soup *la boba*, the "old maid," because no one wanted to try her a second time.

In all of Cuba, clothing is rationed as well, each Cuban allowed only one pair of trousers and one shirt every six months and one pair of shoes every year; prisoners are given only minimal clothing with worn-out shoes frequently not replaced. A not-unusual punishment is to strip a prisoner of his clothes and force him to sleep unprotected on the concrete floor of his cell, his body a haven for the insects and vermin which thrive on filth.

Housing in Cuba continues to be inadequate, with eight to ten people often squeezed together in a one-room apartment. In prisons, as many as ten prisoners share a tiny cell, their bodies cramped and sore from constant contact with one another and with the walls and floor. Solitary-confinement cells, inhabited by those prisoners most adamant in their unwillingness to bow to the system, may be as small as two feet by four, cramping the prisoner in sleep and forcing him to wallow in his own excrement.

General Moya had returned to one such prison that evening after having spent twelve hours in the steaming heat of a sugar-cane field. Upon his return, the General, as he was affectionately known to most Cubans, had ignored his own fatigue as well as that of his cellmates, encouraging them to perform self-imposed nightly duties regardless. He knew that self-discipline was essential if they were to retain their sanity under such barbarous conditions.

And so that night, as they did every night, his fellow prisoners had cleaned their cell as best they could, replenished their small water bucket—they'd been allowed a fresh supply today, a cause for rejoicing—and begun the intricate tapping and coughing which provided communication with the other cells. Such defiance of the restrictions placed on them did much to bolster their morale, a most gratifying thumb in the eye under circumstances that provided few such opportunities.

"Life is short," Moya said, beginning his nightly talk of encouragement.

His cellmates, all political prisoners like himself, sat on the cold concrete floor and leaned against the equally cold block walls, their filthy bodies touching in the cramped space. Even as they listened, they proceeded with the evening ritual of picking lice off one another and squashing them on the floor.

"We each are allotted only our own small reservoir of time to use as we will," Moya continued. "We might be tempted to hoard our moments, saving them for a more perfect time, fearful that by acting we might somehow shorten those days to come. Instead, we should spend them as the golden gifts they are, understanding that their value lies not in the niggardly conservation of them but in the joyous delight of each minute. We must disburse those minutes freely, finding each opportunity for hope, no matter how insignificant in itself."

Moya had long since become used to the stench of prison—bodies unwashed for years, the open latrine pit in the corner of each cell, festering wounds and dying men. His body had also adjusted to the rotten fragments of meat and vegetable floating in fetid broth, which was his only food. But he'd never adjusted to the lethargy and hopelessness that overtook so many prisoners. More men died from despair than from physical abuse, he knew. He was determined that his fellow inmates not succumb to that inner treachery.

"Around us we see unrelenting stone walls, unsmiling faces, gloom and decay. We hear the harsh curses of our captors, the groans of pain, the moans of despair. We smell the stench of filth and hopelessness. We might close our eyes and look no further. In that direction lie failure and despair. Our eyes must be the eyes of the soul. We must see the beauty of hope, hear the hymn of freedom and smell the sweet perfume of promise.

"Our freedom is in our minds; our happiness, in our souls. Stone walls, unfeeling captors, filth cannot enslave us if our minds remain free, if our souls grow, if our wills refuse to bow. Each of us alone holds the key to his own freedom.

"And we *will* be given that opportunity for freedom. Only the hour remains unknown. Tonight. Tomorrow. No man can know. While the timing, the exact moment of release, is immaterial, our attitude, our mental toughness, isn't."

The men were understandably skeptical. But, despite their appalling surroundings, despite every hardship which proclaimed the foolishness of the General's words, their faces now mirrored a certain hope that hadn't existed before Moya's arrival at the prison.

Many of these men had been incarcerated since their late teens and had spent more years in prison than out. They continued to dream of a life shared with loved ones, a life without constant fear and debilitating hardships, but they'd despaired of ever realizing that dream.

Until Moya came, that is. With his calm acceptance of the injustice done to him and his unwavering surety of eventual freedom, he inspired each man he touched, rekindling that man's spark of hope.

Former soldiers, now prisoners, recounted tales of Moya's courage and marveled at his devotion to his men. During prison visits, these stories, as well as Moya's own words of encouragement, were repeated to prisoners' families, who told them to their friends. Thus, the Cubans' admiration for the General grew even as his imprisonment extended into years. Far from silencing him, Castro had provided conditions conducive to the spread of Moya's legend throughout the island.

He was more of a hero now than he'd been when he'd returned from Angola, maybe even than after La Bahía de Cochinos, or the Bay of Pigs, as it's known to the Americans.

"We mustn't allow any moment, any opening, to elude us because we're too tired or too blind or too shortsighted. If we're mentally prepared to fight, if we're willing to take whatever risk is necessary, we will be free. I'm certain of it. We will be free. We must focus on the horizon, watching for the sunrise, not anticipating the sunset.

"But enough. If I continue, the sun will rise before we've gone to bed."

A murmur of easy camaraderie accompanied the ensuing preparations for sleep. Soon each man was alone in his hammock, visions of the sun slowly cresting the horizon comforting his tired mind.

9:00 P.M.
El Palacio de la Revolución
Havana, Cuba

During the evening, María returned to the conference room several times, emboldened each time she saw the contours of the lifeless body under its sheet shroud. Castro's personal bodyguard stood at attention at the head of the couch, his arms cradling his AK-47. María couldn't imagine what he thought he was guarding. His protection had been useless against death and seemed merely pitiful now. His hard eyes followed her as she worked, impaling her with their anger and cruelty. María forced herself to ignore him.

Finally, unable to remain in the room any longer without fear of arousing suspicion, she picked up some broken glass, put it on her tray and returned to the pantry. Edmundo watched as she added it to the trash she was preparing to take out.

Now, if only they'd let her leave! Give me courage, Father, she prayed, taking a steadying breath and squaring her shoulders. She picked up the full wastebasket, opened the door to the corridor and shuffled into the hall.

The soldiers guarding the conference room were tense, their eyes fastened on the door of the room, then darting to scan the recesses of the hall. They held their machine guns more tightly than usual. Each understood that his own future was being decided behind the conference room doors, along with the future of Cuba. Each hoped to ensure the security of his position.

María's heart hammered, begging her to run. But she willed her feet to shuffle, her face to look as simpleminded as possible.

Only one guard prolonged his stare, his eyes following her down the hall, seeming to pierce her back. She despaired of ever coming to the corridor that led outside.

Her breath caught. Footsteps. Behind her. Almost on top of her. Her lungs burned with each stifled gasp. Suddenly a rough hand grasped her shoulder. No! They had to let her leave!

The hand tightened relentlessly, but she kept her eyes on the floor, the basket clutched in her trembling arms.

"Where do you think you're going?" the guard demanded, his voice harsh in the quiet hall. María could feel hot breath on her cheek, smell the stink of garlic and decaying teeth.

As the fingers tightened cruelly, she glanced up fearfully, muttering gibberish about garbage. His eyes continued to hold hers, sadism fighting with laziness. Abruptly, the grip relaxed.

María's feet began moving the moment the pressure on her

shoulder eased. She longed to press her forehead against the cool wall of the corridor and allow her heart time to stop racing, to rub her aching back and shoulders where the imprint of his hand would remain for days, but she kept walking.

Finally turning the corner, she saw only one guard standing between her and Alejandro. He stared at her. Only a few more steps. Her body yearned for the darkness beyond the door.

With a shaking hand, she reached for the doorknob and turned it, leaning her body heavily into the door. The screech of the hinges tore through her. She glanced fearfully from under lowered eyelids at the soldier. His eyes were on her, a hesitation lurking in them. Even as he started to move, she hurried outside, praying he wouldn't stop her. The door closed behind her. María's breath came out in ragged gasps. Conscious of her continuing danger, of the omnipresent eyes of Cuba, which might even now be watching her, she controlled her urge to run and trudged as usual across the cracked and weed-strewn concrete toward the garbage cans piled haphazardly in front of a wooden fence. With the outdoor lights habitually broken, the area was shrouded with dark shadows against an even darker night. Unable to stop herself, she turned to look back at the closed door and blank windows. Nothing. No one appeared to be watching. The guard must have decided she wasn't worth harassing. Her breathing became more normal.

Reaching the battered cans, she searched the gloom. Alejandro's whispered words barely carried above the sounds of the night—the scurrying of rats, the sharp growls of scavenging cats and the skidding of trash carried by gusting breezes. His voice seemed to float on one of those breezes.

"María, I'm here. Your signal . . . What's happened?"

María let out her breath, unaware until that moment that she'd been holding it. "A miracle, Alejandro. Castro's dead—a heart attack, they're saying."

She could hear his gasp.

"Dead? Castro?" He laughed quietly and thumped the boards of the fence. María smiled, her taut body starting to relax. His excitement seemed to fill the air. "This is it, María. Our chance. Tell me everything."

"You can imagine how crazy it was for a while, but all's settling down now. The ministers have ordered everyone to remain in the building until after a meeting at eight tomorrow morning. No one's to know about the death until then, either." She heard Alejandro's muttered "Interesting" as she hurried on. "But, I saw Sergeant Campos, one of the guards, leave for a while. He must've gotten word to someone. He's back now."

"We'd better spread the news ourselves. If they're trying to keep it quiet, then we need to let everyone know. Maybe we can frustrate whatever they have in mind. What about Raul? Is he in charge?"

"No, he wasn't at today's meeting. He's not even in Havana. No one's taken control so far although Registra seems in the best position."

"I wouldn't be surprised if he's preparing to make a move, but what about Valles? Surely he's not just sitting back and taking it."

"Oddly enough, he is," María said, glancing over her shoulder at the huge building looming behind her. Blessedly, the windows and doors still looked empty. "He's said almost nothing, except to persuade them that no one should leave the building. Other than that, he just sits there, watching everyone."

"Then no one's made a real move?"

"That's right. Just a kind of organized chaos. I'm convinced no one anticipated his death. Everyone's in shock or biding his time, probably waiting until tomorrow. Of course, at this point, no one knows what to expect from Raul."

"Until he comes," Alejandro said, "Registra and Valles are the main ones to watch. I don't care how quiet Valles is at the moment, he won't let Raul—or Registra, for that matter—take over without a fight." Alejandro laughed grimly. "Raul may find a surprise waiting for him if he doesn't hurry. Maybe that's why they're being so cagey, keeping the death a secret."

"They haven't said that, at least not while I've been in the room. Makes sense, though. Maybe they'll kill each other off, trying to seize control."

"Pleasant thought, but it would take a real bloodbath to eliminate all of them. We'll see if we can't foment some trouble, maybe when Raul comes. We'll have someone outside El Palacio watching for him." Alejandro's voice became more hurried. "I'll send the information about Castro to Miami right away. Then I'll contact Dr. Llada and the others. We'll have to risk a meeting, tonight if possible. Come to the clinic whenever you can." He paused for a moment. "Anything else we should know right away? You need to get back. Those madmen may get suspicious."

Even as she shivered and looked over her shoulder apprehensively, María felt warmed by his concern. "Nothing urgent," she answered, picking up the basket. "Several ministers seemed to have—"

Suddenly the back door screeched, cutting the quiet of the night. A line of light slowly widened on the scarred concrete. Without thought, María bent over an open garbage can and slowly emptied her basket.

"I'll contact you as soon as I can," she whispered hoarsely.

She turned and began her shuffle to the door, her head once again bowed.

"What's taking so long?" a soldier growled at her as he leaned out the door. "I haven't time to waste on garbage—like you."

María reached the door and was yanked inside.

As soon as the door closed, Alejandro left his hiding place.

Vaya con Dios, María, he thought, taking a last look in the direction she had gone.

He'd grown close to María during the last four years and had come to enjoy being with her. Admittedly, that hadn't been true in the beginning. He'd expected her to be, well, a woman with more physical appeal than brains. His condescension had soon turned to respect. Her reports were filled with insights into the workings of the government as well as with practical ideas about the future of Cuba. He often found himself staring at her, marveling as the vacuous expression and dowdy persona she adopted for her work at El Palacio slipped away to reveal her real beauty. The more she talked, the more attractive she became. Her warm skin glowed in her animation.

Initially, they'd talked only of Castro's meetings with the ministers, parts of which she'd overheard. They'd rejoiced in each scrap of helpful information, each insight into the minds of the men who controlled their country. But gradually they'd begun talking about themselves, slowly revealing secret longings and needs.

Alejandro couldn't believe what was happening to him. He had spent so many years in prison, lost so many of those he loved, suffered such physical and mental anguish, that he'd determined years before to abandon all personal goals and comforts in his quest to rid Cuba of the madmen who ruled her. All his thoughts had centered around La Causa, his personal feelings hidden under a carapace of dedication. María had changed all that. Now his thoughts kept returning to her, a picture of her smile often in his mind, snatches of her words intertwining with his thoughts of La Causa.

He'd finally admitted to himself that he loved her, that lovely brave woman. But Castro's Cuba was no place for love. Being linked with him, a former political prisoner, might well put her life in jeopardy. It would definitely jeopardize her job. He could offer her nothing but increased danger. But he loved her, yearned for her. He needed her as much as he needed freedom. At that moment, he'd decided to do whatever it would take to have them both.

And now Castro was dead! Was this the miracle he'd been hoping for, a miracle for himself as well as for Cuba?

Walking as fast as he dared without arousing suspicion, Alejandro reached El Cerro. This area of Havana had fascinated him for years. The facades of the once-sumptuous homes began at the edge of the sidewalk on either side of the esplanade. Their side walls touched with no lawn, no space even, separating them. In front of the residences stood ornate pillars, a different design for each home. They supported a masonry-and-wood canopy which protected the sidewalks for blocks in either direction. In spite of these similarities, each house was unique, the pillars, the masonry, even the windows and doors a subtle blending of Cuban ingenuity and artistry.

This area now held only the crumbled ruins of the majestic homes of that previous age, an age before the equalities of La

Revolución had caused the decay of so much that was beautiful and proud in the Cuban heritage. Only the stone facades still stood, stark protectors of the ravages within.

El Cerro was the perfect site for his transmissions. The walls shielded him from the curiosity of passersby, and the rubble not only hid the equipment but also protected it from the elements. The area was too decayed, too stripped of all comforts, to be of interest to any but the most destitute. It was now a rabbit warren of hidden passages and isolated rooms.

Alejandro especially admired the House of the Lambs, its outside railing a procession of lambs, twenty in all he'd once counted, their coats appearing softly woolly even in the unrelenting weight of wrought iron. How much the family who'd lived there must have enjoyed their whimsy, he'd often thought, imagining children climbing on them and swinging from their nubby necks onto the sidewalk. Although the lambs remained, battered now but intact, the house they protected, like all those in El Cerro, had become a parody of its former grandeur. The entryway, long since stripped of its door, led into decay.

For once too engrossed to notice the lambs, Alejandro came to his present hideout, one far from the clinic headquarters of La Causa so that if he were discovered—and that possibility was all too real— La Causa itself wouldn't be jeopardized. He clung to the shadows of the canopy before edging inside. Extracting the transmitter from its rocky shelter, he walked to the back of the building and crouched behind a pile of rubble, which would muffle his voice. A ragged opening in the back wall provided another avenue of escape.

The winds of the night gusted through the spaces, snatching up trash and skittering it across the rubble. The faint howl of the wind winding around the rooms and finding freedom through the roofless hole to the sky formed a melancholy background for his message.

His body was painfully tense; his ears, alert for the slightest foreign sound. Rubble, walls, shadows, so innocent in the light, now loomed eerily, their shifting forms sinister in the gloom.

The message was brief: CASTRO IS DEAD. HEART ATTACK PRESUMED. NEW LEADERSHIP UNKNOWN, BUT RAUL LIKELY.

Jumping to his feet, Alejandro began pacing the room. Now for the wait. Within the next five minutes, he'd receive Miami's response. Five long minutes.

9:30 P.M.
Little Havana
Miami, Florida

Four years before, when María had been promoted to her present position on Castro's staff, Alejandro had requested that Miami send him a transmitter. American supporters of a free Cuba had responded readily, raising funds not only for the transmitter but also for a sophisticated receiving station. Located a few minutes from La Calle Ocho in a corporate complex in Little Havana, the receiving station was at the heart of the Cuban-American resistance movement.

Its furnishings were spartan but functional. In complete contrast was the communications system filling the smallest of the rooms, access to which was severely restricted. The equipment was monitored twenty-four hours a day.

T. D. Santos was the Cuban-American on duty tonight.

T.D. was so absorbed in a Louis L'Amour novel that when the message from Cuba began, his chair banged to the floor, almost upsetting him. He raised his eyebrows in surprise. A crisis?

Confirming that the tape-recorder had indeed engaged, he waited impatiently for the transmission to end. Then he typed the message into the computer and waited again, even more impatiently, for the decoder to translate it.

" 'Castro is dead.' " His body stiffened. "Castro's dead?" he whispered. "Can that be right?"

" 'Heart attack presumed. New leadership unknown, but Raul likely.' "

"I don't believe it!" T.D. exclaimed, unable to control his excitement.

Turning to his transmitter, he sent the "message received" signal. His Cuban contact would be anxious to leave, and he had no return message. The next time would, no doubt, be different. He felt a surge of exhilaration at the thought of what that next message from Cuba might be.

Now he needed to call Victor Rojas, head of the Cuban-Americans who supported the resistance group.

One phrase, like the refrain of a broken record, kept repeating itself in his mind: "Castro's dead. Castro's dead."

9:30 P.M.
Russian intelligence-collection facility
Lourdes, Cuba

In a cavernous room housing one small section of the surveillance equipment used at Lourdes, Cuba, Private Stanislav Sebanik scowled as he concentrated on distinguishing the static-laden sounds coming through his earphones. The rows of computerized equipment before him, buttons and screens glowing in ever-changing colors and patterns, were of the most modern design. This listening post, the largest electronic surveillance site outside Russia itself, enabled the Russians to monitor sensitive maritime, military and space communications as well as telephone conversations within the United States. Sebanik reveled in knowing more strategic information and more personal information about individuals in that country than most Americans.

His shift was coming to an end. Just as he was taking off his headset, his hand was stilled by the faint sounds of an unusual transmission. After several months on the job, he'd developed a familiarity with the usual messages of the airwaves, recognizing their cadence, frequency and length. He might not understand the message, but he did recognize the imprint of the anonymous sender.

This message was one he hadn't heard before! His fingers flew over the buttons as he tried to clarify the sounds.

The monitors, printers, keyboards, amplifiers—all the components of the complex listening devices that filled the room—hummed and clattered softly but insistently in the background. The soldiers monitoring the equipment moved restlessly in their chairs, easing cramped muscles, anticipating the end of the shift. A cloud of cigarette smoke enveloped the room. These distractions were blotted out for Private Sebanik. He was intent on his personal mission, the scowl on his face deepening with each silent second. Surely, he thought, the message couldn't have ended already, moments before he could get a clear reading. But it had.

Sebanik could be certain of only one thing: the message had been sent to the United States from somewhere in the vicinity of Havana by an unauthorized, unknown hand. From Havana to the United States. Interesting.

Exhausted, he slumped in his chair, reviewing what little he'd learned. In minutes he'd report his findings to his superior, and Sebanik wanted to have all the facts in order.

9:35 P.M.
El Cerro
Havana, Cuba

Stepping cautiously out of a jagged hole in the wall of the mansion, Alejandro melted into the shadows at the edge of the sidewalk. He would hide the transmitter in a safe spot somewhere in El Cerro, then find his fellow freedom fighters. He needed to arrange to have someone monitor activity at El Palacio, at the clinic, outside the Russian compound—the list would, no doubt, grow with time.

He had good people helping him, a handful whom he trusted implicitly, María included, and more who seemed trustworthy. But were they capable of handling a situation of this magnitude? None of them had ever been in a position of authority; the Cuban government had seized all such powers years before.

His father was certainly able, but . . . The sorrow of his father's illness, a constant grayness over his life, suddenly crystallized. His father was dying, he knew. Dying. The cancer was too powerful, too pervasive for even his iron will to overcome. How much longer could he endure? A few days? A few hours? Why now, with his dream of freedom finally possible? His military expertise might be critical if they were to succeed.

A military confrontation between his fellow patriots in La Causa and whom? Alejandro wondered as he walked, his steps slowing with his tumultuous thoughts. Raul and his henchmen? The Russians, if they were able to get someone of their own in power? Certainly they wouldn't back Raul. And did it matter anyway who ultimately seized power? Could his friends, with their minimal resources, their need for secrecy, their lack of a cohesive military unit—what a grandiose phrase that was; they didn't have that first weapon!— could they hope to prevail against the thugs of Raul or the might of the Russian army or someone else as yet unknown?

And María. Would someone decide she knew too much, that she must be killed?

He stopped walking and rested heavily against the nearest building. He was overwhelmed by the audacity of their plans. His untrained freedom fighters succeeding against such tremendous odds? With General Moya, their leader, still in prison?

Almost against his volition his eyes lifted, encountering across the street the age-softened lines of La Iglesia de Paula. This church, attended by his father's family for generations, had been liberated by the revolution and was now a museum for Cuban music. However, the church spoke to Alejandro not of popular native songs but of the majestic hymns of old, mellowed through the centuries by the intermingling of hundreds of thousands of reverent voices. Alejandro stood motionless, greedily absorbing the memories of a forgotten time, feeding his soul with the comforting promises learned at his grandmother's knee, a faith long buried but not abandoned.

Closing his eyes, he could hear his grandmother's quiet voice, her strength of soul pulsing through each word as she filled him with the wisdom of the ages. "I will lift up mine eyes unto the hills, from whence cometh my help."

"My help . . ." The words warmed him. He remained leaning against the wall a few minutes longer, allowing plans to coalesce, to take on a manageable shape. His face softened. Of course they would succeed. What could he have been thinking?

He smiled ruefully at himself and began striding down the

street. After several blocks, he entered another crumbling mansion and hid the transmitter. Then he went in search of his allies. He needed to give them their orders. La Causa's time had come.

9:40 P.M.
El Brujo Prison
Havana, Cuba

As he did most nights, General Moya lay in his hammock, planning for the time when La Causa could free Cuba. Even he realized that gaining freedom was improbable at best, but he also knew no man's sanity could withstand the horror of a never-ending existence in this hellhole. So each evening, to the sounds of gentle snores, dry coughs and the gnawing of rats, he marshaled his reserves of strength and searched for the answer to Cuba's misery. These were the hours of introspection when only his deep faith gave him courage. "I am the way, the truth and the light." For him, God was the light that illuminated even this seemingly impenetrable darkness.

Years before, as an idealistic youth battling for the rights of the people, Moya had joined Castro in freeing Cuba from its hated dictator. What a dynamic leader Castro had been! His noble words and utopian dreams had uplifted them all. How righteous he had made them feel! Theirs was a future filled with promise.

"Not much has changed in Cuba, has it?" Gregorio Luzan whispered from his hammock, directly above Moya's. "I was just thinking about what you said to us and for some reason started thinking about the beginning. You know—La Revolución, Castro, everything."

"I was, too," Moya said, "and wondering how I could have remained so blind to what happened afterward. The executions, the imprisonments, the Secret Police—how could I have ignored them? I'm not sure I even realized what was happening. Castro seemed to have mesmerized me."

"I know what you mean. I didn't think much about it until I was thrown into prison myself. I'd done nothing wrong so I started wondering about all the others who were imprisoned with me and about those who'd disappeared over the years, supposedly for the good of Cuba."

"For me, the awakening came with Angola," Moya said. "Would you believe I actually complained to Castro about our being there! Obviously I didn't realize what was going on, or I'd never have spoken."

"Must've been a shock to him," Luzan said, laughing. "What'd he do? I'd have expected him to shoot you right then."

"Maybe he was *too* shocked," Moya said. "Actually, he listened politely, nodding and puffing away on his cigar. He talked about supporting oppressed brothers, fulfilling his divine destiny and profoundly shaping the world's future. The next day orders came sending me to Angola, effective immediately."

"Better than prison."

"Agreed, and actually it came as a blessing. On the trip over, I had time to think, to really look at what had been happening in Cuba since La Revolución. I didn't like what I saw."

The voyage aboard the *Admiral Nakimov*, a passenger ship converted to carry troops to Angola, had been long and empty. Moya still remembered the horror he'd felt as his mental numbness was slowly infiltrated by patently treasonous thoughts. How little life in Cuba had changed since Castro had taken power; if anything, it had deteriorated. And prison, the horrible specter of prison always loomed in the background. The more Moya had thought, the more confused he'd become. The old dreams had been difficult to discard for the hard truths he was facing.

"Angola was even worse than I'd imagined," Moya told Luzan. "Not only were brave men dying senselessly on the battlefield, but many had contracted AIDS and carried it back to Cuba. The outrages seemed never-ending."

The General was quiet for a moment, remembering Emilio Loredo, his longtime aide, who'd been killed in a senseless skirmish. All they'd seemed to do was kill and be killed, never gaining any lasting victories, never seeing any reason for the waste.

"I kept asking myself why our men should be sacrificed just to make Castro a hero to the Soviets."

"And found no acceptable answer," Luzan said.

"None that would have kept the firing squad away."

"But your book. Why write that if you knew the consequences?"

"I just got tired of hiding my feelings and of sensing that that cowardice somehow diminished me. Maybe I hoped to atone for my years of blindness. I can't explain it, but suddenly I'd had enough. The book seemed the answer. In the back of my mind, I suppose I thought America would help if they just knew what was happening. Of course they didn't, and I ended up in prison, lucky to be alive."

"Strange to think of how your life has changed," Luzan said. "Now me, I was nothing much before prison so my imprisonment only affected my family. But you, you were a hero, probably the best-known man in Cuba next to Fidel. I remember the parade for you after the Bay of Pigs. I was there cheering. Even understanding the blessing to us if that time had turned out differently, I still get excited thinking about it. We outsmarted the United States—a country as small as Cuba—and you were the one who did it."

Oft-repeated legends had grown up about the way Moya had almost single-handedly defeated the Americans. Using diplomatic channels, playing on that country's fear and hubris, he'd fooled President Kennedy into withholding promised air support for the resistance. What a simple concept but pure genius nonetheless! Psychological weapons were at least as important as materiel. The Bay of Pigs had provided classic proof of that. Military success with little bloodshed, world acclaim, humiliation of the United States—truly a masterful stroke and one duly honored by Castro.

"And now here we both are," Moya said, "praying the United States will come to our aid and not at all sure they'd understand what we need any more now than they did in the past."

11:00 P.M.
The clinic
Havana, Cuba

The clinic of Dr. Jorge Llada served as the headquarters of La Causa, the Cuban resistance movement. Located in San Isidro, one of the poorest neighborhoods in Havana, and the only clinic available to thousands of Cubans, it provided a perfect cover for clandestine meetings and information dissemination. With so many people coming to the clinic legitimately, an occasional extra could blend in unobtrusively, in that way circumventing Castro's prohibition of unauthorized gatherings.

Fidel Castro had recognized the potential problem of such clinics, and, years before, Dr. Llada and others like him had been imprisoned, not for any assumed guilt but to break their spirit. Dr. Llada had been released only when the shortage of doctors in Havana had become acute. Castro hoped the doctor had been properly intimidated, but, just in case, a spy for the Secret Police had been installed in the clinic as an aide. Frequent surprise raids were made by the Secret Police as well.

But Dr. Llada hadn't been intimidated, the aide was too lazy to be a threat and the raids were seldom as secret as the Secret Police supposed. Besides, La Causa's small network was so tenuously held together that little evidence of it existed.

Alejandro Montaner served as a clinic aide.

On the evening of Castro's death, after sending the news to Miami, Alejandro had returned to the clinic, asked several of his friends to monitor any action outside the Russian compounds at San Antonio de los Baños and Lourdes as well as at El Palacio, and arranged a meeting of the leaders of La Causa for later that evening. These leaders had been arriving for the last half hour, for the first time ever daring to meet as a group.

General Paschal Gomez was head of Disinformation and Mind Control for Castro; and, although not a member of Castro's Council of Ministers or elite inner circle, he'd been a frequent and trusted advisor of the late President. Four years before, Castro had decided that the growing discontent caused by increased food shortages could be mitigated if José Moya could be made to publicly support both him and his government. Gomez had been ordered to begin the brainwashing. However, instead of convincing Moya of Castro's worth, Moya had caused Gomez to question the very foundations of his belief. Over the course of the next year, he'd come to embrace Moya's ideas and the promise of La Causa as his own.

Another soldier, Colonel Silvio Sacasa, was one of the field commanders of Castro's western army. While Sacasa didn't have the direct access to Castro that Gomez did, his information about the composition and plans of the military had been helpful in the past and would be invaluable now.

Ines Moya, General Moya's wife, used her job in a sugar cane processing factory to gain access to many of the working people of Havana. The hope was that these people would add their voices to La Causa's when the time came.

Julio Montaner, Alejandro's father, had been living at the clinic for the last several months, ever since his disease had become debilitating. He'd used that time to formulate various contingency plans for the group. One of those detailed actions to be taken if Castro died unexpectedly.

Alejandro was leader of La Causa while Moya was in prison. He was the contact point for those interested in freeing Cuba, and only he knew all their identities.

Tonight, the air of the clinic vibrated with suppressed excitement.

"I don't know what to think about Raul," General Gomez said, absentmindedly stroking his bushy mustache. "You're sure he wasn't at El Palacio?"

"Positive," Alejandro said. "Not in Havana, either, apparently."

"He's such a madman!" Dr. Llada said. "If he takes over, he'll treat everyone so brutally that even Fidel will seem benevolent beside him. Maybe we should wait to act until Raul's been in power awhile; getting allies should be easy then."

"Waiting might work," Gomez said, "but what if it doesn't? Surprise is a powerful weapon, and we may well sacrifice it if we wait. I think we have to prepare as if we were going to act now."

"I agree," Colonel Sacasa said. A small man of slight build, he looked inconsequential. Only his eyes gave indication of his sharp intellect. "That gives us flexibility. But why are we talking about Raul? What about the Russians? Cuba must figure into their plans, or they wouldn't have kept their troops here. Their spying at Lourdes is as blatant as ever. They're bound to have their own man and their own agenda."

"The Russians!" Alejandro laughed dryly. "No, we can't afford to forget them. You'd think with their problems at home they wouldn't bother with us, but most of their troops *are* still here and the spies at Lourdes *are* still all in place. I can't help feeling their threat may be even greater now just because their desperation is greater. They may view Cuba as their last chance both for money and prestige."

"You're thinking of the drug trade?" Dr. Llada asked.

"And arms sales."

"I've heard rumors they're selling intelligence information as well," General Gomez said. "That's why they've stayed at Lourdes."

"So, controlling Cuba may be vital to them," Alejandro said. "What with drugs, arms and intelligence information from Lourdes, we may be a major source of revenue for them."

A pall fell over the room. The Russians might be even more formidable now, the wounded bear struggling for life.

"We have to free José," Julio Montaner said finally, his voice soft. His clothes hung on his emaciated body, but that was true of many Cubans. Only his constant fatigue betrayed the gravity of his illness.

"Yes," Dr. Llada agreed. "The time has come."

"You can leave his escape to me," Gomez said. "Remember, I have regular interrogation sessions with him. I can get him out easily. I'll use your plan, Julio."

"María's still in El Palacio," Alejandro said. "She may learn something which will affect your timing but my feeling is that we go ahead whether she tells us anything new or not. Does everyone agree?" He looked around the table. All nodded. Ines and the doctor looked slightly dazed at the rapidity of events. "Unless I contact you by nine o'clock tomorrow morning, Paschal, go ahead with the escape.

"Ines, you'll need to disappear. When José's escape is discovered, the search will be intense. You'll be the first person they'll look for."

"I'll leave at eleven in the morning, my usual time. That way I shouldn't arouse suspicion." She paused and frowned at Alejandro. Her gray eyes matched her hair, giving her a serious look that was at odds with her relaxed good humor. "But maybe I should wait until Friday morning so I don't precipitate a search."

"No," Alejandro said, "tomorrow is better. The Secret Police won't begin checking until Friday anyway. By then they'll be hunting for the General regardless."

"Then eleven o'clock it is," Ines said. "Tell José I'll hide where he suggested. He can send word to me there."

"Don't tell anyone where you'll be," Gomez said. "Now's no time to become careless. No one's loyalty is certain."

Discovery by Cuban and Russian listening and spying systems, including the one at Lourdes, posed a tremendous risk for the Cuban resistance. However, even more insidious and dangerous was the Committee for the Defense of the Revolution, a network of informants set up by Castro under the Ministry of the Interior. This system was sophisticated in its comprehensive use of computers but elemental in its manipulation of Cubans. Greed and fear motivated Cubans to inform on friends, neighbors and even family, forcing Cuban to be suspicious of Cuban. No one could be trusted. No one. The reward for trust could well be imprisonment or even death. The members of La Causa had lived with those risks for years and had seen several of their members arrested after having been turned in by "friends." Fortunately for La Causa, these unfortunates' membership in an organized resistance group had remained unsuspected. To Castro, they had been merely malcontents.

"That's about it," Alejandro said. "We'll meet again when the General's here."

"I can hardly believe what we're saying," Julio said, shaking his head. "Why, only this morning . . ."

"I know," Ines said. "Everything seems so different somehow. More . . . hopeful, almost like a new beginning."

"But this is only the beginning," Alejandro cautioned. "The odds against us are tremendous. We aren't professionals, and we don't have any weapons. No, General," he interrupted when Gomez started to speak, "I know what you're thinking, but we can't have your position jeopardized by an investigation into missing weapons. So, what do we have? The element of surprise because no one suspects our existence; our agents in key areas, especially María; our access to the military, both their plans and their personnel; the discontent of the people, especially now that food's so scarce; the personal following of General Moya; our contact in Miami and through him our contact with Senator Grant."

"A lot of words," Dr. Llada said. "But in reality, not much."

The room was quiet.

"Poland's free now," Ines said. Radio Martí was heard over hidden radios and the reports repeated by word of mouth throughout Cuba. "Romania and East Germany as well. Even Lithuania, all the Baltic states. Just think of it. Three years ago no one would have believed it possible. It can't have been easy for them, either. They'll say the same about us, that we did the impossible."

Hope once again filled their eyes, the tension easing.

"You're right, Ines," Gomez said. "We have as much chance for freedom as any of those countries."

"Of course we do," Alejandro said, his blue eyes intense. "We just have to use everything to our advantage. Don't try to come to the clinic tomorrow, Silvio," he told Colonel Sacasa. "Whoever emerges as leader will be certain to watch those around him. We need at least one of us whose movements are unassailable."

Sacasa grunted his assent.

"We'd better leave now. It's after curfew as it is. Let's meet here tomorrow morning at eleven-thirty." Alejandro raised his arms. "To a free Cuba."

"To a free Cuba."

11:15 P.M. Havana time (7:15 A.M. Moscow time)
Moscow

Anatoly waited until he'd heard movement for several minutes before knocking softly on the dressing room door. The President was always courteous, but the penalty for mistakes was administered swiftly and severely. Anatoly hoped he wasn't making one by breaking into the President's rigid morning routine.

The President nodded to him from the mirror where he was knotting his tie. Nothing in his demeanor revealed that such interruptions were other than ordinary.

Anatoly cleared his throat. Even though he'd been the Presi-

dent's personal aide for two years—and successfully, too, he reminded himself—he still felt nervous whenever he entered the
presence.

"Sir, General Nestotovski is waiting outside to apprise you of
an urgent situation."

The President finished straightening the tie. Almost imperceptibly he nodded his permission.

At Anatoly's signal, a tall white-haired soldier marched into the
room, his demeanor confident. The President turned from the mirror to watch him. The two men nodded gravely. They were old
friends.

"Mr. President, we've received word from Cuba that Castro is
dead. A heart attack's presumed."

The President raised an eyebrow slightly. "An interesting development. We'll have to move carefully." He motioned the general
toward the door leading outside, picking up an overcoat as they
walked. "We can't afford to commit ourselves prematurely."

"That was the consensus of the Executive Council," Nestotovski said as the door closed behind them. They walked slowly toward
a nearby meadow, their shoes crunching on the snow. Both men
talked softly, their eyes on the ground, their mouths barely moving.

"Are we capable of taking control of Cuba?" the President asked.

"If we move quickly. Fortunately, our troops are still in place."

"Thank God the Americans believed our excuses for leaving
them there. As if inadequate housing here was any reason to delay
removing troops from there." The President snorted his disgust.

"But even at that their number is small."

"As insurance, IBTC has ordered us to send all available ships
into the area. They must have learned of Castro's death even before
we did."

"Has ordered us! I hate all this."

"As do I, but we have no choice."

Both men were silent for a few steps. The changes in their
country had been staggering.

"How important is Cuba?" the general asked.

"How important . . ." the President mused, hands clasped behind his back. They had reached the far corner of the meadow. In

silence, they turned back toward the dacha. "We have to have Cuba. Logistically, it's an asset, of course. If we can't use it, we can sell it." He hit his fist on his palm in anger. "Money. Everything comes down to money. We have to have Cuba. The drugs, munition supplies, covert information—all are important. But the strategic position. Yes, that could be our salvation. We owe too much to ever succeed without a huge influx of money. We have to find a way to break away from those Middle East bloodsuckers."

"And Cuba can provide it."

"Exactly."

"I'll contact Basilov immediately." They began walking more rapidly. "He can set Operation Romanov in motion."

The President put a cautioning hand on Nestotovski's arm. "No one must know of our involvement with Cuba. Any hint and the Americans might discontinue their aid to us. We still need those supplies."

The general nodded his understanding. He opened the door to the dacha. The warmth enveloped them.

"I'll tell the Executive Council of your advice, Mr. President," Nestotovski said for the benefit of hidden microphones. Old practices died hard. "We'll delay any action until you can confer with our American allies."

"That would be well."

The general turned and walked out of the room.

11:45 P.M.
410 A Street, N.E.
Washington, D.C.

Through a haze of sleep, Senator Bob Grant heard the phone ring and felt his wife, Rachel, roll over to answer it. He hoped it wasn't about the Smith child, one of her more seriously ill patients. Rachel had been concerned about his recurring fever on top of chemotherapy.

"Bob, wake up. The phone's for you." She handed it to him.

"Grant here," he growled. This had better be good, he thought. They'd unexpectedly been in session until almost ten, and he'd done little more than talk to Rachel and crawl into bed when he'd finally arrived home.

"Bob, this is Victor Rojas." Rojas was one of the leaders of the Cuban-American community, a successful businessman and a good friend.

"I hate calling so late, but I knew you'd want to know. Fidel Castro is dead."

"What!" Grant exclaimed, instantly alert. Rachel propped herself on one elbow beside him. "What happened? An assassination?"

"Not according to our information," Rojas said. "Natural causes. A heart attack, I'd guess. A pretty prosaic ending for such a man, but he's dead. Thank God, he's dead."

"I'll second that. Any details?"

"No, just the bare facts. The message was short, as you can well imagine, and we have to keep even that confidential. Can't chance anyone discovering there's a resistance movement operating inside Cuba."

"I understand. Have any of the networks reported the news?"

"No. No bulletins, even. It must not have been released yet."

"What about Moya? Any word about him?"

"The message about Castro's death came through Moya's people, but there's no mention of him specifically. He's still in prison—at least I suppose so. Everyone, including the resistance, appears to have been unprepared."

"No one could've anticipated his death," Grant said, "at least not if it really *was* a heart attack."

"No reason to presume otherwise since no one's assumed control. Raul's name was the only one mentioned in the message, but that was it, a mere mention. Sorry I've so little to tell you, but I knew you'd want to know. This will affect the United States."

"It absolutely will," Grant agreed.

"I'm going to begin contacting Cuban partisans in the United States. We may need their help if this is, in fact, Cuba's opportunity for freedom."

"What about Corinne Fitzpatrick?" Grant said, referring to the National Security Advisor for the previous President. "She'd understand the implications. I'd like to get her opinion."

"Perfect. Tell her I'll call the moment I hear more."

Rachel looked inquiringly at her husband when he hung up.

"Castro's dead, Rachel. A heart attack, apparently."

"Dead! What a blessing for Cuba! But how will it affect our country?"

"Security could be a real problem. Would you believe during an interview this afternoon I actually mentioned Castro and discussed the possibility of chemical warheads being directed against our shores!"

"You're going to have every dictator in the world worried if you mention him," Rachel said, laughing. "The kiss of death. But chemical warheads—what a dreadful thought! Surely it won't come to that. What about José Moya? Will this have any bearing on him?"

The Grants had met Moya thirteen years before while Grant, as president of Landsdowne College, had been a delegate to a Pan-American conference on civil rights in Caracas. Moya had been sent by Castro to espouse his own version of civil rights in Cuba. Grant had found the whole show disgusting, had made no attempt to temper his opinion and had been surprised when Moya had asked to come to his hotel room for drinks one evening. Grant had been understandably curious and had agreed.

The three of them—Rachel had, of course, been included—had spent the evening in lively discussion. Grant had asked how anyone in Cuba could talk about civil rights, given the deplorable conditions there. Moya had seemed confused by that viewpoint. Although he'd defended Castro vociferously, he'd seemed intrigued by Grant's observations as well.

Two years later, a large manila envelope from Moya had arrived at Grant's office. A manuscript was enclosed. The cover letter said that Grant had been right, that conditions in Cuba *were* deplorable. He'd written this manuscript, the letter continued, to make some of those conditions known to the rest of the world. He wondered if Grant would read it and, if he found it worthy, arrange to have it published. Once over his initial incredulity, Grant had done just that, using the university press to publish the book. The manuscript had documented the atrocities of Castro, with emphasis on the immorality of the Angolan conflict and the unfair incarceration and barbarous treatment of political prisoners in Cuba.

Through occasional smuggled reports, Moya had kept Grant apprised of the resistance movement he was building in Cuba. The group in turn had informed Grant the moment Moya had been arrested. Immediately, Grant had mobilized Amnesty International behind Moya. Although they hadn't been able to effect his release, they'd prevented his execution.

"Moya's still alive," Grant told Rachel. "At least he was at last report. But who knows what he can do. Right now, our own strategic vulnerability's the main issue."

"But I'm confused, Bob. I thought Castro was a Communist and controlled by the Russians. The Russians are in disarray, and Castro's dead, so why do you look so concerned?"

"The situation was already complex enough with all the changes in Russia, but now . . . I'm having trouble even imagining what might happen. But to answer your question, Castro was a Communist, agreed, even considered himself more pure than his Russian counterparts. But Castro under Russian control? Hardly. He was always something of a maverick with his own agenda. He'd throw an occasional sop to the Russians, the Cuban involvement in Angola, for instance, but controlled by them? Never. They would have loved nothing better than to have gotten rid of him. As to their disarray, I'd feel better if so many of their troops weren't still in Cuba. That and their intelligence facility outside Havana make me leery of their intentions. I know they trumpet their goodwill at every opportunity, but . . ."

"So this may be as much an opportunity for them as for the resistance?" Rachel asked.

"That's what I keep wondering."

"Could it lead to a civil war?"

"Who knows. That's part of what I mean by complex. We can't even be sure who'll be vying for control. In a few days . . ." He shrugged. "Maybe the main protagonists will have sorted themselves out by then. Now you go back to sleep," Grant said, giving her an affectionate pat as he rolled out of bed. "I've got to call Corinne."

Rachel was already asleep by the time he closed the door.

11:50 P.M.
Russian military base
San Antonio de los Baños, Cuba

General Basilov picked up the ringing phone.

"Operation Romanov's to proceed," General Nestotovski told him. "You'll need to move quickly."

"How blatant can we be?"

"Secrecy's essential. The Americans mustn't know we're behind the new government."

"We'll be sure our man appears decidedly proindependence and prodemocracy."

"Good. Our agents in all American intelligence-gathering agencies will subvert any compromising information. Once our man's in power, he'll be there permanently. Americans are reluctant to interfere in established governments."

"How providential that we have this President to deal with and not his predecessor." For a moment, Basilov considered the current American President, a Democrat, the first such in a decade. "Americans are hard to figure, aren't they? Those last few years should have taught them something. Their military strength changed the face of the world."

"Let's hope they continue their present willful blindness. We have to make Cuba ours if we hope to gain economic freedom. Never forget that. What have you done so far?"

"All phone lines have been sabotaged, and a watch was begun at El Palacio," Basilov said. "The messenger sent to inform Raul Castro of his brother's death was eliminated. As we talk, plans for tomorrow morning are being finalized and only await your approval."

"My approval, Basilov? Of course, you have it. Do whatever's necessary to secure Cuba. Just do it quietly."

Midnight
El Palacio de la Revolución
Havana, Cuba

The meeting of the Council of Ministers ended at eleven thirty-five. The ministers retired to their offices either to sleep or to work through the night. As they'd done since soon after the first meeting of the ministers, weary soldiers patrolled the exits, effectively sealing the building.

María remained in El Palacio. She had no choice. The order of the ministers included all personnel in the building. She didn't want to leave anyway. Too much was happening.

At a sound in the hall, she opened the pantry door a crack. The soldiers were moving restlessly. Nothing odd there, she thought. As she started to close the door, she noticed a shadowy movement at the end of the corridor. Sergeant Campos? she wondered as the figure edged into one of the offices, a wash of light momentarily glinting off his red hair. Which minister was he seeing? From this distance, she couldn't be sure.

With a look of vexation, she closed the door. She didn't know which room he'd entered, and she could think of no excuse which would allow her to find out. What good was it to be in the middle of events if she couldn't do even that! She lay back down on the floor with Edmundo huddled nearby. Despite her exhaustion, she was unable to sleep. She knew she needed to rest while she could. She couldn't move around tonight without arousing suspicion, but tomorrow? The next night? Who could say when she might have another chance to rest.

Thoughts of the next day raced through her mind. She needed to gather all the information she could, both as she helped at the meetings and as she cleaned the offices. La Causa would want to know every one of the ministers' plans as well as any potential alliances among them. She'd pay special attention to Raul when he finally arrived. He seemed to be the key, but Valles and Registra were important, too. And Campos—his behavior was decidedly odd. Just what had he been up to? she wondered again.

Slowly exhaustion turned her mind into a tangle of thoughts: of her father, who'd fought beside Castro during La Revolución and whom Castro had subsequently executed, no reason given; of her mother, who'd died soon after, of heartbreak María felt sure; of Alejandro, dear Alejandro, who'd been her friend and her anchor during the last four years of intrigue as she'd worked at El Palacio and spied for La Causa; and coloring it all, Cuba, poor, tormented Cuba, a country of hurt and despair.

But Castro was dead! Even he'd been unable to guard against that eventuality. Wondrous hope, hope for Cuba, for her friends and family, for freedom, glorious freedom, which she'd never known, swept over her. Oh, how she longed to be free, to be able to visit and speak and worship—even to be able to think—without fear. She couldn't remember when oppression and fatigue hadn't ruled her life, dictated her thoughts and feelings.

And now Castro was dead!

Midnight
Cuba

Throughout the night, with help from La Causa, word of Castro's death rumbled inexorably through Havana. The news spread rapidly, as such news invariably does, invisibly but efficiently, gaining new life with each utterance, each reaction different but all uniform in their disbelief that death could have conquered their seemingly immortal leader.

Most Cubans were too enervated by years of suppression to react visibly to the news, even to dare to hope for change. Others remembered the noble promises of La Revolución and, in the face of all evidence to the contrary, saw Castro as the savior who'd yet have brought new glories to their country. These Cubans mourned his passing. But a few Cubans rejoiced in the news and began quiet preparations in hopes that this day would mark the beginning of freedom.

Midnight
Sierra de los Órganos, Cuba

Word of Castro's death hadn't yet spread to the remote hills of Sierra de los Órganos, where Castro's brother, Raul, was staying.

Raul spent much of his time traveling, making unexpected visits to the many branches of his brother's drug and arms operation.

At dawn he would leave for the main exportation point up the coast, to oversee the loading of a shipment of guns for the cartel in Colombia. Normally, communication among the branches of his operation was necessary but not crucial. The present phone shut-down, an annoying but all-too-common occurrence in Cuba, had isolated them but caused no alarm.

After years of unassailable power, Raul had become careless. He was so certain of both his own and his brother's invincibility that he and his entire operation were vulnerable.

But for now Raul was ignorant of any danger.

Like most Cubans, he slept soundly, unaware that his destiny, linked inescapably with that of his brother, had been determined earlier that afternoon.

Midnight
The White House
Washington, D.C.

Rumors of Castro's death had reached the United States, but American intelligence agencies had been so crippled by the micromanagement of Congress that little concrete information was available.

For tonight, the President slept soundly.

Midnight
El Palacio de la Revolución
Havana, Cuba

La Causa's watch on El Palacio proved fruitless. No one entered or left the building. No white paper appeared in the dark second-floor window.

The dawn, so eagerly awaited, seemed far away.

The man who reads nothing at all is better educated than the man who reads nothing but newspapers.

THOMAS JEFFERSON

Day Two

Thursday
January 26

12:20 A.M.
Cynthia Novitsky's home
3604 Cathedral Avenue, N.W.
Washington, D.C.

Cynthia Novitsky was content, even happy. She loved her job, respected Senator Grant, and felt pleasure whenever she thought of her sons, Stevie, a student at Georgetown University, and Dodd, a Georgetown graduate now working in the Middle East. If she still felt lonely, the eleven years since Steve's death had helped dull the pain.

Who would have guessed when she first came to Washington that she would end up not only working for the Senator but serving as his administrative assistant? A long way from her first job as a gofer on the Hill. She and Steve had been newly married then. Eventually the boys had come along, and she'd decided to stay home with them. She'd been afraid that she'd be bored, but they'd provided new experiences. The first tottering step and that first "Mama" with arms held out might not have been as newsworthy as her work on the Hill, but they were undeniably satisfying. She liked to think her presence had been important to the boys as well.

Even at that she'd managed to attend Georgetown Law School.

She'd gotten her degree at the same time Stevie was starting kindergarten. Perfect timing, Steve had told her over a candlelight dinner as they celebrated her passing the bar. What a joyful night that had been, one of those times she brought out of her memory and savored, wrapping herself in the sights and sounds of that moment, cherishing them: the golden candlelight flickering on Steve's hair, the caress of his strong but gentle hands, the faint smell of his aftershave, a smell that still brought him vividly to mind at the oddest moments—a mall, a party—a bittersweet reminder of him, but apart from him.

That first year with her law degree had been among the happiest of their marriage. Steve was rising steadily at the Department of Justice and she in Trade Relations at the Commerce Department.

Suddenly, shatteringly, it had ended.

Steve had been mugged, shot by a druggie. Dead. Her heart, her mind, even her body still went numb whenever she allowed herself to think about that black moment of time.

But she'd held on, pulled herself out of the abyss. Her boys had helped, of course, loving her, demanding her attention, just being there. Above all, her faith had sustained her, there for her even in the quiet alone hours, the empty aeons of the night. Others might trivialize her faith, joke about the "Great Beyond," "the Man Upstairs," scoff at the power of prayer, at the healing comfort of faith. She knew otherwise. She'd been there, had experienced the worst hell on earth, had come back from it whole. Changed, obviously, but somehow she knew changed for the better. Wiser, kinder, more thoughtful and more appreciative. Now she lived for today, not tomorrow or even this afternoon and certainly not for yesterday.

She'd decided early, soon after the numbing pain had released its hold on her mind, that she wasn't going to be ruled by her loss. She was going to live each day in the surety that her years with Steve had been precious, deserving to be remembered, to be seen as the special blessing they undoubtedly were. Those years, the known-to-them-only moments, could be taken from her only with her permission, if she allowed them to be forgotten, if she viewed them as a loss rather than as a special gift to her, the gift of a good marriage joyously and fully lived.

And so she'd retaken hold of her life. Deciding she needed a change, she'd taken a job on Capitol Hill as minority counsel on the Senate Commerce Committee. She'd seized it gratefully and—

The phone beside her bed rang.

"Cynthia." It was the Senator, she realized, picking up a pen and notepad from her bedside table. "Sorry to bother you, but Victor Rojas just called. Fidel Castro's dead."

"Dead! Amazing!"

"I don't know what, if anything, we'll need to do, but we'd both better go in early tomorrow. We can get the staff routine out of the way in case we need time for Cuba."

"Anything I can do in the meantime?"

"You might check out the Bubble first thing tomorrow," Grant said, referring to the room in the Hart Building where intelligence files were kept for the Senate, "but otherwise, nothing. I'm going to call Corinne Fitzpatrick now. If she suggests any immediate action, I'll call you back, but I'm not expecting it."

Corinne Fitzpatrick could put events in perspective, Grant thought as he dialed. As the National Security Advisor to the former President, she'd proven a valuable ally for Grant, especially in regard to relations in this hemisphere, her area of expertise. Even though she'd joined the private sector two years before—this President's embrace of a new world order with little regard for his own country's security was anathema to her—she'd continued to advise Grant on various issues. Now she could give him her insights on Cuba.

"Corinne, this is Bob Grant. I had a feeling you'd be up, you old night owl."

"Hi, Bob. For *you* to be up this late, something big must've happened."

"Victor Rojas just called. Fidel Castro's dead."

"So he's finally gone," Corinne said slowly after a moment's pause. "I'd begun to think he'd be there forever. Odd that there's been nothing on TV or that none of my usual sources have contacted me. When did it happen? And how? Was it a coup? Who's taken over? Is there any—"

"Whoa, Corinne. Slow down. First, he died sometime late yesterday afternoon, presumably of natural causes so no coup and no emerging leader. That leaves Raul, I'd suppose. How solid's his power base?"

"Solid enough if he can keep the military behind him. Whether he can stay in power is a different matter. He'll have problems, both those left by his brother and those he'll create through his own personality. He's brutal and has none of his brother's charisma."

"Is there anyone who might challenge him?"

"Who can be sure? Much will depend on who survives the next few weeks. And survival won't be easy. I'd expect the infighting to be savage."

"What about Moya?" Grant asked. "Or is he even a factor?"

"Moya's as much an uncertainty as anyone. We've no way of knowing his plans or the likelihood of their success. The odds are against him, especially since he's still in prison, or was as of a few weeks ago. He'll have to move quickly, but everyone else will be trying to do the same."

"Does that mean you discount him?"

"Oh, no," Corinne said. "Actually the unexpectedness of Castro's death may be just the advantage he'll need. Not only will everyone be scrambling for position and the power structure in shambles, but the Cuban people may be more willing to support him if no one's there to threaten them. It's too soon even to speculate with any hope of accuracy."

"I'm concerned about the effect on our security," Grant said. "So much depends on who steps in and how stable that government is. Any ideas about what we can do to encourage a prodemocracy leader?"

"At this moment I'm not sure there's anything to do. You know how sketchy our intelligence is. Once we can assess Raul's power base, see the types of challenges thrown up against him, then we can come up with a strategy. These oppressed countries are tricky; much can change in a short time. Any plans we'd make now could be completely inappropriate within twenty-four hours. We may even have a whole new set of characters by then."

"For now," Grant said, "I thought I'd adopt a wait-and-see attitude but gather as much information as I can in the meantime."

"I wish I could suggest something else. I know how hard it is for you just to sit by, but I think waiting would be wise this time. Raul has to make his move, and that in large measure will determine everyone else's moves, the Russians included. I know they assure us of their goodwill, and I know they appear harmless, at least compared to a year ago, but . . ."

"I know," Grant said. They were quiet for a moment, silently considering the ramifications of the Russian situation. Too much was unknown in that country.

"Anyway, we may find our options severely limited just because of the stance the administration adopts. They'll want to control everything and won't be eager for you to take any initiative, especially if it takes attention from them. But you know all that. It certainly happens often enough, but with Cuba . . . Castro being almost a media icon, the hope for democracy . . . I'll bet the administration jumps on it. This will be a high-profile issue. If Moya can do something within the next few days, and if we can get the administration behind him early on, we might be able to quietly direct events. But, again, it's too early to speculate. Keep me informed. I'll make a few discreet phone calls and let you know if I come up with anything."

"Sounds good. I appreciate your input."

"This is turning into quite a night, Bob. Thanks for the good news."

"Let's just hope it's still good news when the dust settles."

6:00 A.M.
Outside El Palacio de la Revolución
Havana, Cuba

Early as it was, the sun already dazzled the eye, reflecting brightly even off the grimy windows of El Palacio. Alejandro had just arrived, hoping for some message from María. However, no signal was in the window, and no note was in their hiding place in the fence.

So many of their plans depended on the actions of Raul Castro. So far, no rumor had been heard about him or his intentions.

Alejandro shifted his position in the alcove that afforded him an unrestricted view of El Palacio. His dark head rested against the stuccoed wall. He looked like any of the thousands of poor Cubans who lounged around the streets of Havana. However, behind the mask of indolence, his lively blue eyes missed nothing.

6:05 A.M.
410 A Street, N.E.
Washington, D.C.

Senator Grant had gone to bed after his talk with Corinne Fitzpatrick, but he'd awakened early, the situation in Cuba instantly on his mind. Now he paced the kitchen, a white terry robe thrown on over his striped pajamas.

Common sense told him that events in Cuba, at least those he might influence, would unravel slowly; even then his contribution would be tangential at best. However, acknowledgment of those limitations in no way comforted him. He wished he could do something.

The Cuban question was really two-pronged: Could Cuba become a free and democratic nation with or without American help, and how would the inevitable power struggle in Cuba affect the security of the United States?

With each bite of bagel and each sip of orange juice, his frustration mounted. Absentmindedly he tossed a crumb to his Labrador retriever, Justice, lying in a black mound next to the table. Justice's soulful eyes followed him as he resumed his pacing.

Raul Castro was the logical successor to his brother, and Raul was the epitome of the trigger-happy madman. Chemical weapons sounded like just his kind of toy. Chemical weapons. Grant shuddered. Even with enhanced Patriot missiles, the United States would be defenseless against such an attack. Sure, the Patriot could destroy an incoming missile, but the chemical component would still fall on the United States, wreaking untold devastation.

And what about the SS-20 missiles that Castro supposedly had imported? Would Raul follow through on his brother's threat to explode U.S. nuclear plants? If only the SDI were in place now and in its entirety. Grant's pacing became more forceful as his mind turned to this oft considered, always disturbing thought. They'd been lucky to keep the Patriot in production, much less the SDI. If only, if only . . .

But what about Cuba? Grant asked himself again, like a squirrel returning to a particularly tough nut. Was the Cuban resistance strong enough to act, especially if Moya was still in prison? Now would seem the time for the United States to give the resistance some help, erase the bad taste of the Bay of Pigs. Grant thought of the present administration and unconsciously sighed. A Cuban resistance could expect little help from that direction. This Democratic President, as was true of the Democratic Congress, had little understanding of either defense or security. If only they could understand the long-term implications of their actions and vote accordingly.

What a tremendous impact a free Cuba would have on the hemisphere! Without Cuban involvement in fomenting revolution, without Cuban involvement in the drug trade, the United States would have a chance to establish some real stability in the region. On the other hand, with the wrong person in power, the hemisphere could be faced with years of strife.

Now was the time for those interested in Cuba to formulate a decisive plan. For that they'd need information. If a request came from the resistance, they'd need to act immediately. But when? A few days or weeks? Even a month or two wasn't improbable. The sorting out in Cuba itself might take some time, hopefully time enough for the resistance to coalesce. Whatever happened, he couldn't do much about it. But what a wonderful opportunity!

Having finished his bagel, Grant headed for the shower. He might as well get dressed and go in to work.

6:17 A.M.
Apartment #323
617 Pennsylvania Avenue, N.E.
Washington, D.C.

At precisely six-seventeen, after a cup of black coffee and two pieces of dry toast, Bonfire, as he was known to his Russian controllers, stood in front of the windows facing Pennsylvania Avenue. His eyes were focused on the third window from the left on the fourth floor of a similar apartment building across the street. At precisely six-eighteen, the shade in that window slowly lowered, then rose again. Something urgent, something that couldn't be sent through regular channels, Bonfire thought, his pulse quickening.

He lowered his shade halfway in answer, then walked to his bedroom to finish dressing.

Leaving his apartment building at six-forty, briefcase in hand, he turned left, taking the long way to the Hart Building. This morning his destination was the bank of pay phones in Union Station. He stepped into the next-to-last booth on the right, wiping off the receiver with his handkerchief before touching it. Predictably, the walls of the booth were defaced with graffiti. Ah, he thought, spying a heart emblazoned with the words JENNY LOVES EDWIN. The thick red inscription was impossible to overlook. The number he needed was written neatly inside the heart, the order of the numbers skewed.

Despite his carefully maintained look of indifference, Bonfire's heart raced as he placed the call. His new mission was about to begin.

"Fidel Castro is dead," a genderless voice, the same one he heard at prescribed intervals, told him after an exchange of identifying codes. Bonfire felt his heart race. Castro dead! Marvelous!

"Operation Romanov has begun," his contact continued. "You must control the information flow about events in Cuba and affecting Cuba. Tell your network to do the same."

The phone went dead. Bonfire looked at his watch, careful to stand away from the dirty walls as he waited the requisite minute to place the second call. The new number was directly under the right side of the red heart.

He thought of his contacts in the CIA, the FBI, and the Defense Intelligence Agency. They'd need to suppress any adverse reports that survived the screening of other agents in foreign countries. Not that they would alter anything physically. No, just hide it in the mass of paper that came in every day. They'd need to promote the right line as well, first by making sure the most favorable reports were easily accessible and second by spreading the right disinformation.

Bonfire dialed. The same voice answered, using new code words. After receiving the correct response, the voice continued his instructions.

"Work with all your contacts. Make sure they understand the correct posture. Learn if any negative comments are being made. Be alert for anyone who seems too bent on finding the truth. We need time to consolidate our power base within Cuba. Remember, no one must suspect our control of events. Even a hint could be disastrous."

Bonfire listened in silence. He would be a major player in events, unnoticed but critical to the outcome. How gratifying to have more real power than the politicians and political appointees who flaunted their positions so pompously, more even than those who purported to control him.

"A great deal rests on your performance," the Russian said. "Keep our involvement absolutely quiet."

When he heard the click at the other end of the line, Bonfire left the booth. He'd almost reached the end of the bank of phones when he moved into another booth and dialed a new number, this one with a foreign exchange.

"International Bank of Trade and Credit. How may I help you?"

Within minutes Bonfire was out on the street.

6:20 A.M.
El Palacio de la Revolución
Havana, Cuba

María had just fallen asleep when Edmundo shook her. She awakened with her heart pounding, aware that something important was happening but unable for a moment to remember exactly what. La Causa. She was instantly alert.

"Help me, María," Edmundo pleaded. "The ministers are already up and demanding breakfast. Minister Escondido is screaming for food. What should we do?"

Escondido always screamed about something, María thought. She touched Edmundo's arm reassuringly. "Please don't worry, Edmundo. We'll manage something."

She reached for the bag of coffee beans. Taking coffee into the conference room would give her an unquestioned entrée into the ministers' deliberations.

6:25 A.M.
A small mountain village
Sierra de los Órganos, Cuba

Castro's drug and arms operation used various facilities dotted around the island. Nestled among the mountains of the Sierra de los Órganos was the main warehouse compound. Here Colombian drugs were stored on their way to the United States and assault weaponry on its way to the drug cartel in Colombia for distribution to communist insurgents in Guatemala, Panama, El Salvador, Honduras, Costa Rica, Nicaragua and, of course, Colombia itself. The precise countries might change with elections or successful coups, but the need for armaments always remained.

The business had been highly remunerative for Castro, who had charged not only for storage but also for use of his ports, in that way collecting from both the country sending the goods and the one receiving them. These countries were willing to pay, albeit grudgingly, to confuse the connection between themselves and the final destination.

Because of its location, Cuba provided a perfect clearinghouse, one the Russians were eager to own. On this issue all Russian leaders were in agreement: Cuba was essential to their own economic recovery.

Near the warehouses, a guesthouse, sumptuously appointed for infrequent stays by Fidel Castro and more frequent ones by his brother, was as well camouflaged as the warehouses. The entire compound was covered with vegetation and surrounded by an inconspicuous but effective fence.

Several small villages ringed the compound at Sierra de los Órganos. Most of the villagers worked in the warehouses or in the delivery of the drugs and weapons to and from the ports, backbreaking jobs which provided them just enough money to survive.

Gabri Echavez, one of the main loaders, had awakened early that morning. The most recent consignment of arms was to be shipped in two days, and that entailed extra time on the job. Gabri's brother-in-law, Ernesto, was due back home at any moment from taking a message to a military base in Havana.

As always, Gabri and Ernesto would travel together to work. Gabri liked riding on the back of Ernesto's scooter. The scooter, the only one in the village, was Ernesto's badge of honor, showing that he was Castro's official messenger.

Gabri could hear the crunch of wheels on the dirt road as the scooter skidded to a stop in front of the hut the two families shared. Strange, Gabri thought; Ernesto was always so careful with the scooter, treated it better than he treated his wife.

Ernesto rushed into the room, stirring up the dust on the earthen floor. The children and their mothers rustled in their sleep before settling back.

"Castro's dead, Gabri," Ernesto gasped, barely able to speak.

Gabri went cold. If this were true, what would happen to Gabri's family? Their survival depended on their work at the warehouse.

Ernesto rushed on, clutching the back of a crude chair for support. "He died while I was in Havana. Everybody says heart attack although I don't know how they can be sure. What should we do?"

Both men were oblivious of their awakening children rubbing the sleep out of their eyes with their fists.

Gabri frowned. "I'd guess Raul Castro doesn't know about the death. If he did, we would've heard by now." He grabbed Ernesto's arm and pulled him out the door. "Come on. We've got to tell El Jefe. Now."

Ernesto picked up the scooter where it had fallen, and Gabri jumped on behind. Several barefoot children, their faces blank, stood in the doorway watching them.

Ernesto urged the scooter to go faster as it struggled up the hill. They reached the fence protecting the guesthouse, where Raul was staying, just as dawn broke behind them.

6:50 A.M.
410 A Street, N.E.
Washington, D.C.

"Rachel, I'm going," Senator Grant called up to his wife as he reached into the closet for his coat. Justice sat at his feet, her eyes begging to go with him. Grant smiled absentmindedly and rubbed behind her ear.

"Just a sec," Rachel called. "I'll be right down."

Grant could hear her moving around over his head. Then her heels clicked rapidly toward the stairs.

"Can you pick up the dry-cleaning on the way home?" she asked, putting in an earring as she walked. "And cash a check? Whatever the bank will bear."

With four teenagers, they seemed perpetually to be cashing checks. Someone always needed something. Or several somethings.

"Thanks. You're a dear," she said with a smile, straightening his tie and brushing a speck of lint from a lapel. "I like this suit on you. *GQ*, definitely. Oh, by the way, Ben Lucas called again. Wants us to reconsider and go to the Symphony Ball with them. Says it'd be a great opportunity. Whatever that means. For you or for him, I'm not sure. Interested?"

"That's tonight, isn't it?" Grant asked. Rachel nodded. "I don't know," he said. "I wish he weren't so persistent. With the uncertainty in Cuba, I hate to commit myself, especially for a night of schmoozing."

"You didn't sleep well, did you?" Rachel asked. "I felt your elbow in my back more than once."

"I'm sorry. I just couldn't get Cuba out of my mind. The strategic problem for the United States, of course, but José Moya as well."

"I know what you mean. His descriptions of Cuban prisons in his book—appalling." She shuddered. "And to think he's been in one all these years. Can we help him?"

"I don't know. We've emasculated all our covert operations so we'll get no help from that direction. And you know the President. No, I'm afraid our only real hope is that some kind of underground network is in place inside Cuba. I know Moya has put a small one together, but how effective it can be . . ."

He slapped his hand against the closet door in frustration. "There's got to be a way! We can't let Cuba lose its chance for freedom once again. Surely even this administration will recognize the opportunity."

"Then it's decided," Rachel said. "The Symphony Ball's out. I'll call Ben."

"Thanks. I'll use tonight to go over some intelligence reports and refresh my memory on what's been happening over there, especially during the past year. I'd like to get a feel for the major characters.

"Love you," he said with a quick kiss. "Mmm," he whispered, pulling her closer and nuzzling her ear. As always, the sweet smell of her warmed him. "Thanks for being so understanding." After another much more satisfactory kiss, he released her. "We'll shut down early because of the ball so I'll be home at a reasonable hour," he said, opening the door. Justice jumped heavily to her feet, shaking her body, her eyes once more plaintive.

"I should be home early, too," Rachel said, reaching down for Justice's collar. "See you then."

Grant shivered as the front door closed to the warm comfort of his home. Pulling his coat collar more tightly around his neck, he set off down the street. Soon he was comfortable, the smattering of snow a pleasant tingle on his face.

No doubt about it, Rachel was special. She understood him and put up with him anyway. But then, he'd realized she was special from the moment they'd met. Almost immediately they'd gotten into a spirited discussion which had led to a meal at the local drive-in. Over hamburgers and fries, they'd fallen in love. Grant always claimed that the chocolate shake, a real treat in those days, had lowered his defenses.

The daughter of factory workers in Ohio, Rachel had worked her way through college, medical school, and finally a pediatric residency. She and Grant had met early in her studies after Grant had received his commission from the Navy. For the next six years, they'd written faithfully (he knew she'd kept his letters, and he had no intention of ever losing hers) and had seen each other on Grant's leaves. They were finally able to marry when Rachel completed her residency. Grant's eight years as a Senator were the longest she'd practiced in one place.

Twenty-three years, he thought with a smile. And to think that each year just got better.

With a mental wrench, he reverted to the conundrum of Cuba, which had frustrated him so much already that morning.

6:55 A.M.
A fortified storage facility hidden in the mountains
Sierra de los Órganos, Cuba

Inside the guesthouse, Raul Castro was mopping up the last of his eggs and tomatoes with a tortilla and talking to his second in command.

"We'll go to Puerto Esperanza today to make final arrangements for sending this shipment. I'm disappointed with our people there. They're too lazy," he said, specks of food spraying out of his mouth. "Time to teach them a lesson. Handle it any way you want." Raul emphasized each word with a jab of his greasy finger. "Just make sure everyone knows I won't tolerate any more problems."

Raul's brow wrinkled, and his eyes almost disappeared under his heavy eyelids. "I want to—"

A tentative knock interrupted him. Everyone knew Raul hated interruptions.

"Come in," he growled.

Ernesto and Gabri stood trembling in front of him, their hands kneading the caps they held.

"El Jefe, I fear we bring sad news." Gabri's voice trailed off. His eyes darted around the room, hoping to find inspiration. How could he tell Raul?

"Sad news?" Raul demanded. "What do you mean? Speak up!"

Gabri licked his lips. "El Presidente's dead," he blurted. "Your brother's dead."

Raul bolted upright in his chair, his beady eyes glowing. Fidel dead? What amazing news! "Tell me all you know."

Gabri's words tumbled together in his haste to finish and leave. "I know little. Ernesto"—Gabri nodded toward his brother-in-law— "was in Havana. He returned as fast as he could. Everyone says El Presidente died of a heart attack."

"A heart attack?" Raul fell silent, his eyes on the floor. Abruptly, he looked up. "But what's happening in Havana? Who's taken control of the government?"

Ernesto started at the harshness of Raul's voice. "Nothing . . . nothing seemed to be happening. Everything was quiet. I left as soon as I heard. Everyone's mourning, of course," he added hastily.

"No one's taken control of the government?"

"Not that I heard."

Waving the men out of the room, Raul slouched in his chair, his hands hanging between his knees. So he was finally to be El Presidente. Too bad his brother had died, of course. Even sadder that he hadn't died more conveniently while they were both in Havana. But no matter. In a few hours he'd take his rightful place at the head of the government.

"Get the men ready," he ordered his aide. "I must leave for Havana immediately."

Raul hastily washed down the rest of his food with beer. Finally he would control Cuba, he thought. With the money from the drug and arms deals, he could expand his power base even more rapidly than his brother had. No one would be able to stop him. No one.

"Vaya con Dios, hermano mio," Raul whispered. He smiled.

7:15 A.M.
Hart Senate Office Building
Washington, D.C.

The Senator was already in, Cynthia realized, looking across the atrium in the center of the Hart Building. Although she couldn't see his private office, which was at the back, away from public eyes, he'd turned on lights in his staff's offices, which overlooked the atrium. Cynthia never saw the wall of windows without remembering the young staffer who'd complained that they afforded him absolutely no privacy. She'd wondered what he wished he could do.

"Looks as if you've been at it awhile," Cynthia said as she walked to Grant's desk. Papers and books were strewn over it. The Senator was leaning back in his chair, oblivious to his surroundings, the high-ceilinged modern office, the Senate-provided antique furniture, even the French doors opening onto a small balcony, his refuge when he needed a moment's peace. "Have you heard anything new?"

"Nothing," Grant said. "What really puzzles me is that Castro's death hasn't been mentioned in any of the papers or on any of the news shows." He gestured toward the muted television in the corner.

"There was nothing on the radio as I drove in, either," Cynthia said, "and no intelligence information in the Bubble just now." She walked toward the door. "Let me access my computer, and I'll check the latest stories on the wires.

"This really is odd," she said when she returned a few minutes later. "The wires don't mention a thing."

"You're right," Grant said. "Something's decidedly odd. It has to have been at least twelve hours since Castro's death, and yet nothing's been mentioned. Why don't you check cable traffic up at Intelligence again when you have a moment."

"Certainly," Cynthia said, jotting a note on her pad. "You don't suppose we've been fed incorrect information, do you?"

"It feels that way, doesn't it? Common sense tells me we're right, though. I've been working with Moya too long not to take any message from him seriously. And Victor would be hard to fool as well. No, I think we're on the right track. I just can't figure out what track everyone else is on."

7:30 A.M.
On the road leading from Sierra de los Órganos, Cuba

A lone man, Pablo Sanchez, swung his machete listlessly. Leaning down to pick up a pile of brush, he paused at the sound of approaching trucks. He could hardly credit his ears. The trucks seemed to be leaving the road and heading straight for him through the sparse trees bordering the field. How could that be? he wondered as he raced for the nearest pile of brush, burrowing well inside. No telling what might be happening, and he surely didn't want to be caught in the middle.

He was barely hidden when a truck crested the slight rise in front of him. Several others followed. All slowed to a halt nearby. The men climbing down from the trucks were dressed like Cuban Secret Police, but the snatches of conversation he could hear were in Russian.

Strange, Pablo thought, more relieved than ever to be safely hidden. He knew he shouldn't be seeing any of this.

After a brief consultation, the men formed several groups and headed toward the highway, each group going in a slightly different direction. What an impressive number of weapons, Pablo thought, even a hand-held rocket launcher. What could they be planning? And was this brush pile really safe?

He chafed at having to stay hidden, but a driver remained in each of the trucks, making escape impossible. Nothing happened for what seemed ages, and Pablo's hideout was growing increasingly more uncomfortable. He'd nearly despaired of ever escaping when he again heard vehicles approaching on the nearby road.

An explosion!

Pablo started, the brush moving around him. Grenades! An ambush! My God in heaven, an ambush!

A machine-gun burst followed immediately, then another and several single gunshots.

Pablo burrowed more deeply into the pile. He must be safe, though, he decided, noting the unconcern of the truckdrivers. One even lounged in the open door of his truck, cleaning his nails with a knife.

As quickly as it had started, the ambush was over, the ensuing silence with its mysteries as disturbing in its own way as the explosions had been. In the distance, Pablo heard shouts and the slam of car doors, followed by two gunshots. Then, just when all seemed quiet, the ground under him heaved, a huge explosion lighting the morning sky.

Pablo licked his lips nervously, his eyes wide as he watched the men dressed as Secret Police come into view. They were talking and laughing as they sprinted toward their trucks and scrambled inside. The last truck had barely disappeared back over the hill when Pablo pushed off the brush, clambered to his feet and ran down to the road.

Several dead bodies lay on the ground, their limbs contorted grotesquely. Only one of the dead, a small man with black hair, wore the uniform of the Secret Police. The others wore Cuban army uniforms. A smoldering mass of metal half in the weeds beside the road was almost unrecognizable but must have been a truck. Several grenade craters pocked the road around it.

Walking closer, Pablo noticed a vehicle partially hidden behind the truck. Its windshield was starred by bullets; its windows, shattered. A body lolled out the back door, blood covering its face, obscuring the features. But Pablo didn't need to see those features to know who was dead. Raul Castro! The white Land Rover made it obvious. No car in Cuba was better known.

Pablo decided he'd seen enough, certainly more than was safe. One minute longer and he'd leave. Walking back to the body in the Secret Police uniform, he began checking the pockets. No telling what might be going on. Probably a waste of time, but maybe he'd find something of interest. He was about to give up when a paper rustled under his fingertips. Unbuttoning the shirt, he found a bag on a string around the soldier's neck. A picture and letter, blood soaked through one corner of the flimsy paper, were in the bag. The writing was Cyrillic, he noticed, recognizing it from the supplies they received from the Russians. He stuffed them into his pocket and loped back up the hill. He'd spent too much time in the open as it was.

Certainly this would make an exciting story, but there weren't many people he trusted enough to tell. He'd heard his brother mention a resistance group once. He'd give the letter and picture to him and tell him all that had happened. Maybe he could use it in some way.

Pablo ran faster. Russians, Cuban Secret Police, Raul Castro. What a day, he thought. What a day!

7:57 A.M.
El Palacio de la Revolución
Havana, Cuba

César Valles sat at the conference table, watching his fellow ministers. He knew all were impatient for the eight o'clock meeting to begin or, more accurately, for it to end.

Dirty dishes and remnants of eggs, black beans and tortillas had just been removed. The maid was bringing in more coffee. Guards leaned against the walls, their weapons held casually.

The autopsy was the only real news, and it was hardly unexpected. Castro's heart had simply given out. As long as Castro was dead, nobody in the room cared.

Valles knew some deals had been struck between ministers during the hours before dawn. Each alliance hoped their combined resources would be enough to grasp control. Each minister secretly planned to have the other killed as soon as the power was secure, seizing absolute control for himself. As they waited for the meeting to begin, the ministers eyed one another slyly, hoping to spy some weakness they could exploit or some strength they could destroy before it destroyed them.

César Valles sat stiffly in his chair, his black eyes hard in his patrician face. His long, delicate fingers steepled at his chin, he watched the transparent machinations of the other ministers. His contemplative profile masked the contempt he felt for them.

The stupid fools, he thought, laughing to himself. They'd been too weak to seize their opportunity. If they survived, they'd be slaves once again; for them, only the master would have changed.

Any minute he should hear . . .

Ah . . .

7:58 A.M.
Outside El Palacio de la Revolución
Havana, Cuba

Alejandro rested against the building, his eyes almost closed. Plans for the next few days wove confused patterns through his tired mind. His legs ached; his back . . .

Alejandro's head jerked up, and his eyes became instantly alert. The sound of heavy engines had reached him. A military truck lumbered around the corner, followed by three other trucks and, at a distance, a nondescript black car.

The trucks shuddered to a halt in front of El Palacio, the rear doors bursting open almost before the wheels had stopped rolling. Soldiers dressed in Cuban uniforms jumped down, AK-47s in their hands and automatic pistols on their hips. The men moved silently though Alejandro frowned in thought as he heard what sounded like a Russian expletive.

The soldiers sprinted up the steps, the first ones slamming open the massive front doors. Several shots exploded from inside as more soldiers raced up the steps, two at a time, their guns at the ready.

When the last soldier had disappeared inside the building and the guns were silent, an aide opened the car door, and a tall gray-blond man in a black business suit emerged. General Basilov! Even out of uniform, the Russian general was unmistakable. So the Russians were making their move, and incognito as well.

The general, stiff-backed and formidable, mounted the steps. He ignored the stunned crowd filling La Plaza. The thud of the doors closing behind him rang hollowly down the street.

Alejandro whistled silently through his teeth. This certainly wasn't a diplomatic call. The Russians had wasted no time in staking their claim to Cuba, and emphatically at that. Who had they chosen as their figurehead? he wondered. Had Raul entered El Palacio unobserved during the night? Or was it Registra? The head of the Secret Police would have many of his own men to support him. Whether that would be an asset in Russian eyes, Alejandro wasn't sure. Could it be Valles? Although he didn't have a ready-made force as did Registra, he certainly was cunning enough to take advantage of Castro's death. Whoever, the first press conference would make it clear even though the Russians would, obviously, be nowhere in sight.

The question of when to undertake General Moya's escape might just have been answered. Alejandro had forty-five minutes to decide.

Once Moya had escaped, they were committed.

8:00 A.M.
El Palacio de la Revolución
Havana, Cuba

When the shooting started, the men in the conference room became silent. Manny Escondido stopped talking in midsentence, his mouth forming an O of astonishment.

The Cuban guards, clumsy with surprise, clutched at their holsters. Before most could pull out their weapons, the double doors to the room crashed open, and soldiers stormed in. Chairs banged to the floor as Registra and several of the startled ministers jumped up and turned toward the door. Others, among them Escondido, flung themselves under the table.

Castro's personal bodyguard, finally finding a target for his impotent rage, fired his machine pistol indiscriminately at the rushing mass of uniforms. His body was cut in two by return fire almost before he could press the trigger.

More soldiers fanned into the room, guns before them. All Cuban resistance vanished.

As soon as the dead and injured had been removed, General Basilov strode in, grimly imposing even out of uniform. His hard eyes seemed to flash in the light. He stopped just inside the doors and surveyed the room. By then all the ministers were standing, staring at the Russian. He turned to Valles. A smile touched his lips, never reaching his eyes.

"Presidente Valles, I extend my congratulations to you on your new position," Basilov said in a gruff voice, his Spanish fluent. The two shared a charged look. The Russian regarded the Cuban with equal parts of approbation and caution; Valles was fastidious and coolly in charge even under these stressful circumstances. Walking toward the table, Basilov made a mental note to keep a close watch on him. Those in Moscow would need to apply relentless pressure if they hoped to control the Cuban.

Heads swiveled toward Valles, then back to Basilov. Only Registra's face remained impassive. César Valles, new President of Cuba, imperceptibly straightened his shoulders and walked around the table toward the Russian general, extending his hand.

"General Basilov, I welcome you on behalf of the people of Cuba."

Basilov nodded, his thick eyelids lowered. At his signal a dozen Russian soldiers, again in Cuban military uniforms, marched into the room. They formed a loose circle around the conference table, their submachine guns trained outward.

"Slowly, put your weapons on the floor," Valles ordered the Cuban bodyguards, his easy manner indicating his absolute control. "Now."

Weapons clattered on the marble.

Valles turned to the guard who for so long had been his main contact with the Russian compound. "Sergeant Campos, for now you will command my special forces. Eliminate any of those men whose allegiance could be questioned."

Campos walked around the room slowly, examining each man emotionlessly. He chose quickly but with deliberation, sending those he rejected to the door, where they were removed by Russian soldiers.

When the doors had closed behind the last unfortunate guard and the guns on the floor had been redistributed or removed, Valles turned to General Basilov. "You're acquainted with these men, no doubt?" He gestured dismissively toward the ministers. Their faces were bleak with fear.

Valles savored his triumph. What a glorious moment, he exulted, worth every degradation, every slight he'd had to endure. He stared at each minister in turn until his eyes finally rested on Registra, his longtime enemy and the greatest threat to his power. Surely he detected a tiny spasm of fear, Valles thought. He hoped so.

The tense silence was broken by Basilov.

"El Presidente, we're here in friendship to ensure the peaceful transfer of power to you." Basilov's presence was commanding; his personal raw power, palpable. Regardless of problems in the motherland, regardless of Moscow's vow to remove their troops, Cuba had seen little diminution of Russian strength. Basilov represented that strength.

Both Basilov and Valles knew exactly what would happen next. They had made their plans months before, in anticipation of Castro's death.

With a bow toward Basilov, Valles spoke. "We feel an indebtedness to you, General Basilov, which we can never repay. Because of your heroic actions today on behalf of all Cubans, our nation will once again be controlled by a strong government, one which will do the will of the people while at the same time forging a new policy of coexistence under world socialism. We look forward to working in peaceful unity with our Russian friends.

"Cuba will be embarking on a noble future, one in which the old and ineffective must be destroyed to make way for that which is new and innovative.

"As you know, General Basilov, it has become obvious that several of these men who sit before us, these leaders who have purported to support the goals of Cuba, are actually traitors, placing their personal interests above those of the state."

Valles's voice was low now, his eyes holding those of the other ministers as they leaned forward to hear.

"These men, these traitors, are part of the debris which must be swept away if we're to place Cuba at the forefront of world power."

Valles paused, savoring the mounting fear in the eyes before him.

"It's my duty as the new President of Cuba to treat these traitors as they deserve. In their punishment they will serve as examples to others that such traitorous behavior cannot and will not be tolerated."

No one in the room seemed to move, to blink, even to breathe. Valles could feel his power swelling, just as he could feel the mounting fear in the room. Each brought him pleasure. When the air fairly screamed, he resumed, his smooth voice devoid of menace, its urbanity increasing the horror.

"These men must be eliminated immediately as must all others who'd do irreparable harm to our great country."

Once more he paused. Deliberately, he looked at each of the ministers. Each stared back, transfixed by his words and his cold eyes, barely daring to breathe for fear of drawing attention to himself.

Valles's eyes finally rested on a balding, hawk-nosed man at the end of the table.

"Gonzalo Petrón," he intoned softly, "you stand accused of betraying the people's trust." Valles mentioned no specific crime. These men must understand that his word alone was sufficient.

Petrón's face blanched, and his eyes skittered around the room, seeking some avenue of escape. His mouth opened and shut like that of a fish gasping for the essence of life.

At General Basilov's signal, two soldiers seized Petrón from behind and, half dragging, half pushing, forced him toward the doors.

The other ministers sat motionless, their eyes darting from Valles to Petrón to Basilov and back again. Expressions of shock, incredulity, horror, all suffused their faces. Only the ragged breathing of Manny Escondido and the ticking of the clock violated the silence.

Once again Valles spoke.

"Marcelo Avalar, you stand accused of betraying the people's trust."

Avalar eased up from his seat as if in a trance. Held upright by the soldiers, he stumbled around the table. Before they reached the doors, the soldiers were dragging his limp body, the toes of his boots slithering across the floor.

All breathing had ceased. Even Escondido was silent. Each man's face betrayed the same frightening thought, a certainty that his name would be next. Like birds before a cobra, they stared, mesmerized, at Valles.

"Manny Escondido, you stand accused of betraying the people's trust."

Escondido groaned hoarsely, sweat pouring from his face, spreading visibly on his shirt. "No, César. I mean, El Presidente. Please. You're mistaken. Please. Don't do this to me. I beg of you."

Escondido was pulled around the table toward the doors. His agonized pleading embarrassed the air, making a mockery of all the times he'd ridiculed those who'd begged him for mercy.

Listening to the fading cries, the remaining ministers seemed to shrink, hoping by sheer willpower to escape notice. Registra alone seemed unmoved.

Two more men were accused. Two more men, distraught and desperate, were forced from the room.

Valles felt his power grow with each name. The fear of the others, these most powerful men in Cuba, uplifted him, strengthened him, added armor to his invincibility. Even his fertile imagination hadn't truly conceived of the ecstasy of ultimate power. To be able to determine whether a man lived or died—to be able to do so for every person living in Cuba!

His eyes held Registra's. The fool's face was expressionless! Why wasn't he groveling? Anger swept over Valles. Didn't Registra realize that death was staring him in the face, and that death was even more unflinching than he?

Registra didn't blink. For the first time, Valles's voice betrayed his loathing of the men before him and his primitive exultation at his supremacy over them. He gave to Registra's name the hatred that the years had fostered.

"Arturo Registra, you stand accused of being a traitor to your country. You have brutally murdered Raul Castro."

The ministers gasped at the news. Registra smiled bitterly, seeming to admire the audacity that had beaten him.

Valles's hate for Registra overpowered him. He choked out the last words. "You are a disgrace to your people and to your high calling."

Registra stood abruptly and marched out of the room, his back straight, his head held high. Only a slight stiffness in his carriage gave any hint of his thoughts.

Valles was enraged. The arrogant bastard hadn't even allowed him the satisfaction of showing no mercy. He took a deep breath to steady himself. By the time the echo of Registra's footsteps had faded, Valles was again in control.

He addressed the eight surviving ministers. "Members of the Council of Ministers, you must decide. You may remain in this room and become a loyal part of my government or you may leave. The choice is yours, but the decision is irrevocable."

The ministers sagged in their chairs. They'd live. They would live! Hope replaced the dull emptiness in their eyes. Their compliance had been secured the moment Valles had made his offer. They'd willingly agree to anything, anything, to remain alive.

Valles waited with patent patience, knowing the thoughts racing through their minds, pitying them their weakness. "You've chosen wisely. Don't jeopardize your decision by betraying my trust. Be assured that I will know. And be assured that I will take appropriate action."

The pause this time was less charged, the threat more familiar, having been uttered by each man to whom it was addressed. This familiarity made it no less dangerous.

"You and I share this moment of destiny," Valles said. "We will be the architects of a glorious future for our country. We'll rule without opposition, with the gratitude of the Cuban people and with the admiration of the world."

He turned to Basilov. "General Basilov, thank you for your aid in our time of need. We will not forget."

Basilov bowed his acknowledgment. After an enigmatic glance at the ministers, he left. A dozen Russian soldiers dressed in Cuban uniforms remained. All spoke fluent Spanish.

The first phase of Operation Romanov was at an end.

8:35 A.M.
Outside El Palacio de la Revolución
Havana, Cuba

The heavy doors of El Palacio burst open. Alejandro strained forward, motionless, as soldiers wrestled several Cuban guards down the steps and shoved them into one of the waiting trucks. Four more men were brought out similarly, one grabbing the side of the truck in a desperate struggle to escape. Immediately, rifle butts pummeled his cringing body, continuing their staccato beat long after he was senseless. The soldiers tossed his body heedlessly in with the others. His hand dangled over the truck bed and was smashed by the closing door. The soldiers ignored it.

The doors of El Palacio opened once more. Arturo Registra was propelled down the steps, his arms pinioned by two soldiers, one shouting orders in Russian. So Registra wasn't working with the Russians, Alejandro thought. Was it Raul, then? Valles? Someone else?

Two soldiers slammed the truck doors shut, another hoisted himself into the passenger's seat, and the truck lumbered off down the street.

Alejandro stared after it. The fury of the Russians, their secrecy, the gunfire, Registra, even the period of quiet, all seemed ominous. Was María safe? With the violence of the last hour, who could know? What on earth was happening?

Slowly, Alejandro turned back toward El Palacio. Within minutes the doors opened again, and General Basilov and a number of soldiers emerged into the sunlight. They climbed into their vehicles and roared away.

Were the Russians in complete control of Cuba now, or had something else happened that he couldn't even imagine?

Whatever the last hour meant exactly, his decision about General Moya's escape was no longer in doubt. With the Russians already moving decisively, La Causa couldn't afford to wait. The General had to be free to lead them. Thank God the escape plan was already in motion.

9:15 A.M.
El Palacio de la Revolución
Havana, Cuba

María made herself concentrate, forcing her mind to focus on the words being spoken by César Valles—El Presidente, she thought with scorn. She wouldn't allow herself to become hostage to the horrors of the morning. The staccato bark of the guns, the tormented screams of the wounded, the frenzied pleading of the ministers: those sounds would haunt her forever. She felt isolated, surrounded by people with alien principles, strangers who placed no value on life, who loved personal power above integrity. She longed to talk to Alejandro. But she couldn't dwell on any of that now if she hoped to help La Causa.

Edmundo had become so drunk after the shooting that he could do nothing. Good. That meant she would be the one working in the conference room.

As she walked around the table, refilling glasses and clearing away debris, she listened and memorized. Periodically, her glance was drawn to the blood staining the floor and splattering the walls. Even cleaning up the gore would be a small price to pay for a few moments longer in the room, moments which might reveal the words that would guarantee the success of La Causa.

Valles was visibly savoring this first meeting with the remaining ministers. "Temporary ministers," he'd reminded them more than once.

"The funeral, which you'll oversee," he said, "is more important than the public viewing. However, my public inauguration, which will take place immediately afterward, is obviously of greater importance than either. All three will mark a new age for Cuba. The eyes of the world, or more accurately the eyes of the media of the world, will be focused on us for that brief time, and we must capitalize on that exposure.

"Therefore, the funeral ceremony must begin at exactly eleven-thirty on Saturday, the anniversary of José Martí's birthday and a perfect reason for forgoing a long mourning period. Our haste will appear correct to the world; they'll applaud the symbolism of honoring two great liberators on the same day. My ascension to power will be seen as the culmination of the efforts of both Martí and Castro."

Valles then gave the ministers detailed instructions for the three events. They would, he knew, meticulously carry out his orders.

Their lives depended on it, and no one understood that better than the ministers themselves.

"We'll meet back in the conference room at two-thirty," Valles said.

The meeting disbanded, and with obvious relief the ministers returned to their offices. Guards followed each man and then stood outside his open door.

As soon as the room was empty, María hurried to the pantry. She had to get this new information to Alejandro. The Russians, Valles, the death sentences of the ministers, Raul's death, the details of the funeral, all were of vital importance.

She'd already jotted down the developments of the night and early morning, using the code she and Alejandro had devised. Now she added a few words about the funeral and dropped the paper into the wastebasket, securing it to the side with her thumb. If only she'd been able to put the signal in the window; but the guards, like everyone else, were jumpy. She'd been afraid to call attention to herself by going past them twice. With a deep breath, she opened the pantry door.

Hostile eyes followed her as she walked down the first corridor. They watched as she walked toward the door. They watched as she walked across the concrete parking area.

María could feel the eyes cutting through her. Her hands were slippery with tension. Her blouse clung to her back. Finally, she heard a thud as the door was closed behind her. With a relieved sigh, she whispered Alejandro's name.

He didn't answer.

Her body sagged against the fence. Well, she couldn't do anything about it now, she thought as she forced herself to move. If she could, she'd put the signal in the window when she went back inside. She felt sure he'd look for a message even without the signal, but . . .

With shaking fingers, she pushed the paper into the cavity in the fence, their secret repository, positioning her body to block the view from the building. Almost in the same motion, she reached toward the garbage cans and dumped her trash. Wiping her damp forehead, she turned to walk back into El Palacio. Back into the lion's den. She thought of Daniel and divine intervention. Her pulse throbbing in her throat and a prayer in her heart, she began her slow shuffle.

9:30 A.M.
Russian military base
San Antonio de los Baños, Cuba

General Basilov's office at San Antonio de los Baños, though not luxurious, was much more comfortable than those of his staff. The sofa against one wall converted into a bed, the liquor cabinet was well stocked and his love of classical music had been indulged with a sophisticated sound system.

Basilov was leaning back in his leather desk chair, the strains of Tchaikovsky forming a fitting background for his disturbing thoughts. Valles was too sly, too pleased with himself. Just what was he planning and with whom?

Colonel Tuporov buzzed on the intercom. "General Basilov, sir, Presidente Valles is on the phone."

"Your ascension to high office went well," Basilov said, wondering how to direct the conversation so that Valles would reveal his intentions. "We had surprise on our side. We may not be as fortunate in the future."

"We may not have surprise," Valles said, "but we do have everything else: the armies of both Cuba and the Russians, the power of the presidency, the fear of the people, the difficulty of effecting a change now that I'm firmly in power."

"Nevertheless," Basilov said, "you're not yet President of Cuba in the eyes of the world. Until then your position isn't secure."

"If Castro was good for anything," Valles said, "it was in destroying all defiance. Right now my men are rounding up Raul and Registra loyalists. That should quash any threat from those directions. Trust me, I've considered all threats and am watching for any others. I appreciate your concern, General, b—"

"Cuba *is* our concern, El Presidente," the general said, cutting him off. "Make no mistake about that.

"You must court the Americans," he continued after a significant pause. "They'll be vital in securing worldwide approval. Get their President to attend the funeral. Make him feel he's instrumental in bringing freedom to Cuba, that he's witnessing the final burial of communism. He's gullible, but he's no fool. Give no hint of our involvement. Emphasize that freedom is your goal. Any questions of our continued presence can be tied to our economic problems— no housing for soldiers if they return to Russia."

"I plan to relay such information to the American press within the hour," Valles said. "Peter Evans of the *Washington Herald* will be eager to report the news and in a way most beneficial to us."

Evans was so naïve, Valles thought with amusement, that had he been given proof he still wouldn't have believed how carefully their initial meeting had been engineered and how assiduously their relationship had been nurtured during the following years. Basilov knew of the relationship, of course, had actually worked to ensure that Valles had as many contacts with Evans as possible. Fortunately, Basilov appeared unaware of other of Valles's contacts. Soon, unknown to him, the general and all his countrymen would be back in Russia, housing shortage or not.

" 'The burial of communism' is apropos," Valles said, ending the conversation on his own terms. "Yes, the Americans will like that."

9:30 A.M.
A sugar cane field
Outside Havana, Cuba

A drab brown jeep skidded to a stop on the edge of the sugar cane field. The driver stuck out his arm, a paper in his hand.

From his position near the edge of the field, General José Moya watched with concealed interest. Was he to be taken to Gomez's office for his periodic brainwashing session? he wondered. He hoped so. That would give him a chance to talk with his friend. He enjoyed their sessions and the mental stimulation they provided. The break from prison was also welcome.

But why was the prison guard arguing with the driver? The jeep door opened, and an angrily gesticulating soldier got out. Not fat old Pedro. Moya frowned, surprised that the usual driver hadn't come.

Moya's heart jumped into his throat. The driver was his old friend Sal Mendez, one of the first to join La Causa! Sal, and in a uniform!

As Sal talked to the guard, Moya watched him casually scan the prisoners working in the field. His eyes passed over Moya without the slightest hint of recognition.

His escape plan was under way! Moya's hands felt slippery on the machete. Why had La Causa decided on today?

He saw Sal thrust a paper at the guard and then wave his arms angrily. Did the guard suspect something?

Moya felt a sharp jab in his back. He jerked around. "Get to work," a guard ordered.

Moya began swinging his machete, turning so he could watch Sal, who was still arguing with the guard. Thanks to Paschal Gomez, the orders would be real, with only the signature a forgery. So what was wrong?

When Moya looked again, Sal and the guard were moving his way. He could hear snatches of their conversation.

"Why are you alone?" the guard was asking. In the past, two men had always come for him, Moya realized.

Sal jabbed at the orders. "These are General Gomez's orders. I'm just the messenger." Pray the guard would consider the consequences of thwarting a general as powerful as Gomez. The guard stopped walking and looked at Sal with resignation.

"Hey, you! Moya!" he finally yelled. "Over here!"

"Come on, Moya." A guard grabbed his arm and shoved him. "Move it."

The General stumbled forward, eyes downcast. Had Sal convinced the guard? Would they let him leave?

"Get in the jeep," Sal ordered Moya. The guards watched grimly. "Who knows how long they'll keep him this time," Sal shouted over his shoulder as the jeep's gears grated and the vehicle moved forward.

"Welcome to the free world, General, at least the relatively free world," Sal said when they were safely away. "Castro's dead."

So that was it, Moya thought. Castro was finally dead. Now they could begin.

9:40 A.M.
Outside El Palacio de la Revolución
Havana, Cuba

El Palacio rose above Alejandro, the white stone walls impressive even in their present state of disrepair. A grin broke out on his face. The white paper had just been put in the window.

The signal! María was all right, and she had news. He moved out of the alcove and took a circuitous route around the building to the fence. No one seemed to be paying him undue attention. He looked through a crack between the boards. María wasn't there, he realized with disappointment. He felt in their hiding place. But a paper was there!

He scanned the message. So Valles was the Russian stooge. How would that choice affect them? Stuffing the paper into a pocket inside his pants, he walked away toward El Cerro.

9:40 A.M.
Guillermo Sorzano Air Force Base
Outside Havana, Cuba

If their plan had worked, General Gomez thought as he paced his office, Moya should now be in Havana. If not . . . Gomez stood still at a knock on his door. Had something gone wrong? he wondered, even as he realized that no one would connect him with Moya's escape, at least not so soon.

"General Gomez," his aide said, "you've been ordered to report to El Palacio de la Revolución. Presidente Valles wishes to see you."

Presidente Valles, Gomez thought. So Valles had managed to turn Castro's death to his benefit and quickly, too. What did that bode for La Causa? Of more immediate concern, what did this summons bode for him personally? Had La Causa been betrayed somehow and his part in it as well?

Gomez walked toward his car. Too many imponderables. He'd know the answers soon enough. Gomez shivered in the warm sunshine.

9:40 A.M.
The Washington Herald Building
Washington, D.C.

As was his custom upon arrival at his *Washington Herald* office each morning, Peter Evans was organizing his day, jotting notes in his planner. Lunch was a question mark. The White House Mess? He was the only journalist with presidential permission to eat there whenever he wished, but he had no need to underscore his influence today. Today was a day to see and be seen. He'd better go to Dukes. But with whom? He'd call . . .

The intercom buzzed. "Mr. César Valles for you on line two, Mr. Evans."

"César, I'm so pleased to hear from you," Evans said. "It's been too long."

Evans liked Valles, liked his cosmopolitan personality and quick wit. He'd realized from the beginning that Valles was a man of promise. His good looks, his intelligence, his mellifluous voice, his commanding presence, all assured him future prominence.

Evans was an impressive figure in his own way. His morning workout ensured that his Savile Row suits hung perfectly on his toned, six-foot-tall body. His wavy brown hair was styled straight back and accentuated his chiseled features. His appearance was always impeccable. Without question, he was a force on the Washington social scene.

Evans had met Valles six years before in Geneva at the annual meeting of the International Association of Media Resources, Evans in his capacity as newly appointed executive editor of the largest paper in Washington, D.C., and Valles as Cuba's Minister of Communications. Valles had been unabashedly pleased to meet him, and a firm friendship had been formed over drinks and tennis during the rest of the week.

"I wanted you to be the first to know," Valles said. "Fidel Castro died just a few hours ago. A heart attack."

"But, César, I'm, well . . . Castro seemed indestructible. His impact on Cuba—nay, on the entire world—can't be denied." The eulogy for the paper began composing itself in his head.

"No one knows his past greatness better than I," Valles said. "The deterioration over the past few years has been distressing. Regardless, his death has come as a shock to my country. To forestall any problems, the Council of Ministers just met and elected me the new President of Cuba."

"César . . . no, I mean Presidente Valles, let me extend my heartfelt congratulations. Cuba will be well served."

"Thank you, my friend."

Evans was pleased and a little smug to note that Valles still referred to him as his friend. "But," he said hesitantly, "I'm somewhat confused as well. I'd assumed that Raul Castro was the heir apparent."

"So did we all; however, I'm saddened to report that the tragedy of Fidel's death has been compounded by the ambush and killing of his brother."

"No! What happened?"

"During the confusion following Fidel's death, Arturo Registra, the head of the Secret Police, moved quickly to eliminate what he perceived to be the biggest threat to his power, Raul Castro. Early this morning, the Secret Police, on Registra's orders, ambushed Raul outside Havana. Raul as well as all his aides were slaughtered—"

"And then you were named President?"

"Yes, I immediately had Registra and his confederates arrested. He had no idea that we knew of his treachery or even that the Council of Ministers had met, and so we were able to subdue him easily. He and his supporters will be tried for murder."

"You've handled the situation deftly," Evans said, "just as I would have expected."

"Thank you. This has been, to say the least, a trial by fire. Fortunately for Cuba, my countrymen have enthusiastically embraced my presidency. I look forward to justifying their faith. I need not say that everything I do will be for their benefit and for the furtherance of democracy.

"I'd be pleased to have you attend the funeral and inauguration this Saturday as my personal guest."

"I'd be honored to do so."

"Good. I would also like to grant an exclusive interview to any reporter you choose."

"I'll send someone immediately."

"I'm determined—and I know you are also—to foster friendship and understanding between our two countries. Destroying Castro's drug empire and abolishing his arms-running scheme, those are but two parts of my plans."

"Wonderful ideas! The U.S. will certainly take that as proof of your sincerity."

"I'm glad you think so. The burial of communism in this hemisphere—that's how I view the events in my country. I'm eager for the world to learn of the new order in Cuba. But I must go. We'll speak again soon, I promise."

As soon as he hung up, Evans punched an inside line. The associate editor should have everyone in the conference room in twenty minutes. Further, he should cancel the front page of the bulldog edition and hold it for a major story.

What a scoop this would be for him personally as well as for the paper! Evans thought. He needed to get his information out on the wires as quickly as possible if he wanted to be the first. Within two hours the whole world would know the news, and he wanted to be, he had to be, the one whose personal imprint dictated the viewpoint of every subsequent news account. Even the networks would follow his lead if he were first.

He reached forward and rewound his tape recorder. He'd better listen to Valles again and get the facts firmly in mind. Then he needed to make some phone calls.

10:00 A.M.
El Palacio de la Revolución
Havana, Cuba

When General Gomez arrived at El Palacio, a guard at the entrance told him about the seizure of the ministers by the Russians. Gomez wasn't surprised—such actions were to be expected during any take-over—but he was shaken. The enemy was moving quickly.

Now he sat tensely, only the desk separating him from César Valles. Why didn't Valles speak? Gomez wondered. What had gone wrong? Did it have something to do with Moya's escape? Or with La Causa itself?

Valles hadn't said a word since Gomez had entered the room, hadn't even looked up from his papers. Gomez could feel beads of sweat forming on the back of his neck.

"General Gomez."

Using his full title. A bad sign?

"I'm sure you've been told of the death of Fidel Castro," Valles said. "I won't waste time with words of sorrow because we both know that Castro was badly out of control. He'd lost sight of the goals of La Revolución. For years we've needed a progressive leader, and now we can have just that."

Gomez relaxed. Valles was telling him too much to be contemplating execution.

Even as he considered his precarious position, Gomez was cynically amused by Valles's view of Castro. The newly dead leader had certainly undergone a radical transformation from hero to villain, the Stalin of the Caribbean.

"The Council of Ministers has named me the new President."

Valles paused for Gomez's congratulations.

"I'd like for you to be my Minister of Defense."

Gomez blinked once, quickly controlling the shock that jolted through him. From fear of death to a major position in the new government. His black eyes danced at the irony.

"I'm indeed honored, Presidente Valles," he said solemnly. "I'll gladly serve you in any capacity."

"Good. Your first priority will be to plan the military's role in the funeral and inauguration. We need to pay our final tribute to Castro, obviously, but the whole event has only one purpose: to show that the leadership of our country is unquestionably in my hands, and rightly so."

"Certainly, sir."

"For the moment we'll be working with the Russians. Our basic military operation must be reworked with that alliance in mind. We'll be receiving some help from other sources as well. However, our ultimate goal is self-sufficiency. Cuba must become a world power in its own right.

"We'll meet again at one this afternoon," Valles continued. "I'm looking forward to hearing your suggestions. Today is but the beginning. Cuba will soon be the power base for this hemisphere, a leader in the social order."

"The very thought is overwhelming, sir," Gomez said as he rose to leave. "I'll be here at one. Thank you again for honoring me with your trust. I'll do my best for you and for Cuba."

Gomez smiled to himself as he left El Palacio. Obviously, Valles had chosen him because of their long association. As Castro's expert on brainwashing techniques and propaganda dissemination, Gomez had worked closely with Valles, the Minister of Communication, devising effective ways to present information both to the foreign press and to the Cuban people. In the past Valles had found Gomez's advice to be sound. He would expect the same now. The military was the vulnerable link in any government. Under the wrong leadership, it could do much damage, could even topple the government.

Gomez laughed.

10:00 A.M.
The Washington Herald Building
Washington, D.C.

He needed to call the President, Peter Evans thought, reaching for the phone. Since the United States didn't have diplomatic relations with Cuba, the President would appreciate getting direct information. Yes, this was one call that needed to be made.

Lyn Birkla, the President's longtime secretary and protector, was her usual self, pleasant but efficient. "I'm so sorry, Mr. Evans. The President is in a meeting now, but I'm sure he can get back to you in a few minutes."

Evans hung up, certain that the President would return his call at the first opportunity. No politician in recent times had made better use of the power of the press than did this President, and no one appreciated or courted the media more assiduously. He'd known exactly where he was heading from that first congressional campaign; and now that he'd arrived, he intended to stay. He made sure the media knew he appreciated their help.

The President was an astute politician. He was careful to emphasize his Kentucky heritage; he was just a good old boy. Funny how few had keyed on his real history: boarding schools in the East, Ivy League college, first jobs in the East as well. But then the media had been careful to nurture his Kentucky background for him. And why not? He had the same background as many of them and had attended the same prestigious schools as some of the most influential. He really was a good old boy, if not in the traditional sense. These media leaders liked having one of their own kind in power.

Hadn't Evans himself been one of the most helpful, painting the President, only a presidential candidate at the time, as a dynamic and concerned leader? Actually, he'd been nurturing the President's career for years, first giving considerable national prominence to the then Senator from Kentucky. Now was payback time.

While he waited for the President to return his call, Evans placed a call to Senator Trent Westlake, Chairman of the Senate Select Committee on Intelligence. Westlake, too, needed to be reminded of Valles's importance to the United States. Besides, Evans enjoyed the irony of talking to the husband of his current lover, not that Westlake knew.

The conversation was developing just as Evans had planned, with Westlake properly grateful at his inclusion in the inner loop. The intercom buzzed.

"White House on line one, Mr. Evans."

"I've got to go now, Trent," Evans said. "Call from the President on another line."

He punched line one.

"Peter Evans here."

"This is the White House operator. Please hold for the President of the United States."

Evans heard clicks as the President was put on the line.

"Peter, Lyn tells me you called."

"Mr. President, I'm sure you've been informed of the interesting events in Cuba?"

"Yes, the news was sent over a few minutes ago. Interesting, indeed. Nothing we can do, though. Just wait for events to unfold. Wouldn't do to interfere in another country's affairs."

Evans could picture the President smoothing the graying hair at his temple with the ends of his fingers, a newly acquired habit.

"I admire your grasp of the situation, sir," Evans said. "I called to let you know I spoke with César Valles a short time ago. We've been friends for years. He assures me that they're experiencing a smooth transition of power. Valles has the complete support of the Council of Ministers as well as the people of Cuba."

"I'm pleased to have my evaluation of the situation reinforced," the President responded. "Valles seems a good man. Prodemocracy. Not a renegade like Castro."

"I agree, sir. He'll be a valuable ally, and our strength in the Caribbean will be greatly enhanced. President Valles has asked me to attend the funeral and inauguration. Being a witness to the burial of communism and the emergence of an ally certainly is appealing."

The President was silent for a moment. "An intriguing thought, Peter. I hope to see you tonight at the Symphony Ball."

"Yes, sir, I'll be there. Wouldn't miss it."

Evans hung up, satisfied. Only time would tell, but he'd bet that the President would support Valles, as indeed he should. Valles deserved the support of the United States.

Evans returned to the eulogy he'd written on Castro for the front page. It didn't need much polishing, but he wanted it to be especially good.

After a few changes, he saved what he'd written and retrieved that day's editorial from his computer's memory. In it he'd mentioned Valles in supportive terms, to give the Western world the proper introduction to him. That, coupled with the news story about his election to the presidency, would help establish Valles as a creditable world leader.

Leaning back in his chair, he thought about how best to present the information about Cuba to his staff. Coverage in the paper must be both dramatic and factual. One sold papers; the other was the essence of good journalism. He'd have to make sure that everyone understood what was necessary. Valles had given Evans an information bonanza. He'd better make the most of it.

10:15 A.M.
The White House
Washington, D.C.

"The Cuban situation is shaping up nicely," the President said to his Chief of Staff, M. Eugene Corforth, as he hung up the phone. "That was Peter Evans. He and César Valles have been personal friends for years, and Evans agrees that Valles is a man we can deal with. I honestly believe we are witnessing the burial of communism in this hemisphere, maybe the end of communism everywhere." His smile was beatific. "We need to cement such a change. Normalizing relations between our two countries as soon as Valles has established his right of leadership would seem a logical first step."

The President rose from his chair and walked from behind his desk. His quick, agile movements were a carryover from his days as a successful college wrestler. Although he was of average height, his broad shoulders and large head made him appear more physically commanding on TV than in person.

He began pacing in front of the multipaned windows that looked out over the Rose Garden. The view was bleak. Cold winter days had made the normally green and flower-filled expanse barren. Actually, few roses grew in the enclosure; but, in season, other flowers filled the void.

Corforth's eyes glittered in his ruddy face. "Mr. President, this could be a momentous event not only for Cuba but for us, too. If we position you properly, we could give you credit for bringing freedom and democracy to Cuba."

The President had stopped his pacing and gave Corforth his full attention.

"Your reelection would almost be assured," Corforth continued. "Castro has been an albatross around our neck for too long. If his successor is pro-American and prodemocracy . . . All we have to do is maximize the situation."

"Put together a statement for me," the President said, moving away from the marble mantel where he'd been leaning. "The press are probably writing their stories already, and we need to put the right spin on this from the beginning."

The President, ever punctual, was already walking Corforth to the door. His tailor would be arriving at ten-thirty to fit two new suits, and this President never kept anyone waiting.

10:38 A.M.
The Capitol
Washington, D.C.

Bob Grant walked out of the Senate chamber and entered the Republican Cloakroom. Absentmindedly he picked up a box of raisins from the basket by the door, opened it, and popped several into his mouth. Good thing they didn't have just candy bars; he had enough trouble with his weight as it was.

"Senator Grant." A Senate page stopped deferentially in front of him. "You have a phone call." He pointed to a booth at the end of the room.

With a "Thank you," Grant walked over and picked up the phone, not bothering to close the door. Out of the corner of his eye, he watched one of the all-news networks on the cloakroom TV.

"Senator, this is Victor Rojas. Cynthia suggested I call. We've just received another message from Cuba."

Grant moved into the booth and closed the glass door.

"According to the message, César Valles has been named President of Cuba, and Valles is actively supported by the Russians."

"César Valles? He was Minister of Communication, wasn't he?"

"Yes."

"And he's backed by the Russians? They've certainly moved quickly, especially since they're supposed to be harmless these days. But what about Raul? Surely he'll have something to say."

"Raul's dead."

Grant whistled in surprise.

"Apparently he was killed on his way to Havana. The story being circulated is that he was ambushed by the Secret Police on orders of Arturo Registra, their head."

"Then how do the Russians figure in?"

"The ambush must have been Russian led. At around the same time Raul was being eliminated, the commander of the Russian military installation in Cuba took some of his troops into El Palacio. The soldiers were in Cuban uniforms, and Basilov, the commander, was in a suit, but our informant recognized him. Said he was sure it was a Russian squad trying to look otherwise. Anyway, shots were fired, and several members of the Cuban Council of Ministers, Registra among them, were led out, thrown into a truck, and taken away. When it was over, Valles was President. The timing of the events . . . well, it just couldn't have been coincidental."

"Just a minute, Victor," Grant said, his eye caught by Castro's picture on the TV screen. "Something about Cuba's just come on the TV."

Grant opened the door and listened.

"I don't like this," he said when the report had ended and he'd once again closed the door. "The President just extolled Valles, saying he's a man we can do business with. You're sure about this Valles-Russian connection?"

"As sure as I can be. You know how accurate Moya's information has been in the past."

"His people certainly knew about Castro's death long before it was known here. There's over a seventeen-hour discrepancy, isn't there?"

"About," Rojas said.

"Enough time for Valles and the Russians to get their plan under way. Is that how you read it?"

"Sounds logical," Rojas said. "Even if they had the plan prepared, it'd take time to put it in motion, especially since they couldn't know where Raul would be."

"We'd better play this low-key for the moment," Grant said. "We don't want to compromise our contact in Cuba by being too well informed. Why don't you come to the office? In the meantime, I'll search out Trent Westlake, our venerable chairman, to see if we can convene the Select Committee on Intelligence and get some answers from that direction. I don't like what's happening, especially the apparent Russian involvement. Too many odd inconsistencies about the whole thing. We need to figure out what's really going on."

The Senate Select Committee on Intelligence was the oversight committee for all intelligence operations of the government. Comprising twelve members, each serving a maximum of eight years, this committee was one where a less-senior Senator could be chairman or ranking member because of the required rotation of membership. For the last year and a half, Westlake had been chairman and Grant ranking member.

Pushing through the double doors that opened directly onto the floor, Grant scanned the chamber. Luck was with him. Westlake was just crossing the well and heading for the far door.

Westlake smiled at Grant as he approached.

No, he told Grant with a friendly slap on the back, he didn't know much about Cuba. Yes, Castro had died, that had been reported. But the Russians in the picture, he doubted that. They weren't about to break their pledge of peace. Well, if Grant was so concerned, he'd do him a favor and call a meeting. Eleven-thirty. A waste of time, probably.

10:47 A.M.
The Washington Herald Building
Washington, D.C.

The executive editor's office was breathtaking in its understated elegance. Peter Evans knew that first impressions were crucial. Further, he wanted his visitors to feel inferior to the man who could command such opulence in a business not usually concerned with personal comfort. Hence, the modern sculptures, the authentic Frank Lloyd Wright furniture and finally the Picasso in lonely splendor on the far wall. The couch under it was cause for even more comment, however. Reputedly, it was used most often in a horizontal position and not for naps. Evans's conquests were the making of legends.

At the moment, Evans was lounging in his leather chair, white shirtsleeves rolled up to expose his Piaget, the phone at his ear. With no pause in his conversation, he motioned Amy Averitt, one of his reporters, to a chair.

"Sure . . . sure. Just make certain the picture's not only in a prominent place but big, at least five columns, more if you can . . . eyes above the fold . . . right." Hanging up, he turned to Amy.

"Think you can be ready to leave for Cuba in two hours?" he asked.

"Yes, sir," Amy replied.

Evans hoped he'd been right in choosing her for the assignment. Her fluency in Spanish made her the logical choice, but women . . . No telling what they'd do, especially on a major story. Fortunately, the thrust of this story was self-evident.

"Good," he replied brusquely. "Pick up the tickets at the desk when you leave." Pausing, he smiled at her encouragingly. Amy smiled in return.

"This is an important assignment, you know, and I personally chose you."

Amy smiled again.

"Now, don't get the wrong idea," he continued. "You'll be writing the stories, but everything will come through me. President Valles is a personal friend." Evans paused for another acknowledgment—pauses were an important ingredient in his conversations with subordinates. "And so I have a special insight into the events there. Valles has given us an exclusive—you can finalize arrangements when you arrive this afternoon—and I expect you to take full advantage of it.

"Show why Valles is a good choice for President—the young leader taking up the gauntlet, bringing back the hope of the revolution. Castro had lost his vision. Valles has it. You know what I mean, don't you?''

"Yes, I think I understand."

"Interview the people. Emphasize Valles's popularity. We want to make Valles sound good—because he is. I'll expect you to call me personally, morning and evening. Leave a message with the foreign desk if I'm not around."

He reached for a pen. "Call the desk when you arrive. I want general first impressions for tomorrow's edition. A country at the dawn of a new age. The usual local color.

"Oh, and I'll be at the funeral myself, guest of President Valles, so I'll cover it personally.

"Don't blow this, Averitt. The story will practically write itself."

Evans looked down at the paper in front of him and began writing.

10:48 A.M.
The Capitol
Washington, D.C.

Smiling and nodding at the Senators he passed, Westlake walked toward the front of the chamber and took the door to the left, which led to the Senators' lounge. He would call Edmund Miller right away. Miller had been on his staff for fourteen years, almost from the beginning, and could anticipate just what was needed. When Westlake had assumed the chairmanship of the Senate Select Committee on Intelligence, Miller had asked to be made majority counsel. The Senator had agreed but with the proviso that he continue his administrative-assistant duties as well. Miller had managed both positions adroitly.

Westlake picked up a phone on one of the tables in the lounge. "Edmund, we need to call a meeting of the Intelligence Committee. Bob Grant's concerned about what's going on in Cuba. Line up someone from the CIA to brief us if you can. Eleven-thirty."

"Did Grant express any special concerns?"

"No, just a general need to know. You don't have to focus on anything specific."

"I'll take care of it."

Westlake glanced at the ormolu clock on the mantel at one end of the room. Miller would have just enough time to set up a meeting and inform the appropriate Senators of the time.

10:48 A.M.
The clinic
Havana, Cuba

A knock! Ines Moya ran to the door. She must come to the clinic immediately, she was told; her medicine was ready.

What had happened? she wondered as she grabbed her purse, which was already crammed preparatory to leaving at eleven. This summons to the clinic . . . Why the change?

She slammed the door and hurried down the street, unanswered questions and unnamed fears filling her mind. Her threadbare cotton dress molded to her thin figure, and her short gray hair blew back from her small-featured face. With relief she saw the clinic at the end of the street.

As she followed an employee to a small examination room at the back, her heart raced wildly. She heard the door close behind her, but her eyes were held by the gaunt figure before her, her husband, José. José really was standing before her.

With a cry, she threw herself into his arms, sobbing as she pressed her cheek tightly against his chest. Moya kissed her hair, her eyes, her wet cheeks.

They pulled apart slightly, each needing to see the other's face, to reassure himself. José, José, Ines's mind sang. It really was he. Each savored the closeness of the other, trying to prolong the moment. To see each other—and without guards or prison walls—was a miracle, a moment to hold in memory against future separation.

Their eyes closed as they pressed their bodies together fiercely. Ines could feel her husband's bones digging into her. How thin he'd become! She knew he must be discovering the same about her. So much had changed, but so much was the same.

"Oh, José, I can't believe you're really here," she whispered, holding his face in her hands. "You're all right, aren't you?" He smiled; she searched his face. "Yes, I can see you are." He'd aged terribly, but the light of hope was in his eyes, she saw with gladness.

"And you, my sweet one," Moya said, running his finger lightly over her lips, "you're lovelier even than my dreams of you. If only we could spend these minutes enjoying each other. Oh, my darling," he whispered, one hand caressing her face, his other arm holding her protectively, "I want to hold you, to feel your nearness. You're so dear to me, so truly precious. But . . ." His arm tightened. "As always, we've so little time."

Ines pulled back gently from the circle of his arm. "You're right, of course, but be prepared when the time's finally ours." The light of mischief sparkled in her gray eyes. "You have many years to make up for, you know."

Moya shook his head in wonder. How amazing his wife was and how amazing her love. She'd suffered so much. They both had. Years of separation, of torture, of want and sorrow and betrayal. And yet, through it all, she'd retained her humor and her enjoyment of life.

"Ines, my love." Moya brushed the back of his hand against her cheek and then led her to the table. "We need to make plans while we have the chance, before our meeting with the others. I'd hoped you wouldn't have to come to the clinic this morning."

She smiled, and he squeezed her hand. "I know," he said, grinning; "I'm certainly not complaining, but"—his face became sober—"being here compounds your danger. However, I couldn't chance your going to Umberto's. We don't know what happened, but he disappeared a short while ago. Alejandro thinks it has something to do with his being in the Secret Police. Whatever the reason, we couldn't risk it. Instead I want you to stay with Vincente Aguirre. You'll be safe there. Because we've never served in the same army unit, no one will suspect that Vincente and I are friends. He's crucial to our plans as well, and the two of you can work together. But, Ines," Moya cautioned, "tell no one where you'll be, not even the members of La Causa."

"How will you contact me?"

"Alejandro's taken care of it. He can explain his plan to you. If I'm forced to leave here, I'll join you at Vincente's."

For a moment they stared at each other in silence. So much could go wrong.

11:25 A.M.
Senate Intelligence Committee's Hearing Room
Hart Senate Office Building
Washington, D.C.

"Encouraging news about Cuba, isn't it?" Grant felt Stan Yarbonski's hand on his arm, a big man to match a big voice.

Yar, a second-term conservative like himself, was one of Grant's closest friends on the Hill. He saw Congress's role in the same way as Grant. The less Congress governed, the better.

"Castro's death, you mean," Grant said.

"Well, sure. I must say, you don't act overjoyed. I thought you'd be euphoric."

"About Castro, of course. But I'm not as enamored with Valles as the President seems to be. Things have moved too quickly. Everything's too pat. I'll be interested in hearing the CIA briefing. Hope Westlake got someone good to come."

The two men arrived at the glass doors leading into the area where the SIC meetings were held. Intelligence reports stored in this area were highly classified, so access was carefully monitored. The room was secure, impervious to microwaves or other listening devices. Those who worked on the Hill referred to it as the Bubble.

When Senator Grant had become ranking member of the committee, he'd requested and received a code-word clearance for his administrative assistant, Cynthia Novitsky, thereby giving her access to all information up to that clearance. Security was understandably restrictive, with even some Senators not read into certain programs. Security levels ranged from "Classified" to "Top Secret" to "Code" to "Eyes Only." Few people, even on the Hill, had clearance for "Eyes Only" documents.

Grant did as did Senator Westlake. Edmund Miller, of course, as majority counsel, had complete clearance. These men were given any file they requested, but that file contained only the documents the majority counsel chose to include. Most of the documents were stored in huge general files.

Grant had already been to the Bubble once that morning. The most recent reports in the Cuba file had presented little more than had been on TV.

"Senator Grant. Senator Yarbonski. You may enter." The guard opened the reinforced doors leading into the hearing room.

Most of the twelve Senators who made up the Senate Select Committee on Intelligence had already arrived. They began taking their seniority-determined seats around the horseshoe-shaped table at the front of the hearing room. Their aides took seats directly behind. While he waited for the meeting to begin, Grant leafed through the fact sheets about Valles and Cuba that Cynthia had sent via his intelligence staffer.

When Trent Westlake finally entered the room, Grant felt a familiar stir of irritation mixed with affection.

Westlake was the epitome of a Senator. His tall, slightly paunchy body and mane of white hair were perfectly complemented by a resonant voice and telegenic smile. He was frequently described as a teddy bear of a man, and so kind. He *was* kind, Grant agreed, if kindness was measured by the amount of someone else's money he could give away. And, boy, did he give it away! There wasn't a program except defense that he wasn't ready to fund, no questions asked, no accountability demanded.

But it was hard not to like Westlake, deplorable as his voting record was. He'd been friendly to Grant from the beginning, making him feel welcome in the Senate. And he certainly wasn't deliberately strident and obstructive like some. Not that their actual words ever made it into the permanent record; most Senators and Representatives were quick to "revise and extend" their remarks before they were made part of the *Congressional Record*. A deplorable practice to Grant's mind, the so-called recorded debates having never taken place.

Grant had trouble reconciling Westlake's adherence to the liberal agenda with his affectionate personality, almost as if he didn't really understand the implications of his votes. Grant had often wondered if he just wasn't bright, but even that didn't explain everything. The Senator was hard to figure. Of course, his ambitious wife explained a lot.

Yar leaned over. "I hope we get some information this time. I'm tired of being spoon-fed pap."

"My sentiments exactly."

As always in public, Westlake spoke confidently, content to follow the script his administrative assistant had left at his place. In his opening remarks, he mentioned Castro and then praised the new President, César Valles, "choice of the Council of Ministers and also of the Cuban people," "a friend of the United States" and "a most urbane and intelligent gentleman."

"Christopher Rhynehart, Deputy Director of the Central Intelligence Agency, will now brief us on the Cuban situation."

"Thank you, Mr. Chairman," Rhynehart began from his seat at the testifier's table. "Events have taken a favorable turn in Cuba. Through reports from our intelligence network, we've reason to believe that a government with prodemocracy leanings is being established there. Our sources have further confirmed that Arturo Registra, head of the Secret Police, was planning a coup with Raul Castro's assassination as the first step. César Valles and the Council of Ministers acted immediately to arrest Registra and his confederates before . . ." Grant's mind wandered. Rhynehart's report added little to information already available through the media. "We're receiving no contrary or negative information about César Valles or his government," Rhynehart concluded.

"Mr. Rhynehart," Grant asked when he was finally recognized by the chairman, "do any of your reports cast doubt on the legitimacy of the Valles presidency or in any way link him to the Russians or to any other country?"

"No, Senator, absolutely no linkage exists between Valles and the Russians or between Valles and any other country."

Edmund Miller, seated directly behind Westlake, began writing furiously.

"Do we have any information about increased Russian activity in the area?" Grant asked, phrasing the question in generalities so as not to compromise Moya's activities.

"No, Senator, other than increased communication between Moscow and the Russian military base near Havana, we've no reports of unusual Russian activity. Naturally we've noticed little activity by the Russians anywhere this last year. Cuba is no exception."

"Do you—" Grant began.

Miller leaned forward and deftly placed a paper on the table in front of Westlake. The act was well practiced and hardly noticeable.

"My esteemed colleague," Westlake interrupted after glancing at Miller's note, "we've been assured that the Valles government is as honorable as it appears. To belabor the point seems unproductive. Does anyone else have a question germane to our discussion . . . ? Then thank you, Mr. Rhynehart."

What was going on? Grant wondered, staring at Westlake with a puzzled frown. Why truncate the hearing? Wasn't now the time to be asking questions, now when any potential problems could still be averted? How frustrating to be the minority party at the mercy of the shortsightedness of those in the majority. There was no such thing as equality among Senators.

"In summary," Westlake said, "we're all aware that the United States has the best intelligence-gathering network in the world. We know for a fact that President Valles has been selected virtually unanimously by his country's Council of Ministers. We've been assured that he has the support of the Cuban people as well. He's a friend of the United States and a personal friend of our President. We are fortunate to have him in power instead of someone less eager to be a part of the free world."

Grant sat back in his chair, disgusted at the trivialization of a potentially serious problem. A personal friend of the President, he thought sardonically. Now wasn't the time to deal in personalities. Now they should be looking at the facts, wondering at the inconsistencies. Why had the lost seventeen hours in reporting Castro's death not been mentioned? Or the presence of the Russians when Valles took office? Or the convenient timing of Raul's death? Angrily, he began stuffing his papers into his briefcase. Why was Westlake using the prerogatives of the chairman to adjourn the meeting before all questions were asked and answered?

Westlake had been right for once, Grant thought as he left the room; the meeting *had* been a waste of time. Resignedly he stepped onto the elevator.

"Pretty worthless meeting, wasn't it?" Yar asked. "Not that I expected different. Why is it that we seldom know more than the media?"

"A good question. I can't help wondering what's really going on in Cuba. Are the Russians involved in some way? If they are, I want to know why. I'm going to find out who's heading the CODEL to Cuba and see if I can join it."

Congress always sent a congressional delegation to any major event, usually headed by a committee chairman. In this case, the Chairman of the Foreign Relations Committee would, no doubt, be working up a list.

"Do you think that's wise?" Yarbonski asked as the private Senate subway station came into view. "Won't it look as if you're giving tacit approval to Valles? Trent's evaluation of Valles may be wrong. Just his saying it makes me wonder."

"That's exactly why I need to go. Someone's got to keep Westlake and his cohorts in line. They might be tempted to compromise us completely—in the name of brotherhood and world peace, of course."

11:30 A.M.
The clinic
Havana, Cuba

Ines rushed to hug Dr. Llada as he and Alejandro walked into the room.

"Thank you, Jorge," she said, holding his hands tightly. "Thank you for delivering my husband to me. Or me to him," she added, laughing. "You've been wonderful."

Dr. Llada squeezed her hands in return. "Don't thank me. I

just took him in when he appeared on my doorstep. A more pitiful specimen I've seldom seen. What else could I do? Throw him back on the street? A bath and clean clothes seemed more to the point."

While Ines and Dr. Llada talked, Moya and Alejandro conferred in undertones. They'd had only a few minutes together before Ines's arrival.

"May I join you?" Julio Montaner asked from the doorway.

"Of course, of course," the doctor said, bustling to pull up chairs.

"You're just in time," Moya said. "We need to discuss our plans. Paschal hasn't arrived yet?"

"No," Alejandro answered, "but I'm not surprised. The streets are crowded. Everyone's coming for the funeral. María confirms it'll be Saturday at eleven-thirty, followed by the inauguration. Valles is wasting no time in establishing his claim to the presidency. He wants to make the event into as big a media statement as possible."

"No doubt the American media will be at the funeral in full strength," Ines said, laughing dryly. "If they liked Castro, they'll love Valles."

"No doubt," her husband said. "But maybe we can use them to our advantage. If we have everything in position by Saturday, they'll be forced to show the world the free government of Cuba. Of course"—he shrugged—"if we fail, they'll give increased credibility to Valles. Is our network in place, Alejandro?"

"As in place as it can be with so few of us. We have to overcome so much—fear of Valles and the Russians, fear of change, for that matter, and then the suddenness of it all. Hopefully, the news of this morning's barbarisms at El Palacio will increase people's willingness to act. They'll want to avoid another Castro. But the Russians . . . They may say they're now peace loving, but their troops are still here. We'll need many more people helping us than we have now if we hope to overcome them."

"The Russians? But what about Raul?" Ines asked, obviously confused.

"I thought you knew," Alejandro said. "He was ambushed and killed this morning, supposedly by the Secret Police."

"Why 'supposedly'?"

"One of our friends outside Havana says that the Russians were behind it," Alejandro said. "His brother saw it happen. We're told he has hard proof and will get it to us as soon as possible. He's frightened for his family, but I'm hoping he'll help us because Miami's last message said they needed proof—Raul, Valles, the Russians, even the legitimacy of our movement."

"Tell our people to be on the lookout for anything that corroborates the truth," Moya said. "After all, I might be a Russian plant, and Valles, the hero. We'll have to come up with proof of Valles's Russian alliance because proving I'm prodemocracy will be impossible. Of course, convincing the West that the Russians still have teeth won't be easy, either."

"I'll send out the word," Alejandro promised. "María may be able to find something, especially as she cleans the ministers' offices."

"For now let's firm up our plans. Securing the support of the military is of paramount importance. We'll need soldiers who are loyal to us, enough soldiers to defeat the Russians. That won't be easily done. Finding means to contact the bases is a problem in itself. I'd hoped—"

A knock cut through his words. Alejandro opened the door to admit a stocky man dressed in peasant clothes.

"Paschal!" Moya cried, walking to the newcomer and embracing him. "I'm glad to see you. We'd begun to worry, you were so long in coming."

Gomez laughed. "You won't believe what has happened." He shook his head as he laughed again. Moya and the others watched, puzzled.

"I still can't believe it. I was summoned to César Valles's office—have you heard he's proclaimed himself President, with the help of the Russians?"

They nodded.

"Well, I went to his office prepared for the worst, sure he'd found out about La Causa. I admit it—I was so afraid, the sweat literally dripped off me. Then, believe it or not, Valles made me Minister of Defense."

"What! You can't mean it!" Moya exclaimed.

"Astounding, isn't it?" Gomez smiled. "I had trouble not giving myself away, I was so totally unprepared. Still seems too amazing to be true."

"The possibilities are limitless," Julio Montaner congratulated him. "This will make our job a thousand times easier."

"It is overwhelming," Gomez agreed. "The rest of my news is just as good. I'm to plan the use of the military during the funeral and the events surrounding it."

"An answer to prayer," Alejandro said. "Nothing else could help us more."

"I've come up with the skeleton of a plan," Gomez said, "one that I think will appeal to Valles."

The others looked at him expectantly.

"I was considering a military flyover at the beginning of the ceremony, two groups of four planes, one comprising backfire bombers"—Gomez smiled at their murmurs of appreciation—"and the second, MiGs. Each group would perform the missing-man maneuver, honoring Castro and signifying the end of military rule. I shouldn't have any trouble convincing Valles of the appropriateness of that symbolism. The maneuvers would put our people in the air and allow them to fly in different directions without alarming anyone."

"We'll have to pick our targets carefully," Alejandro said, "coordinating times and distances, but the ceremony makes for the consummate camouflage. You've hit upon the perfect combination."

"The quicker we control the air," Moya said, "the quicker we own the ground. Paschal, can you meet with Silvio Sacasa and formulate a plan, one that includes informing our people at the various bases?"

"Obviously, as the new military commander, I must personally make my presence and my authority felt at every installation," Gomez said with a grin. "I'll suggest to Valles that I tour all our bases tomorrow." Alejandro and Dr. Llada laughed softly. "That should take care of our communication needs."

"Because he's a field commander for the western army, Silvio would be a logical choice as your deputy and contact man," Moya said. "Suggest that Valles make that appointment. Then Sacasa will have the freedom to move our people around without arousing suspicion. Everyone will be expecting Valles to make changes and will be fearful of questioning anything."

"Crippling communications on all military bases immediately before the attack has to be a main priority," Gomez said.

"Without damaging the equipment unduly," Alejandro added. "We'll need it as soon as you're named President, General."

"Right. Julio, would you begin working on that?"

Julio Montaner nodded.

"Jorge, you and Ines need to coordinate our popular support at La Plaza," Moya told Dr. Llada. "Make sure our people are prepared to support us as vocally as possible. Try to maximize our impact on the media. I know we haven't many materials to use, but do what you can."

"I think many will be excited about helping," Dr. Llada said. "The spark for that support is already evident. More and more of my patients are openly complaining, something they've feared doing until the recent shortages."

"We'll make sure that by Saturday everyone knows of your escape," Ines added, "and of your determination to lead us to freedom."

"What about our military network, Paschal? Are you satisfied with the officers we presently have supporting La Causa?"

"As much as I can be," Gomez replied, "considering how seldom I've spoken with them. I'll feel everyone out when I tour the bases tomorrow. We'll need to add more to their number, though, if we hope to succeed."

"If you can stay for a few minutes after this meeting, we can discuss some possible contacts," Moya said. He stood as he brought the meeting to a close.

"Alejandro, you'll continue coordinating all phases of the operation. Jorge and Ines, you'll oversee the nonmilitary events surrounding the takeover. Paschal and Julio, you'll develop the military aspects, with you, Paschal, relaying the plans to our network on the bases. Hopefully, Silvio will be in a position to coordinate all of that. And I'll continue formulating plans for the administration of our new government."

The takeover plan had to succeed; it was of supreme importance and their primary goal. But the ultimate success of the takeover would depend on his handling of the crises that were sure to follow. Moya knew he'd need much support and many voices at the time of triumph. He'd need a few strong ones at his right hand in the days that followed. Those first days would be crucial.

"We shouldn't plan on meeting again, so Alejandro has set up a communication system for us. After this meeting, all messages and requests will be relayed through him. I'll remain at the clinic for as long as it seems safe."

12:05 P.M.
The Senate side of the Capitol
Washington, D.C.

Cynthia was once again racing down the tunnel connecting the Hart Building with the Capitol, only this time she was accompanied by a breathless Victor Rojas. As they climbed the single flight of stairs that would lead them to the subbasement corridor where the Senator's hideaway office was located, Edmund Miller passed them unnoticed. Miller cocked his eyebrow at their intent conversation, making no effort to interrupt them. He was late for a meeting in the Hart Building.

"We'll turn left down this next corridor, and then we're almost there," Cynthia told Rojas. "It's always amazed me how the Senate was able to find private office space for each Senator down here. It's a great place to work when several votes are being held and it's impossible to leave the building. It's also a good spot," she said with a laugh, "if you don't want your staff to know with whom you're meeting.

"Here we are." She rapped on the nondescript door they faced. It was opened by Grant.

"Victor, I'm glad you got here so quickly." A desk, sofa, coffee table and chairs were on the right; but Grant ushered Rojas and Cynthia toward the conference table at the other end of the room.

Rojas had heard about these most secret and private offices, but this was his first visit to one. Senators knew how to pamper themselves, he thought. Not only was this office furnished with Chippendale-style furniture, but it had the most advanced of telecommunications equipment, handsome bookcases, artwork and even a small refrigerator, well stocked, no doubt. Quite a nice little hideaway, he thought cynically. Then he looked at Grant and amended his thoughts. A good Senator deserved the extra convenience. Too bad all Senators weren't—

"Victor." Grant's amused voice brought Rojas back. Not many people ever saw a "cubby," but their thoughts were always equally transparent. "The President's convinced that Valles is going to be a valuable ally, the CIA concurs, and I'm not getting any reports to the contrary. In fact, I don't have anything that supports the information you've given me."

"Senator, our contact in Cuba is the same one Moya's always used. He's proven himself totally reliable in the past."

"Before we go any further, let's make sure I have all the facts on Moya's group," Grant said. "Cynthia, you need to stay. You'll be the sole point of contact in our office. The need to know has to be limited to protect the resistance. Now, Victor, tell us anything you think would help."

"Before he was imprisoned," Rojas began, "Moya put together a resistance network, and he still heads the group. They call themselves La Causa. Since Moya's imprisonment, other Cubans have joined them. At the same time, some of the original members have been imprisoned or have died, including several key members who were executed at the time of Moya's imprisonment for knowing him. The group is small, has no espionage training and no way of receiving any, and has been forced to work within the confines of a totally repressive society. Meetings aren't allowed; neither is ownership of much of anything. Wholesale spying and random arrests are the norm. La Causa has no weapons. Their only equipment is a transmitter/receiver set we sent them."

"What makes Moya think he has a chance now?" Grant asked.

"Almost from the beginning, La Causa has had a plan in readiness. That plan includes provisions for Moya's escape, for control of the military and for generating widespread support of the people.

I, and now you, are the only ones outside of La Causa who know such a plan exists, and only the leaders of La Causa know the details or even who the members of the group are. Secrecy has been absolutely vital to their survival and is an integral part of their plan to gain freedom. Because the Cuban government has no idea such a group exists, Moya feels they can succeed if they can move quickly before anyone can discover and destroy them."

"So we can't divulge any information that could have come only from someone inside Cuba," Cynthia said.

"Exactly. The Russians have too many friendly ears in too many places. And remember, their strength in Cuba, for whatever reason, is as great now as it's ever been. Even the intelligence facility at Lourdes appears fully operational."

"But couldn't the information about Castro have come from our own intelligence sources inside Cuba?" Cynthia asked.

"I wish the answer were yes," Grant said, "but remember a few years ago when the media got self-righteous and exposed much of our intelligence network around the world?"

Cynthia nodded.

"Not only were many agents and informants killed as a result, but you can imagine the problems for recruiting. Cuba was severely affected. We had few resources there to begin with—Castro had seen to that—and we lost those we had. Nobody knows this better than the Russians. They'd know the information had to have come from a resistance group within that country. But back to Valles. Who is he really, Victor? And what are his intentions?"

"He was the Minister of Communication for Castro. He'd earned his way up the ranks, receiving most of his training in Moscow and Eastern Europe, with a short tour in China—at least that's according to one unconfirmed report. He's known for waiting quietly to see what can help him personally before making any kind of move. He was one of Castro's favorites and definitely part of the inner circle. For example, he's the one minister whom Castro trusted enough to send to foreign conferences. As a result, he's cultivated friendships with a variety of influential people around the world. For the last few months, he's been unusually quiet at ministry meetings, almost as if he were trying to take attention away from himself."

"How do you know all this?" Grant asked. "I thought those ministry meetings were ultrasecret."

"This is Moya's work, Senator," Rojas replied. "He has people in several strategic areas. Don't get me wrong. We're only talking about a handful, but their information has been accurate. We've tried to keep their existence secret. So far, we think we've succeeded.

"Now, about Valles in relation to the Russians," Rojas continued. "Before its downfall, the Soviet Union had readied a takeover plan in the event of the death or removal of Castro. Whether the Russian Republic has equal interest or capability to continue with that plan, we just don't know. Obviously, Valles is working with them to some extent. The events this morning at El Palacio prove that. I don't trust either Valles or the Russians. Whatever they plan, it won't be good for Cuba."

"Which brings up something else," Grant said. "Where are the Russians getting their money? Just keeping troops in Cuba has to be a drain. Now that they've committed themselves to Valles, how can they hope to find funds to stabilize Cuba's economy as well as prevent a revolt by hungry Cubans? All that takes money, more than I'd have thought they could spare."

"I've heard no talk of finances, but I'll put out feelers. Financial trails are notoriously hard to follow."

"So the bottom line on all this," Grant said with a look at his watch, "is that we take Moya at his own valuation and work to expose Valles and get Moya in power?"

"We're dealing on faith here," Rojas said. "But has anyone presented proof of what Valles says? The choice is between accepting the word of General Moya and his people or the word of a member of Castro's inner council."

"The choice isn't quite so simple. If the last few hours are any indication, Valles already has several powerful forces aligned with him: the media have embraced him; we're saddled with a President who's easily influenced; the Russians have put their military behind him; and the personality of the Cuban people will work in his favor. They've been subjugated for so long that they'll be reluctant to oppose him."

"All true," Rojas said. "The inexperience of the members of La Causa and their lack of weapons must be considered as well. And what does Moya have? Next to nothing, and he's in prison, at least we have to assume so. I don't know, Senator; put like that, the odds seem overwhelming."

"They are," Cynthia said. "They're frighteningly one-sided, but they were in 1776, too. That's corny, I know, but it's true. Just having freedom as the goal, that changes the odds, doesn't it?"

"It does, indeed, help to even things," Grant said. "And we mustn't forget that those same odds apply to the security of our country. While I'd like to see Moya succeed for Cuba's sake, my primary concern is for the United States."

He leaned forward, his arms on the table. "At this point I'm not sure what we'll be able to do, but I know I need more information. I want everything we can find on Valles, on the current situation in Cuba, on Moya's whereabouts and the true extent of his operation and on the Russians and any interesting meetings they might have had in the past six months, especially in the last twenty-four hours, with countries or individuals who have money to spare and a presumed agenda against the United States. The more we know, the better chance we'll have of helping Cuba.

"We need to educate the media, the Senate and, if it comes to that, the President personally about the true situation. Facts—we have to have significantly more than we have right now. Ideally, we need concrete proof from Cuba, the sooner the better, about the Valles-Russian alliance and about the reason for the Russian involvement there to begin with. And we have to do all this without compromising La Causa."

Grant smiled. "Now that's what I call a challenge."

12:15 P.M.
A government-controlled radio station
Havana, Cuba

IN A UNANIMOUS SHOW OF SUPPORT, THE CUBAN COUNCIL OF MIN-
ISTERS IS PROUD TO ANNOUNCE THE NEW PRESIDENT OF CUBA,
CÉSAR VALLES. PRESIDENTE VALLES IS A FRIEND OF THE PEOPLE
AND A CHAMPION OF THE RIGHTS OF THE PEOPLE. HE PROMISES
NEW PROSPERITY . . .

12:40 P.M.
Hart Senate Office Building
Washington, D.C.

So, Grant was nosing around, Bonfire thought as he hung up the
phone. His contacts would want that bit of information right away,
certainly before his usual time. They'd need to get Grant muzzled
immediately.

The emergency number was answered on the sixth ring, as
prearranged.

"Has Mrs. Green returned from her Bahama vacation yet?" Bonfire asked, knowing these words would verify his identity.

"She'll be distraught to have missed you, but she'll be in the
office tomorrow," came the correct response.

"Would you give her a message for me? I have a friend from
Georgia, a junior basketball star whose home court is the Dome.
He's not sure just what he wants to do, but he's definitely interested
in island business. He's already contacted their Miami connection,
Big Red. We may need to run some interference. Can you steer
him in the right direction?"

"Not us," came the clipped reply. "You. Keep him busy for the
next few days, so busy he can't cause trouble. We'll keep an eye
on him from our end as well. Plan on a noon meeting tomorrow,
usual place."

"That sounds reasonable," Bonfire said. "Tell Mrs. Green I'm
sorry to have missed her. I'll plan on meeting her tomorrow for
lunch."

12:42 P.M.
Private hideaway office
The Capitol
Washington, D.C.

Grant wished he knew what had happened in Cuba during those lost hours of the night. He snapped his fingers. Champ DePaul, an old friend, was commanding officer at Guantánamo.

"Cynthia, see if you can run down Admiral Champion DePaul at our naval base at Guantánamo, Cuba, please," Grant requested over the intercom.

Getting DePaul on the phone took longer than he'd expected. At least Cuba and D.C. were in the same time zone. Not having it that way was one complication they could do without. While he waited, Grant began signing some letters Mary Lee, his secretary, had sent over.

"You old son of a gun." DePaul's voice boomed over the miles. "Glad to hear from you. You still surviving among those SOBs on the Hill?"

Grant smiled at the sound of his old friend's voice. Nice how friendships forged in the discipline of the academy seemed to grow stronger in spite of prolonged absences.

"Cuba," Grant said. "That's what I'm calling about. The whole situation has me puzzled." He wished he could explain the Valles-Moya scenario to DePaul, but he couldn't break that trust.

"I had a feeling your call might be in reference to the late, totally unlamented leader of this island paradise. I'll tell you what I can. Just remember, Castro made sure we're pretty much isolated on this end of the island. I get most of my information through hearsay and rumor."

"Understood. Just fill me in on anything you have—unusual communication interceptions, all that you know about this Valles character, especially his relation with the Russians and his own military and, I suppose, the general mood of the people."

"You don't ask for much, do you," DePaul said, laughing. "First thing, Castro died yesterday afternoon, but the news didn't get out

112

even in Cuba until early this morning. Further, our informant thinks that Raul's death and Valles's ascension are connected, especially after seeing the Russian brass enter El Palacio just before Valles was named President. The soldiers wore Cuban uniforms, but their leader was Basilov. He's hard to mistake even out of uniform."

"That confirms my information."

"The Russians moving in Cuba . . . I've wondered why their forces have remained here—didn't make much sense with their problems at home. Lourdes is running as usual, too, but our contacts have picked up rumors that they're selling much of the information they're learning through that spy network. Helping to shore up their economy, I'd guess. Not nice, but makes sense."

"Any suggestion of to whom?"

"The usual guesses—our friends in the Middle East, China."

"I'd be interested in hearing more if you learn anything. But about the current situation."

"Something odd happened last night, an almost universal phone outage. However, we did detect some traffic from the Russian compound at San Antonio de los Baños. Nothing else. Wouldn't have given it much thought since the phones are regularly on the fritz around here, except it's never happened so comprehensively before, usually just one section of the island at a time."

"How do the times fit in with everything else?" Grant asked.

"Let's see." Grant could hear DePaul rustling through his reports. "Here we are. We first noticed the outage at 22:08, and communications had resumed by 08:07."

"The times sure would fit, wouldn't they, if someone wanted to isolate his opposition while he consolidated his own power?"

"Just remember," DePaul cautioned, "before today we heard no rumors about Valles and the Russians. Remember General Ochoa? Castro said he executed Ochoa because of his involvement with the drug trade. Hornswoggle. Rumor had it that Ochoa was in league with the Russians; others swore he was a bona fide freedom fighter. As far as Castro was concerned, all that mattered was that Ochoa was against him so Ochoa was dead. In Valles's case, Castro wouldn't have tolerated any treachery, either. If Valles is hand in glove with the Russkies, then he's one very smart fellow to have pulled it off without detection. Wherever you're headed, my friend, watch your back."

"With those words of comfort, I'll ring off," Grant said, laughing grimly, "but do call if any information comes your way. I'd appreciate it."

"Glad to do what I can," DePaul replied. "Sure don't like the idea of any but a friendly controlling Cuba. It's much too close to home. Besides, I must admit I've had a hankering to tour the whole place. Some nice people here, I'll bet, if given half a chance."

Grant hung up, knowing that DePaul would do all he could. He was a good man, brave but not foolhardy, able to judge events and act, or not act, accordingly. Grant hoped the United States wouldn't have to take action in Cuba, but if they did, DePaul was the right man to have on the spot.

Grant looked at his watch. He had time to make one more call. Maybe Tommy MacKinsey would know something. As head of the naval arm of the Defense Intelligence Agency at the Pentagon, he should.

Like Champ DePaul, MacKinsey was pleased to hear from Grant. "I've been wondering what was going on in Cuba myself, Bob. Considering my job, you'd think I'd be one of the first to know, wouldn't you?" MacKinsey's voice was grim. "Used to be, we knew things almost before they happened. We prevented plenty of headaches that way. Today, we don't have enough data to defend us from an armada of rowboats."

"Frustrating for me as well, I assure you."

"I can appreciate that. Whatever you do, Bob, don't give up trying to change things on the Hill. We need you. But as far as Cuba goes, is there anything specific that interests you?"

"I've received information that indicates the Russians are behind Valles. The source has always been reliable so I'm treating it with utmost seriousness. Have you heard anything of the sort?"

"No direct confirmation, but that's not to say it isn't true. Even with the mess in their own country, it'd be logical for them to have been prepared and to have moved quickly. After all, they've kept their troops there for some reason."

"That's what I've been thinking," Grant said. "The funeral will be Saturday with the inauguration immediately after so we're looking toward Saturday as the last day that the Cuban resistance has a realistic shot at controlling the country."

"Forty-eight hours, maybe even less. We're not talking much time, are we?"

"No, Tommy, we're not."

"What's coming out of the White House?"

"They've jumped on the Valles bandwagon. I'm concerned the President's rushing things by going along with the media push for Valles. His thinking is predictable, though. Why should he propose his own agenda when Valles seems a ready-made choice? But just in case I've misjudged him"—Grant could hear Tommy mutter a sarcastic "Surely not"—"I've asked for a meeting. If time weren't so short, I'd be willing to wait, but with this President, I could be kept waiting for days. I'm not optimistic that he'll give me a hearing, but I'll keep pushing."

"The whole thing's ludicrous. We've got to know what's going on before everything hits the fan. If you're right, this could become a genuine security crisis."

Grant's mouth went dry as the potential danger, a danger that seemed to be escalating frighteningly, washed over him once again. "Yes, that about says it. Sobering thought, isn't it? I'm not about to gamble the security of our country on the possible success of someone else."

"Why don't we try handling this in the simplest way possible," MacKinsey said after a moment's thought. "We certainly don't want an open confrontation with anyone. Do you know James Lawrence, about four classes behind us at Annapolis?"

"Sure. We were stationed in San Diego at the same time. A quality officer. What about him?"

"Well, Lawrence might be just the man you need. He's fleet commander in the Caribbean. They've completed an open-water exercise and will be in port in Panama for a few days. He may have a lead for you."

"I'll get in touch with him," Grant said.

"You might also check Navy reports on the location of ships—Russian or any other for that matter—in the Caribbean. We're as efficient as ever in that area."

"Will do. You're a friend, Tommy. I'll give Lawrence a call right away."

As soon as he hung up, Cynthia buzzed through on the telephone intercom. "Remember, you're meeting the president of the Georgia state Chamber of Commerce and her delegation for lunch in fifteen minutes."

"Is it that time already? Can it be rescheduled?"

Cynthia remained silent. She knew the Senator was much more interested in issues than in working at being reelected. Part of her job was ensuring that he did both.

"I guess you've heard that one before. I promise I'll behave and go directly to the dining room. But first tell me what you've learned about Cuba."

"It's been an odd experience," she told him. "Defense didn't have much to say about Russian military deployment. I asked for it worldwide, including information about naval activities for all countries. They finally agreed to send what they could, but I wouldn't expect to hear before next week. A lot of foot dragging, it seemed to me, but maybe I was expecting too much."

"Don't be too hard on yourself," Grant said. "You're so good at wangling information, you're taking their reluctance too much to heart."

"You may not be so sanguine when you hear the rest of it. No new information from any of my contacts in the House—weekend recess, and you know how I feel about that."

Grant knew she'd never been able to understand how the members of the House thought they could run their offices efficiently when they shut down every Thursday afternoon for a weekend recess and didn't resume business until the next Tuesday morning.

"Senate contacts a washout as well," Cynthia continued.

"You really did strike out, didn't you? I'm surprised."

"It gets worse. I finally reached Edmund Miller. According to him, the committee has received only the same information that's already in the public domain. That in itself seems odd, doesn't it?"

"It certainly does. I don't understand it. No hint about the Russians or anyone else?" Grant thought about DePaul's report.

"Not a word, according to Miller. Of course, I haven't made a dent in the mass of paper up there. Anyway, I'll keep digging."

"Good. As you have time, start probing into financing as well. Bank transfers, rumors in Switzerland, the Bahamas or even Hong Kong. You know the drill. I don't expect much in that direction, but it's worth a try."

Grant was soon in the Senate dining room, charming his guests. Even as he listened, he mulled over what he'd learned about Cuba. Disturbing that they couldn't get any information from sources inside the government, even negative information. He could think of no obvious reason why the official reports were so at variance with those of the resistance, but something was decidedly odd.

Maybe Champ had picked up something new by now, and James Lawrence was certainly worth a call. His position in the Caribbean was ideal for some on-site evaluation. With the administration's overtures toward Valles, he'd better get on the phone right away. The longer the President held to his views, the harder it would be for him to abandon them.

1:00 P.M.
El Palacio de la Revolución
Havana, Cuba

Life was a superb challenge, Paschal Gomez mentally philosophized as he entered El Palacio for his meeting with Valles. So many forces were pushing and pulling against each other, each one trying to gain ascendancy, each creating only a small imprint on the whole, with one force eventually taking the whole as its own. The surface gave no indication of these underlying forces, the anger, hatred, jealousy, greed, even love, that ultimately gave shape to events. But their influence was immutable.

Gomez was intimately involved in two plots, each designed to shape Cuba's future and each diametrically opposed to the other. Only one would prevail. What whim of human nature, what small unexpected happening would determine which one?

Gomez mentally shook himself. He enjoyed these silent debates, but now was no time to lose himself in his mind. He had to be alert. Valles would be.

Already showing small proprietary airs—the removal of Castro's pictures, the rearranging of furniture—Valles received Gomez in Castro's old office. Valles's attitude had changed as well. The two men were no longer equals; Valles was the gracious leader consulting with a trusted advisor.

"I propose we continue to have three separate army units," Gomez began at Valles's invitation. "As demonstrated in the past, this separation prevents a military coup."

Years before, to guard against just such an uprising, Castro had divided the Cuban military into three entirely autonomous units: the eastern army, which primarily monitored the United States' activity at Guantánamo; the middle army; and the western army, this last the most important because it protected Havana and monitored Russian activity at both San Antonio do los Baños and the Lourdes communication center.

"With this in mind," Gomez continued, "I suggest that all three divisions be represented at the ceremonies, ensuring that no group brings too many forces. Unless we're prepared, the funeral might provide ideal conditions for a coup."

Valles nodded, his chin resting on his steepled fingers.

"I propose to visit each base on the island and personally choose men loyal to you. There must be no question about their allegiance. I'd like to have Colonel Silvio Sacasa as my second in command. He's an excellent officer with proven loyalty."

Valles nodded again, reminding himself to get a background check on Sacasa. He'd better increase Sacasa's surveillance as well.

"Further," Gomez resumed, "I propose leaving at least one emissary at each base to continue on-site coordination of our plans. Each of these men will report to me, either directly or through Sacasa. In that way there will be no misunderstanding of plans, and I'll be informed immediately of any unusual activity."

"A good idea," Valles said thoughtfully. "I'm pleased you're being so thorough. How many men do you propose to have in Havana?"

"With your permission, El Presidente, I'd like to wait until tomorrow to decide. We must ensure that all commands are led by men dedicated to you. I want to leave a sufficient number of loyal officers at each base as well as send only loyal ones to the ceremonies."

"Do whatever is necessary," Valles responded. "All my resources are at your disposal. Keep me informed as your plans firm."

"I wonder if using the Americans at Guantánamo during the funeral"—at Valles's look of skepticism, Gomez hurried on—"in a token manner, of course, might further disarm that country."

"You mean why would I invite them if I had anything to hide?"

"Exactly."

"I'll think about it. I'd feel more secure with Russian troops close by. Their presence has such a quelling effect; but, of course, I realize that would cause a great deal of Western anxiety. I'm relying on you and our own military to ensure that events go smoothly. The scope of my authority must be beyond doubt. Do you have other suggestions?"

"I'd recommend we key on media coverage. We must grab the cameras' attention and hold it. First, on the dot of eleven-thirty, two groups of our aircraft, four MiGs and four Backfire bombers, should fly overhead in two missing-man formations, breaking off to fly in different directions. In your opening remarks, you can point out the symbolism—a tribute to Castro, our lost leader, as well as a sign that we'll no longer need force to maintain control.

"Second, as soon as the sound of the planes has diminished, our national anthem should be played over the loudspeakers. Then, after a suitable interval and with suitable fanfare—flags, banners, cheering, whatever—you will be announced. You must be seen immediately while the drama is high. The ritual of the funeral can follow, beginning with a eulogy delivered by you. Your inauguration will then commence, a fitting conclusion."

"I like your ideas," Valles said, gazing at the far wall as he visualized the ceremony. "The more pomp and patriotism and ceremony we have, the more readily I'll be accepted as President." He stood. "Report to me as soon as you've visited the bases."

Each man left the meeting feeling satisfied. The whole which would be Cuba was slowly taking shape.

1:30 P.M.
Hong Kong

Ten men sat around the oval conference table. Their words, spoken in Arabic, were muted by the ancient Persian carpets which glowed richly on the floor. The ostentatious wealth implicit in the decor of the room—the best of Middle Eastern painting, gold work and sculpture—in no way intimidated them. Their own palaces were equally sumptuous. The men were dressed in Western suits, rich fabrics combined with impeccable tailoring. Each exuded power. Ruthlessness was inherent in the proud tilt of their heads, the contemptuous turn of their lips.

This meeting had been called hastily, and they'd arrived within the last hour. Their discussion seemed emotionless, but suppressed passion underscored their words. Their minds worked with business-like precision, but their eyes burned with religious fervor.

"Appropriate funds have been sent to Valles?"

"Early this morning, long before the rest of the world learned of Castro's death. Food supplies are being sent as well."

"Valles's position is secure?"

"The Russians have seen to it. They know they must support him if they wish to keep Lourdes. Selling their intelligence information is a major source of revenue for them now."

"What fools! To have lost their immense power and only because they refused to keep their people satisfied. The additional unrest we fomented in their country was almost unnecessary."

"Their assets—how many of them are presently in our hands?"

"Artillery, over half; ships and submarines, the same. Already all those previously home-ported at Vladivostok have been transferred to Chinese slips. The Chinese hope to establish themselves as a force throughout the world, but they are no better than their Russian neighbors. Soon they, too, will be begging us for more than mere money. Soon the whole world will bow before us."

"Allah be praised!"

"The West has no idea the Russians have sold the ships?"

"Of course not. They believe this new euphoria of world peace. They've accepted the Russians' pledge to abandon all weapons. As if the Russians wouldn't grasp any source of revenue. They've lost power; acquiring money and assuaging their people are all that remain to them."

"And the balance of the ships?"

"We've paid the Russians to keep most of them in the Atlantic."

"The Americans haven't protested their presence so close to their shores?"

"We paid for Castro to say he needed them to prevent imperialist aggression and for the Russians to say they were needed to provide world stability. The Americans seemed to find that logical. They are easily fooled. Even now the ships are converging on Cuba."

"Allah be praised!"

"Russian recon satellites and receiving stations—have we completed negotiations for them?"

"All that remains is the transfer of funds."

"And their spy network?"

"We've bought parts of it, including a main agent in Washington. He's already begun subverting information for us."

"Is he trustworthy?"

"He enjoys the power, but he's easily bought. No doubt the Russians are still using him."

"No matter. As long as he does what we ask. Nothing can stop us now."

"But controlling Cuba is essential. Valles has agreed to continue the drug agreement we instituted with Castro?"

"Yes. He negotiated the plan for Castro, understands it completely and is eager to continue it. He hints at an increase in payment from us, but he is merely flexing his new power. He'll soon realize the money we propose is enough. If not, we'll replace him."

"Laos, Burma and China are sending quality drugs?"

"Quality, yes, and in increased quantities."

"Good. Our network in the eastern United States has expanded even more rapidly than we'd hoped. Castro was good to his word in setting up an efficient delivery system for us."

"And Valles should be even better. He hasn't Castro's egomania, at least not yet. Actually, the plans for the drug network were developed by him."

"Promise him the nuclear weapons he's hinted about. We need them there anyway, and in the meantime that'll keep him content. We must ensure that he saturates the United States with opium, heroin and ice."

"And as quickly as possible. Even that fool in the White House might wake up to the threat if we take too long."

"Drugs to weaken them, nuclear weapons poised off their shores—soon they will be ours. Our money gives us the power. Allah gives us the divine right."

"Allah be praised!"

"The pieces are almost in place. Within the year, the Persian Empire will regain its rightful place as supreme power of the universe. The infidels will beg our mercy, and we will destroy them. We will rule the world once again."

"Allah be praised!"

2:15 P.M.
Hart Senate Office Building
Washington, D.C.

Too many matters vied for his attention, Grant thought impatiently as he signed letters and approved staff proposals. These matters were genuinely urgent, but their importance seemed to pale in the shadow of the Cuban situation.

He put through a call to Champ DePaul. DePaul was on another line. How critical was each second, each empty moment, Grant chafed as he watched more of them tick away. He was jolted back to the present by the ringing of the phone. Good. It was his direct line.

"Sorry to have kept you waiting, Bob," DePaul said, "but I was talking to the White House. The bad news is that the President's considering going to Cuba."

Grant groaned.

"Sure. But what did you expect? He wants to ensure Valles's position. The White House military office came right out and said it."

Grant grunted dismissively, too disgusted to reply.

"Anyway," DePaul continued, "the good news is that now I have a legitimate reason for sending men to Havana. Security for the President. My men should be able to nose around."

"Good. Call me with their reports, would you? The sooner the better. But why on earth is the President in such a hurry to back Valles? It wouldn't hurt to wait a few weeks before recognizing the new government. I just don't understand what's behind the rush."

"Who knows," DePaul said. "But we might as well make the most of it and hope his decision turns out to be right."

"All I know is that at this moment it seems monstrously inappropriate." Grant paused. "Where do you suppose the Russians have found funds for a serious commitment in Cuba?"

"Good question. Our money, you think?"

"I doubt it although we've certainly poured more money down that hole than most people realize. Financing our enemies—World War One and Two revisited. But that doesn't seem applicable here. And the funds can't be theirs. Since they've lost so many of their sister states, their resources are stretched to the limit."

"So where's the money coming from?" DePaul finished for him. "Has to cost plenty, mounting a takeover, even if they do have troops already in place. Surely they've taken into account possible resistance from the Cuban people. They'd have to crush it immediately. All that costs money."

"Not to mention the cost of keeping the new government in place once they succeed. I can't imagine how they plan to do it. We're talking a major investment. Think they're paid front men for someone else, someone with money? A Middle Eastern country maybe?"

"What a thought!" DePaul exclaimed.

"I've heard nothing along those lines," Grant reassured him, "but the prospect did cross my mind."

"Peace at any price could prove costly indeed," DePaul said, "if someone in the Middle East is in league with the Russians. A hostile Arab state in Cuba—we can't allow that. Think about how close some of them are to having nuclear weapons."

"Whoa, Champ. We're talking a worst-case scenario. Not impossible but far from probable. The money could come from hidden Russian resources for all we know—selling art works, increasing production, depleting reserves of diamonds, uranium, platinum."

"Or be a colossal bluff on their part, hoping that the appearance of strength will stifle any opposition."

"Sure. We just don't know. Wherever it's coming from, or if there's even any money coming in—either way, we've got to know. That kind of partnership would compound the threat to the United States. It may mean nothing, but it bothers me."

"My men leave for Havana within the hour. I'm assuming they'll be well received. That'll give them latitude for some serious investigating. I'll keep in touch."

DePaul rang off.

Admiral Lawrence was easy for Grant to track down.

"So our Russian friends seem to be backing Valles, do they?" Lawrence asked. "Can't say I'm surprised. They'd be fools not to move quickly, and no one's ever accused them of being that.

"For the moment all's quiet here in Panama. However, as you know, the situation in Nicaragua isn't as pleasant. These naval exercises may be the only thing keeping events from escalating out of hand. I hate to think what might happen if a terrorist group gained a headlock on Cuba. To give Castro credit, he kept everyone off balance. From what you're saying, Valles would be a totally different proposition, in bed with the highest bidder and enjoying the experience. What a mess! What can we do at our end?"

"Probably not much," Grant said. "I'm just trying to get enough information to slow down the administration's rush into a potentially dangerous situation. When does your fleet return to Pensacola?"

"We were due to pull out Saturday morning, but a couple of

hours ago we were given a heads-up we might have to move in close to Cuba if the President decides to attend the ceremonies."

Grant let out his breath. If those orders were actually given, not only could Lawrence provide a steady stream of up-to-date information, but he'd be in a position to monitor any movement in the area. Maybe some good could come out of the President's visit after all.

Grant hung up feeling better than he had since he'd first been told of Valles's presidency. Only that morning, he thought. Time had gained added urgency in this age of instant communication.

2:56 P.M.
The clinic
Havana, Cuba

The walk from El Palacio to the clinic was taking longer than usual, María thought, forcing her way through the remarkable throng of people. Everyone in Havana seemed to be outside; some were actually sleeping in the streets, she realized with surprise. Of course. They'd come for the funeral. Already. She was startled not to see the usual line of people in front of the America Theater, but of course it would be closed in mourning.

She began walking faster, worming her way through the crush. The circuitous route she followed was eating up precious time; however, she had no choice. She had to shake any surveillance. Much as she wanted to hurry, she mustn't lead the enemy to the clinic. What had happened with La Causa while she had been isolated in El Palacio? What was being planned? How futile to be in the center of events when she knew so little that was really important. She had to see Alejandro. He'd know everything.

When she arrived at the clinic, she stood at the back of the waiting room, confused by the unusual number of patients. Were these friends or informers? Nothing she saw gave any indication.

The shrill noise and hot bodies grated on her already exhausted mind. She couldn't let them distract her. This might be a trap.

Her turn at last, María was led down the dark hallway to the last cubicle, the most isolated one. What awaited her behind the door?

As she opened it, she felt a weight lifting. This was no trap. La Causa was safe.

Alejandro stood before her, surprise filling his tired eyes. María rushed to him, throwing her arms around his neck. He enfolded her slight body, hugging her tightly and stroking her hair.

She suddenly pulled away, her dark eyes holding a hint of embarrassment. "Oh, Alejandro, you must think I'm a fool, throwing myself at you like that. So much has happened today. I'm sorry," she finished lamely, feeling vaguely disturbed by the excitement she'd felt when he'd held her. Alejandro was so serious, so dedicated to La Causa. She hoped he hadn't been offended by her sudden display of affection at such a critical time. How could she have forgotten La Causa even for a moment? She searched his blue eyes and was absurdly relieved when he took her hands in both of his, kissing her fingertips.

"My poor María," he said, realizing with sadness that her headlong rush into his arms had been occasioned not by love but by her need for comfort. Ah, well, he thought, at least that impetuous embrace was a distinct improvement over conversation. Given time . . . He smiled slightly, momentarily forgetting his resolve to ignore his love until all risk had passed.

"Here," he said, pulling up a chair. "You must be exhausted."

María rushed into speech, her thick black braid hanging down the front of her blouse as she leaned forward.

"The funeral's definitely set for Saturday at eleven-thirty in La Plaza de la Revolución. The inauguration will follow immediately. Valles refers to the Russians often. They seem to be telling him what to do."

"Have you learned any specifics?"

"Not as many as I'd have liked. You know how those meetings are—more talk than substance. However, I did learn a little. The casket will be on a raised platform at the center back of the stage. The Cuban dignitaries will be seated on the right as you face the stage; foreign leaders, on the left. Valles and the American President if he comes, and they seem fairly confident that he'll—"

"Valles thinks he's bought the prodemocracy line?" Alejandro interrupted, frowning.

"That's what he implied."

"What a blow if the United States supports Valles! We've got to get proof of Valles's Russian backing. Senator Grant will have to have it."

Proof, María thought, tucking the idea in the back of her mind. Surely she could find something.

"He may not come," she said, "but they talk as if it's just a matter of time. They laugh about how easy he is to manipulate."

"We'll have to hope they're wrong. Any more on the funeral?"

"Valles and the American President will be seated at the front center of the stage. The rest of the delegation—they call them the minor dignitaries—will be in the seats facing the stage. Valles keeps stressing visual impact. He's media-obsessed."

"And rightly so. He's counting on the media to give him legitimacy."

"A lot was said about that, not much of it of any use to us. Scaffolding's being erected. The media—actually, almost everyone who's arriving—are being housed at La Habana Libre."

The old Hilton in downtown Havana had been renamed the Habana Libre after the revolution. Foreigners were routinely housed there, where Castro's people could keep an eye—and ear—on them.

"What a madhouse that'll be!" Alejandro said with a laugh.

María grinned with him, glad for a reason to do so.

"That's all I've learned," she said. "I've found nothing in the wastebaskets, even those in Valles's office. Either nothing's being written or else it's being destroyed."

Alejandro leaned forward. "Much has happened here that'll work well with your information."

"I'm so glad! At times this morning I felt almost overwhelmed. Valles seems so powerful and confident, and we . . ." Her voice faded.

"We've more strength than you realize," Alejandro said, his eyes soft with compassion. He reached for her hand.

He told her about Moya and his escape and about Gomez's plans for the military. María listened raptly, her eyes glowing with renewed optimism. Faint footsteps sounded in the corridor. They whirled to face the opening door.

Moya walked into the room.

"You must be María," he said, smiling. "Alejandro's told me about you. We are indeed in your debt." As he spoke, Maria stood, a shy smile on her face. "I'm glad you're safely here," Moya continued. "Alejandro's had us worried that something might have happened."

Alejandro gave her a wink and a wolfish grin.

María's heart jolted. Blushing, she shook the General's hand. "I'm honored to finally meet you, General Moya. Just seeing you— free from prison—gives me renewed hope."

"Why, thank you," the General said. "Your news about Castro's death was instrumental in my escape. What have you learned since then?"

"Mainly plans for the funeral," she said as they both sat. The General leaned forward, his forearms on his knees, a look of concentration on his face. "They're about what you'd expect. The big news is that Valles is confident of persuading the American President to attend the ceremonies. He believes that tacit support will give credibility to his presidency."

"That's unfortunate news," Moya said, his mouth grim. "I'd hoped to keep our struggle internal, at least as internal as the Russians will allow. But we can't do anything to affect the actions of either the Russians or the Americans. We need to concentrate on solidifying our own plans. When do you return to El Palacio?"

"The ministers reconvene at eight o'clock, but I need to return early to prepare. Alejandro told me a little about your plans, but I'd feel more confident if I knew what specific information you need."

For the next few minutes, Alejandro and Moya explored various avenues of action. The more they talked, the more they found that they were unsure exactly what to suggest. Their plans were too tentative, too dependent on the events of the next two days.

María laughed. "In other words, listen to everything, read everything and remember it all."

3:00 P.M.
Hart Senate Office Building
Washington, D.C.

Edmund Miller crossed the deep-pile carpet of Senator Westlake's office—golden-colored like the wheat fields of Iowa, God's country, the Senator was fond of telling visitors—and stopped deferentially at the side of the Senator's massive mahogany desk.

Westlake waved him to a chair. "The Intelligence Committee meeting went well."

"Yes, sir. As always, you brought lucidity to a fast-breaking event. I especially liked the way you presented Valles. He seems a good man."

"Quite right, Miller. No doubt at all about Valles's credentials."

The Senator's voice sounded almost childishly pleased as he continued. "I had a call from Peter Evans earlier. He had to cut it short because the President was on another line."

Miller tried to look impressed.

"Evans confirmed my own judgment. Says Valles is sound. Couldn't be better for Cuban-American relations. I assured him I'd do all I could to promote him. Now may be the time to speak out about normalizing relations between our countries."

"I've arranged just such an opportunity," Miller said. "Since you're the preeminent Senate authority on Cuba, Rob Reese wants to interview you for tonight's news. Then, tomorrow morning, you'll be on 'Wake Up, America.' Tonight, you should be prepared with a short statement to reel off if the opportunity arises as you walk into the Symphony Ball. The President will be there so the press will be, too."

"Excellent, Miller. I'll need a few ideas jotted down, major points to target as well as a few interesting facts to spice up my presentation."

"Senator, there's one thing that disturbs me."

"Go on."

"If you're to be recognized as the preeminent Senator on Cuban affairs, then it's imperative you regain control of the Intelligence Committee. Senator Grant mustn't be allowed to insist that the

Committee convene. He may be the ranking member, but *you're* the chairman. I don't need to tell you how important appearance is. Grant has to be controlled. You're the only one who can do so."

"I've been thinking along those lines myself. Valles needs our help now, and Grant's the only one off the reservation. The sooner I set him straight, the better I'll feel. Those interviews are the place to start."

3:15 P.M.
The White House
Washington, D.C.

"And so," M. Eugene Corforth told the President, "if we want to retain control over the Cuban situation and use it to our advantage, you must be the one making the definitive statements. We can't let the initiative appear to come from the Hill. The leadership must come from the White House."

"A press conference?" the President asked, pausing in his pacing.

"More like a statement at the Symphony Ball, I was thinking. I know"—Corforth held up a cautionary hand—"an elitist image, but it'll give the statement a certain class as well as show that Cuba poses no threat. Would you attend a social event, even one for charity, if it were otherwise? You'll make the eleven-o'clock news and the morning shows as well."

The President leaned against the mantel, crossing one ankle over the other. It was white tie that night, and he knew how impressive he'd look. The women's vote was important, after all.

"I think you're right," he said. "I need a meaty phrase I can use, one that'll stick in voters' minds. Something to go with 'the burial of communism.' " He resumed his pacing. After a minute he stopped, a smile growing on his face. " 'The awakening of freedom.' That's it."

3:55 P.M.
Guillermo Sorzano Air Force Base
Outside Havana

Gomez looked up as Lieutenant Balbino Ruiz came to attention in front of his desk. Ruiz was one of several young officers whose careers Gomez had personally but unobtrusively nurtured, making sure they'd been trained as fighter pilots. They were all bright, hardworking men with the ability to think for themselves. They had no idea of Gomez's long-term interest in them. Now he had to persuade them to join La Causa.

Gomez stared at Ruiz thoughtfully. Had he judged the young man correctly? Ruiz for his part became increasingly uneasy under the scrutiny. The general finally broke the silence.

"Lieutenant Ruiz, you've heard, of course, of the death of Fidel Castro and, I hope, have given thought to its effect on our country. We're faced with two choices. We can either continue our present form of government under César Valles, with the Russians, for reasons only they can understand, even more intimately involved in our affairs; or we can place the man of our choice in power, a man who would truly liberate Cuba."

Ruiz blinked once in shock but said nothing. A good man, Gomez thought. Most would have blurted their surprise.

"I know you're wondering why I, a supporter of Castro and a member of Valles's inner circle, would speak such words unless it were some kind of trap. You must forget your preconceived ideas about my allegiance.

"I'm about to put my life in your hands. You could report what I will say to any Valles loyalist. We both know what would happen then." He paused to give Ruiz a chance to consider his words.

"For several years, I've had the privilege of knowing General José Moya," he continued. "Since soon after I began my Castro-ordered interrogations of him, the General and I have planned for the day when Cuba could be freed."

Gomez smiled for the first time at his bemused subordinate. "I know you're startled by what I'm saying, but I'm convinced that Cuba's time has come. This morning General Moya escaped from prison and is even now gathering compatriots dedicated to freeing our country. The risks will be great, but I believe the rewards outweigh those risks. I've sensed that you love Cuba as we do and would rejoice as we will to have her free. I'm hoping that you'll choose to join us. You'll wish time to consider. Take a few minutes, but we haven't the luxury of more than that."

Gomez swiveled his chair to face the window. The ticking of the clock on the far wall was loud in the quiet room.

"General Gomez." Gomez turned back around. "I'm going to put my life in your hands as well. I hope we both know what we're doing."

Gomez smiled, pleased at Ruiz's composure. He'd be a good ally, Gomez thought once again.

"I think you'll be surprised at the number of soldiers who are dissatisfied with conditions in Cuba," Ruiz continued. "In the barracks, we've spent hours speculating about our futures now that Castro is dead. Naturally, no one's spoken openly against Valles; however, General Moya's name has been mentioned often, but only sadly, as someone who could have led us were he free. Many trust him. I feel sure many will follow him if given the chance.

"I'm honored that you've trusted me. I'll do what I can for General Moya and for Cuba."

Both men relaxed visibly now that they were openly committed.

"I feel sure neither of us will regret his decision," Gomez said.

For the next few minutes the men discussed whom else to approach as possible confederates.

After Ruiz left, Gomez remained at his desk, waiting for the next officer he hoped would join them. Tomorrow, he would recruit more men on other bases to add to those already in place. Gomez's plan centered around a small coterie of like-minded officers who'd been members of La Causa almost from the beginning. These men would be in a position to control the men under them; some would willingly support Moya while the others would just as willingly follow orders, either out of ignorance or out of fear of reprisals.

Because Gomez himself was stationed there, the majority of the men in his plan belonged to the western army centered around Havana, a fact that increased the chances of the plan's success. Not only must Havana be secured, but the communications facility at Lourdes would have to be crippled and the Russian troops at San Antonio de los Baños immobilized as well. All were in the west.

Time was so short, Gomez thought, wondering if he could organize everything by Saturday. Now that he'd openly committed himself, La Causa had to succeed. He wouldn't survive otherwise. None of them would.

5:30 P.M.
Hart Senate Office Building
Washington, D.C.

Time was getting away from him, and Bob Grant couldn't seem to do a thing about it. He'd had to attend the luncheon with the chamber president; he couldn't have ignored the bells signaling Senate votes; and what with a debate on defense appropriations, he'd ended up spending the rest of the afternoon on the floor of the Senate. Defense was his area of expertise, and he had much he wanted to debate, but his mind was preoccupied with Cuba.

Finally back in his office, he sank wearily into his chair.

"I've some good news for you," Cynthia told him. "Looks like you could use some."

Grant gave her a tired smile.

"I found Admiral DePaul's report about Valles and the Russians. It was in the Cuba file, but tucked in the middle of some especially tedious reports. DePaul mentions General Basilov's appearance at El Palacio with Russian troops, but he gives no details. He cautions that he's found no evidence, only rumors."

"Only rumors? Too bad."

"The Chairman of the Foreign Relations Committee is heading up a CODEL to Cuba and is pleased the 'ranking member of the Intelligence Committee, a Senator of your stature, would want to accompany them.' "

Grant chuckled at her broad mimicry of his colleague.

"His office will keep me informed as things firm up."

"Good," Grant said. "The more I learn—or don't learn—the

more I feel compelled to go to Cuba. Too bad Champ wasn't able to get some concrete proof to support the rumors. Anything else?"

"Just negative news. Corinne Fitzpatrick left a message that she'd learned nothing new. Her original assessment still stands."

"So her contacts aren't any more forthcoming than ours. Interesting. We'll just have to keep digging. Get Chet Houston at Homestead Air Force Base on the phone, would you, please. Being in southern Florida, he just might have heard something."

Houston was one of Grant's oldest friends. They'd met as guards on opposing high school basketball teams back in Atlanta. Subsequently, Grant had gone to Annapolis, and Houston had gone to the Air Force Academy. After graduation they'd shared one tour of duty and made a point of getting together whenever they could.

"Chet, I'm worried about Cuba," Grant said. "There's not enough hard information and too much uncertainty. Any chance you've heard something sub rosa?"

"Aw, Bobby," Chet began in his slow southern drawl, "I hate to disappoint you, old buddy, but we just don't know much at all. Hell, we're only ninety miles from that li'l ol' island, but gettin' news from there is like gettin' sugar from a rattlesnake—dangerous if not downright impossible. Was there anything specific on that crazy mind of yours?"

"What about Russian involvement with Valles," Grant asked, "or unusual troop movement by the Russians or unusual comings and goings out of Cuba to not-so-friendly countries? Do you have anything along those lines?"

"So that's the way your mind's working, is it?" Houston said after a pause, his drawl conspicuous in its absence. Everyone knew when Houston was serious. "Last night we noticed an islandwide telephone outage lasting about ten hours. And the lines between Moscow and Cuba have been fairly busy today, which, of course, is to be expected. It's a complicated code, so we may never know what was said. Obviously, the Russians are being careful. Does any of that help?"

"It's not new, but it does give credence to some information I've already received."

"What a situation!" Houston declared, frustration heavy in his voice. "Do nothing and the Russians waltz in and take complete control of a strategic military asset right on our doorstep. But why are the Russians intent on controlling Cuba when they're so busy convincing us of their friendship? What's in it for them? It just doesn't make sense."

"That's why we'll have trouble convincing anyone that they're other than pure of intent—not only why would they do it but how are they financing it?"

As Grant had hoped, Houston understood. "So we need to ensure that the Cubans have the chance to choose for themselves. We have some planes down here that just might need some ninety-mile test runs. That should give our Russian friends a moment's pause if they're planning anything. Help us prepare for the President's possible visit, too. We'll commence some practice tomorrow. I'll keep my people on the alert."

Grant suddenly was glad that the President was considering going to Cuba. Preparations for a presidential trip, whether the trip was actually taken or not, would provide an excellent cover for everyone.

5:45 P.M.
The clinic
Havana, Cuba

"Papa," Alejandro chided, "you're supposed to be resting."

"Resting? You don't know what you say," his father replied, his gaunt body propped up on the cot. "I'll have all eternity to rest, but now I have work to do—logistics, troops, attack points. I've almost finished the plans for the communication blackout before the funeral. Paschal and Silvio will want to begin implementing them tomorrow." He tapped a gnarled finger on the papers he held. "The General needs so much help."

"You're right, of course," Alejandro said, straightening the covers on the cot. "He needs María, too, but I worry about her. She's more vulnerable than any of us."

"She's assumed those risks willingly. To try to shield her would

135

be to deny her bravery and her commitment." He coughed. "You're being careful about the messages you send?"

"Of course. The Secret Police and the Russians at Lourdes . . . they'd like nothing better than to catch me. Why?"

"I wasn't thinking about your physical safety, Alej, more about the safety of La Causa. We can't put Cuba's future into the hands of others." Julio waved his hand when his son started to speak. "I realize the General knows this Senator Grant and is convinced we can trust him, but we've tried that before."

"You mean the Bay of Pigs."

"Yes, the Bay of Pigs. We may ultimately need the help of the United States, but not yet. Be careful not to allow anyone so much information that he can destroy La Causa."

"I'll remember." Alejandro placed a tray in front of his father. The food was meager, but at least the broth would be warming. His father seemed perpetually cold.

"Try to eat. You must keep up your strength."

"You're a good son," Julio said. "But food is of little use to me now. I must depend on the food of my soul for strength."

Alejandro looked at his father speculatively, nodding his head. "I think I understand."

"Yes, I believe you do," Montaner replied, relieved to realize it was true. Death could be difficult, especially for those forced to helplessly watch its advance. "But enough—we both have work to do. Go now and leave me to mine. And I'll drink the broth," he added with a smile.

6:00 P.M.
Potomac, Maryland

Why couldn't they stay home for a change? Patsi P. Evans asked herself. Just this once. She longed for a family evening, just Pete, herself and Pauline and Patricia, enjoying those family activities she cherished from her childhood, roasting marshmallows, popping corn, working jigsaw puzzles. She couldn't remember the last time they'd done anything as a family. Pete was so seldom at home.

He'd started complaining that she was too self-centered, too wrapped up in her own world to enjoy any meaningful social life. Maybe he was right, she thought. Lately, she'd found herself feeling vaguely dissatisfied most of the time.

And that was plain stupid. After all, she had a good life, and if Pete wanted to go out every night, then he should be able to do so, without listening to complaints from her. He worked hard at the paper and deserved his relaxation. Resolutely she pushed back the thought that she deserved something, too.

Patsi continued to search desultorily through her evening gowns. Too bad she'd gained those extra pounds. Nothing seemed to fit anymore. But what did it matter? Pete liked her just the way she was. Could any woman be luckier? She smiled to herself as she pulled the pink chiffon from the closet and struggled into it, the sides almost refusing to zip together. She'd start a diet tomorrow, she promised herself, just as she promised herself every night.

She turned as her husband walked into the room. "Pete, honey, you're home."

Peter Evans had long since stopped listening to his wife. She always said the same things: "Pete, honey, you're home." "Pete, honey, do you think we could possibly stay home tonight?" "Sweetheart, the girls really would like for you to stop by their rooms if you have time."

"Don't you think that dress is too tight?" he asked without much interest, rummaging through his closet. At least she'd remembered to go to the dry cleaners, he thought, taking his tails off the hanger.

"Fix this button, would you," he said. "Seems to be loose." He threw the jacket in her direction.

Patsi was hurt by his remark about the dress. She'd thought the pink chiffon stole camouflaged the tight fit nicely.

"Hurry up, would you," Peter said. "We need to be leaving." His mind was on Constance Westlake. She'd be at the gala, too.

Constance was an attractive woman, no doubt about that, and entertaining in bed. But her real attraction came from the tidbits of information she repeated, frequently verbatim, from her conversations with her husband: gossip from the Senate Cloakroom, the strategies of his party on any number of issues, even the goings-on of the Senate Intelligence Committee. Wouldn't the Senator be surprised to know how much Evans knew—and the source of that information!

6:00 P.M.
Kalorama
Washington, D.C.

Trent Westlake and his wife, Constance, were also preparing for the Symphony Ball but taking considerably more time than the Evanses. As he looked in the full-length mirror, Westlake was pleased with the image that smiled back. He didn't look bad. He really didn't. Still distinguished enough to bring in the votes. Distinguished, he wanted; but old, he fought determinedly. The fight became more time-consuming each year. Constance was so much younger than he was, he thought with a sigh.

"Hrumph," he said to cover the sigh. "Constance, do you think Philip cut my hair right? It looks a little uneven over the ears."

Constance barely glanced away from her image in the mirror above her dressing table. "You know he always styles your hair perfectly. You're turning into such an old woman, Trent."

Westlake sighed again, making no effort this time to disguise it.

Constance was habitually short with her much older husband; he was such a bore. This evening she felt even more impatient than usual. She was concerned. The lines at the corners of her eyes were definitely more noticeable. She'd be forced to resort to plastic surgery soon. Savagely she rubbed special cream into the offending skin, using the circular massage she'd been taught.

The Westlakes' marriage was fairly typical, at least by Washington standards. Seventeen years before, Westlake had met Constance, Miss Iowa in the Miss America pageant. He'd been immediately entranced and had made a point of including her in as many of his Iowa events as possible.

He'd divorced his wife of twenty-three years and, after a decent interval, had married the beautiful Constance. Ever the politician, the Senator had carefully gauged the voters' reaction to both the divorce and the remarriage before doing either.

"Be sure to compliment Melissa Secoulas on the decorations tonight," Constance said. "She and Reba Perkins are co-chairs. Melissa's quite wealthy, you know, and the most interesting people have started attending her dinners."

For Constance, interesting and wealthy were synonymous. She knew Trent would charm both women. He liked being seen at the right places just as much as she.

"Melissa bought that place on Foxhall, the one with the spectacular wrought-iron fence. She's spent millions remodeling it and loves showing it off. She'd do almost anything to get us to attend her parties. She's such a name-dropper, but amusing, too."

Westlake carefully evened the ends of his bow tie, leaning toward the mirror for a better view. "We might want to tape the eleven-o'clock news," he told Constance. "Rob Reese interviewed me earlier. He promised it wouldn't be cut to less than fifty seconds. And tomorrow morning I'll be on 'Wake Up, America' so I'll need to leave early."

Constance turned toward him. Trent was getting old, but there was still time for him to become President if he got the right media exposure. "That's wonderful, darling."

"They want to interview me on Cuba. I can fill them in on César Valles. The Senate Foreign Relations Committee will give its full support to him, of course, and I plan to push for appointment of an ambassador to Cuba. The sooner we reestablish diplomatic relations, the better. Valles comes highly recommended. As a matter of fact, Peter Evans knows him well."

The mention of Peter's name by her husband always provided Constance with an exhilarating high, similar to the ones she'd felt as a teenager when she'd gotten away with some particularly sneaky piece of work. Trent wasn't the only one who wanted to speak to Peter, she thought with amusement.

6:15 P.M.
Washington, D.C.

Although most staffers on the Hill had left early, using the Symphony Ball as a pretext, Bonfire had remained in his office. Charles Kendall wouldn't return to their apartment complex until seven, after his regular Thursday-night workout at the Y. Bonfire looked at his Rolex. He had plenty of time to get to the apartment and initiate a seemingly innocent meeting.

Kendall was an aide on the President's staff attached to the National Security Council. Bonfire wanted to press the merits of having the President travel to Cuba, suggesting that the majority of Senators supported the idea. He could talk up Valles and find out what was being said in the White House. The opening on the National Security Council staff might make its way into the conversation as well. That position was one he coveted.

Yes, seeing Kendall would be a good move all around.

Often in the past, Bonfire had made use of the residents of his apartment building. Near the Hill and relatively inexpensive, the building attracted many young staffers. Someone was always coming to him for advice or to gossip. Bonfire encouraged them. Naturally they were flattered by his attention. He was an important man. If at times they wondered if they'd spoken injudiciously, they dismissed the thought; his clearances were at least as high as their own, after all. They were pleased, as well, to repeat much of what he said, frequently prefacing their statements with "According to one who knows."

Bonfire was generous in helping to further the careers of his protégés. Even after they moved, he kept in touch. As a result, he had listening posts in many offices in Washington, some at fairly high levels. They'd proven valuable in the past. Tonight, with the unexpected development in Cuba, they'd be doubly important.

After priming Kendall, he would drop by Clyde's, a hangout for many of his young friends. He'd continue to spread the word about Valles and pump them for information in turn.

If only he had someone in Grant's office. He'd like to know

what was really going on over there. He'd remedy that oversight when this crisis ended.

Bonfire headed for the door. His meeting with Kendall needed to be timed perfectly.

6:30 P.M.
Hart Senate Office Building
Washington, D.C.

"So you checked the Bubble again and found nothing new," Grant stated.

"Succinctly put and sadly true," Cynthia agreed. "I only had time to check today's files on Cuba and the Russian Republic, but I found nothing that isn't a repeat. Oddly enough, there weren't even the tidbits of information I've come to expect from the intelligence community. None of the big things—Moya, Valles and the Russians, financial backing—and none of the little indicators, either. The whole thing is screwy, so screwy I can't figure out what's happening."

"I'd feel better if we could find something although this lack of information is telling in itself, almost as if someone's clamped down on our sources."

"I'll give the Bubble a look again first thing in the morning. Maybe something will have come in during the night."

"How does the schedule look for tomorrow?" Grant asked. "I'd like to have some time to do some digging on my own."

"I'm afraid you may have trouble with that," Cynthia told him. "Senator Westlake plans to offer a series of amendments from the floor to the defense appropriations bill. He's tied things up for the better part of the day. He may be trying to slow things down—you know how he is about money for defense—or maybe he wants some TV time."

"Poor old Trent," Grant said, chuckling. "I'm afraid that wife of his has grand ideas. Wants him to be President and thinks TV is the way to get him there." He cocked his head in thought. "Curious timing, though, isn't it, Westlake tying things up when I need to spend time on Cuba."

7:00 P.M.
Sheraton Hotel
Washington, D.C.

When Peter Evans had become executive editor of the *Washington Herald*, he'd instituted a policy of buying two tables in the paper's name at all big charity functions. Before each event, he and his eighteen guests would meet in an upstairs suite for drinks and conversation. Many profitable relationships had been nurtured during those informal gatherings. As a matter of fact, he'd first met Constance Westlake at one.

Although tonight's guest list had been drawn up weeks in advance, Evans was pleased at how well it fit into his plan to promote Valles. Tonight, he easily got Trent Westlake and George Avery, a popular political columnist, into a discussion on Cuba. Avery professed surprise at the emergence of Valles since he'd been so much in the background during Castro's rule.

"But, George," Westlake interjected, "everyone was in the background. Castro may have been the most charismatic leader of this century. Anywhere. But Valles is good. Don't make a mistake about that."

Chadwick Stevenson, the National Security Advisor, overheard. "Trent's right, George. We'd have been in a mess if someone with Russian backing had taken over or that crazy brother of Castro's, for that matter."

The group was joined by Craig DeVine, a movie star who championed many popular causes. Not surprisingly, he was followed by Mitchell Tucker, president of the paper's biggest advertiser. Tucker loved being around anyone from Hollywood.

"Wouldn't Castro make a terrific movie role?" DeVine said. "He was so much larger than life. Too bad he didn't die more spectacularly, though, something to make a truly stunning conclusion. Blood, intrigue, maybe a little sex and a social message, of course."

"I wonder if Valles would be interested in having a plant down there," Tucker said. "Would the Caribbean Basin Initiative apply, do you think?"

"Could be that it will," Stevenson said. "The Valles government seems stable at this point. And pro-American. This isn't for public consumption, you understand, but the President's considering attending the ceremonies so he can show support for Valles. Peter, didn't I hear that Valles is a friend of yours?"

"That he is. I've known him for years, first met him in Geneva at a media conference. He impressed me then, and he still does."

"But can we deal with him?" Avery interjected. "That's the question."

Evans's voice was as serious as he could make it. "I've always found Valles sympathetic. He's serious about establishing a democracy and plans to implement immediate economic reforms. His ideas about social reform are interesting, too." Evans smiled broadly. "And he plays a wicked game of tennis."

8:00 P.M.
El Palacio de la Revolución
Havana, Cuba

At the eight-o'clock meeting at El Palacio de la Revolución, Valles received a report from each minister detailing preparations for the events on Saturday. María poured coffee and then stood unobtrusively by the serving table.

"We have to ensure the support of the United States for our government," Valles said. "Therefore, I'll be inviting a delegation from the United States naval base at Guantánamo to participate in the ceremonies. They should find that gesture disarming."

When the meeting ended, María headed toward the clinic. General Moya would want to know about Guantánamo.

Out of the corner of her eye, she thought she glimpsed a guard leaving behind her. She couldn't be sure.

8:30 P.M.
Sheraton Hotel
Washington, D.C.

Peter Evans and his guests joined the receiving line for the President and First Lady. As usual, both were chic and sleek, he in white tie and she in the latest couturier fashion. The media never tired of using phrases such as "the always stunning President and First Lady," "their style combining elegance with a dash of flair," "magnificent models for American haute couture."

A crush of people sipped champagne in the lobby as they awaited their turn. The women's jewels were refracted as myriad prisms by the crystal chandeliers; their silk and taffeta rustled as they moved.

Tonight's benefit was as good as a command performance for those in the upper echelon of Washington society and a coveted billet for the hangers-on. The symphony was one of the First Lady's pet projects.

Unfortunately, this was a typical grip and grin, and Evans had no time to mention Cuba to the President. He'd call him in the morning, he decided. One last prod about attending the ceremonies might be all it would take.

8:50 P.M.
Sheraton Hotel
Washington, D.C.

As soon as the President shook the last hand, his Secret Service agents hustled him into a back hallway toward his holding room. Both he and his wife had seen more back hallways and out-of-the-way entrances than they'd ever imagined existed.

Security demanded that his entrance and exit to any event be as protected and unobtrusive as possible. The attempted assassination and wounding of a previous President outside a hotel down the street had mandated that precaution. Had this President possessed any sense of humor, he'd have chuckled at the thought of getting lost deep in the bowels of one of the buildings, a sort of Hansel and Gretel political story. But he didn't. The security only irritated him.

Before the President and his entourage reached the door leading into the ballroom, he stopped to have a word with the mass of reporters, photographers and cameramen waiting for him in a roped-off area. His most thoughtful expression firmly in place, he turned toward the bright lights and jabbing microphones. He was in his element now.

"I'm pleased to recognize César Valles as the new President of Cuba." He concentrated on caressing the cameras with his eyes. "Furthermore, the United States recognizes the full import of the events in Cuba. We're privileged to witness the end of an era . . ." pause for effect, "the downfall of oppression in this hemisphere . . ." pause for effect, face even more solemn, "the burial of communism . . . and the awakening of freedom."

After another meaningful pause, his somber eyes staring into the cameras, the President turned, waited for his wife to join him and walked through the door into the ballroom, ignoring the frenzied questioning of the reporters.

Through the door came the strains of "Hail to the Chief" and the announcement, "Ladies and gentlemen, the President of the United States and Mrs. . . ."

9:10 P.M.
Sheraton Hotel
Washington, D.C.

Peter Evans held Constance Westlake close as they swayed to the music of the dance band. Huge gilded blossoms festooned the walls and ceiling of the cavernous ballroom, making surreal a normally unremarkable room. Constance was certainly better suited to this milieu than poor Patsi, Evans thought. He relished holding her in an intimate embrace like this, in front of hundreds of people, including his wife, maybe especially his wife.

"I'll be at the Watergate tomorrow evening after nine," he whispered, admiring the way Constance's bright red dress clung to her body and emphasized her white complexion and black hair. "If I'm late, just let yourself in. I'm not expecting to be, but you know how it is. Cuba could turn messy, and I'd need to handle it myself."

Constance smiled up at him lazily. "Don't worry. I'll be there. I'll tell Trent I'm going to New York."

Soon after her marriage, Constance had begun her own business. She procured intriguing and, needless to say, expensive objets d'art for the many wealthy people in and around Washington. Her taste was excellent; her manner, charming; and her husband, influential. Now, no residence in Washington was complete without at least one Constance Westlake acquisition.

Constance made frequent buying trips to New York although not as frequently as her husband supposed. She spent even more time at Evans's apartment at the Watergate. Evans was one of *her* favorite acquisitions.

"You wouldn't believe how excited Trent is to be the 'lead Senator on Cuba,' " Constance mimicked.

"That's fine with me," Evans said, "as long as he understands what's what. Valles really is important, you know. You'd like him, Constance."

Evans knew Constance would realize that having Westlake support Valles was important. She would keep her husband in line. The Senator might be laughable personally, but he made his presence felt on the Hill.

From one of the two tables the newspaper had reserved, Patsi P. Evans gazed fondly at her husband. "He's such a dear," she told Representative Goldberg's wife, Sophie. "He's so good about making sure that everyone gets to dance, that no one feels left out."

Even as she said it, Patsi felt a stab of disquiet, its intensity frightening. If only Peter didn't hold Constance quite so closely. If only he held her that way. She wondered if Peter would even remember to dance with her. He frequently didn't.

Evans returned Constance to the table, where they joined Westlake, who'd just returned from dancing with Craig Devine's starlet girlfriend. The Senator was addressing her avuncularly, but his eyes were drawn continually to her daring décolletage.

There was plenty of life in the old boy yet, Evans thought, laughing to himself. Constance had better watch herself.

9:15 P.M.
Havana, Cuba

The streets of Havana were filled with people, but for María the crowds made them no less threatening. Was she being followed? she wondered, again glancing behind her. She saw no one but couldn't be sure. She'd already tried every stratagem she could think of to lose any surveillance. If only she could be certain she'd succeeded.

She had to get to the clinic. General Moya would want to know about Guantánamo. Besides, she needed to find out what else she could do. But whatever she did, she mustn't jeopardize La Causa by leading the enemy there.

People jostled against her, impeding her progress, holding her back. She could barely move, barely breathe.

Ahead, she saw an alley that led behind the clinic. It was a dark, narrow mire of dust and garbage. It would be perfect. She could go down it and reach the clinic quickly without anyone noticing her. If someone were still following her—she'd surely lost them by now, hadn't she? she thought, twisting to look behind once more—she'd know positively and be able to steer them away from the clinic.

She sidled into the alley, her eyes adjusting slowly to the gloom. Garbage squished under her feet and flies buzzed around her, but the alley was blessedly free of people. She could hurry. Even in her haste, she paused several times in concealing doorways. All seemed safe.

At last she could see the back of the clinic at the end of the next block. She ran toward it. Footsteps sounded behind her. She paused. They continued, seeming to gain speed.

A blackened alcove was just ahead. She dodged into it, crouching low. She held her body tightly, ready to spring if she were attacked. The steps quickened and came closer. Her skin felt icy despite the heat. Why had she been so intent on coming to the clinic? She wasn't close enough to have betrayed it, was she? She glanced in that direction, appalled at its proximity.

She stared from her black hole. Her pursuer was almost on her.

She clasped her shaking hands tightly in front of her. She saw the scuffed shoe first, then the edge of a tattered trouser. Not a uniform, she realized with relief.

The figure was revealed and gone before her mind registered its identity.

Alejandro!

She sprang from her hiding place, all danger forgotten, and ran after him, his name caught wordlessly in her throat.

Alejandro whirled toward the footsteps. María threw herself into his arms, laughing and crying at once. Her words were incoherent, pent-up stress and fatigue bursting from her.

"I thought . . . I thought you were a soldier from El Palacio, following me. I tried to hide, but your boots . . . I wasn't sure if . . ."

As she looked up into his face, the words slowly faded. Their eyes held. He bent his head and kissed her. The kiss became more passionate, blotting out the noisome alley, La Causa, even the immediacy of their danger. Alejandro! He'd been in her heart all this time.

Slowly they pulled apart, their arms still around each other. With one hand, Alejandro gently cupped her face and turned it up to him. "You're safe now." His look was tender. "But we mustn't stay out here."

María seemed to awaken to their position. "Of course," she said, smiling as she fit her body against his. He put his arm around her shoulder, giving her an affectionate squeeze as they began walking. They reached the back door of the clinic, eased inside and walked to a back room.

"Now," he said, pulling out a chair for her and seating himself, "tell me what's happened."

"I haven't much to tell, I'm afraid, at least nothing major."

"They're not about to reveal anything dramatic. But every scrap of information helps. What happened today?"

"A food relief, an airlift, has been promised. The planes should arrive tomorrow. Valles hopes to make us sympathetic to his government."

"How clever! With everyone so hungry, Valles will be a hero. I wonder if the Americans will see it as a sign of a Russian-Valles alliance."

"Probably not," María said, "because no mention will be made of the source of the food. I'm not sure the Russians are behind it anyway. Several allusions he's made . . . I'm just not sure."

"You think someone else may be helping Valles?"

"I've gotten that impression, but that's all it is, an impression. However, he's adamant about Cuba's official attitude toward the Russians. He keeps reiterating the same theme, that all Russian help must appear temporary and of little real value, as should the Russian military presence. He's even invited United States military representatives from Guantánamo to help with the ceremonies."

"I'll tell our Miami contact about all of this in tomorrow's transmission," Alejandro said, picking up her hands and caressing them, "but that's not what frightened you. I know you wouldn't be alarmed without reason. What happened?"

"It was probably nothing. I saw a guard leaving El Palacio behind me, and in the dark, I don't know, suddenly I thought I might not have lost him. You have to admit your footsteps were dreadfully loud. I'm tired, and I overreacted."

They swung around as the door opened.

"María," Moya said, "you're a welcome sight. What's been happening at El Palacio?"

"An airlift of food is scheduled to reach Havana tomorrow afternoon."

"So he's trying to bribe us, is he?" Moya said. "I'm sure he'll succeed with some. Ines and Jorge are working to ensure that our popular support is solid. This sudden influx of food will make their job harder. Can we use it to link Valles with the Russians?"

"I'm not even sure the Russians are involved. Valles may be receiving aid from someone else as well."

"Wonderful!" Moya said with disgust. "So the odds against us are increasing. Not that I'm surprised. Cuba is ideally suited for any anti-American factions, a strategic location with military installations already in place. But we can't worry about that. Valles has to be stopped regardless of who's behind him. Has my disappearance been reported?"

"No."

"They're bound to discover it soon, and while they may not act immediately—I've been interrogated overnight before—we need to be prepared to leave the clinic at the first hint of trouble. You worked out codes as well as alternate meeting places and message drops, didn't you, Alejandro?"

"Yes, it's all in place." He turned to María. "Use the fence drop if you need to contact us; just don't call attention to yourself. We've taken Edmundo to a safe house, where he'll stay until after the ceremonies. If suspicion centers around someone at El Palacio, Edmundo's disappearance will make him the likely suspect."

"I know you need to get some rest, María," the General said, "but before you go, I'd like you to write an account of everything that you've witnessed at El Palacio so far."

María frowned. Why write something when it might be intercepted?

"I wouldn't ask you to do this," the General said, "but Senator Grant needs proof, both of our political position and of Valles's Russian backing. Your statement will help." He turned to Alejandro. "You know the evidence about Raul's assassination you mentioned this morning?"

Alejandro nodded.

"It was brought to me a short while ago, a picture and letter taken off the body of one of the men who ambushed Raul. The writing's Cyrillic. The soldier was Russian."

"Is it conclusive evidence?"

"Not by itself. That's why María's account is so important. I'm going to write a letter explaining my position, the position of La Causa and that of Valles. I've also asked the man who witnessed the ambush to write his account. Maybe taken together, it'll be enough to discredit Valles. I just wish it weren't so circumstantial."

"Combined with their own intelligence reports, surely it'll be convincing."

"I hope you're right, but I'd feel more confident if we had solid proof, something not open to misinterpretation. You know how clever even our own Communists are at using disinformation. We'll have to be equally clever if we hope to stop them."

"I'll write my account now," María said, wondering for a moment how long she could function with so little sleep.

"Thank you. Be sure to phrase it so that you can't be identified. I've asked Jorge to copy it when you're finished. A man's hand might further the deception. He's going to translate everything into English as well. Alejandro, you need to devise a way to get the packet of information to Miami, by tomorrow morning if possible. We've got to get it to Senator Grant."

"I'll do what I can. Maybe use a motorboat, one of Raul's. The security around them is bound to be more lax than usual. I'll start working on it right now." Alejandro moved toward the door. "Unless there's something else I need to know?"

"No, nothing. The packet will be ready when you return."

9:30 P.M.
Hart Senate Office Building
Washington, D.C.

"My men in Havana just called in," Admiral DePaul told Grant as soon as he answered the phone. "They picked up an interesting rumor. Your friend José Moya has escaped from prison and is leading an opposition force against Valles."

"Hallelujah!" Grant exclaimed, sitting bolt upright.

"You understand this is all highly unofficial," DePaul cautioned. "But apparently they've heard enough to believe it's true."

"Official or not, I'm just relieved to hear it. So José's free. Does he have much of a following?"

"I'm not sure, but as of twenty minutes ago, my men were reporting frequent mentions of his name."

"That's encouraging, anyway," Grant said. "What about the Russians? Any change in that direction?"

"The Russians are lying low, no sign of them anywhere, at least no uniforms. On the surface, Valles is behaving well. However, we're picking up plenty of phone traffic between El Palacio and the Russian compound and, interestingly enough, between El Palacio and Hong Kong and the Russian compound and Hong Kong, for whatever that's worth."

"Interesting. Any indication that Valles is after Moya?"

"Not directly," DePaul replied, "although my men have heard rumors of wholesale arrests. The word is that they're after terrorist agitators, but they could just as easily be after Moya's people or Registra's or Raul's. Who knows? Moya won't have an easy time regardless of their target."

"No, he won't, but if he really is free, at least he'll have a chance, and Cuba will have a choice. Moya and Valles couldn't be more different."

"If your reading of both of them is correct."

"I feel confident I'm right about Moya. Valles, I'm taking on the evidence. The Russian presence at his back is too pronounced to be coincidental, as inexplicable as it might be. No, I think I've pegged both of them correctly. I just wish we knew more about what's happening there. It's almost as if someone's put a stranglehold on our intelligence network."

"My men are good," DePaul said. "They should have something for us by tomorrow. They're having to work with Valles's Secret Police to set up the security for the President so they're under constant scrutiny, but if there's anything out there, they'll get it. Hold on a minute, Bob. Something just came in."

Grant could hear talk in the background.

"An interesting development," DePaul said. "Valles has invited us to send a small complement of troops to take an active part in the ceremonies—a sign of his goodwill."

"He's clever, isn't he? Send as many men as you can. Who knows? We might need them."

9:55 P.M.
Sheraton Hotel
Washington, D.C.

Just as Peter Evans was rising to escort another of his guests to the dance floor, a messenger tapped him discreetly on the arm. "A phone call for you, sir."

Excusing himself, Evans slowly made his way through the tables, an attractive, self-assured man stopping for a word or a wink with several people on the way. The mood of the ball was noticeably more relaxed now that the presidential party had left. The more cynical watching Evans's progress wondered what story could be important enough to pry the dashing editor from Constance's side.

Unaware of the speculation but well aware of the interest in his movements, Evans walked out into the hallway. The *Herald*'s foreign editor was on the phone.

"Averitt just phoned in. She reported rumors of an active insurgent movement against Valles."

"How accurate is her source?"

"General talk. Barroom banter. So, who knows? The name Moya was attached to the rumors. Our library says a José Moya was a general under Castro but was imprisoned years ago."

After further discussion, Evans replaced the receiver and stood by the phone in thought. Averitt's information was disturbing. Should he call Valles and warn him of the rumors? But surely if there were any basis in fact, Valles would know already.

He couldn't take the chance, Evans decided, reaching for his credit card. He had to call. What a disaster if Valles's government were threatened just because Evans hesitated to disturb him.

10:00 *P.M.*
Hart Senate Office Building
Washington, D.C.

Papers littered Grant's desk, and several books were open facedown on top of them. Where was José Moya? Grant wondered. And what was he doing? Phone calls back and forth to Hong Kong, both Cuban and Russian—what could it mean?

The Senator's eye kept returning to a map of Cuba as if he hoped it might tell him something. Only ninety miles from Florida—this litany repeated itself in his mind.

Fidel Castro's visage appeared on the TV in the corner. Grant turned up the sound and settled back to listen, hoping he'd hear something interesting. Finally. And from the media, not intelligence. What a sad commentary.

A solemn-faced President filled the screen.

Grant sat motionless, appalled by what he was hearing. Not only was the President giving his support to Valles, but he was saying that communism in Cuba was dead.

How could he! Grant fumed. And the media! Where were the so-called investigative journalists?

Now Trent Westlake appeared on the screen, echoing with pompous sincerity the President's words. The burial of communism, Grant thought with disgust. Where had they come up with that wretched bit of imagery? And didn't they realize that that might not be the only threat?

Grant began pacing the room, his step heavier the madder he became. What was going on? Valles's credibility seemed shaky at best. Certainly the rapidity of his assumption of the presidency was reason for skepticism, and the National Security Council had to realize that. So why all this pressure from the White House?

The phone rang.

10:03 P.M.
El Palacio de la Revolución
Havana, Cuba

César Valles listened thoughtfully as Peter Evans recounted his conversation with the foreign editor. Then he answered quietly, his smooth voice betraying none of his inner turmoil.

"You say your reporter overheard some talk, something about opposition to my government?"

Valles had expected some grumbling about his power takeover, of course, but enough that a *norteamericano* would remark on it? Why hadn't his men reported such talk? He needed to know more.

"That's what she said. Some conversations with the name Moya attached to them. Does that mean anything to you?"

General José Moya. How could it not mean something! He was one of the few men Castro had feared. But wasn't Moya in prison? Or dead?

"Moya! The man's an abomination to all freedom-loving Cubans!"

154

Valles said, improvising as he spoke. "He's thrown in his lot with the Russians, and together they're attempting to take over the country."

"But the Russians . . ."

"I know it sounds strange. I know their whole country's in chaos, but believe me, it's true. For some reason, the Russians are backing Moya. I don't know why, but they are, almost as if they see it as their last stand in the international arena."

"This Moya's a Russian pawn? As you say, hard to believe. What do you know about him?"

"He was a distinguished general at one time, but Fidel imprisoned him years ago, thought he was too friendly with the Russians even then. Moya's a clever man to have survived all these years."

"Moya sounds like their man; I'm just surprised they've decided to meddle," Evans said.

"I don't understand either, but it's imperative they be stopped."

"It certainly is. I wish you luck. You'll have your hands full."

"You're right. Trying to establish a new government is never easy. You needn't fear that we'll fail, however. As long as I can establish a stable government, we'll be all right. After that, Moya or anyone else can run for President for all I care. I know the people are behind me. I know I can defeat anyone easily. But I won't have Moya throwing Cuba into chaos."

"You can count on our help, El Presidente," Evans said as he hung up.

Valles laughed aloud at his own audacity. Now he could hunt Moya openly and with the blessing of the United States. He'd better call Campos. Moya! How odd to have his name surface after all these years.

"We may have a problem," Valles told Campos. "General José Moya is rumored to be planning an uprising against me."

"But isn't Moya in prison?"

"So we thought. Check to see if he's still there."

While he waited, Valles called Basilov at the Russian compound. The story that Moya was backed by the Russians needed to be substantiated by solid facts through legitimate channels. Basilov should be able to take care of it, but, Valles decided, he'd call IBTC as well just to make sure.

Two hours later, word came down to Valles. Moya wasn't in prison. No one knew where he was. He'd been taken away that morning, but none of the guards presently on duty at the prison knew the details. No alarm had been raised because he was frequently away for intensive interrogations.

"Find him!" Valles ordered.

An all-out manhunt was begun.

10:25 P.M.
Hart Senate Office Building
Washington, D.C.

"Did you happen to catch the President's statement about Cuba just now?" Victor Rojas demanded of Grant after getting him on the phone. "I could hardly believe what I was hearing."

"Appalling, wasn't it?" Grant agreed. "I was just sitting here wondering what on earth he could have been thinking. Or if he was thinking at all. I'm heading home now. Why don't you meet me there. Twenty minutes. We need to talk, and I'm never quite happy talking about anything sensitive on the phone."

"I'll be there."

10:30 P.M.
The Sheraton Hotel
Washington, D.C.

"Well, well, Peter," Trent Westlake said, throwing his arm around the editor's shoulder. "That was one long call. Any late-breaking news?"

Constance smiled at Evans sardonically, raising an eyebrow toward her husband. She began examining her nails to hide her amusement.

"Actually, Trent," Peter Evans said, shooting his cuffs so that his solid gold presidential cuff links, a personal gift from the President and the ultimate status symbol, were clearly visible. On his way back to the table, he'd decided to share the news. He was too late to make any of his own editions, and he wasn't about to allow anyone else to break the story. "I did learn something rather interesting. From President César Valles himself, as a matter of fact."

All faces turned to Evans. This was why they loved Washington!

"César has just learned," Evans said, "that the Russians are making a play to take control of Cuba."

"Was a name mentioned?" Chad Stevenson asked.

"As a matter of fact, yes. A General José Moya, a member of the Cuban military under Castro. He was imprisoned by Castro several years ago for being too chummy with the Russians."

"But why have they resurrected him now?" Avery asked. "The Russians are peaceful."

"Maybe psychologically they can't give up this last vestige of their former power," Evans said. "One final grand gesture."

"If you'll excuse me, please." Stevenson rose from the table. "I need to use the phone."

Good, Evans thought. The President needed to know about the threat. Between them, they'd make short work of this Moya.

10:35 P.M. Havana time (6:35 A.M. Moscow time) Moscow, USSR

"So our friend Valles has suggested that this General Moya is being backed by our government," the Russian President said. "A clever move—much too clever. Unfortunately, we've been given no choice but to support his story."

"IBTC?"

"Yes. Make sure evidence of such collusion is relayed immediately through our most reliable sources. However, do what you can to make our part in it seem only possible, not probable. Have them say Moya is a renegade terrorist. That way, the Americans may be willing to believe our assurances we're not involved. We'd better prepare a statement saying just that. We'll need it tomorrow to counter the Americans' predictable indignation."

"I'll take care of it, Mr. President. The United States will be pleased to learn that Moya's the enemy, won't they? They like being assured of such things. Valles's position should be impregnable once this intelligence reaches the White House."

"Let's hope so. For all our sakes, Valles has to succeed. IBTC has made that clear. But we'd better watch Valles closely to make sure he's not planning to force us out of Cuba when his position's secure. I don't trust him."

10:40 P.M.
The White House
Washington, D.C.

On the second floor of the White House in the family quarters, the President, wearing his favorite silk robe, sat on the edge of his bed, frowning petulantly.

"Why do people keep bothering me with their problems? That's what staff is for," the President told his wife, hardly bothering to look at her. A stack of just signed letters rested in a manila folder on his lap. "That was Stevenson just now. He's been told that the Russians are trying to undermine Valles with their own man, a General Moya. I told him to look into it, of course, and bring it up at the meeting tomorrow. Don't know what he thought I could do about it tonight."

The First Lady lounged against the ruffled pillows of her own bed, her Siamese cat, Nefertiti, curled in her lap. She paid little attention to what her husband was saying. He didn't really talk to her anyway, just talked at her.

The twins had been in for their obligatory ten minutes and were now off finishing homework. Or so they said. She couldn't help feeling relieved that the older two were on their own now and that the twins would leave for college in the fall. She would have sent them all to boarding school years before if she hadn't been afraid of being labeled an elitist or, much worse, an insensitive parent, at odds with their image of a happy family.

Looking at her husband, she wondered what had happened to that dream, because it had been their dream. A happy family. Those first years after college when they'd met and married, those had been incredible times, full of promise and passion.

So many years had passed. So much bitterness and emptiness had replaced the joy. Was she remembering the past as it had been or as she'd wanted it to be? No, she was sure she really had been happy, genuinely in love with her husband. She remembered the joy, remembered her scudding heart whenever they were together, remembered so many good times, even as she remembered the cramped apartment and the scrimping they'd seemed to revel in.

Estelle wasn't sure when the happiness had begun to dissolve. Suddenly they were all strangers, the children, her husband, herself, each living his own narrow life. The endless bickering, neglect, backbiting: when had it replaced the love and happiness? She wasn't at all sure that any of the love remained. She felt more a prisoner of convention and inertia than of love.

If only her husband weren't so obsessed with power. If only he cared about her as much as he cared about the opinions of others.

With a sigh, she reached for the illustration pad and stylus she kept by her bed.

10:40 P.M.
410 A Street, N.E.
Washington, D.C.

Victor Rojas had arrived a few minutes earlier, and the two men were sitting in Senator Grant's study.

"More to the point," Rojas said, continuing their discussion, "I spoke on the phone with several former political prisoners who now live in Miami. They revere Moya. Say he's a great man. According to them, he's extremely popular, and deservedly so."

"Is he popular enough to take control of Cuba, given Valles's advantage?"

"Popular enough, yes," Rojas replied. "Strong enough to take on both Valles and the Russians, I don't know. That's why I was so appalled to hear the President publicly endorsing Valles. How could he?"

"Who knows?" Grant said, taking a sip of his drink. "I'll try to talk to him tomorrow, but I'm not expecting much, especially considering how little he likes me."

Grant had never been able to decide if the President disliked him because he was conservative, retired military, or black. Probably all three, he thought wryly. Not that it mattered. For Grant, the President embodied all that was wrong with many politicians. Arrogance, avarice, laziness and stupidity were too prevalent in all facets of government, probably in most facets of life. But the awesome power of a President or even the lesser power of a Senator or Representative exaggerated those traits to frightening proportions. Power, or more accurately the love of power, was a subtle corrupter.

"Do you have any suggestions other than going to the President? Something with a greater probability of success?"

"That's a tough one, Bob. We've been tossing around all sorts of ideas, but few are practical. For one thing, time's so short. I can't help thinking that Moya will have to be on his own, at least as far as what goes on inside Cuba. We just can't do anything down there. But even without our help, given his military background and his base of support, he might just pull it off. That is, if the Russians don't interfere."

"That seems to me to be the key," Grant agreed. "Keeping the Russians out of it."

"You're the military expert. Do you have any ideas of what can be done to neutralize them? Obviously, they'll do all they can to keep Valles in power."

"I've put out some feelers," Grant said. "The Russians have increased naval activity among the ships they have left in the Caribbean, just as would be expected, but our fleet is planning to move around some themselves, preparing for a possible visit by the President. We should be able to keep the Russians from landing additional troops, but I don't see how we can do a thing about troops already there."

"Well, at least that takes care of one threat," Rojas said. "I'd heard rumors about Russian naval movement, too. It's good to know it won't be a factor."

"The Russian navy won't affect Moya's strategy, anyway,"

Grant said. "Maybe his ultimate success, but not his plans. My guess is he's already spread pretty thin, too thin to worry about a threat that might not materialize. He has too many crucial problems to contend with as it is.

"This heavy-handed support by the President, that has to be our major concern, and without something concrete to prove the Valles-Russian connection, I haven't a prayer of changing his direction."

Midnight
Situation Room
The White House
Washington, D.C.

The Situation Room at the White House was a repository for all intelligence reports gathered by U.S. agencies worldwide and the President's eyes and ears on the world. In the secure room, a senior duty officer read the most recent transcription, unscrambled now, that had come across the cables. It was from Jordan.

RELIABLE SOURCE INDICATES THAT A RUSSIAN-BACKED GENERAL NAMED MOYA IS TRYING TO WREST CONTROL FROM PRESIDENT VALLES. MOYA IS A SOVIET SLEEPER WHOSE TIME HAS COME. NO DETAILS BUT SOURCE POSITIVE OF INFORMATION.

A similar report, this one from Hong Kong, arrived within minutes. Bits of corroboration from around the world continued to come in throughout the night.

During the night
Havana, Cuba

Gunshots. Crescendoing screams. Wails, curses and groans. Noise and fear and pain. These filled the tense silence that had been hanging over the apartment building Ines Moya had left earlier that day. Two truckloads of soldiers had arrived fifteen minutes before.

Even when the answers never changed, the soldiers refused to believe that Ines Moya and her husband weren't hidden in one of the squalid buildings nearby. They refused to believe that no one had seen Moya for years.

The soldiers finally left. One man was dead; many were brutalized; five people had been dragged away to be interrogated further. The soldiers' visit wouldn't soon be forgotten.

The same carnage was taking place throughout Havana. Every known associate of Moya was being questioned. No part of the city was left unscathed. Even those in prison felt the scourge.

General Moya would be found. No matter the cost, he would be found.

Bear welcome in your eye,
Your hand, your tongue: look like the innocent flower,
But be the Serpent under it.

Macbeth,
WILLIAM SHAKESPEARE

Day Three

Friday
January 27

6:45 A.M.
Hart Senate Office Building
Washington, D.C.

The Senator's office lights were on again, Cynthia realized as she walked through the reception area. Didn't he ever sleep? She tapped softly on the door.

"Any news?"

"No, nothing," Grant said, "other than the President's statement last night."

"As if that were based on fact!" Cynthia said, laughing. Her cynical amusement was immediately replaced by puzzlement. "He gets the same reports we do so how can he be so sure of Valles? Does he have some outside source, do you think?"

"Could be, but I can't imagine what would make him commit himself so publicly. What's in it for him? If we knew that, we might understand what's happening. Of course he may just see the media value—'the burial of communism.' " Grant's mouth curved in a disgusted grimace. He rustled through the papers in front of him, picking up several. "Let's get office business out of the way so we'll have time later today to do some more digging on Cuba. We need to tap some more of our own sources."

163

They'd been working on that day's schedule for several minutes when the news at the top of the hour appeared on the muted TV in the corner. Simultaneously, they turned to watch; Grant turned up the sound.

The lead story included a clip of the President at the Symphony Ball, extolling the virtues of César Valles. Cynthia smiled sympathetically at the Senator's snort of disgust.

The station then segued to their man in Havana:

"News reports here in Havana indicate that former Castro general José Moya is heading a Russian-backed attempt to topple the newly formed and popularly supported government of President César Valles. The people of Cuba as well as highly placed members of the Valles government have given assurances that nothing will deter them from their pursuit of freedom and democracy. As you can see from the crowds in the background already forming for Saturday's funeral and inauguration, the mood is optimistic, with the majority of Cubans hopeful of finally attaining what the Cuban revolution began over thirty years ago. Brian Brent, Havana, Cuba."

"What are they talking about! How can they say that!" Grant bounded from his chair. "Russian-backed! Moya! I never truly wanted to believe the amount of disinformation that goes over the airwaves, but this . . ." He turned to Cynthia, raising his arms helplessly. "This is so blatantly wrong, such an incredible lie. How could anyone have fallen for—"

The face of Eleanor Allen-Warren, the presidential Press Secretary, appeared on the screen.

"The White House deplores any intervention on the part of any country in the internal affairs of Cuba. The Cuban people, and they alone, have the right to determine their own destiny. César Valles is their obvious choice. The United States' ambassador to the Russian Republic earlier this morning hand-delivered to the office of the Russian President a communiqué strongly protesting their supposed involvement in Cuba. The Russian President gave assurances that his country is appalled at any attempt to oppose Valles. They deny any dealings with—to use their words—'that terrorist Moya,' and they stand with the United States in supporting Valles and his democratic government."

Grant stared in disbelief. "Oh, no, surely not." He paused in dismay, shaking his head as if to clear it. "This is unbelievable. The administration has bought the whole friggin' thing. What idiocy!" With a final glance at the screen, Grant strode back to his chair. "Even if we can discredit Valles—and that's looking more improbable by the minute—the administration will ignore Moya. They've been so successful with their character assassination, his credibility has been destroyed. The forces against Moya and against Cuba are greater than any of us could have dreamed. We're going to have to work quickly, Cynthia. The information linking Valles to the Russians has to be in some intelligence report somewhere." Grant slapped his palm on the desk. "All our intelligence operations can't have been totally compromised. All contradictory information can't have been diverted. You're going to have to go back and look through every file, even those only remotely tangential to Cuba. Scour them. Look for nuances, hints, anything. There's got to be a kernel of information somewhere. If we can find that first bit of truth, we'll know where to continue our digging."

"I'll get on it right away," Cynthia said, glancing at her watch. "Oh, my gosh, Senator. Your Georgia Rotary breakfast. You'd better hurry. Then you'll have to go straight up to the floor. They're starting early today. They want to bring up those promised amendments from Senator Westlake right after morning business."

"Please call Rojas," Grant said as he put on his suit jacket. "Tell him we've *got* to have hard evidence. Too much is happening to wait much longer. It's almost as if the whole world's against us.

"José Moya and the Russians," he muttered as he walked to the door. "How could they have bought it? What fools!"

7:00 A.M.
Hart Senate Office Building
Washington, D.C.

Edmund Miller was skimming through the intelligence reports that had come into the Bubble during the night. Their sheer mass was impressive; their value was not.

Miller sorted the reports as he did every day, assigning them to folders according to subject matter and importance. The direction of the debate in the Senate on issues requiring intelligence information, including foreign affairs and defense, was in large part dictated by the reports found in this room.

Today, Miller paid special attention to the folder he was compiling on Cuba. Interesting, he thought as he tucked the reports into the appropriate files.

Finished, he handed them to the guard for relogging.

7:00 A.M.
El Palacio de la Revolución
Havana, Cuba

"What do you mean, you haven't found Moya?" César Valles screamed at Carlos Campos. The night before, Valles had made Campos the new head of the Secret Police with rank of colonel. One of his first duties had been to find Moya. "You've had hours. What have you been doing?"

Campos's hands were clenched in tight fists at his sides. He stared at a point just above Valles's head. "We've brought in and interrogated most of the prison guards who were on duty yesterday. They agree that a lieutenant came out to the field, presented an order signed by an officer—obviously official—and took Moya off in a military jeep. No one paid much attention because Moya has been taken away often in the past. The guard who actually okayed the request couldn't be found last night—the crowds here for the funeral made it difficult—and he hasn't arrived at work yet. When he does, we'll know the name of the officer on the order as well as the name of the one who picked up Moya."

"And the prisoners. What do they say?"

"No one knows anything. We'll continue questioning them, especially his cellmates. Moya can't remain hidden much longer."

"You've gone to all areas where he's known to have contacts?"

"Yes, sir, and found nothing. Strange things are going on. People aren't where they should be, including some of our best informants. Then, the crowds here for tomorrow . . . they've complicated the situation. I don't understand it; nothing points toward either Moya or his hideout. His wife has disappeared as well. She hasn't been at work, and no one's seen her at her apartment."

"Let's try something else," Valles said, his eyes unfocused in thought, the angry red of his face fading. "I'm releasing some prisoners today—a gesture for the Americans. Make sure Moya's cellmates are among those released—any other known associates as well—then have them followed. I'd be surprised if they don't lead us to him."

7:30 A.M.
El Palacio de la Revolución
Havana, Cuba

"Mr. President, I'm honored by your call," Valles began, his whole being focused on the man at the other end of the line. And he was honored. The Russian President was well known for initiating conversations only with those he felt held the power. This call was Valles's sign of acceptance. "As heads of state it's incumbent on us to work together. I take that obligation seriously."

"Ah, yes," the Russian President replied. "The Russian Republic is pleased that Cuba will be aligned with us." His voice held a gentle reminder. "I congratulate you on your handling of the Moya situation. Your plan was well conceived. Of course, I'll deny any involvement with Moya. The Americans will be unsure what to believe, but should they be so foolish as to curtail their aid to us, IBTC has agreed to make up the difference. Cuba is of paramount importance to them."

"I realize that," Valles said, "and have implemented several plans to ensure my success. This morning the *Washington Herald* will announce the release of a number of political prisoners. Such a gesture will have broad appeal. That, combined with the announcement yesterday that I'm halting all Cuban involvement in worldwide drug activity, should convince the Americans of the good intentions of my government."

"Still," the President said, "as long as Moya's free, you're in jeopardy. Remember, support for you hasn't come cheaply. Our mutual alliance with IBTC is important and must be protected. Their support is crucial to both of our economies. We must succeed in controlling Cuba."

"I understand," Valles replied. Indeed, he did. "Moya should be in our hands momentarily. I personally—"

"Yes," the President interrupted, "you personally are responsible for your own future. With or without you, Cuba will be ours." After a tense silence, he continued, his tone once again matter-of-fact. "The Russian Foreign Minister will be arriving in your country late this evening. He'll represent the Russian Republic tomorrow, not I. I cannot in good conscience attend the funeral of a man who continually insulted and defied me."

"I quite understand."

7:55 A.M.
Las Villas Army Base
Outside Havana, Cuba

When the plane landed at Las Villas Army Base, the first stop on General Gomez's list, a group of nervous officers waited on the tarmac to greet him. All were anxious about this first meeting with the Minister of Defense, the personal representative of the new President. Their survival could hinge on the outcome of the next few hours.

Many of the officers were hard-line Communists, pleased that the Russians were rumored to have taken over the government. Others supported Valles just as they had Castro, hoping to be suitably rewarded for their loyalty.

Captain Emil Guerrero, a pilot in the air force, belonged in neither of these camps. Instead, he hoped the death of Castro would mean a dramatic shift in government, a move toward sanity.

But here was General Gomez, an avowed Communist, coming to the base as the personal emissary of the new President. If Valles had sent Gomez, then the rumors of Russian control of Valles must be true.

During Gomez's meeting with all officers on the base, Guerrero sat at the back of the room. He was sick with disappointment. The Russians were truly in control of Cuba with Valles as the figurehead President.

Would this horror never end? Castro was dead, finally, but nothing else had changed. If anything, conditions would deteriorate. What did the Russians care about Cuba other than to use it for their own purposes? Cuba—and all Cubans—would be expendable.

But what was this? Gomez was reading a short list of men he wanted to remain in the room. Emil Guerrero's heart stopped. His name was one of the first.

Sweat beaded on his forehead. Had his feelings been more obvious than he'd realized? Had La Causa been infiltrated? Was he about to be condemned? Were all those on the list?

He felt numb.

As soon as the door closed behind the departing men, Gomez asked those remaining to move to the front and be seated.

"Brothers," Gomez began, "what I'm about to say will shock you. And well it should. For now, you must take my words on trust. Presently, I'll offer proof that my word is good, that what I say is honorable."

What was Gomez talking about? Guerrero wondered. Trust? Proof? Brothers? If Guerrero hadn't known better, he'd have sworn that Gomez looked nervous.

"You needn't fear that this is a trap," Gomez continued, "although being intelligent men, I would expect you to show no reaction to anything I say.

"No doubt word has reached you that President Valles is controlled by the Russians. That word is true. You've been told that I represent Valles. That is true also, but not the whole truth. What you don't know, what only a handful of people know, is that I hate the Russians and what they've done to our country."

Several men gasped in spite of Gomez's caution. Guerrero struggled to keep his face impassive.

"Of course you're shocked," Gomez said, "and you do well to be skeptical."

The rustling in the room was more audible now as men moved

uncomfortably in their chairs. Guerrero was as dubious as the rest. He longed to believe, but he was too much of a realist, too often disappointed in the past.

Gomez was a master manipulator, wasn't he? Guerrero asked himself. He'd visited this base often enough in the past, trying to ensure their loyalty to the Marxist-Leninist ideals of Castro. Wasn't it much more logical that this was just another mental exercise, one formulated to uncover any latent threats to the new government?

"I've joined forces with General José Moya and others to free Cuba from all outside influences. Those of you who know General Moya know of his courage and integrity."

Several men looked at each other stealthily at the mention of the General. Guerrero had heard rumors of his escape. But Gomez and Moya? A most improbable alliance.

"Even now as I speak," Gomez continued, "the General is organizing to take control of Cuba. His goal is to create an independent, democratic government. I, too, am dedicated to that goal. We ask you to make that same commitment."

The men listened intently, motionless now, their eyes never leaving Gomez's face. Guerrero's body tensed, knowing they'd reached the crux of the meeting.

He glanced at the men Gomez had brought with him, recognizing Colonel Sacasa, field commander of the western army. Only a few men had accompanied Gomez, he thought, certainly not enough to detain them all. But who could tell how many of the other men in the room were actually in collusion with Gomez? He wouldn't allow himself to be taken quietly.

"Each of you in this room was chosen carefully, either because the General recommended you personally or because I thought you would support a change in Cuba. Some of you have supported the General and his ideas actively for a number of years."

Several eyes opened wide in astonishment at this information.

"You're all good soldiers. As such, you must have become disenchanted with a government that treats its people so shamefully. And as soldiers you can appreciate the qualities in General Moya that make him a worthy leader."

Gomez paused to look around the room, taking time to examine each man before moving to the next. The men returned that look warily, many turning away in confusion. They weren't at all convinced, Guerrero realized. He himself didn't know what to believe.

"If you don't agree with me that our country deserves freedom, you may be tempted to report me. Be warned that I have total control over the military. I'll be the first to hear of your betrayal. Be assured I'll take appropriate action."

Gomez walked to the back of the room for a moment, giving the men time to think. Every eye followed him. He returned to the front and resumed speaking.

"But now the proof I promised. Colonel Sacasa serves as liaison between La Causa and General Moya."

Sacasa walked to the front of the room.

"Like me and the rest of the men I've brought with me, Colonel Sacasa supports General Moya and his dream of a free Cuba.

"General Simplico and General Blanco," Gomez said, addressing two commanders at the base.

Guerrero was sitting next to Blanco. He could smell the man's fear, see the faint shaking of his hands.

"You both served under General Moya. The General has sent each of you a message verifying my words, asking that you trust me. Included in each note is an incident or words only you and the General could know.

"Knowing General Moya, you'll know also that he'd never betray you and that his message was sent voluntarily. If after reading the note you agree with the contents, I ask that you tell the others. Colonel Sacasa."

Sacasa walked over to each of the men and gave him a sealed envelope.

Simplico tore open his envelope impatiently, read the contents quickly and nodded once as he finished.

With shaking hands, General Blanco examined his envelope and then opened it, reading the message slowly. When he finished, he put it back in the envelope carefully and cleared his throat.

Guerrero had been unable to read Blanco's note. However, he could see the general begin to relax. Was the message really that persuasive? he wondered. Was there cause to hope?

"What you've said is true, General Gomez," General Blanco said, his voice overloud in the tense silence, startling Guerrero. Blanco stood and turned to face his fellow officers. He held up the envelope. "Only General Moya could have written this note. Of that I am convinced. The General supports General Gomez and trusts him completely. I know General Moya well and am pleased to accept his valuation. I hope each of you will feel the same. General Gomez," he said, turning to face the General, "I am ready to follow your orders."

Simplico had been shaking his head in agreement during Blanco's statement. When Blanco finished, he, too, stood. "I agree with General Blanco. My message could have come only from José Moya. He asks that we support him and help free our country. I make that same request." He leaned toward the men, his voice charged with emotion. "We've already waited years too long. Years too long." With an obvious effort to control his passion, he turned to Gomez. "I'm pleased to join forces with you, General Gomez." He walked to Gomez, shook his hand, then returned to his seat. Blanco did the same. Tension visibly left Gomez's body as he clasped each man's hand.

"Thank you," Gomez said, his head light with relief. He took a deep breath and addressed them again. "I'll give the rest of you a moment to consider. You must commit yourselves freely and understand that success is in no way guaranteed. We're pitted against a ruthless dictator who has the power of the Russian army behind him. He'll use all that power and any other he can amass to try to crush us. Make your decision, and then we'll begin our plans. The future of Cuba, the freedom of Cuba, is in our hands."

Guerrero shook his head in wonder, a grin spreading on his face. Rather than dying, he was being given new life, maybe even a free life. He leaned forward expectantly, waiting for Gomez's next words.

8:05 A.M.
The White House
Washington, D.C.

Chadwick Stevenson, the President's National Security Advisor, was on his way to the Oval Office for his daily briefing of the President. As he did every morning, Stevenson considered how best to present his material to a man of facile understanding but huge ego. So much depended on the President's mood.

This morning, Stevenson felt confident. The statement by the President at the Symphony Ball had received excellent coverage on the late news. Nothing of note had happened during the night so the clips had been retelecast that morning.

Stevenson almost wished he had more to report. The President should be receptive to anything.

M. Eugene Corforth, the Chief of Staff, was speaking when Stevenson entered the Oval Office. Both the President and the Vice-President laughed when he finished. Stevenson had predicted accurately. The President rarely relinquished center stage. Today should be a good one.

Presently the President's face assumed the look known to voters around the country, intelligence combined with concern.

"Gentlemen," he intoned. "Let's begin."

Toward the end of the briefing, Stevenson brought up Cuba. "Although most of our reports confirm that Valles is as he appears, an independent, prodemocracy, popular leader, and that General José Moya is a renegade being promoted by the Russians, we've received one report from Admiral DePaul at Guantánamo to the contrary, suggesting that Valles may be under Russian control. DePaul admits his source is hearsay, but given the—"

"I know Valles," the President interrupted. "DePaul's source isn't reliable this time. We've heard nothing else to corroborate it, have we?"

"No, Mr. President, but—"

"Chad"—the President cut him short—"that Valles is as he appears is the only thing that makes sense. Further, we need to ensure that this terrorist Moya doesn't get into power. We know we can work with Valles; Moya . . . I fear not."

"You're right, Mr. President," Stevenson said, back-pedaling hastily. "We've received information that Valles is already setting in motion his plan for a free election."

"There, you see?" the President interposed, smiling benignly. "I knew I was right. Valles is a man of vision." He paused. "I've decided to attend the ceremonies. Not because of Castro, of course. He's a problem we're well rid of. But because of the symbolism of the burial of communism."

"I agree, sir," Stevenson replied, unwilling to voice any opposition in the face of such obvious enthusiasm. "We just received a cabled invitation from Valles through our Interest Section in Havana. Valles is most effusive in his praise of your understanding of Latin America as a whole and of the Caribbean in particular and emphasizes his admiration for the United States."

The President nodded.

"He says that he's determined to turn his country into a democracy and is hopeful of normalizing relations with the United States. We certainly need to put Cuba in our column from a strategic standpoint. Attending the ceremonies might be the perfect first step."

"And media coverage will be extensive," Corforth added. "You couldn't ask for a better stage."

"My thoughts exactly." The President beamed at his advisors. "I feel it would be a strong move, one with many positive benefits and with little or no chance of negative repercussions. As long as there are no hiccups in the system, I'm inclined to think it's the thing to do."

8:15 A.M. *(9:15* P.M. *Hong Kong time)*
Hong Kong

"Valles has continued with his plan to implicate the Russians with Moya?"

"Yes. Since we propose eliminating the Russians soon anyway, this merely simplifies our plans. They make an appropriate scapegoat."

"But they still believe we're solidly behind them?"

"Of course."

"Valles asks if we wish to send a representative to Cuba for tomorrow's events."

"No. No one must have any suspicion we're involved. When the drugs have had time to further weaken the Americans, when the missiles are in place, then we make our presence known. Then we make our demands."

"Then the Persian Empire will once again rule the world."

"Allah be praised!"

8:50 A.M.
The Senate Intelligence Committee Room
Hart Senate Office Building
Washington, D.C.

As soon as she had the office routine under way, Cynthia went up to Secure Documents. By now General Moya would be mentioned, and somewhere at least one report had to exist exposing the Russian-Moya connection for the lie it was.

Sergeant Guinn was manning the door as usual.

Like so many who worked in the Capitol, Guinn was always pleasant, treating everyone with equal respect. He'd seen too many politicians and too many staffers come and go to be impressed by anyone's position. *He* might not be impressed, he often told his wife, but all too frequently they were.

Cynthia asked for and was given that day's folder on Cuba, which she took to a reading cubicle. In less time than she'd hoped, she was finished. As Sergeant Guinn checked to be sure that everything had been returned, Cynthia thought about what had been or, more accurately, had not been in the reports. Instead of new insights into events in Cuba, she'd found only confirmation of what she'd been told by Miller the day before and what had been on TV that morning: Moya as a Russian figurehead.

There had to be more. Somewhere in this mass of paper, Cynthia thought, surveying the rows of cabinets behind the glass wall, there had to be more.

"I need to use the phone," she told Guinn, who pointed toward an enclosed room.

Cynthia went inside and closed the door. She'd call Edmund Miller again. After all, he was the one who determined what information was put into what file. Maybe he could suggest where to look.

"I don't know what I can tell you," Miller said after a friendly greeting. "I sort the reports as logically as I can and put every significant report at the front. Trust me. I want the Senate to be as well informed as possible. This General Moya has been mentioned often, but that's to be expected considering his Russian connection. I don't read every word of every report, of course, but I just don't remember seeing anything to contradict that. I'd say you're looking for something that doesn't exist."

All right, Cynthia thought as she walked back to the file section, she'd have to do it the hard way. Miller couldn't be expected to notice everything. He was right—there were just too many unremarkable reports.

"Sergeant, I'm going to go through every file you have, starting at the beginning of the alphabet. I want every piece of paper that's come in since Tuesday. I'll have to work in short shifts so I can keep things going at the office, but, fair warning," she said with an apologetic shrug, "I'll be keeping you busy today."

9:20 A.M.
El Palacio de la Revolución
Havana, Cuba

After a general briefing at La Plaza, while the other journalists were herded into the buses for the return trip to La Habana Libre, Amy Averitt was escorted to El Palacio for her exclusive with Valles. The article was almost written; she just needed a few quotes from Valles. She'd phone in her finished draft as soon as she got back to the hotel.

"Señorita Averitt, I'm so pleased you were able to come," Valles said, rising behind his desk.

How handsome he was, and how aristocratic, Amy thought, immediately impressed. She'd been expecting someone more on the order of Castro. The difference was striking.

"Please, take this chair," he continued, indicating one pulled up to the side of the desk. "Can I offer you some coffee, perhaps, or some rum?"

Amy gladly accepted the coffee, using the brief interlude to study her host. His black hair touched with gray, clear brown eyes, Castilian features . . . and he fairly oozed charm. He was an impressive man, without doubt.

"Now, Señorita Averitt," Valles resumed, "perhaps it would be best if I give you general information first and then you may ask your questions."

Amy took out her pad and pencil and switched on her tape recorder.

"You, of course, are well aware of the great service Castro rendered our country during the revolution," Valles began. "He liberated our people and formed a government responsive to them. Unfortunately, in the last few years, he'd lost his revolutionary vision. You can see the results around you—decaying buildings, crowded housing, little food.

"Castro became paranoid as well, convinced against all reason that his life was in danger. As a result, he imprisoned many Cubans, needing no proof to back his accusations. Realizing the injustice of those actions, I ordered the release of those prisoners this morning. Even now they're being reunited with their families."

What an extraordinary man! Amy thought, her pencil flying over the page. She'd have to be sure her prose captured the essence— the scope—of the man.

"I deplore the restrictions placed on us by communism and view the events of tomorrow as a burial of that repressive system. Indeed, I've extended an invitation to your President to attend the funeral and inauguration. This information is confidential," he said with an air of candor, "but I'm hopeful that he'll view these events as the beginning of a new accord between our countries."

"This morning, I noticed people receiving food rations," Amy said at a nod from him. "If such rations are necessary now, how do you plan to change your country to eliminate that need?"

Valles smiled, his tone when he spoke complimenting her on a question well chosen. "You've pointed up a very real problem. Until our rebuilding is complete, we'll be forced to rely on others, including some less than desirable sources, for our basic needs. I, of course, will work to hasten the day of total independence."

"Are you suggesting that you plan to ask the Russians to leave Cuba?"

"Yes, although the transition won't be as immediate as I might wish. The present uncertainties in their own country have made some changes difficult. Certainly, their military presence is an embarrassment to our country, one we hope to eliminate soon. The moment they have adequate housing in their own country, the Russians will be leaving."

"Now that you're personally able to determine the course of your country," Amy asked, pencil poised above a clean page, "do you plan to hold free elections?"

"That is my goal. I rejoice in the thought of a free Cuba. Obviously I'd be honored if I were the people's choice, but I'm determined that the choice be theirs."

"Much has been said both in this country and in the rest of the world about General José Moya. How does this man factor into your plans? Since he's obviously backed by the Russians, are you attempting to apprehend him? And do you expect him to be a candidate in the elections?"

"As you say, Moya *is* backed by the Russians. My concern is that he'll disrupt the natural order of events and force his way into power. But, have him on the ballot once we have free elections? Absolutely. The people have the right to decide. I have every confidence that Moya would be soundly defeated. When given a choice, people choose democracy." Valles leaned forward, speaking earnestly. "General Moya is a menace to the cause of freedom in Cuba. I love my country and am dedicated to establishing a new order here. Moya won't be allowed to interfere with that order."

He stood and walked around the desk, extending his hand. "I regret that I must end this interview, but so much remains to be done."

Amy smiled her understanding.

9:30 A.M.
Russian military base
San Antonio de los Baños

The music filling the room was more turbulent today, in keeping with Basilov's mood. Tuporov's knock on the door announced the beginning of the morning briefing.

"Little has changed in the Moya situation," Tuporov told his superior. "He's rumored to be leading a resistance movement, but no actual evidence of such a group has surfaced. Valles doubts it could exist, but he's confident of capturing—"

"In other words, he has no more idea of Moya's whereabouts than we do. However, for once I agree with him. This Moya will be found soon. Someone's bound to betray him.

"We've been given a mandate to secure Cuba irrevocably, regardless of cost. Many people are counting on big things from Cuba and, therefore, from us. Make sure Valles understands. Tell him Lourdes is on the alert for any insurgent messages. His men must be ready to move immediately if we uncover one. The insurgents must be captured. I think Valles is wrong to underestimate the power of Moya." Basilov slammed his fist on the desk to accent his words. "Moya . . . must . . . be . . . crushed."

9:30 A.M.
A government-controlled radio station
Havana, Cuba

. . . IN HIS FIRST ACT AS CUBAN LEADER, PRESIDENTE VALLES ANNOUNCES A MASSIVE AIRLIFT OF FOOD WHICH WILL REACH CUBA THIS AFTERNOON. THIS ABUNDANCE OF FOOD IS A SIGN OF THE NEW ORDER FOR CUBA UNDER THE NEW PRESIDENT. . . .

9:35 A.M.
The White House
Washington, D.C.

He'd call Peter Evans and get his input on the whole Cuba situation, the President decided. Evans would know how much support Valles needed from the United States; he'd appreciate the political implications as well. And he'd be honest. At times the President had doubts about his political advisors, carefully chosen as they were. They tended to get bogged down in details.

"Mr. President, what can I do for you?"

"It's Cuba, Peter. What have you heard about the Russian interference down there? One of our usually reliable sources says Valles is the Russian figurehead, not Moya. Is there any substance to it, do you think?"

"Sounds like typical disinformation to me," Evans said. "I've known César Valles for years, and I can personally guarantee he'd have nothing to do with the Russians. His goal is democracy, pure and simple. For what it's worth, our reporter in Cuba concurs. Says that the terrorist involvement with Moya is the talk of Havana. I spoke to César last night, and he assured me he has everything under control. Why not call Valles yourself? For that matter, why not attend the ceremonies?"

"That's exactly what I suggested to Corforth. I have to show my support of democracy in Cuba. The picture of my presence at the burial of communism would come to symbolize throughout history the emergence of a totally free and democratic hemisphere on the cusp of the twenty-first century."

As he spoke, the President envisioned his face on the cover of *Time*: "Man of the Century."

"Since you're planning on going to Cuba anyway, Peter, why don't you join me as a member of the official party?"

"I'd be honored, Mr. President. You're most generous to ask."

Bonfire stared at the pink message slip as he dialed Charles Kendall's number. Had Kendall learned something new about Cuba? Maybe their discussion in the apartment lobby the night before would prove as fruitful as he'd hoped.

"I knew you'd want to know," Kendall said, "that the Man has decided to go to Cuba. He just told my boss." Kendall's boss was Chadwick Stevenson, National Security Advisor to the President.

"That's great," Bonfire replied. So, the President was making it official. "He won't regret it. Valles is worth supporting."

"The consensus of the Senators that the President *should* go may have made the difference," Kendall continued, referring to Bonfire's information during their "accidental" meeting. "Whatever, the final arrangements are being made right now. That'll be a real headache for someone. Security has to be extra tight."

"No sense in taking chances," Bonfire agreed. "If anything happened, it would ruin Valles."

Kendall was nonplussed for a moment. It *might* ruin Valles, but it would sure as hell ruin the President. He must've misunderstood, he decided, before forgetting the words completely.

"I'm pleased with the President's decision," Bonfire went on. "In the spirit of bipartisanship, you might want to make Senator Bob Grant a member of the official party. I've heard he's asked to be part of the CODEL so it'd be a symbolic transfer. A great stroke as well."

"I see your point," Kendall said. "As one of our most outspoken critics, having Grant along would make the 'burial of communism' analogy seem even more credible. I'll work on it. By the way, your name came up in our meeting. The boss said your credentials are just what we need. I agreed, needless to say."

Bonfire smiled to himself. A position on the National Security Council staff was sure to be his and even sooner than he'd hoped. Dominance of the policies of that corridor of power wouldn't be far behind.

"Charles, I had no idea," he replied. "Obviously I'm pleased. Thank you."

"No problem. I'm just glad you're being considered. You'd enjoy it over here."

"I'm sure I would."

10:30 A.M.
The Capitol
Washington, D.C.

During a lull in the debate on the floor, Grant went to the Republican Cloakroom and placed a call to James Lawrence. After a static-filled delay, he was patched through.

"James, anything interesting happening down your way?"

"Quite a bit, all of it pretty much as expected. We'd barely gotten into Cuban water when we located ships on our radar, incredible sub action, coming in fast behind us, and heading straight for the island."

"So they *were* planning to give Valles some support," Grant said.

"Not *some* support. They were bringing in everything they have in the area."

"And did they get into position?"

"Let's just say the matter's under control," Lawrence said with a laugh. "At this point they can't break wind without our knowing it."

Grant chuckled. "So I can assume that you're sitting off Cuba, and they're sitting in your sights?"

"Exactly, and they're not about to get any closer." Lawrence paused, and when he continued, his voice was grave. "We didn't get here a moment too soon, Bob. I hate to think what they plan in Cuba itself if they're willing to commit this much firepower on the periphery.

"The whole thing is screwy," he continued. "Why on earth are they so concerned with Cuba when they're barely hanging on in their own country? And how can they afford to do anything anyway?"

"I can't figure it, either. But you're sure they're there?"

"I'm sure. Believe me, that's no mystery."

10:30 A.M.
El Palacio de la Revolución
Havana, Cuba

"Please hold for the President of the United States."

Valles could hardly believe it—the President was calling *him*.

"President Valles, I wish to offer my personal best wishes and the best wishes of my country for a long and prosperous relationship between Cuba and the United States."

"Mr. President, I'm indeed honored. I can think of nothing that would benefit my country more than the normalization of relations with yours."

"We will certainly be looking into that," the President said. "We've received reports that indicate the Russians are trying to take control of Cuba. They deny any such allegations."

"Regardless of what the Russians say, your reports are accurate, Mr. President. I don't understand their motives—their own country is in such obvious chaos—but they *are* backing Moya and Moya *is* attempting to control the country. I'm determined to root out that threat. Moya will be stopped. I'm determined to remedy many other injustices as well. This morning I'm releasing hundreds of political prisoners whose only fault was to disagree with Fidel Castro. Today I also began implementing plans for free and democratic elections."

"I applaud your stand on both human rights and democracy," the President said. "I'm sure that within a matter of weeks our Congress will agree to include you on the list of those receiving developmental aid. That is but the first step in welcoming Cuba into the fold of all democracy-loving countries. Further, in the spirit of international cooperation for peace, I accept your invitation for tomorrow."

"Sir, my country would indeed be honored. Might I suggest that we have a four-eyes meeting afterward to discuss the specific programs you might suggest for Cuba?"

"Certainly. I'll look forward to it."

10:30 A.M.
El Cerro
Havana, Cuba

As he neared the crumbling mansion which held his transmitter, Alejandro's pulse quickened. Why were so many Cuban troops patrolling the streets? Admittedly, the manhunt for the General was extensive, but why so many in this particular area? Had his messages been intercepted and El Cerro pinpointed?

With a last look down the street, he sidled into the mansion and picked his way through the rubble to the hiding spot for the transmitter. He knew he was alone, but he couldn't shake his uneasiness. He'd been sending too many transmissions. If they hadn't already, Lourdes was sure to key in on him soon.

He unfolded the antenna and sent the message:

OUR MAN HAS LARGE POPULAR SUPPORT. ENEMY RECEIVING SUBSTANTIAL MONETARY HELP FROM EAST. EXACT SOURCE UNCLEAR. HOPING TO FOOL AMERICANS INTO SUPPORT. STOP HIM AT ALL COSTS. STORK EN ROUTE. CODE GREEN.

Miami would know that "stork" meant a letter or package and that "code green" was one of several potential locations for the pickup. The "stork" should be arriving in Miami at any moment, Alejandro thought, too late for anyone to intercept it if they happened to understand the transmission. Soon La Causa should be receiving help from the United States.

10:36 A.M.
Russian intelligence-collection facility
Lourdes, Cuba

"I have it!" Private Sebanik shouted, throwing off his earphones and striding toward Colonel Sumorov's desk in the center of the room. Triumphantly, he waved a sheet of paper in front of him.

"I've located the insurgent, Colonel Sumorov."

Saluting smartly, Sebanik handed over the now-decoded message.

The colonel read it quickly. Was the insurgent waiting for an answer? He might yet betray himself if that were so.

Sumorov picked up the phone. "Get me Colonel Campos in Havana, immediately."

He drew on his cigarette impatiently until Campos came on the line. "We've located an insurgent or insurgents sending a message to Miami," Sumorov said. "Just shut up and listen. Send your men to . . ."

Sumorov looked over at Sebanik, who was standing in front of a map of Havana, checking coordinates from a paper in his hand. Sebanik gave the colonel the names of four streets encompassing a half-mile area.

Within minutes, five truckloads of Cuban soldiers were racing through Havana. In ten minutes they would combine with troops already in the area and have the insurgent surrounded.

10:41 A.M.
El Cerro
Havana, Cuba

Alejandro's shoulders ached with tension. He sat staring at the floor, mesmerized by the splotches of sunlight filtering through chinks in the roof. Light in the darkness, he thought. Would they find light even in this darkness?

With each second, the room became more menacing, more of a prison, a dungeon where he was condemned to wait. Unbidden, images from his years in prison pervaded his mind. He shuddered and felt immeasurably cold.

Hurry, he admonished his contact silently, forcing his mind away from the horror and emptiness of the past.

He was afraid to move to a safer hideout, to leave even this travesty of a room. He couldn't risk missing a return message.

Come on, Miami.

10:42 A.M.
Little Havana
Miami, Florida

The moment the message arrived, T. D. Santos called Victor Rojas. Three minutes passed before Rojas came on the line. Three long minutes, each second increasing the Cuban's danger.

T.D. read Rojas the message.

The clock on the wall ticked loudly, inexorably, in the tense silence.

Finally Rojas spoke. "Send this answer: 'Need proof of intentions of both their man and yours. Stork appreciated. If possible Redbird arriving tonight. Usual nest.'

"Hurry," he told T.D., who was already speaking into the microphone. A little more than six minutes had passed.

10:42 A.M.
Russian intelligence-collection facility
Lourdes, Cuba

The operations room was quiet, cigarette smoke weaving eerie patterns through the charged air. Sebanik hunched over his console, punching buttons with tension-stiff fingers. The return message would be brief. He'd have little time to identify the coordinates.

Sebanik stiffened, then wrote furiously on the pad in front of him even as he began pushing away from his console. Colonel Sumorov hurried forward. Sebanik, poised halfway out of his chair, punched letters into his decoder.

"The coordinates, Private!" Sumorov barked. "Give me the coordinates."

Sebanik thrust a paper at the colonel.

Sumorov yelled the coordinates into the phone. A one-block area, he thought. If Campos hurried . . . If the insurgent didn't . . .

10:44 A.M.
El Cerro
Havana, Cuba

Alejandro sat huddled over his receiver, cupping it in clammy hands. The dial was set at the next agreed-upon frequency. He checked the dials again just as he had every few seconds of the last interminable four minutes.

Come on. *Come on!*

What was delaying Miami? Had his transmission been intercepted and then jammed so that Miami had heard nothing? Even now were troops closing in on him?

He scanned the room, his eyes lingering on the archway, his escape route.

The set crackled. Alejandro hunched closer, squeezing the transmitter.

The new code word was spoken.

His breathing steadied. It was all right. They'd gotten the message.

So Redbird was coming. Alejandro felt profound relief. He would set up a surveillance at La Habana Libre, the "usual nest" for foreign visitors, and then arrange some kind of message drop. He wouldn't risk a face-to-face meeting unless Redbird insisted.

He folded the antenna and stowed it in the special pocket inside his pants leg. He'd keep the equipment with him from now on. He turned and worked his way through the rubble toward the door to the street. Before he went to the clinic, he'd go by El Palacio to see if María had left a message.

He eased out onto the sidewalk, fumbling with his zipper, just a poor, destitute soul having relieved himself in the putrid ruins. Everything looked safe. A soldier stood a little way down the street, but his back was turned.

Plenty of people crowded the street. Good. Another block and his anonymity would be complete.

A truck's wheels screeched behind him. Alejandro whirled toward the noise.

Soldiers, dozens of them, jumped from the truck. Their curses and the thud of their gun barrels as they slashed through the crowd hovered above the now-hushed street. Alejandro saw soldiers grabbing people and frisking them.

His radio transmission! They must have intercepted it. Covertly, he scanned the area for a place to hide the transmitter, which now weighed so heavily in his pocket. The crowd which had seemed providential just minutes before now made concealment impossible.

Most of the Cubans around him kept moving. They knew better than to draw attention to themselves. Alejandro stood motionless a moment longer. He watched as the soldiers formed a wedge and moved down the street in the opposite direction.

In the opposite direction!

They were too late this time, Alejandro thought, turning and walking away, but the enemy was getting perilously close.

11:00 A.M.
The Press Room
The White House

"All right, everybody," Eleanor Allen-Warren, the presidential Press Secretary, said with bored exasperation. "Get in your places. You have to be seated and quiet before the President will come in. You know the drill." When relative order had been achieved, she intoned gravely, "Ladies and gentlemen, the President of the United States."

The press grumbled as they rose to their feet.

The President strode in and stood at the front of the long room, which still retained the shape of the swimming pool it covered. President Roosevelt had built the pool, President Kennedy had enjoyed it and President Nixon had filled it in and housed the White House press corps over it.

"Ladies and gentlemen, earlier this morning I had the opportunity of speaking with César Valles, the new President of Cuba. President Valles assured me that at the earliest possible moment during his term in office, he plans to hold free and democratic elections. Because of this assurance and because of my admiration for what President Valles has set out to do in the areas of human rights and the eradication of drugs and armament running, I'm pleased to announce that I will be traveling to Cuba tomorrow to attend the funeral of their former leader and to be present at the inauguration. At that time, I will initiate discussions with President Valles with regard to the normalization of relations between our two countries.

"Thank you."

As the President left the room, a barrage of questions was screamed in his direction.

Eleanor Allen-Warren returned to the podium.

"Come on, guys. You know the ground rules. The President doesn't take questions after he's read a statement. You've got all you need."

11:05 A.M.
The Senate
Washington, D.C.

When news of an imminent presidential pronouncement was made, Senators who were on the floor for the debate retired to the Senate Cloakrooms to watch it on TV.

Grant's eyes flashed with anger as he turned from the set, all thoughts of the defense appropriations bill wiped from his mind. He stormed to a phone booth at the other end of the room.

"Victor, did you hear the President's statement?" he asked as soon as Rojas came on the line.

"Hear it! I'm still in shock."

"Every time I think we're making some headway, something happens to negate it. We can't let it go any further. We have to convince the President of the truth. *I* know we're right, but we have to have some evidence."

"Senator, I just received word that a packet of information from Moya has arrived in Miami. I have a plane standing by down there ready to bring it here. I should be able to deliver it to you by two this afternoon."

"That doesn't give us much leeway. The closer to the funeral, the less likely we are of changing the President's mind. I'll try to set up an appointment with him for this afternoon at around three if possible. Any idea what's being sent?"

"No, only that a cover letter from Moya indicates it should be delivered to you personally."

"That doesn't tell us much, does it?" Grant said, wondering why the information hadn't been faxed from Miami. Maybe they were afraid of a leak on their end. Or on his. "Bring it over here the moment it arrives. Let's pray it contains irrefutable proof."

"I'll keep Cynthia posted. Wish I could speed things up, but . . ."

"I know. We'll just have to do the best we can."

This stuff had better be good, Grant thought as he put through a call to M. Eugene Corforth. He was laying his credibility on the line with only Moya's unread information to support him.

Finally a break—Corforth took his call immediately.

"Senator, what can I do for you?"

"I have grave concerns about the Valles government, Eugene. Since time's so short, I urgently request a meeting with the President where I can present hard evidence about Valles's Russian connection. The President must be prevented from making a grievous error that will not only endanger our national security but will have the effect of crippling his presidency."

"Oh, come on, Senator. The facts are indisputable. Let's not emotionalize an obviously clear-cut situation. What could you show us about Valles that our intelligence people haven't already?"

"Eugene, I've never bothered the President unnecessarily. All I'm asking now is for a few minutes of his time. I believe he's making a monumental error, and I have the facts to prove it. I can be at the White House anytime after three. Allow the President to hear me. Allow him access to all available information."

"All right, Senator, you've made your case. I'll check with the President and get back to you. We'll see if we can work you in, but I make no promise."

"That's all I ask, a chance for a fair hearing. I'll wait for your call. For all our sakes, I hope the President finds the time."

11:20 A.M.
Russian intelligence-collection facility
Lourdes, Cuba

"General Basilov," Colonel Sumorov said as soon as his superior answered the phone, "we've intercepted a transmission from the insurgents and have contacted Colonel Campos. He should be arresting them at this moment."

"And the message?"

"Actually two. The first was from Havana to Miami: 'Our man has large popular support. Enemy receiving substantial monetary help from East. Exact source unclear. Hoping to fool Americans into support. Stop him at all costs. Stork en route. Code green.' The return message came six minutes later: 'Need proof of intentions of both their man and yours. Stork appreciated. If possible Redbird arriving tonight. Usual nest.' "

"I'll send copies of both messages to Moscow for interpretation," Basilov said, "but any fool can tell we have a problem. I'll contact Valles."

Why didn't Campos call? Sumorov fumed after Basilov hung up. He paced impatiently, lighting one cigarette from the stub of the last. He squinted in the smoke as he tried to make sense of the messages. He'd enjoy interrogating the insurgents when they were brought in, he thought viciously.

The phone rang. Sumorov grabbed it. He listened, his cigarette arrested in midair. After a minute, he slammed down the receiver.

How could they have escaped! Campos was a fool! Those Cubans couldn't be trusted with anything!

All they'd found was one knife and four suspicious peasants. What a mockery! Whom were these Cubans trying to fool, Sumorov thought, throwing such laughable sops to hide their total failure.

"Listen to me," he yelled into the room, startling everyone into immobility. "The Cubans have failed; the insurgents have escaped. It won't happen again. We'll remain in this room for as long as it takes to capture them." He took a drag on his cigarette. "Don't allow these traitors to send a message undetected."

11:35 A.M.
San Antonio de los Baños, Cuba

"Word has come," Basilov told César Valles, "that the Redbird mentioned in the insurgent's message may refer to a Cuban-American with strong revolutionary ties with this country. Victor Rojas."

"Rojas. Redbird. Of course!"

"Issue Rojas an official invitation to the ceremony tomorrow. Much better to have him under our eye and within our control. We may need to use him."

"I'll see to it immediately."

"And, Valles, find Moya. This is getting out of hand. You don't want the Americans seeing through our subterfuge."

11:40 A.M.
El Palacio de la Revolución
Havana, Cuba

The contents of Valles's wastebasket were spread out on the counter in front of María. Even though she'd been unable to empty it since early that morning, the basket held nothing that would be helpful to La Causa. She'd found a list of events to take place after the ceremonies, and she'd put that on top. But nothing helpful about tomorrow.

Her body stiffened, her breath catching in her throat. The hairs on the back of her neck tingled. Someone was in the room with her. Slowly she turned.

The guard was there, the one who kept watching her, the one who kept stopping her. His eyes were cold and implacable; his mouth, a venomous straight line.

María clutched the wastebasket with shaking hands. She cleared her throat. "Señor wishes something?"

The guard continued to regard her silently, his eyes moving from the papers still on the counter back to her. Surely he'd give her a chance to explain. And surely he'd believe, at least long enough for her to escape.

The silent seconds mounted.

"What are you doing?" he finally demanded. María saw his hands balling into fists, the tendons standing out on his neck.

"Doing?" Her voice trembled.

"The wastebasket, wretch. What are you doing with the papers in the wastebasket?" He took two steps forward, punctuating his last words with a brutal shaking of her shoulders.

"Oh," María said, her eyes wide, hoping to sound relieved and frightened at the same time. "Earring, my earring," she said, reaching one hand toward her ear.

The guard gripped her shoulders harder, his fingers digging into her flesh. She would have fierce bruises. If she lived.

"I lost my earring. I couldn't find it. I'm looking for it. My only pair."

"You were looking for an earring?" The guard's voice remained skeptical, but he looked at her ears, noting the tiny gold hoop in one, the empty hole in the other. María had taken out one earring that morning to provide an excuse for just such a situation. She'd felt melodramatic then. Now she blessed her foresight.

With an eagerness assumed only with considerable self-control, she rummaged through the papers on the counter. "See," she prattled. "I looked hard. But I couldn't find it."

The guard continued to regard her.

"Do you want something?" she asked. "Drink? Rum, maybe?" She made her smile sly as she reached toward a bottle.

The guard pushed her hand away from the bottle although he eyed it hungrily. "No drink," he said. "I have orders for you. You're to have Presidente Valles's office ready for a visit by the American President." He turned and spat on the floor at the name. "You can clean it during the funeral. Be prepared to serve drinks as well. Can you do that? All must be perfect."

"Tomorrow. Clean El Presidente's office. Yes, I can do it." She grinned at him. "It will look real good, too. I'm a good cleaner."

The soldier shook his head with disgust. "You won't forget?"

"No, I won't forget."

The soldier finally left, pausing for a last puzzled look at the papers on the counter before closing the door behind him.

As his footsteps receded, María sagged against the counter, the peril of her situation reflected in her huge, dark eyes.

He suspected. He might do nothing now, but he'd continue thinking about what he'd seen, and eventually even his dim mind might question her story. Or, of more immediate danger, he might tell someone who would understand.

María thrust the trash back into the wastebasket but palmed Valles's memo. If she were stopped, she'd release it to become part of the trash. She opened the door to the hallway.

She'd been frightened before, but it had been a formless fear, a fear of the unknown. Now she knew the face of the enemy. The threat now was both real and personal.

María shuffled down the hall, her head lowered. She wanted desperately to look around, to see if anyone was paying her undue attention.

She came to the hallway leading to the outside. All was clear except for the guard at the door. He was leaning against the wall, his eyes closed. As she came even with him, she reached for the doorknob. A hand snaked out and grabbed her arm, twisting it. A jolt of pain seared through her body. She bit her lower lip on a scream and squeezed her eyes shut. She held the wastebasket partially hidden behind her back, the memo still under her fingers.

"Where do you think you're going?" the guard demanded.

"Trash. Take out trash," María said with a gasp, tears forming in the corners of her eyes. A pulse beat erratically in her neck.

Once more the guard twisted her arm, a half-smile on his face. María's knees started to buckle; his smile became a feral grin. She forced herself to stay upright, clenching her teeth against a wave of pain and nausea.

Suddenly tiring of his game, he pushed her toward the door. "Okay. Okay. Get on with it," he ordered. "Just come right back."

María stumbled out the door and shuffled toward the garbage cans, her mind blank with pain. Alejandro. His name filled the vacuum of her mind. Alejandro. If only he were here!

"María, thank God you've come!"

Alejandro! María sagged against the fence, put down the basket and began massaging her arm.

"I just heard from Miami," he said. "They want more information. We've *got* to have more."

More information. "Didn't the packet arrive?"

"I don't suppose we'll know for sure until this is all over. But with this new disinformation that General Moya is controlled by the Russians, I'd bet what we sent won't be enough."

"I've brought you a handwritten list from Valles which outlines his plans for the next few weeks. He names those he plans to execute, the system of punishments he plans to introduce and his own plans for the prisons. The Russian presence is integral to it all. Will that help?"

"Is it signed? Is there any way of knowing it's his?"

"No," María said. "Just a plain sheet of paper with writing on it."

"By itself, it's not enough, but it sounds interesting. Slip it through the fence, and I'll take it to the General."

"Maybe I can find something else when I go back inside," María told him. Inside. A spasm of desolation shuddered through her. "If I can, I'll come to the clinic at eleven," she continued, her voice subdued. "Maybe I'll have found more by then."

"Let's hope so. If anything happens, I'll leave a note in the fence. You do the same. I love you, my sweet one."

María's heart leapt. He loved her. She'd known it, had cherished the thought, but to hear him say it . . . "And I love you," she whispered, smiling. She could hear his footsteps receding. As she dumped the garbage, a leaden weight replaced the euphoria brought on by his words.

She leaned for a moment against the fence, her head bowed. A fervent prayer for courage formed in her mind. She picked up the basket, and, rubbing one bruised arm with her free hand, she walked toward the building.

11:45 A.M.
El Brujo Prison
Outside Havana, Cuba

The sun blazed down on the thousands of prisoners lined up in ragged rows in the sweltering courtyard. El Brujo Prison outside

Havana was a hellhole at the best of times. The noonday heat merely intensified the odors while the dazzling light spotlighted the decay and filth.

Gregorio Luzan, José Moya's confidant in prison, hardly knew what to think. Camp gossip had it that Castro was dead. Castro dead! And the General had disappeared as well. Already that morning, all prisoners who knew him, including himself, had been tortured and questioned about the General's friends and his hideouts. Thank God he had never revealed details to anyone! And now this assembly and in the middle of the day.

"Line up, you scum," shouted the guard nicknamed the Pig. He pushed Luzan and his cellmates into the front row, smashing a nearby prisoner with the butt of his rifle. Luzan could hear groans throughout the courtyard. He himself felt weak with pain, his body throbbed so from his beating.

The commandant emerged from his office and began reading to the huge assembly from a paper in his hand. Contempt and loathing distorted his features.

" 'President Valles is concerned about what the world perceives as Cuba's lack of response to the question of human rights. One hundred prisoners will be released immediately.' "

The commandant wadded the paper and threw it to the ground.

"You vermin in the first two rows, step forward. No more than one hundred. Get your foul bodies out of here within ten minutes."

He wheeled and stalked to the barracks. The slam of the door was lost in the roar of disbelief which swept through the lines of men. The stunned prisoners in the first two rows were herded into a group and counted. The twelve men too many were sent back to their cells with the rest.

One hundred men stumbled out of the gates. They could see their friends' faces lining the prison windows; they could hear their shouts of encouragement eddying down the road behind them.

Viva La Causa!

Viva La Revolución!

Gregorio Luzan was one of the chosen few.

12:00 Noon
The Capitol
Washington, D.C.

Senator Grant called his office during a break in the defense appropriations debate.

"Cynthia, anything from the White House?"

"Corforth's office just called. The President will see you at three for fifteen minutes."

"Three o'clock. That doesn't give us much time. I don't suppose the packet's arrived?"

"No. Probably not before two. Victor called to say he'd been invited by Valles to attend the ceremonies."

"Any reason given?"

"They've asked several prominent members of the Cuban-American community as a sign of Valles's good intentions. Victor plans to leave tonight and will try to meet with the resistance. He sent Moya a message to that effect several hours ago, at that time just hoping he'd find a way to enter the country."

"We'll have to wait until after my meeting with the President to decide what to tell Moya," Grant said. "Anything else?"

"The resistance sent another message." Cynthia read it to him, explaining the code words as Rojas had explained them to her.

"I wonder whom they mean by the East. Did you find anything in the Bubble that would explain?"

"Not a thing. I'm eating with Estelle at the White House today," Cynthia said, referring to her monthly lunch with the First Lady, her college roommate, "but I'll be sure to be back by one-thirty and start looking again."

"Maybe Estelle could get the President to start asking the right questions," Grant said. "If you feed her some information about Moya and Valles, do you think she might repeat it to him?"

"I don't know, but it's sure worth a try. I'll do what I can."

12:00 Noon
The Whodunit
Washington, D.C.

During the fifteen-minute taxi ride from the Hart Building to his assignation at The Whodunit, a book shop on Dupont Circle, Bonfire considered how best to neutralize Grant's threat. He was still addressing the puzzle when the taxi stopped.

"Ah, sir"—the owner beamed above his half-glasses as Bonfire entered—"so pleased to see you. I've been holding a book for you, an obscure turn-of-the-century first edition."

Bonfire was a bona fide collector of mystery novels, enjoying the intricate plots and the mental agility of the characters. His collection was well known on the Hill, and his frequent lunchtime visits to the book shop elicited no comment.

His routine while there never varied. The owner had learned early on that his patron expected absolute adherence to that routine. For the first ten or fifteen minutes, Bonfire roamed through the stacks, examining those books that caught his eye, occasionally selecting one to buy. At some time during his seemingly random wanderings, he always opened the last volume on the second from the top row of the books of literary criticism. The book varied depending on current inventory. Its contents varied as well.

If his contact had a message for him, it would have been placed in the book only minutes before Bonfire's arrival. If Bonfire had a message to send, he would put it in the same book.

The message Bonfire brought today was urgent, an encoded copy of a memo from a CIA operative high in the leadership of the Cuban-American community in Miami, detailing the messages that Alejandro had sent from Havana. It also pointed to high-level complicity in Moya's escape as well as in the plans for his takeover. How fitting, Bonfire thought, that an American agent would be helpful in ensuring enemy control of Cuba, however unwittingly.

He opened the book to page 63 and deftly palmed the small paper lying between the pages. Turning to page 37, he inserted his own message. He replaced the book and moved slowly down the aisle.

He hoped the message he'd just received was as interesting

as what he'd sent and that he'd be entrusted with an assignment commensurate with his abilities. Such wasn't always the case. So much tedious detail work had to be endured.

After five more minutes of browsing, he made his way to the front of the store. The book the owner held for him was worthy of inclusion in his collection, he decided after examining it. He carried it conspicuously, neatly wrapped in butcher paper and tied with twine, when he returned to the Hart Building.

12:30 P.M.
The White House
Washington, D.C.

No matter that she came here once a month. No matter that every corner of the place was thoroughly familiar to her. Cynthia still felt a rush of wonder every time she walked up the broad stairs inside the White House.

The building wasn't ostentatious; no one would argue that, especially no one who'd seen the splendors of Europe or Buckingham Palace, but it was perfectly right for the United States. Noble but not regal, comfortable but not provincial, it was a reminder of the stability and integrity of the glorious country it symbolized. Cynthia loved this house, but even more she loved all it stood for.

The First Lady often suggested that she take the elevator, but Cynthia always demurred. Part of the joy of her visits was in seeing the varied vistas of the White House, each red-carpeted stair exposing another facet of the whole.

Besides, the practical side of her admitted, she needed the exercise.

As usual, Estelle was waiting for her under the curved window of the small study at the end of the second floor, a page in her sketchbook coming to life under her pen. Cynthia paused for a moment at the edge of the room, reluctant to break her friend's relaxed mood. The First Lady had too little time for the things she enjoyed.

Cynthia understood that one of the reasons Estelle continued their monthly luncheons was that she felt comfortable with her. They'd been friends for years, almost inseparable as college roommates. They'd hung on to their friendship through marriage, children, even the growing rift in their political views.

Cynthia liked Estelle, not as devotedly as in college, but with the easy comfort of a long and intimate association. Now, with the sun streaming through the window and highlighting her golden hair, Estelle looked like a softened shadow of the girl of college days. She was still lovely, but a brittleness hardened her mouth and seemed to reach into her eyes. Motionless, as she was at the moment, the mantle of years was obvious, seemed to weigh her down.

Suddenly, the stillness ended as Estelle felt Cynthia's presence in the archway. With fluid grace, she stood and walked forward, her arms outstretched, a delighted smile on her face. She looked ten, even fifteen years younger, her vivacity hiding many of the signs of age.

"Cynthia, I'm so glad you've come." She smiled, clasping Cynthia's hands in her own. "The President had hoped to be here to greet you, but he's in a meeting."

Cynthia was amused that even with close friends Estelle never used her husband's name. And since the President had been similarly unavailable every other time she'd visited, she wasn't at all surprised that he wouldn't be making an appearance today.

"Look at the fun I'm having with this new illustration."

Cynthia smiled at the clever sketch. The flowing lines and intricate details gave fascinating depths to the gently humorous characters. Estelle had studied to be an illustrator for children's books but drew now for her own pleasure.

The waiters, dressed in black suits and ties, were standing at attention in the family dining room. Sometimes Cynthia wondered if this pampering was one of the reasons she kept returning. Admittedly, she reveled in the unaccustomed luxury.

"I was so afraid this Cuba situation was going to force me to cancel our luncheon," Estelle said, "but everything worked out just right."

Cynthia looked at her inquiringly. "What happened?"

"The President came up after his National Security briefing, and was he mad! He'd about made up his mind to go to Cuba, and here was this briefer questioning the President's assessment of the situation. That didn't last long.''

"But are you sure Valles really should be supported? We're moving awfully quickly there, aren't we? I can't help thinking too much is happening we don't understand.''

"There you go again,'' Estelle said, laughing. "You and that Senator of yours are always trying to resurrect the cold war. What with the sweeping changes in Russia, their whole thrust has changed. Besides, Moya's the one we should be watching. The President says there's no doubt about him.''

"I don't know, Estelle. Senator Grant has known General Moya for years and is convinced he'd have nothing to do with any terrorist movement. Someone in Cuba is lying.''

"We're too careful for a mistake on our part. The President thinks Valles is really special, just the type of ally we need. As a matter of fact, we're attending the ceremonies tomorrow. The President just decided.''

So the President was going, Cynthia thought. The Senator would want to know as soon as possible.

"Political problems aside, Cuba will be hot and squalid,'' the First Lady said, wrinkling her nose. "Why can't we ever go someplace nice? Don't look at me like that, Cynthia,'' she said crossly. "I know we go to lots of nice places, but I mean, really go, see something besides back hallways and rear entrances, walk by ourselves without a parade of agents. Maybe things would be more like they used to be. Remember what fun the four of us used to have?''

"Of course I remember. But don't give me that, Estelle! You know you thrive on all this. You'd wilt away if you weren't surrounded by all the hoopla.''

"Maybe you're right''—she smiled—"but I still wish things were different somehow.'' She took a bite of salad. "Whatever brought this on, anyway? We've hardly talked about you at all. Say, isn't Dodd still in the Middle East?''

"Why, yes,'' Cynthia said, thinking longingly of her elder son, "and loving it. Just got a raise, as a matter of fact. He'll be home for a month at the end of May. I can hardly wait.''

"I'm so pleased for you." Estelle smiled, squeezing Cynthia's hand. "I thought of him today. Seems some of his Arab friends just paid a visit to Moscow. Trading sand for snow, I suppose. Can't you just see them in their burnooses, or whatever they're called, trudging through the mud and snow, unsure what either is. Just the thought of it makes me want to laugh. Much funnier than imagining the inscrutable Chinese in the same situation.

"And imagine this," she continued before Cynthia could say anything. "The Russians have sent a delegation to the desert as well. I can just picture those unsmiling Russian mucky-mucks sneaking in and out of some high-class tents in the middle of all that sand. I mean, really."

"Come on," Cynthia said, laughing. "That all sounds too bizarre to be true. Are you sure you're not letting your imagination run wild?"

"Cross my heart. This is hush-hush, of course, but I felt you'd enjoy knowing. The tents may be a bit of an exaggeration—you know me—but I swear the rest is absolutely true. You needn't worry that this might be a problem for Dodd—he never goes to Hong Kong anyway—but I thought you might be interested."

"You're nice to tell me," Cynthia said. "I'm not worried, and I do find it interesting." And indeed she did.

Lunch over, Cynthia walked slowly down the steps, preoccupied with Estelle's information. The Russians, the Chinese and the Middle East with an oblique reference to Hong Kong. Was this the connection Senator Grant was hunting? If the President already had been briefed about such possible collusion, the reports had to be somewhere in the Senate intelligence files as well.

1:30 P.M.
Hart Senate Office Building
Washington, D.C.

Grant had to be stopped. Maybe Peter Evans could help.

As usual, Evans took Bonfire's call immediately.

Their association had begun years before with Evans's famous

CIA exposé. Bonfire, through his position with the Foreign Relations Committee, had provided the "facts" which had made the exposé possible. The exposé in turn had led to Evans's Pulitzer and subsequently to his powerful position on the paper. It had also led to the virtual emasculation of the United States' intelligence operation.

"Good to hear from you," Evans said. "How've you been?"

Bonfire wondered how hard Evans had to grit his teeth to sound so pleasant. The publisher was grateful to him for numerous bits of inside information, but they were far from friends.

"I'm fine, thanks, keeping busy over here. I've enjoyed the *Herald*'s editorials on Cuba. Your personal touch was evident—all the right nuances, as usual."

"Glad to hear you liked them, but that's one story that's pretty much written itself. Valles is obviously the right man in the right place."

"Absolutely," Bonfire agreed. "By the way, I heard a heads-up for the paper."

"What's that?"

"The Russians have made a play in Cuba. They're backing someone named José Moya, a general who was imprisoned by Castro, apparently for being too buddy-buddy with the Russians."

"I've already heard, from César Valles himself, as a matter of fact. But thanks. Can't figure why the Russians would care about a two-bit general in Cuba, though."

"Maybe it's just Moya talking, trying to gather some support from Cubans who still admire the Russians. Maybe it's no more than that," Bonfire said. The apparent reason for his call now out of the way, he could concentrate on his real concern. "Have you heard that Bob Grant's been stirring up trouble, trumpeting all sorts of negative comments about Valles? He's even been meeting with leaders of the Cuban-American community, Victor Rojas in particular. You know what extremists they are."

"Grant's gotten that involved? And against Valles? Though I can't imagine why I'm surprised. Grant has a rather plebeian understanding in most areas of international relations. Anybody listening to him?"

"So far he's being ignored," Bonfire replied, "but that hasn't stopped him. I'm concerned that someone will believe him. Too bad we can't know exactly what he's doing before he does something really stupid."

"But maybe we can," Evans said. "I have an idea. Suppose I send a reporter to interview Grant—'the opinions of the ranking member' sort of thing. If Grant thinks he has something, he'll want everyone to know."

"Great idea," Bonfire answered. "I'll be interested to hear what you learn."

2:00 P.M.
A government-controlled radio station
Havana, Cuba

. . . AS A FURTHER INDICATION OF THE CHANGES TO BE MADE FOR THE PEOPLE OF CUBA, PRESIDENT CÉSAR VALLES HAS AN-NOUNCED THE RELEASE OF POLITICAL PRISONERS. THESE RE-LEASES ARE EVEN NOW TAKING PLACE. CONDITIONS IN CUBA WILL CONTINUE TO IMPROVE AS PRESIDENT VALLES WORKS FOR THE BETTERMENT OF THE PEOPLE. . . .

2:00 P.M.
The Capitol
Washington, D.C.

Grant ran down the outside steps of the Senate, cut through the parking lot and headed through the park toward the Hart Building. He wanted time to go over Moya's information before his meeting with the President. Two o'clock. Surely the packet had arrived by now.

Oh, no, Grant groaned to himself as a disheveled young man carrying a tape recorder and notebook ran up alongside him.

"Senator, Senator. Bradley Thomas from the *Washington Herald*. May I have a word with you?"

"I'm in a hurry," Grant said, picking up his pace, "but if you want to tag along, I won't stop you."

"Why don't you agree with the President about the sincerity of Valles?" Thomas asked, trying to match his much shorter steps with the Senator's strides. "And why would you endorse this terrorist Moya? What's the connection between you, Victor Rojas and Moya?"

Rojas, Moya and himself, Grant thought with surprise, wondering at the reporter's source. Why were his movements of such interest? Or was it Rojas who was being watched?

"As the father of our country cautioned, we must be wary of rushing into entangling alliances," Grant said, trying to reveal as little as possible. "We have a duty to ask questions, to consider all possible ramifications."

Grant approached the intersection, relieved that the light remained green. Without breaking stride, he crossed the street and entered the Staff Only entrance to the Dirksen Building, leaving the reporter yelling questions after him from the sidewalk. He'd walk through the corridors to the Hart Building, any ruse to lose the reporter. He took the stairs two at a time up to his office.

"Where's Victor's packet?" he asked Cynthia as he sat down beside her desk. "We don't have much time."

"It's not here." Grant blew out his breath in disappointment. "I've tried his car phone, with no response. His secretary called to say he left about one-fifteen, saying the packet was about to arrive, and he'd have it here by two o'clock, two-fifteen at the outside."

"Great," Grant replied, hitting the arm of the chair in frustration, "but I guess nothing can be done to speed things up. Have you found anything I can use?"

"I've come up empty in the Bubble. Nothing but the official line. But Estelle said something interesting at lunch; she thought I'd want to know because of Dodd. Seems the White House has received reports of increased activity between the Russians and a Middle Eastern country. I don't know which one; she was vague. Could even be more than one, I suppose. I didn't feel I could press—not that she'd know much more even if I did."

"At least it's something," Grant said. "I'll just quote an unnamed source to the President."

"Let's just hope he believes himself," Cynthia said with a dry laugh. "Estelle mentioned China and Hong Kong as well. China I can understand, but I wonder where Hong Kong fits in."

"That's something we need to discover."

2:10 P.M.
Russian military base
San Antonio de los Baños, Cuba

"What's going on over there?" Basilov barked without preamble as soon as César Valles was put on the secure phone. "One of our agents sent us a CIA report from Miami which indicates you have a security breach on your end."

"What do you mean?" Valles demanded, outraged.

"Just that. The information came from one of our top assets in the United States. Without doubt, it's genuine. He says someone with high-level knowledge has to be aiding the insurgents."

The silence was tense.

"So you're saying a traitor. What exactly was in the report?"

General Basilov intoned his information as if it were an indictment. "Information about Castro's death reached Miami soon after he died, long before we allowed any outside communication. They knew much of what's been discussed inside El Palacio since yesterday morning, information mentioned nowhere else."

"In other words," Valles said thoughtfully, "information only someone privy to council meetings or intimate with someone at the meetings could have known."

"Since the information reached Miami so quickly, you must assume someone actually in the conference room on both days. Nothing else would fit. That narrows your choices considerably. Find the traitor."

"I will."

"What's the status of Moya?"

"He's still at large, but we're closing in. I assure you we'll have him soon."

"You'd better. Time's running short."

Reaching for the intercom, Valles was consumed by a cold fury.

Basilov was too condescending. Didn't he know Russia's days in Cuba were numbered? He'd destroy Moya all right and anyone else who got in his way, including Basilov if it came to that.

2:15 P.M.
The clinic
Havana, Cuba

"Gregorio Luzan's here," Dr. Llada told the General.

"Gregorio? Here?"

How had he gotten out of prison? the General wondered as Luzan was escorted through the door. Moya strode across the room and hugged his old cellmate.

"Is it really you?"

"I do look a little different, don't I?" Luzan laughed. "Your dragon in the front room wouldn't let me see anyone until I took a shower. She didn't seem too partial to lice. Nice of you to provide some clothes for me."

"What's happened?" Moya asked, putting an arm around his friend and leading him to a group of chairs beside the ancient examining table. "How'd you get out?"

"I'm not sure," Luzan answered. "All I know is the commandant came into our yard and released one hundred of us. You should have heard the response that got! He read something about Valles wanting to end violations of our human rights. As if releasing one hundred would begin to make a difference. Not that I declined to leave, mind you," Luzan said with a grin.

"I should hope not," Dr. Llada said. "But what a clever move on Valles's part."

"I'm wondering why he chose you," Moya said. "He must have known you and I are old friends."

"They obviously had their reasons. All your former cellmates were beaten this morning and released this afternoon."

"You weren't followed here, were you?" Dr. Llada asked, his face pinched with worry.

"Followed, yes, but not here. Several men—I presume Secret

Police—stayed near me, one even posing as a prisoner—as if I wouldn't know, the fool. When we reached the crowds in Havana, I lost them."

"But—"

"No, doctor. There's no way I could be wrong. Believe me, I wouldn't be here if I had doubts."

"And the others?" Moya asked. "Were any of them followed?"

"Of course. All those in our cell. They were interrogated about you this morning as well, but since they knew nothing of the clinic, they could reveal nothing. May those fools follow them until they drop dead."

"They're coming too close," Moya said. "And they aren't forgetting a thing. They'll be watching your family, Gregorio."

"I know. I won't go home until this is all over. I can wait a while longer after all these years."

"Good," Moya said. "I'm glad you're here. We need your help."

"Just tell me what to do."

2:30 P.M.
Hart Senate Office Building
Washington, D.C.

After his abortive interview with Senator Grant, Bradley Thomas went to Senator Westlake's office to get some quotes from the Senate expert on Cuba. The Senator was out, he was told, but Edmund Miller would answer his questions.

The interview was ending when the reporter alluded to his interview with Grant.

"Hard to believe Grant actually has any credibility at all, isn't it?" Miller said, shaking his head. "I just hope his loose mouth doesn't jeopardize Valles's position. We need Valles in power. Valles understands the importance of a democratic government."

"Grant shouldn't be allowed to take such random shots. What's in it for him, do you suppose?"

"Who knows." Miller shrugged. "He's a reactionary, always going off on some tangent. None of them make sense."

"He won't get any satisfaction from me," Thomas assured him. "This story is more credible without him."

"I don't know. The people need to know the truth. If we keep covering up for Grant, we may be doing a disservice."

"The sin of omission, you mean. You're right. Grant's irresponsibility needs to be exposed for what it is."

2:40 P.M.
El Palacio de la Revolución
Havana, Cuba

"We've had a break," Campos told Valles. "The men following Moya's cellmates have yet to report in, all but the one following Gregorio Luzan."

"He was Moya's confidant in prison, wasn't he?"

"Exactly. And he managed to elude our men."

"Then what's this big break?" Valles demanded, his eyes narrowing angrily.

"The men following Luzan decided to canvass some of Moya's former haunts. One of them feels sure he caught a glimpse of Luzan on Calle Benuto in San Isidro. He disappeared in the crowd, but—"

"Concentrate the search in that area. I want Moya."

2:45 P.M.
Hart Senate Office Building
Washington, D.C.

"What could be delaying Victor?" Grant asked Cynthia rhetorically as he gathered up the papers on his desk. "I have to leave. The President waits for no one." They walked toward the elevator. "If Victor arrives in time, try to get the packet to the White House. I don't care what you have to do, interrupt the meeting, whatever, just do it. I'll stall, give the President what we have, but he's too committed to change his mind easily. I need Moya's information regardless of how late it arrives."

Grant and Cynthia had reached the bank of elevators that led down to the garage.

"I'll do everything I can, Senator. I'm sure you'll do well."

His "I hope you're right" was barely audible as the doors closed on the Senators Only elevator.

"Cynthia!" She looked back toward the office. Mary Lee, Grant's secretary, was running toward her. "Did I miss the Senator?" she asked breathlessly. "Victor Rojas is on the phone."

Cynthia ran toward the office. "The Senator just left," she yelled over her shoulder. "Try to catch him if you can. I'll take the call."

She raced into the office reception area and grabbed the first available phone. "Victor, the Senator just left. Do you have the packet?"

"Yes. I'm in my car just leaving Butler Aviation at National."

"Do you have a pen and paper?"

"Just a sec . . . Okay."

"The Senator's car phone number is 202-555-0635. I told him you'd call if you could to arrange a pickup point on the way to the White House. I'll give you four minutes, then I'll call the Senator myself just in case you can't get a connection. If he hasn't talked to you, I'll have him wait in his car on Pennsylvania Avenue across from the northwest gate."

2:47 P.M.
Constitution Avenue at Pennsylvania Avenue
Washington, D.C.

What a debacle this was going to be, Grant thought as he drove toward the White House, a meeting with the President and only his own unsupported word for evidence. One thing was certain: this was the last private meeting the President would ever agree to have with him. He'd think Grant had lost his mind. Should he cancel? he wondered. No, the situation was critical. Evidence or not, he had to try to convince the President.

The car phone rang.

"Senator, this is Victor."

"Victor! Thank God!"

"I have the packet, and I'm on the parkway heading for Memorial Bridge."

"I've just passed the intersection of Ninth and Pennsylvania," Grant said. "Meet me at the southeast corner of Lafayette Park. I'll pull over and wait. I'm in a blue Olds."

"I'll get there as soon as I can."

"Do you know what's in the packet?"

"No, I haven't had time to open it. The plane was kept in a holding pattern over National so it just arrived. Sorry I couldn't get to a phone."

"Couldn't be helped. I just wish I felt better prepared. I'll be waiting for you."

Grant turned onto Fifteenth Street, waited interminably for the light to change and turned back onto Pennsylvania Avenue. He pulled over to the curb at Lafayette Park. He sat leaning on the steering wheel and staring at the White House.

His car phone rang again.

"Senator, this is Cynthia. Did Victor get you?"

"Yes, I'm waiting for him now. Unfortunately, he doesn't know what Moya sent. I only hope I have a few minutes to look it over."

"You'll do a great job. I'll be by the phone if you need me."

In the rearview mirror, Grant saw a black Cadillac pull up behind him. Rojas was out of the car almost before it stopped. Grant rolled down his window as Rojas sprinted toward him.

"Here it is, Senator," he said as he thrust the package through the window. "I hope it's enough."

"So do I," Grant said, putting the car in gear. "Thanks." He pulled away from the curb.

Grant drove half a block farther down Pennsylvania Avenue and turned into the White House gate. As officers of the uniform division of the Secret Service checked his ID and searched his car, he ripped open the packet and glanced through its contents. He found a cover letter from Moya, a picture, a letter written in Cyrillic, a letter from Moya describing his plans for Cuba as well as the Valles-Russian connection, one from someone detailing the Russian

involvement in Valles's takeover and one about the ambush of Raul
Castro. Each had an English translation attached.

The gates opened. Grant slid the papers back into the packet,
drove in, parked his car, and walked between two uniformed Marine
guards to the reception area of the west wing of the White House.

He had only seconds to spare. The President's personal aide
was just entering the room from the other direction.

Grant followed him down the hall to the Oval Office. At least
he'd had a moment to familiarize himself with what he'd be presenting. It was all circumstantial, but taken as a whole, it might be
enough. Regardless, it was bound to be a tough sell.

The President came around his desk and greeted Grant, mo-
tioning him toward one of the wing chairs that flanked the fireplace.
Chief of Staff Corforth, National Security Advisor Stevenson, the
President's head of Congressional Affairs Sam Breeze, and Press
Secretary Allen-Warren seated themselves on the two couches that
completed the seating group.

As with every meeting in the Oval Office, the White House
photographer took the official photographs that were its historic documentation. That finished, the President opened the meeting.

"I understand you have some information for me, Bob. Please
proceed."

"Mr. President, I'm concerned that the United States may be
jeopardizing its own security by rushing into a relationship with a
man who may not be as he seems. I have evidence that suggests
Valles is being actively aided by the official army of the Russian
Republic."

Grant pulled out the information from Havana, handing to the
President María's account of Basilov's meeting with Valles as well
as the translation.

"This first is an eyewitness account of the takeover at El Palacio
which put Valles in power."

The President glanced through María's account, then handed it
to Stevenson.

"From the details, you can tell that the anonymous writer was
actually in the room. You can also tell that Valles's alliance with the
Russians is beyond doubt."

The President looked at him expressionlessly.

"This next is an account of Raul Castro's ambush, explaining in detail the Russians' participation. This picture and letter, written in Cyrillic, were taken from the body of one of the assassins, proving beyond doubt that he was, in fact, a Russian soldier."

Grant handed them to the President, who glanced at them before giving them to Stevenson. His expression remained impassive. Grant's chest tightened. Was the man even paying attention? he wondered.

"In addition, I have a personal letter from General José Moya, whom I've known for the past thirteen years, detailing what has transpired in his country. Further, I've received information from an informed source—and I'm sure you were briefed on this earlier—indicating a close relationship between the Russian Republic and at least one of the more aggressive and less friendly Middle Eastern countries. All of this combined with reports of wholesale Russian troop movement in the waters off Cuba should give you reason to pause, I'd hope, in what appears to me to be your precipitous embrace of the Valles government."

The President left Moya's letter lying in his lap.

He'd done no more than look at it, Grant thought despairingly. He wasn't planning to consider any of it. Grant pressed on.

"Mr. President, at the same time that General Basilov was at El Palacio greeting Valles as President with his own Russian soldiers ensuring Valles's position, other Russian soldiers—not the Secret Police—were ambushing and killing Raul Castro." Grant's voice was heavy with emotion, as persuasive as he could make it. "Arturo Registra, head of the Secret Police, is now dead; General Moya was in prison when all this occurred; the only person who could have coordinated it all and who's benefited from it is César Valles. The evidence can lead to no other conclusion. Further, any government that has been able to come to power so easily in a country that was under the iron-fisted control of a dictator has to be suspect."

The room was quiet as the documents were examined. Grant watched, recognizing with despair the blank looks on their faces.

"Bob, no one would ever question your sincerity or your patriotism," the President said, leaning forward and looking Grant in the eye, "but all you've given me is circumstantial evidence and hearsay. There's nothing in these papers, in and of themselves, individually or collectively, that's even remotely able to bring into question the abundance of evidence supporting Valles and supporting this administration's position. Moya may be appealing to those who revere the Russia of old by purporting to have their support, but the Russians aren't about to jeopardize their present good standing with us, not to mention our aid, by intruding on Cuba's internal affairs. The Russians have entered a new era of freedom and democracy. Wake up, Bob. The cold war is over. The age of peace has begun. Valles is the man of the people, the democratic choice.

"I want to help you understand. I'm so confident of the direction our country is taking that I'd like for you to come with me to the ceremonies tomorrow so you can meet Valles and realize the rightness of my position."

Grant's jaw set. He'd failed. In spite of the proof, he'd failed. He had to give himself an opening.

"Thank you, Mr. President, I accept your invitation. If by then I can present irrefutable proof of my contentions, will you agree to see me to examine what I've found?"

"Of course. If you can find concrete proof at any time between now and the funeral, I'll be glad to look at it. Just don't bring me any more of these uncorroborated statements. They're too easily forged; they're too often lies."

"Thank you, Mr. President. I appreciate your giving me so much of your time. I hope you're right about the shape of events in Cuba, but at this moment I honestly fear for my country's security."

3:20 P.M.
The White House
Washington, D.C.

"I don't like this, Eugene," the President said to his Chief of Staff. The two men sat with several National Security Council staffers in the Oval Office, discussing the meeting with Grant. "Why would Grant be stirring up trouble about Cuba when everything's so clear-cut?"

"Other than pure cussedness, Mr. President?" Corforth asked with a tight smile. "Maybe it's because Moya's his friend. Grant's been championing him for years through Amnesty International. He may be reluctant to admit he's been wrong about him."

"That's probably it," the President said, getting out of his chair and beginning his habitual pacing. "I've never known him to be so impassioned, but if he's emotionally involved with Moya, that would explain it. From what he suggested about Russian naval movement, he must have been checking with some of his military buddies."

"No doubt," Stevenson agreed. "Security has reported he's made inquiries into our military capabilities. Those of other countries, too, for that matter."

"We can't have him interfering," the President said, stopping his pacing to stare out the window. "Democracy is worth promoting wherever possible. We have to give the Cubans their chance. Tell the military that all information about Cuba will only be released by direct request of the National Security Council. I want our most restrictive security classifications applied." The President turned back from the window and resumed pacing. "That should prevent Grant from unknowingly causing an international incident."

"And at least slow down his meddling," Corforth said. "No one will talk to him now."

3:40 P.M.
The White House
Washington, D.C.

"What kind of reactionary nut do you have over there, anyway?" Charles Kendall asked from his National Security Council office at the White House as soon as his friend Bonfire got on the line. Not that he knew his friend was anything but a loyal supporter of the administration.

"I don't understand," Bonfire said.

"Grant, Senator Grant. That's who I'm talking about."

Bonfire laughed. "The Senator's been called many unspeakable names over here, too. What's he up to now?"

"You won't believe what the guy just did. Brought over a bunch of papers, no better than trash, and said they proved that Valles was being controlled by the Russians."

"You're kidding! What did he have?"

"Accounts written by supposed eyewitnesses to the ambush of Raul and the 'Russian invasion' of El Palacio. Russian invasion. Can you imagine?"

"I wish I could have seen his 'proof.' " Bonfire sneered as he said the last word. "Did it look authentic?"

"Actually, it wasn't bad. I'll fax you a copy if you'd like."

"Like? Of course I would. Maybe it would help me understand Grant better. We've got to work with him, you know."

"Grant didn't stop there. He's even contacted military sources. The nerve of the guy. Can't you control him?"

"Believe me, we've been trying to control him for years. He goes off half-cocked about half the time. Sorry he's giving you such a hard time."

"Not me. I hardly see the guy. It's you I'm sorry for. I know you'll be relieved to get over here. The word's come down you're definitely in."

"You're saying the National Security Council staff position is mine?"

"You aren't supposed to know yet, but, yes. Congratulations. We'll be looking for you."

"Thanks, Charles. Thanks for everything."

3:40 P.M.
The clinic
Havana, Cuba

Dr. Llada stood in the middle of an examination room. A tall Cuban soldier, his grizzled beard jutting belligerently over his uniform, stood at his side. With their backs to the open door to the hallway, the two men faced General Moya across a table cluttered with the accoutrements of medicine.

"You claim to be a patient?" the soldier asked, leaning forward aggressively. "Show me your papers. You just might be our man." He thrust out his hand.

"Yes, sir. Of course, sir," Moya stammered. "I have my papers right here." He fumbled with his back pocket. The soldier moved a little closer.

While Moya patted and then searched through his pockets, a look of dismay and fear growing on his face, Alejandro slipped into the room through the open door.

The General, his hands clumsy with tension, kept his eyes on his clothes. He increased his stammering, willing Alejandro on, willing the soldier to concentrate on his antics. Only a few more steps.

The soldier wheeled, his hand grabbing for the gun at his hip. Alejandro sprang toward him, the side of his open hand thudding on the soldier's neck just above his uniform collar. Like a figure in a slow-motion film, the soldier slid to the floor. His fingers released the gun, which clattered down beside him.

With several long strides, Alejandro recrossed the room and checked the corridor. No other soldiers were in sight, no one to raise the alarm. He closed the door softly.

"Was anyone with him?"

"No," Dr. Llada replied as he knelt by the body, feeling for a pulse. "At least no one came in with him. Several soldiers have been checking all the buildings in this block. He's alive," he announced, reaching for the gun and handing it to Moya.

"You've got to get away from here, General," Alejandro said as he and Dr. Llada wrestled the soldier onto the cot and covered him to the chin with a sheet.

"You're right. I'll get—"

The men whirled as the door opened. Julio Montaner stood in the doorway, clutching the door frame to hold himself upright.

"You shouldn't be up," Alejandro said, lines of worry immediately etched around his eyes.

His father waved him away impatiently. "So you were able to subdue him," he said. He lowered himself carefully onto a chair. "How much time do we have before they come again?"

"Not much," Moya told him. He opened a cardboard box and rummaged through the garments half-filling it, taking out a frayed straw hat and a faded but gaudy shirt.

"Dressed like this, maybe no one will notice me," he said grimly as he buttoned the shirt. It ballooned around him, camouflaging his gaunt body.

"Margarita can go with you," the doctor said, referring to an elderly worker at the clinic. "She'll add credibility to your disguise."

"Disguise!" Alejandro exclaimed, shaking his head. But what else could they do? "I'll check the hallway."

"I'm not leaving yet," the General said, stopping him. "As long as the soldier is here, La Causa's in danger."

"But we can't get him away from here, and we can't hide him from even the most cursory search."

The silence became oppressive. The trap was closing. Alejandro slid over to the door and again checked the hall. Clear.

"You *all* must leave," Julio Montaner said.

"But—"

"None of you can stay. Consider La Causa. Each of you is vital to its success. I'll stay and pose as the doctor. You can help me look the part," he told Dr. Llada. "The soldiers won't discover their mistake for many hours. If I can stall them here, make them think they're closing in, you'll have enough time to get our plans in place. La Causa will be preserved."

The silence was profound.

"You'll never survive an interrogation," Alejandro said, echoing all their thoughts.

"So be it," Julio replied. "I'm about to die anyway. No one can doubt that. Now I'll die on my own terms."

Moya laid a hand on his friend's shoulder. "I can't tell you . . ." He cleared his throat. "Thank you, my friend. Our prayers are with you."

"The honor is mine," Montaner said, putting his hand over the General's. "Now you must leave."

Moya moved toward the door. "We'll meet as we'd planned? Eleven o'clock?"

The other two nodded.

"The meeting with Rojas has been arranged?"

"Yes," Alejandro said. "Margarita will get the message to him at the church."

"Good. Right now, make sure the clinic is clear of people. We mustn't put anyone in danger needlessly."

"I'll explain the risks," Julio Montaner assured him. "The decision to stay or leave must be theirs."

Alejandro once again checked the hall, and the General walked out.

"We've had good times, haven't we, my friend?" Dr. Llada said, hugging Montaner. "I plan on seeing you tomorrow as soon as La Causa has succeeded."

Dr. Llada, too, left the room.

"Don't grieve for me, Alej," Montaner said. "I'm happier now than I've been since this disease began devouring me. Take care of yourself, of María, most of all of Cuba. I love you, my son."

"And I love you, Father." Alejandro held his father gently. "Thank you. I can't . . ."

The words caught in his throat. He turned, and he, too, walked from the room.

3:45 P.M.
The White House
Washington, D.C.

"I just had a most disturbing meeting with Bob Grant," the President told Peter Evans. "I don't agree with him most of the time, but I've never known him to go off the deep end before. Is there anything to his claim that Valles is being manipulated by the Russians?"

"Not a thing. I don't care how much supposed proof he has, that doesn't change the truth. I know César Valles; he's a friend of mine, and I know he's an honorable man."

"You're right. I know you are, and not just because of Valles. This whole Russian thing just doesn't make sense." His voice sounded perplexed. "They're making such strides toward democracy; why would they jeopardize that by taking sides in the internal struggles of a country on the other side of the world? Besides, they don't have the money to launch anything."

"I'm as puzzled as you. Valles was, too. All he knew for sure was that Moya claims he's backed by the Russians. Anyway, none of it really matters since Valles will be President, and we know he's prodemocracy."

"True. At least there's no doubt about that. I've invited Grant to be a member of the presidential party attending the ceremonies, to see Valles firsthand. Maybe you could talk with him on the plane, convince him of the merits of a Valles government."

"I'll try, Mr. President. Another thought—you might want to consider making Trent Westlake a part of the official group as well. He's diverting media attention from you. If he's with you, his importance will pale, and stateside journalists won't have access to him, either."

"Good idea, Peter. Thanks."

4:00 P.M.
Washington, D.C.

Bonfire stood in a phone carrel near the Capitol, his back to the street, his voice low.

"Our southern friend is interested in military movements, both ours and theirs, and has brought further proof of a spy in Valles's inner sanctum. I need an immediate meeting. Thirty minutes."

His contact would come to The Whodunit, ready to receive the latest news about Grant and Moya.

Bonfire deposited another quarter—one more call to make.

4:00 P.M.
Hart Senate Office Building
Washington, D.C.

"The meeting was a disaster," Grant said, ushering Cynthia and Victor Rojas into his office. "The risk the Cubans took to get the stuff to us, and the President barely glanced at it, told me I was a good boy and invited me to accompany him to the ceremonies."

"As a member of the presidential party?" Cynthia asked with surprise.

"Ironic, isn't it? The President's convinced that all I have to do is meet Valles and I'll love him."

"You don't think he was swayed at all?" Rojas asked, unwilling to concede the futility of their efforts.

"Never! The man practically patted me on the head and told me to go out and play."

"What about the eyewitness account of the meeting between Valles and the Russian general?" Cynthia asked. "How could he ignore that?"

"He threw it all back into my lap, saying it was hearsay, inadmissible. Couldn't be right anyway, he said, mentioning peace and the end of the cold war. Talked like Moya may just be saying he's supported by the Russians to get the backing of those Cubans who still admire the Communist agenda, that the Russians are as appalled by his contentions as we are. A real tangle of accusations, countercharges and blindness. One piece of good news—he didn't close the door on another meeting if I can bring him incontrovertible proof."

"That's something," Rojas said. "We'll just have to get it. Here's that background check on Valles you wanted." He handed Grant several dozen sheets of computer printout. "He made numerous trips out of the country, doing business for Castro. It's all there. Maybe you can find something."

"Maybe," Grant said, flipping through the sheets. "I'll go through this tonight. When do you leave for Cuba?"

"Six-twenty. Should be there by nine."

"You'll have to get word to the resistance that we need hard proof. Written accounts aren't enough."

"Moya knows I'm coming, and he knows I'll be staying at the Habana Libre. I'm sure he'll contact me."

"They've got to come up with something so conclusive that the President can't ignore it. And get it to us well before the funeral.

"I'll tell General Moya what we need," Grant said, leaning forward to pick up a pen. "Contact him tonight if you can and give him my letter. You'll have to be careful. I know that's self-evident, but if they intercepted the transmission and decided you're Redbird, their invitation may be an attempt to keep you under surveillance or even out of commission. Valles is a diabolically clever man."

4:30 P.M.
The Whodunit
Washington, D.C.

"Thought I'd take another look at one of the books I saw today," Bonfire told the owner of The Whodunit. "Decided I might have made a mistake passing it up."

The shop owner looked at him in surprise. Never before had Bonfire come back so soon, certainly not the same day. And never had he concerned himself with supplying justification.

Damn, Bonfire cursed to himself. The Cuban situation was getting to him. He made his way to the literary criticism section.

He opened the prearranged book and put in a copy of the report Charles Kendall had sent him. They'd better make good use of this, he thought angrily as he turned away.

Now he had to find a book that would justify his return to the shop.

4:35 P.M.
Hart Senate Office Building
Washington, D.C.

"James," Senator Grant greeted his friend. "I knew I'd been hard to track down this afternoon so I thought I'd call to see what's been happening."

"Look, Bob," Admiral Lawrence said in a tired voice, "you and I are friends, aren't we?"

"Well, of course. What are you trying to say?"

Grant's stomach muscles knotted at the ensuing silence.

"There's no way to sugarcoat this," Lawrence finally said. "All information regarding Cuba is now classified. Your questions must be directed to the National Security Council."

"Oh . . ." Grant said, his face lengthening. So that was what they'd done. "I appreciate your telling me. I know you didn't have to take my call."

"Let's get together when all this is over."

"Yes, let's," Grant agreed. "When all this is over."

Grant threw down his pen. Another avenue closed. What was left? He wouldn't waste time calling Champ.

The administration was making things as hard for him as the enemy was.

6:00 P.M.
Kalorama
Washington, D.C.

Westlake arrived home to find Constance packing an overnight bag.

"A trip to New York?" he asked, kissing her gingerly on the cheek so as not to mess her makeup.

"I'm afraid so," she said, pulling her mind away from Peter Evans and the night they would spend together. She turned toward her husband and slowly began unbuttoning his jacket. She slipped her hands underneath it and stroked his back and chest. "I know it's Friday, and you know I always try to stay home on Fridays." She pressed her body against his and nibbled his ear. "It's so nice having you come home early. What a bore that I have to leave." She ran her tongue around the lobe. "But this trip really is an emergency. My man in New York has found the perfect antique for Melissa Secoulas, and he can't hold it past tomorrow. I'm devastated, you know that." She put a whisper of a kiss on his lips.

"I'm sorry you won't be here," her husband murmured breathlessly, fumbling with the buttons on her blouse. "I'll miss you."

Constance gently disengaged his hands. Smiling wistfully, she pulled away and returned to her packing.

He sighed. "It may be just as well." He paused for a moment

to let the fire go out. "I'm flying to Havana tomorrow with the President. I have to be at Andrews by six-thirty, and I'd hate to disturb you so early."

"Well, well, darling," Constance drawled, "I'm so pleased. So you're part of the official party, are you? I'll be looking for you during the ceremonies. Be sure you make your presence felt."

6:15 P.M.
Potomac, Maryland

As she rinsed a soapy plate under the steaming faucet, Patsi P. Evans whistled under her breath. She and the girls had just finished making cookies, and she was cleaning up the mess. How they could get sprinkles all over everything, she couldn't imagine, her exasperation more from affection than annoyance.

Patsi loved doing anything with her girls. She just wished Pete had more time to join them. He was gone so much, especially lately, she thought, then resolutely pushed the thought from her mind.

She absentmindedly answered the ringing phone, her mind still on her husband.

"Pete, how extraordinary," she bubbled. "I was just thinking about you. Oh, dear"—her voice lost its ebullience—"I hope this call doesn't mean you're going to be late again."

"I'm afraid that's just what it does mean," Evans snapped. "I have to stay in town tonight." Patsi heard him take a steadying breath before he continued more moderately. "I've been asked by the President to go to Cuba with him tomorrow, and I have to be at Andrews early. You know it doesn't make sense for me to come home and then turn right around again at the crack of dawn."

"All right," Patsi replied quietly. "I'm glad you've been asked, but I wish you were coming home. It seems like we never see you. The girls baked cookies as a surprise, and they'll be especially disappointed. You promised you'd be home tonight for sure." Suddenly she felt immeasurably tired.

"Quit carrying on," Evans said, unaware of his wife's despair, of her sudden realization that he'd never intended to come home.

"There's nothing I can do about it. I'll eat the cookies tomorrow night—if you haven't eaten them all yourself."

Patsi admitted numbly that that was exactly what she'd do. She always ate when she was unhappy or lonely. Lately, she'd been eating all the time.

"I have to go now." Evans hung up.

Patsi remained standing by the phone. What had happened to them? she wondered, staring sightlessly in front of her.

Pete didn't love her. He didn't want to be with her, didn't really care about her at all.

A shudder racked her body. She threw her hands to her face, trying to force the hurt back in.

He was probably with someone else. She wouldn't think about that. She squeezed her eyes shut, tears seeping out at the corners. Unbidden, the image of Constance Westlake loomed before her, the huge red mouth laughing, cruel, gaudy laughter. About her. About the joke of her marriage.

Pete was gone.

Patsi stumbled out of the kitchen.

7:00 P.M.
El Palacio de la Revolución
Havana, Cuba

By the time he returned to Havana, General Gomez knew that they had a chance of success. One of his emissaries had remained on each base, ostensibly to oversee plans for the ceremonies, actually to work for La Causa. Much could still go wrong, but for once, time was on their side, surely too little time for their plans to be uncovered. Only seventeen more hours.

When Gomez entered the presidential office, Valles greeted him coldly.

"Are you ready for tomorrow?"

"Our plans are in place, El Presidente," Gomez replied. Why was Valles so distant? he wondered. Worry gnawed at him. He worked to keep his voice steady. "I've ordered several elite corps to arrive in Havana this evening. However, the majority will be here by five tomorrow morning so that they can control the crowds as well as set the proper tone for the ceremony. My goal is to be so prepared that the perfection of the events will be commensurate with the historic significance of the day. I hope you'll be pleased."

"I'm convinced," Valles said dryly, "that tomorrow will be a day long celebrated by the people of Cuba."

They discussed plans for the ceremonies for several more minutes. Gomez felt his unease increase with each of Valles's cold words.

"One moment, General Gomez," Valles said, their conference all but ended. Gomez had already risen and was turning toward the door. "Please be seated."

The silent minutes mounted.

Valles stared at Gomez for far too long.

"I've discovered a traitor among us," he finally said, his eyes holding Gomez's.

Gomez felt his face freeze, his mind denying the meaning of the words. He forced his body to remain relaxed. Had he been betrayed by one of the officers that morning? Or by someone at the clinic?

"A traitor?"

"Yes, General, a traitor. One whom I've trusted, someone of importance in my government, is aiding, maybe even leading, Moya and his revolutionaries."

"How can that be, sir? Certainly no one I spoke with today indicated anything but support for you. I feel sure I would have noticed if it had been otherwise."

"I'm sure you would," Valles said, hidden meaning underlining his words. "No, I refer to someone who's seemed to support me while actually plotting against me."

Surreptitiously, Gomez examined the room. They were alone, but Valles was protected by the desk, his foot no doubt near the buzzer that would immediately summon help. If he had to, Gomez would try to seize Valles and use him as a shield. He certainly wouldn't surrender.

Valles continued to stare at him, saying nothing. Gomez began to sweat, only with effort refraining from licking his dry lips.

"You requested that Moya be brought to your office immediately before his escape." Valles's voice was emotionless. Gomez watched a pulse throb in his forehead.

"Moya?" Gomez asked, his voice puzzled, trying to hide his relief. His story about Moya's escape would survive scrutiny. His work in La Causa was safe—at least for the moment. "I asked him to my office?"

Valles stared at him. Unblinking. Silent.

"What are you talking about? I never called for Moya."

"The soldier who took Moya away brought an official order signed by you."

"I never signed an order," Gomez said angrily.

"You never sent for Moya?"

"No. *Castro* had ordered that I interrogate Moya. You know that. But not this week. Obviously, not this week. What about the soldier who picked up Moya? Who was he? What does he say?"

"He's disappeared. No one's certain of his identity. The jeep he was driving was found abandoned in Havana."

"Has anyone checked the log in my office?"

"Yes, and there was no record of anything. Your clerk knew nothing."

"What a clever move by Moya! If I've learned one thing during my interrogations of him, it's that he's treacherous. He must be found."

Gomez stood abruptly. "The arrogance of the man! Using my name! I'll find him myself."

With relief, Gomez saw Valles begin to relax.

"I understand how you feel," Valles told him. "But your skills are needed elsewhere. I do ask that you check your interrogation notes for any hints as to his whereabouts, anything at all suggestive."

"I'll get them to you," Gomez assured him, sitting back down, "but the list will be short. Moya was too smart to incriminate his associates." He slammed his palm on his knee in anger. "He's got to be caught. You mentioned a traitor in the inner circle," he continued more moderately. "Why do you think that?"

"The Russians have received CIA information as well as a detailed written report that could only have come through someone involved in the meetings of the Council of Ministers."

Gomez shook his head in disgust. "It's already started, hasn't it, the jealousy and power grabbing. Thank God your government is well entrenched. These things—Moya, the traitor—are problems, but they shouldn't threaten your ultimate success."

"I value your opinion, General, but I'll feel better when they're both captured."

Valles stared thoughtfully at the door after Gomez left. Gomez had been his friend for years, had spent a year with him at Tomorrasov University in Moscow, and was one of the few men he'd ever thought of trusting. In no way could Gomez be involved in the escape. His name had been forged on the order. It *had* been a forgery; that had been verified. And Gomez had been with him in El Palacio during the time of the escape, a meeting that was completely spontaneous, at least on Gomez's part. Gomez's anger just now had been genuine, just as he'd expected it to be.

No, Gomez wasn't involved. Of that, he could be reasonably sure.

7:00 P.M.
Hart Senate Office Building
Washington, D.C.

Grant finished jotting a last note on his pad and leaned back to review what he'd written. He studied the notes for several minutes; then, frowning, he sat up and again read through the computer printout from Rojas, verifying the tenuous thread that ran through it. Valles had met with eight different sheiks during the last three years, presumably at Castro's behest. He'd visited several of those men on more than one occasion. Was this the key for which they were searching?

"Cynthia, get Benjamin Dashev on the line for me, would you please? The Israeli Embassy." Dashev was ostensibly the deputy chief of mission, but Grant had worked with him several times in the past and felt sure he was connected somehow with Mossad. Maybe Israeli intelligence could explain Valles's Middle East visits. They certainly kept a close eye on that area. Thank God.

"Sorry to bother you, Benjamin, but I've come across some names and wondered if they mean anything to you." Grant read the list of those whom Valles had contacted.

"If they mean anything!" Dashev exploded. "We've been trying to get your people to listen to our reports about them for months. You've just listed half of the board of directors of the International Bank of Trade and Credit."

"I've heard of it, but why the anger?"

"That bank is the major bankroller for every terrorist group in the world today. Outwardly it seems a legitimate banking concern, but in reality—brother! You're talking major power brokers."

"What exactly do they do?"

"Money to terrorist groups, of course, even the small ones; laundering of drug money worldwide and facilitating drug dispersal, especially the heavy stuff from the Orient; and lately brokerage of assets for the Russians."

"Assets? What do you mean? Weapons? Ships? Food? What?"

"All that. For example, Russian ships at Vladivostok have been sold to the Chinese with money provided by IBTC. The Russians are even selling some of their intelligence assets, including agents and even information. Everything—well, probably that's an exaggeration—but most of what their spies learn is for sale. Lourdes is one of their most lucrative capitalist ventures."

"I had no idea." Grant felt as if a floodlight had been directed on the murky facts he'd been slogging through for the last few days. "That explains so much."

"You'd have understood much sooner if your people would just listen to us. We've been trying to alert you, but our credibility is zilch. Nobody seems the least concerned."

"The world is one huge family now, all peace loving. Hadn't you heard?" Grant's voice dripped frustration. "What proof do you have about IBTC?"

"Only paper documentation, I'm afraid: names of the members of the board of directors, those attending meetings, probable results of those meetings—the paper trail—about what you'd expect."

"What I'd expect from *your* people, you mean," Grant said

dryly. "*Our* reports have suggested none of this, not even a hint. Was Castro in their pay?"

"They had an arrangement. The influx of hard drugs into the United States—you've read the reports about the increase in their availability on your eastern seaboard—came from China, Burma, Laos, through Castro, facilitated by IBTC."

"And Valles?"

"He was Castro's front man," Dashev said. "Organized the operation and met with the money men."

"So that's why he had so little trouble getting into power— IBTC was already behind him."

"Can't tell you that for sure, but it seems a reasonable surmise."

"What's this group after?"

"You've got to remember the whole world order is changing. The Russians have left a huge void in what might be termed the superpower arena. Whether IBTC helped accelerate Russia's downfall . . . Regardless, they're ready to step in. IBTC was formed and is now run by wealthy businessmen from Syria, Libya, Iran, Iraq, Jordan, all the obvious ones and a few others. They think of themselves as the Holy Alliance, bringing the Persian Empire back to its rightful place as ruler of the world."

"Hell!"

"Exactly. Death to the infidel. If you don't wake up, the United States may get a taste of what we've been facing for years."

7:30 P.M.
El Palacio de la Revolución
Havana, Cuba

"No, El Presidente," Colonel Campos said. He stood at attention in front of Valles's desk. "We haven't found him yet. But we've found his headquarters, a clinic in San Isidro as we suspected. Several people have confessed to seeing him there. Luzan as well."

The interrogations had been brutal.

"Even now my men are there. They'll bring back anyone they find for interrogation."

"You'd better hope they're successful," Valles said. "And the traitor within my cabinet?"

"I'm not sure he's in your cabinet," Campos said. He tugged at his collar nervously. "We've received word that Edmundo, the servant here at El Palacio—you may remember him, tall, thin, rather timid?—this Edmundo has disappeared."

"He has, has he?" Valles sat up expectantly.

"Yes, sir. No one's seen him since last night or has any idea of his whereabouts. We're searching for him now."

"Inform me as soon as he's found."

7:30 P.M.
Outside the clinic
Havana, Cuba

The soldiers had been in the clinic for twenty minutes. Alejandro watched the closed door from the shadows of an alleyway across the street.

Twenty-three minutes.

He sucked in a breath and stamped his feet. More than anything he wanted to go in. How could he stand by while his father suffered? He clenched his fists and hugged his chest tightly. But he had no choice. He couldn't sacrifice himself as well as his father to Valles's soldiers.

Twenty-six minutes.

Was his father alive? Had he been able to husband his strength so that he could give La Causa some extra time? Minutes so far. Could he hold on for hours?

Thirty-three minutes.

"Bring them with us," a soldier shouted as he backed out of the clinic door.

Several people were shoved out onto the sidewalk, one holding an arm, another rubbing a bloody nose. A soldier cursed and clubbed an old woman when she stumbled. Alejandro cringed with each blow even as he strained to see. Then he caught a glimpse of a man in a dingy white clinic jacket being shoved into the waiting truck. Julio Montaner was barely visible between the two soldiers who lifted him, but his eyes were open. Alejandro closed his own. His father was alive.

7:45 P.M.
Hart Senate Office Building
Washington, D.C.

Grant had been poring over the reports about Cuba they'd accumulated in the last few days, viewing them in the light of Dashev's frightening revelations about IBTC. Now that he knew what to look for, he could discern the coalition's imprint on events, but he could find no proof that these sinister forces were behind Valles, certainly nothing that would merit further talk with the President.

With surprise he heard a knock on his door. Cynthia was in the Bubble, hunting for any information on IBTC. Only his wife, Rachel, knew he was still at the office, and she wouldn't knock. "Come in," he said, his hands on the chair arms preparatory to rising.

"Tommy." Grant's face split in a smile of welcome at the sight of Tommy MacKinsey, his friend from naval intelligence. "What's brought you down here? And at this time of night?"

"I know it's late," MacKinsey said, lowering himself into the chair Grant indicated, "but Rachel said you were here. Some satellite recon photos just came in, and after our talk about Cuba, I thought you might want to see them."

Grant's eyebrows rose inquiringly, a gleam of hope in his eyes.

"Now, don't get too excited," MacKinsey cautioned. "They have nothing to do with Cuba—I couldn't show them to you if they did—but they're certainly odd."

Grant had opened the envelope and was slowly looking through the pictures, a frown growing on his face. "I hate to admit it, but these mean nothing to me."

MacKinsey bent down and pointed to various parts of the pictures as he explained. "This is Russia, the port at Vladivostok. Looks fairly much like you'd expect, doesn't it? Ships docked, just a normal port. That was taken last week; this one, last month; and this, a year ago." He spread the photos on the desk, and Grant leaned over, examining them. "See the differences? Far fewer ships in the latest photos and no reports from the Russians about any naval maneuvers. What with the new spirit of friendship and cooperation, they've been most forthcoming about all their plans. This disappearance of ships just doesn't fit into that."

"What are the other pictures?"

"These were taken along the Chinese coast. Compare the ones taken most recently with those from several months ago."

"The shoreline has changed a little in several of the ports, hasn't it," Grant said slowly, "as if ships are being hidden to look like extensions of land. So he was right; Russia *is* selling its assets."

"What do you mean?"

Grant told MacKinsey what Dashev had told him. MacKinsey slumped back in his chair when Grant finished, weariness in every line of his body. "How can all this have been kept from us? A threat of this magnitude, and we don't even know . . ." His voice trailed off.

"Then you think it's true?"

"Oh, yes," MacKinsey said, trying to rouse himself from his depression. "It explains much of what's been bothering me, what hasn't made sense for the last few months. No, I'm wrong. The signs have been there for several years."

"Any concrete proof?"

"Not that I know of."

"But you think the threat is real?" Grant asked.

"Damned real."

8:15 P.M.
The conference room
El Palacio de la Revolución
Havana, Cuba

María had served coffee and was standing at the side of the room, next to a table of refreshments she'd set up earlier. So far she'd heard nothing of interest, nothing which would prove Valles's Russian connection. Nothing less would suffice.

"The American President will be attending the ceremonies," Valles said. He paused for a moment to survey the room, enjoying the ministers' amazement. His glance returned speculatively to María.

Her heart jumped. No one had treated her with any suspicion during the day, but what if the guard had mentioned his meeting with her? What if . . .

Valles finally looked away and resumed speaking.

With shaking hands, she put some cups on a tray. She'd serve more coffee, anything to appear to have a reason to stay.

"The President's arrival will, of course, mean—"

Valles stopped abruptly and stared again at María.

"What are you doing in here?" he demanded. Everyone swiveled to look at her. Every sound, every rustle of paper or cloth, every clink of coffee cup against saucer, was stopped. María cleared her throat.

"Serving refreshments, sir, coffee and rum, sir."

"Well, get out of here. I don't want you in this room at all unless you're specifically called. Do you understand?"

"Yes, sir. As you wish, sir." María picked up her tray and started for the door.

"Leave the tray here."

María replaced it on the table. She thought her seared lungs would burst.

Valles stared her out of the room. The silence behind her was absolute.

9:30 P.M.
The Senate Intelligence Committee Room
Hart Senate Office Building
Washington, D.C.

Grant walked into the Bubble, catching Cynthia stifling a yawn. She'd been going through files for almost three hours.

"Any luck?" he asked her kindly as he pulled out a chair and sat down beside her.

"One more report confirming Moya's and Champ DePaul's accounts of the Russian takeover at El Palacio," she said. "It had been filed near the back of the last general-information file. A strange location. The report's too sketchy to be much help."

"Anything on IBTC?"

"Plenty of innocuous references, nothing else. They've certainly been busy all over the world, branches of the bank, of course, but also meetings, some with heads of state."

"Maybe what I just learned will help you know where else to look." Grant told her about the satellite pictures. "Try the China file." A speculative look came into his eyes. "If Russia has already sold some of its ships, what about those that are in the waters off Cuba? Are they really Russian? Chinese maybe? Or does IBTC control them? I wish Lawrence hadn't been warned not to talk to me. He needs to know what may be happening, and he might be able to pick up something, revealing radio transmissions from the subs, something."

Cynthia looked at him sympathetically, rubbing the small of her back as she nodded toward the folders on the table. "I'll hunt for some indication about the ships although these people seem too careful to have left much of a paper trail, at least not one that will implicate them."

"I'm afraid you're right. I'm going to call Senator Yarbonski," Grant said, remembering his colleague's interest in joining the CODEL. "Maybe he can think of something we've missed."

Yarbonski listened sympathetically.

"Look, Bob, if you're right—and I tend to think you may be— you're taking on some major players. Their disinformation campaign alone would have to involve the highest levels of our government. You've got the intelligence community against you, the media, your own committee and the President of the United States. Weigh that against what you have—some circumstantial evidence, most of it smuggled to you from a group of suspect revolutionaries based on the word of a man you've only met once and who's been isolated in prison for years. That, a few iffy satellite pictures and the intelli-

gence reports of another government. Give it up, Bob. Think of
your credibility. All this directed by a group of Arabs with allegiance
to no single country! How many people would believe that? If you
get the reputation of a wild-eyed reactionary, you'll never be taken
seriously in this town again. We need you on other issues. Don't
jeopardize your career on something as unsubstantiated as this. Wait
until you have substantive evidence before you put up your fight."

Grant hung up and rubbed tired hands over his tired face. Was
Yar right? Was this one fight that just couldn't be won, at least not
in time to keep Cuba out of enemy hands? Should he give up for
now and hope to find enough evidence to topple Valles's government at some later date? Might he be more effective then anyway?
What a mess! And so unnecessary. He sat beside the phone for
several minutes, his head bowed in thought.

"Come on, Cynthia," he said as he walked back into the intelligence reading room. "Something more has to be here. We're going
to find it, and we haven't much time."

9:30 P.M.
The White House
Washington, D.C.

"What's the problem now?" the First Lady asked her husband with
a sigh.

She lounged on her bed, Nefertiti under her stroking fingers.
The President sat at the foot of the other bed, his nightly file of
work partly finished on his lap.

"Does this have anything to do with Cuba?" she asked, her
shapely hands caressing the cat's ears, its face turned to her in
rapture. "I wondered if you hadn't acted rashly, deciding to go to
Cuba."

"Do you really think I made a mistake? That's what Bob Grant
told me today. He believes that César Valles is controlled by the
Russians."

"Maybe he's right."

The President stared at the floor in thought.

"It's too late for you to change your mind about going, you know," the First Lady told him. "You've made too big a deal out of it with the media."

"You misunderstand me. I still want to go. Valles will need our support if he hopes to establish a democracy. This is one time it's important for me to be proactive. Grant's wrong, and I must help Valles."

The President looked at his wife for signs of appreciation, only to find her feigning sleep, the cat curled under her hand. He hung up his robe and pulled up his covers. He'd finish his work first thing in the morning.

As he burrowed his head into the pillow, the phone rang.

"The President of Cuba, César Valles, is calling," the White House operator said.

"Put him through."

Now what could Valles want? The funeral was only—he looked at his bedside clock—fourteen hours away.

"Mr. President, I wouldn't even consider bothering you if a critical situation hadn't arisen. We've just received reports of a major military coup being planned by José Moya with the active participation of the Russians. The information we've received indicates that their strength is just too great for my people to counteract."

"What exactly are we talking about?" the President asked, sitting up in his bed.

"A major military move, using Russian military equipment. We have no exact details. All we know is that the force could be large."

"Hard to believe the Russians would involve themselves so deeply, but . . ." The President paused. "Look," he said, "I'll keep my people on standby. I'll give orders that they should put down any unusual or threatening military activity. That should take care of any potential problem. Surely the Russians aren't actually involved—maybe some renegade Russians without the knowledge of their leaders—but regardless, we'll keep Moya under control. He's the danger."

"Mr. President, I can't begin to express my appreciation for your support of democracy in Cuba. My countrymen thank you as well."

The President disconnected and punched the button for the White House operator. "Get me Chad Stevenson," he said.

After a few minutes the National Security Advisor was put through.

"Chad, I just received a phone call from President Valles requesting our military support if a coup should arise. I gave him my word that the United States would do all we could to prevent such a coup. You and the Secretary of Defense will need to get together immediately to look into our options. In the meantime, we'd better put our forces in the area on alert. Get the tape of my conversation with Valles transcribed so you'll know exactly what his request was and what I promised. I'll expect a report at my early morning briefing before we board the helicopter for Andrews."

The President lay in bed, thinking about Cuba. Strange that Bob Grant was so blind to the truth. He was frighteningly out of touch.

10:15 P.M.
La Habana Libre Hotel
Havana, Cuba

Victor Rojas sauntered into the lounge of the hotel. He hoped he looked more relaxed and unconcerned than he felt. Quite a crowd, he thought, stopping inside the door to survey the room. Two men stopped in the lobby behind him and moved to either side of the room, keeping him in view. They'd been at the airport when he arrived in Havana and had been dogging him ever since. Were others keeping him under surveillance as well? he wondered. He couldn't tell by looking so he might as well go in. He'd just have to act as if everyone had him under observation and do all he could to confuse them.

He expected to be contacted by Moya's people somewhere around the hotel, but so far no one had approached him. That wasn't surprising. His hotel room was too risky as well as too vulnerable to observation. Probably bugged as well. The lounge made better sense, especially now since it was crowded with foreigners.

Rojas elbowed his way to the bar, murmuring apologies. No one looked at him furtively or nodded toward the door. He laughed shakily to himself. He'd been watching too much James Bond. Real life wasn't nearly so obvious. And the good guy didn't always win.

No one bumped him or put a paper in his hand.

"Red Label on the rocks," he told the harried barman, "my favorite drink in Miami. Hope you have it." He said the code words loudly to be heard over the shouts and laughter. While he waited, he leaned his back against the bar and continued to survey the room. No one seemed to pay him any attention.

"Your drink, señor." Rojas turned to smile his thanks. "The ambrosia of the redbird. For you."

Rojas's hand arrested in midair before he continued reaching for the glass. The drink sloshed as he picked it up.

After pouring several drinks at the other end of the bar, the bartender moved toward Rojas again. Rojas leaned forward, waving an unlit cigarette. "You wouldn't have a match, would you?"

The bartender flipped a packet to him without breaking stride.

Rojas lit his cigarette with shaking hands, dropped the matchbook into his pocket and finished his drink.

10:30 P.M.
The office of the President
El Palacio de la Revolución
Havana, Cuba

The meeting between César Valles and General Gomez had barely begun when Colonel Campos was announced.

"I'm afraid we have bad news, Presidente Valles," Campos said. He shifted his weight nervously from one foot to the other.

Valles just stared at him.

"The doctor in charge of the clinic where Moya's been hiding died minutes ago."

Julio Montaner was dead, Gomez thought with sorrow. The death of a martyr.

"What did he reveal?"

"Very little. He just kept repeating treasonous litanies. He was out of his head much of the time."

Well done, my friend, Gomez thought. Well done.

"He was our last direct link with Moya. The others arrested with him were patients and knew nothing. They would have admitted anything after they saw the first of their group die. We're continuing our search, but so far nothing."

"Nothing," Valles said, looking down at the pencil he bounced in the palm of his hand. "And the traitor? Have you learned nothing there as well?"

"Not exactly nothing," Campos replied, running a forefinger around the inside of his collar. "We're convinced Edmundo's our man. If we can find Moya, we feel we'll find this Edmundo hiding with him."

"Then find him, you incompetent fool!" Valles roared, springing to his feet and leaning forward on the desk. "Widen your search area. Increase your interrogations. Find him and bring him to me."

"Yes, sir," Campos said, gulping. Beads of sweat stood on his forehead. He saluted, turned smartly and marched out of the room.

"You've every right to be angry, El Presidente," Gomez said after a tense silence. "However, if we can just hold Moya at bay until noon tomorrow, he'll be unable to act. Your men may not have found him yet, but they've run him to ground. He's like a fox cowering in his hole. He can't leave, and no one can come to him. He's effectively neutralized as long as the pressure remains."

"You may be right," Valles said, again seated and bouncing his pencil, "but I'd feel more secure with him under my control. I spoke to the American President a few minutes before you came and explained the situation. He was concerned that a renegade like Moya might take control of Cuba." Valles laughed mirthlessly. "He volunteered to come to our defense militarily at the first sign of an uprising."

Gomez's heart plummeted. He forced himself to speak. "Masterful! You've won if Moya's captured, and you've won if he remains at large. I bow before your skill."

"It's rather amusing, isn't it?" Valles laughed.

"Indeed, it is. I just wish I could have heard the conversation. I can't imagine how you managed such a colossal stroke."

"You can hear it," Valles said, rising from his chair and walking to a nearby cabinet. He took out two tapes, removed the rubber band that held them together and replaced one. "Here it is."

Gomez chuckled appreciatively at the American President's comment that "that should take care of any potential problem."

"That was choice, El Presidente," he said at the tape's conclusion. "Simply wonderful! You must enjoy listening to these tapes," he continued as Valles bent down to replace it. If only Valles would reveal the location of a compromising tape, Gomez thought.

"They do prove entertaining. Here's another one you might enjoy." Valles put on a second tape.

"The Russian President?" Gomez asked respectfully, after the first few words. Valles nodded.

" 'Still, as long as Moya's free,' the Russian President was telling Valles, 'you're in jeopardy. Remember, support for you hasn't come cheaply. Our mutual alliance with IBTC is important and must be protected.' "

The proof! Gomez thought. Here was the proof to give to the Americans. No one could doubt Valles's allegiance or Moya's innocence after listening to this tape.

Valles put the tape back in the cabinet, replacing the rubber band which held the two together.

"I feel honored that you'd share these with me," Gomez said.

Valles smiled and leaned back in his chair. "Now tell me," he said, "what do you know about this woman who cleans El Palacio?"

"The woman who cleans?" Gomez frowned. Surely he didn't suspect María.

"I've noticed her serving at several meetings," Valles said. "I know Campos suspects this Edmundo, but what if he's wrong? What if the traitor is still among us?"

"I understand what you're suggesting, but I have to agree with Campos. Getting one spy into El Palacio would be difficult enough. But two? I doubt it. I don't know much about the woman, I'm afraid. She seems hardworking but somewhat simpleminded, too much so to be a threat, I would have thought. There should be a file on her somewhere. Would you like me to see what I can find?"

"Might be a good idea," Valles said. "I have a funny feeling about her."

10:30 P.M.
The Senate Intelligence Committee Room
Hart Senate Office Building
Washington, D.C.

They'd been going through file after endless file for hours, checking for IBTC, money transfers, sales by the Russians, anything that might help.

"This is no good," Grant said finally, stretching and covering a yawn. "They've covered themselves too thoroughly. We might as well go home. I need to get my thoughts organized before I board *Air Force One* in the morning."

"You go ahead. I'm going to stay a little longer." Cynthia stretched her back tiredly as she talked. "IBTC frightens me. Surely someone somewhere has recognized their threat. I'll keep looking."

10:45 P.M.
Iglesia y Convento Santa Clara de Asis
Havana, Cuba

Victor Rojas slid into the eleventh pew on the right side of the church. An elderly woman, her head covered in a black cloth which fell almost to her waist, was seated in the middle of the pew. He assumed his shadowers were moving into pews behind him, for he'd made no effort to lose them since leaving the hotel. Instead, he'd strolled leisurely through the streets and greeted everyone he'd passed. He'd had no idea what kind of contact to expect from Moya at the church, and he was laying the groundwork. Surely all those people, those innocent bystanders, couldn't be arrested just for talking to him, he thought with a cold shudder.

Following the instructions written on the inside of the match-book cover, he'd entered the church of his youth at exactly ten forty-five and now here he sat in the eleventh pew. How well he remembered coming here as a boy, awed by the beauty and solemnity. And how faded it seemed now, faded but somehow still potent.

Despite the late hour, several dozen worshipers were in the pews; others were lighting candles or gazing at the few remaining reliquaries. So much had disappeared over the years.

Still following instructions, Rojas left the pew and moved slowly toward the shrine near the front of the church, joining those who prayed there. The anxiety and weariness of the past three days slowly dissipated as he allowed himself to relax.

He lit a candle and added his prayers to the prayers of those beside him, watching the elongated flame and the slender stream of smoke rising to disappear in the darkness of the arched ceiling.

No one approached him.

He returned to his seat. The pew was empty now. He saw the elderly lady lighting a candle at the front.

Time was running out. If he weren't contacted soon, he'd be forced to leave. He could try to return later, he supposed, but that was bound to seem suspicious and to draw suspicion to anyone near him.

He reached for one of the ancient hymnals in the holder in front of him. His body stiffened. The back of one of the books was facing him. His heart hammering, Rojas picked up the book and let it fall open. A slip of paper rested between the pages, a tiny caricature of a bird in one corner. Redbird! They'd managed it! Moving only his thumb, he slid the paper to the edge of the book and palmed it. He reached into his pocket and brought out his handkerchief, leaving the paper from Moya in his pocket. He put the cloth to his nose and blew, hoping no one had noticed the paper from Grant he'd extracted from the cloth.

Grant's message safely in the book, Moya's message safely in his pocket, Rojas replaced the book and, after a final prayer, left the church.

The lady in black shuffled out of the church a short time later, the letter from Grant hidden in the folds of her skirt.

11:30 P.M.
Vincente Aguirre's apartment
Havana, Cuba

"Our people are in place at La Plaza," Dr. Llada said, his eyes dark with fatigue. He and Moya had begun the final run-through for the next morning. María, Ines and Vincente Aguirre were there as well. "They're nervous but determined. I feel sure that many more will join them once you appear."

The door opened, and Alejandro edged in. "Margarita just gave me the message Redbird left for us at the church."

He handed a paper to the General, then sat next to María and draped his arm over the back of her chair. At her smile, he squeezed her shoulder and forced his thoughts away from his father.

"No problems?"

"No, General, none at all. Margarita was certain she'd aroused no suspicion, and I noticed no surveillance around her. She saw Redbird take your message for Senator Grant and leave."

"Excellent."

The door opened again, this time to admit Gomez.

"Paschal, what are you doing here?" Dr. Llada exclaimed. No one had expected him to come.

He paused for a moment as he sat down, his face grave. The others looked at him tensely. "The American President has agreed to use his country's military to stop any aggression against Valles. Our planes will be destroyed before the first bomb reaches the ground."

"What!" Moya exclaimed. Alejandro threw down his pencil and slumped in his chair, arms folded across his chest.

"There can be no doubt, I'm afraid," Gomez said, rubbing his eyes wearily. "I heard a tape of Valles's conversation with the President. The Americans are convinced you're a terrorist in league with the Russians, General, or at least with Russian renegades. They're committed to having Valles as President."

"Can he be defeated?" Dr. Llada asked.

"Only with hard evidence—at least that's what Redbird's note from Senator Grant says," Alejandro told them. "And that was before all this. We've got to find something conclusive and get it to Senator Grant with enough time for him to present it to the President. This is Grant's time schedule for tomorrow"—Alejandro handed Moya the paper—"with Redbird's suggestions for contacting him."

"That evidence does exist," Gomez said. "I heard another tape, this one between Valles and the Russian President. It leaves no doubt as to who's backing Valles."

"Finally! Just what we need," Moya said. "Is it accessible?"

"Yes, in a cabinet in his office."

"I can get it," María said softly.

Gomez's head jerked up. He opened his mouth to tell them of the tremendous suspicion already leveled at María. She gave him a warning glance. He closed his mouth and stared down at his hands.

"Can you get it in time?" Moya asked her.

"Yes, I'm sure I can. I've been ordered to clean Valles's office tomorrow morning—he's planning a private meeting with the American President after the ceremonies. No one should question my presence."

"Alejandro," Moya said, "you'll need to get the tape to Senator Grant. María can deliver it to you."

"I'll wait at the usual place from seven o'clock on," Alejandro said, his voice steady. The skin on his face was taut. Oh, María, María, his mind wept. To what depths had Cuba fallen that they must put her in such danger?

"The crowds will be tremendous tomorrow," Gomez warned. "You'll have to allow adequate time to walk even that short distance. You won't be able to cut behind the buildings, either. The American Secret Service has sealed off that area. Believe me, no one will be able to get through. We can get you an army uniform, though, and make you a member of the security detail. You won't be able to get in areas secured by the Secret Service, but you'll have some flexibility. Remember, as soon as the presidential motorcade arrives and the President leaves the car, getting to Senator

Grant will be virtually impossible. Security will be absolute, and our people have no authority to change any of it. A uniform won't make any difference."

"Our timing must be perfect, then," Moya said. "The Senator has to get the tape to the President and then convince him of its importance. Then the President has to countermand his orders to attack our people. All of that will take time."

María and Alejandro looked at each other.

"By ten o'clock, María?" Alejandro asked, wanting to give her as much time as possible. The closer to the time of the ceremonies, the less chance that the theft would be discovered.

"Yes, by ten o'clock."

"The tapes," Gomez said, "are in the cabinet on the far side of the room. They're the only ones held together by a rubber band. They're labeled, in case you're unsure."

María nodded.

"You should take them both," Moya said. "Paschal, will you be in a position to get the tapes from Alejandro and give them to the Senator?"

"Yes," Gomez said. "Given the crush of the crowd, plan to meet me as close to the platform as you can, Alejandro. You can use the statue of José Martí as a guide. I'll be looking for you near it."

"Alejandro, you must get word to Grant early tomorrow so he'll be looking for the tapes. He'll need time to arrange for a tape recorder. A Russian interpreter as well. Unless we can get them for him?"

No one said anything.

"Then he has to know in time to get them himself."

"Getting a message to the Senator will be almost impossible," Alejandro said, "at least early enough to do any good. His plane doesn't land until after nine, and he'll be inaccessible to us until the presidential motorcade arrives at La Plaza. But I can have Margarita get the message to Rojas. He can tell the Senator."

"I wish we could contact the Senator personally," Moya said, "but go ahead with your plans. We'll hope Rojas can get through. If not, we'll give Grant the tapes cold and hope the Americans come prepared for anything. Be sure the message to Rojas doesn't reveal too much of our plan too soon."

He turned to Gomez. "Were you able to learn anything else?"

Gomez looked at Alejandro with compassion. "Julio Montaner is dead."

Alejandro's body became rigid. María leaned over and clasped his hand in hers.

"He kept their attention away from us for many hours and died without revealing anything."

"He was a patriot, and he died a patriot's death, bravely and with honor," Moya said. "I grieve not only for you, Alejandro, who has lost a beloved father, but for Cuba, which has lost a courageous son."

He slammed his hand down on the table. "We will succeed," he declared. "We have to be so prepared that we cannot fail."

The others murmured their agreement.

"The pilots are standing by for their orders, I presume?" he asked Gomez.

"That's correct. We'll give them their flight plans immediately before takeoff to avoid any breach of security."

"Have Sacasa wait until eleven to inform them. That will allow enough time to reach everyone, won't it?"

"Just enough, I'd say, and not enough for word of our plans to reach Havana. The communications systems on all bases will be sabotaged by eleven-ten. Julio, God rest his soul, finished those plans early yesterday."

"And the motorcade?"

"Those plans are in order," Vincente Aguirre told him.

Moya looked at all of them. "Then we're ready."

Midnight Cuban time (8:00 A.M. Moscow time)
Moscow, Russia

". . . And the Ivy Halls network? What have you heard from that direction?" asked the Director of Intelligence.

"Bonfire sent two interesting reports—a copy of a CIA memo

from Miami as well as eyewitness accounts of our involvement in Cuba since Castro's death. All were accurate—disturbingly so—and indicate a mole in Valles's government. Fortunately, the Americans have been persuaded to ignore the reports. Valles has been informed of the potential danger."

"Good," his superior said, nodding. "Tell him exposing this mole is a top priority. Apply more pressure if Valles seems reluctant to press the issue. His allegiance has been brought into question by Basilov.

"These reports came through Bonfire? His information always brings a high price. Is he working for others?"

"We sold his identity to our benefactors—I'm sure he signed on."

"We need to keep him satisfied and keep his best information coming to us. How close is he to moving into the executive branch?"

"Groundwork was laid several months ago, as you ordered. We just received word that his appointment is about to be announced. The National Security Council staff."

"Perfect."

If you feed the people just with revolutionary slogans, they will listen today, they will listen tomorrow, they will listen the day after tomorrow, but on the fourth day they will say, "To hell with you!"

NIKITA KHRUSHCHEV

Day Four

Saturday
January 28

2:00 A.M.
The Bubble
Washington, D.C.

"Senator, I've found another report," Cynthia told Grant as soon as he came on the line.

"IBTC?"

"Not by name, but it certainly sounds like them. An asset in Libya reports significant money transfers from there to Hong Kong. He mentions several names. One is a director of IBTC."

"Good work, Cynthia. Was that today?"

"No, last week. We should have found it in one of the Libya files, but someone had put it in with Third World food shortages."

"We need to check into this filing problem. Too many inconsistencies. Anything else?"

"I checked for the same type of transfer in China, thought it might have been those ships. A new report had just come in indicating a huge influx of money over the last several months. Hong Kong is listed as the source of the transfers. IBTC isn't mentioned, no names at all, but the dates are interesting."

"This won't help Moya, but if they defeat us, it'll help undermine Valles's credibility."

"They won't defeat us, Senator."

"I hope you're right, but time is running out. We need to be thinking about what we'll do if the worst occurs."

4:30 A.M.
Vincente Aguirre's apartment
Havana, Cuba

Moya slumped forward in his chair, his forearms resting on his thighs. He knew he'd be revitalized by events later that day, but right now he was tired, so dreadfully tired. He'd endured too many years of physical abuse and too many hours without sleep.

"We've heard nothing more from the Americans?" he asked wearily.

"No," Alejandro said. "Redbird's been silent. My feeling is that it's too late to expect a change in American policy without the tapes."

"I think you're right. But even if María can't get them, we have to go ahead with our plans. We can't let the actions of the Americans affect what we do. Have you decided how to get the message about the tapes to Rojas?"

"Yes. Margarita will deliver it to him as he leaves the hotel this morning. Paschal got her a set of media credentials so she can blend with the crowd in the lobby without arousing suspicion." Alejandro stood. "I must go now."

"The Lord be with you, my friend."

"And with you." Alejandro closed the door softly.

Moya turned to Gregorio Luzan, who stood in front of a cracked mirror, tugging at the coat of the Cuban army uniform he'd just put on.

"Not a bad fit," he said as he walked around his friend, pausing to adjust a shoulder. He forced himself to shake off his weariness. Luzan would need every bit of self-confidence he could give him. "You did well to get one so close to your size."

"You needn't be so polite," Luzan said with a laugh. "The

uniforms of most soldiers would fit twice around this stick of a body. I feel quite impressive, actually. I can't help wishing I had a few of those prison guards within easy reach right now. They'd be forced to listen to me."

"Now don't get carried away," Moya said, understanding Luzan's need to talk away some of his nervousness. "Do you have any questions?"

"No questions about what to do or say," Luzan said. "You're sure they'll believe me? I have visions of them looking at me like I'm some kind of fool."

"I understand our soldiers. They've been trained to obey without question. If you say what I've told you, they'll think your orders no more unusual than many others they've received. Much less strange than some. You should go. I look forward to the next time I hear your voice."

Luzan shook the General's hand. "I, too, look forward to that moment."

"He'll be all right, won't he?" Ines Moya asked her husband as the door closed.

"Yes, I believe so. He's a tough old boy, as good as they come."

So much could go wrong, Moya knew, but he'd learned long before the futility of worry. He'd done his best. The plan and the patriots who labored were now beyond his help. He'd gladly entrusted them into the care of Another, much wiser and more powerful than he.

How did others survive, he'd often wondered, when they depended only on themselves for strength and support, for their very survival? How did they remain sane, knowing as they must their own frailties and inadequacies?

In large measure, Moya's strength came from an understanding of his own weaknesses and his willingness to seek help. He treated others fairly, always expecting much, never asking more than he himself was willing to give. However, his calmness, his strength in crisis, came not from the people around him—he knew they were as flawed as he—but from his faith.

No one in Cuba understood better than he the tremendous risk he was taking and asking others to take. No one else realized fully the many small pieces that formed the fabric of this fight for freedom, any piece of which could fail, causing the failure of the whole.

And yet Moya was truly relaxed, truly confident. As he had often done during the last bleak years, he remembered David and Goliath. David, too, had faced seemingly insurmountable odds; David, too, had been warned of certain failure; David, too, had faced his enemy boldly and without fear.

"The battle is the Lord's," David had said as he slew the giant. Moya remembered those words as he prepared for his own great battle, this battle which would determine the future of Cuba.

5:45 A.M.
Washington, D.C.

The cupola atop the great dome of the Capitol was unlit; neither house of Congress was in session. As he did every time he saw the darkened dome, Grant smiled, remembering his family's long-standing joke that at least that meant the country was safe for a few more hours—no new laws were being passed.

He glanced again at the magnificent dome silhouetted against the dawn sky. Could a long-range missile armed with a nuclear warhead one day soon be targeted on it? The image of a Russian SSC-X-4 loomed in his mind, the dome exploding under it. Had the Russians sold those missiles?

Grant picked up the car phone. Cynthia didn't answer.

5:45 A.M.
The Bubble
Washington, D.C.

Cynthia sat at the table, thumbing through yet another folder, her fingers clumsy with fatigue. She really ought to leave, she knew. Her mind was so numb that she wasn't doing any good by staying.

Stubbornly, she read the next report. Why she was looking in this file she couldn't imagine. Brazil had no connection with anything. Her hand arrested as she started to turn the page. She'd found it! She sat up, excitedly scanning the message.

An asset in Colombia reported a huge shipment of food from that country. He'd heard talk that it was going to Cuba. And the purchaser was one of the directors of IBTC! A direct link between IBTC and Valles!

She ran to the phone. The Senator had already left for Andrews, Rachel told her. She tried calling his car phone but couldn't get a connection.

Shifting from one foot to the other, she waited impatiently for Sergeant Guinn to check through the file. The moment he finished, she raced down the hall. She'd have to drive to Andrews. She couldn't count on getting a connection to the Senator's car phone, and reaching him by phone at Andrews was iffy at best.

The report wasn't conclusive by itself, but combined with the others . . . ?

6:00 A.M.
El Palacio de la Revolución
Havana, Cuba

María backed out of the room she was cleaning, dragging a bucket of water. She glanced down the hall toward Valles's office. A shiver slid down her spine. That guard, the brutal one, was standing outside Valles's door, he and several others. She'd have to be especially careful. She knew he was already suspicious.

If only she could have cleaned Valles's office when she'd first arrived. But the guard had been standing there even then. He always did when Valles was inside. This guard was the one who'd ordered her yesterday to clean during the funeral, not before. He had been so specific. She'd just have to wait. If it got too late, she'd chance going in, but not yet.

María wiped a straggling hair out of her eyes with the back of her hand and carried her cleaning equipment into the next room.

Four more hours.

6:38 A.M.
Andrews Air Force Base
Prince Georges County, Maryland

By six-thirty Andrews Air Force Base outside Washington, D.C., was alive with activity. Secret Service agents, conspicuous in their conservative dark suits, spoke to one another through microphones hidden in their sleeves, checking that all areas were secure for the President's arrival. The two Marine Corps members who would stand guard at the door of *Marine One*, the President's helicopter, were talking quietly, waiting to assume their official duties.

By six thirty-five most members of the President's official party were waiting in the VIP lounge at the end of the regular terminal. Peter Evans, a mug of coffee cupped in his hands, talked desultorily with a member of the House, one of the President's oldest friends. The Cuba trip was bound to garner some good publicity, possibly enough to make a difference in the Representative's race. He needed every advantage he could find in order to overcome a ground swell of voter discontent with his long tenure and dubious ethics.

"Cuba's eclectic population combined with its predominantly Spanish ancestry . . ."

Evans stopped listening but continued to smile and nod at appropriate intervals. He felt a hand on his arm.

"Nice to see you here, Peter," Trent Westlake said as he and several others joined the group. Most carried a glass of the lemonade that was so ubiquitous at Andrews. "Pleasant morning, isn't it?"

"It certainly is," Evans answered with amusement, remembering an especially erotic interlude with Constance which had made the start of the morning undeniably good for him.

"I'm looking forward to the ceremony—not that a funeral is something to look forward to," Westlake added hastily, not wanting *that* quote to appear in the paper, "but I'll be glad to have Valles in power. He's a good man."

"No doubt about it," Evans said, leaning down to put his empty coffee cup on the table beside him.

"Say, Senator," Evans said with a chuckle, patting Bob Grant's shoulder as the Senator walked by. Grant looked at him under hooded eyes. "*Still* finding commies under your bed?"

Grant saw several heads turn their way.

"I looked under mine," Evans said, grinning. "Nothing there."

With a wink and a slap on Grant's back, he walked away, joining the crowd gathered around a grouping of leather couches and chairs.

What a horse's ass, Grant thought in disgust. The top side of a bed Evans might know intimately, but under it? He wouldn't know where to look. Interesting that he knew of Grant's concerns about Cuba, though. Was the President that much in Evans's pocket? Or was the information coming from somewhere else?

An Air Force officer approached the assembled group. "We need to board *Air Force One* now, please. *Marine One* will be landing shortly."

By six fifty-eight all passengers and crew were on the plane. *Air Force One* would take off the moment the President was on board. No one except the Secret Service could board after him, no matter the circumstance.

At seven o'clock precisely the President of the United States, the First Lady and a retinue of staff and Secret Service agents walked the short distance from the helicopter to the plane. The First Couple climbed the stairs at the front while the others hurried to the rear stairs.

Before boarding, the President and the First Lady turned to wave to the assembled members of the press waiting in a roped-off area on the tarmac. This footage would make the morning news shows.

The doors closed behind the First Couple. Within moments *Air Force One* was heading down the runway. Smoothly, the blue and white 747 soared into the air.

7:00 A.M.
Andrews Air Force Base
Prince Georges County, Maryland

Cynthia raced out of the terminal, her eyes searching the runway. In the distance she saw *Air Force One* disappearing.

Her body sagged. Fatigue engulfed her.

She'd been too late. She'd keep trying to contact the Senator, of course, but *Air Force One* . . . Cuba . . . Her chances of reaching him were slim. Not that her information was vital by itself. She'd have to hope Moya's people had found something conclusive.

7:40 A.M.
El Palacio de la Revolución
Havana, Cuba

Valles was still in his office, María realized with disquiet as she pulled her equipment out of another clean office. He had to leave soon. He had to!

Two hours to get the tapes to Alejandro. Only two.

8:15 A.M.
La Plaza de la Revolución
Havana, Cuba

At La Plaza de la Revolución, laborers were still working on the platform, their movements increasingly hampered by the swelling crowd around them. Several bureaucrats stood on the periphery, shouting and hectoring but in no way speeding the ponderous movements of the workers.

Only the areas where the dignitaries would sit and where the motorcades would arrive were free of people. No one wanted to tangle with the American and Cuban soldiers ringing them.

The imposing statue of José Martí in the center of La Plaza and the considerably taller, obelisklike tower behind formed the backdrop for the funeral service. The platform in front of the statue had been completed two days earlier. Now draped in red cloth and elevated to be visible for several blocks, it would serve as the temporary resting place for Fidel Castro. The body would be moved into position at ten o'clock.

In front of this platform, divided by a center aisle, were rows

256

of chairs, those to the left for the Cuban delegation and those to the right for the Presidents and chief dignitaries of the attending countries, including Basilov and the Russian Foreign Minister. The President of Cuba and the President of the United States would sit side by side in the center of the stage in front of Castro's platform. Long sheets of bulletproof glass stretched in front of the seats.

The front rows in the amphitheater itself, forming a semicircle facing the platform, were reserved for dignitaries of lesser rank. The American delegation would be sitting in the first row.

At that moment, a distracted functionary was consulting a seating chart and taping a name to each seat. On occasions of such international import, nothing was left to chance. The host country was responsible not only for the safety of the visiting dignitaries but also for their comfort. For the planners, an embarrassing situation could be almost as disastrous as a security breach.

Behind the chairs but before the area for the general public, a huge scaffold had been erected for the media. Already journalists were crawling over it, like play figures on a giant erector set. Places had been assigned as Valles had demanded, with television cameras from networks around the world placed strategically on the upper levels. Print journalists would be on the lower levels but with equally unobstructed views. A position had been assigned to each journalist according to his importance, but none was above moving around to gain an advantage. Gaining an advantage—the unwritten code of the journalist. The scaffold would be overflowing long before the ceremonies began.

Arriving early for a meeting with President Valles, General Paschal Gomez stopped to watch the preparations. He was pleased. All would be finished in time, would be imposing on TV and would work neatly into Moya's plans. The whole panoply would make a fitting backdrop for the new President.

Gomez ran up the steps of El Palacio two at a time. For a moment he paused in the doorway and looked back at La Plaza. He considered the throng of people already assembled and the soldiers overseeing it all. He thought of the huge challenge—and responsibility—facing the new President.

So much should be done for them, all these people who were

such slaves to the will of their leaders. Only a special type of man would have the foresight and understanding to bring Cuba back to its former glory.

Thoughtfully, Gomez walked into the building. He must use the next few minutes to placate Valles, or Moya would have no chance to be that man.

With luck, María would already have the tapes.

8:30 A.M.
La Habana Libre
Havana, Cuba

As Victor Rojas got off the elevator in the lobby, a surge of people rushed on. An old lady pushed by him breathlessly, her bag banging against his leg and slipping from her hands. He reached down to pick it up and felt a tightly folded piece of paper being forced into his hand.

His palms were instantly sweaty. He tried to keep his breathing even as he muttered an apology, stood and walked toward the door. His shadows fell in behind.

8:45 A.M.
El Palacio de la Revolución
Havana, Cuba

Little more than an hour, María realized with a lurch of her heart. Would Valles never go! At least General Gomez was with him now. Maybe the general could get him to leave.

"I hope this meeting doesn't last too long," María said to one of the soldiers guarding the door. She leaned on her mop as she spoke. The brutal soldier, who seemed to have appointed himself her enemy, glared at her from across the corridor. María made herself ignore him. Her back was as wet as the water in the bucket. Sweat trickled between her shoulder blades.

"I have to clean the office. The American President, you know. He's coming."

The guard looked at her appraisingly.

"I want to impress El Presidente," she continued. "I'll lose my job if I don't. He's terribly particular."

The guard looked at her more sympathetically. He could understand her concern. "Look," he told María in an undertone, "if I can, I'll let you know the minute he leaves so you can start cleaning right away."

María beamed. "Thank you. Thank you very much."

Little more than an hour.

9:00 A.M.
Air Force One

The President of the United States greeted the members of his official party as they arrived for the customary chat in his private sitting room on *Air Force One*. Air Force stewards served coffee.

Grant settled restlessly in one of the seats, only half-listening to the President's small talk. Instead, he was reviewing the totally predictable conversation he'd had with Peter Evans a few minutes before. Talk about myopia! Evans wouldn't tolerate any suggestion that his assessment of Valles could be wrong. What an attitude for a journalist! Grant realized that the President was addressing his guests.

"Isn't this plane fantastic," he said with a smile, referring to the specially designed 747. "It has everything: conference rooms, sitting rooms, bedrooms, even a shower, in addition to every state-of-the-art communications system you can imagine. Sure could spoil a body," he said, grinning. "But, down to business.

"This trip is momentous for each of us here. We're privileged to be participating in a truly historic moment, witnesses to the end of the last totalitarian dictatorship in this hemisphere.

"It isn't a matter of public record yet, but let me tell you, César Valles is so eager to be our ally that late last night he asked if I would have our military ready to put down a Russian coup attempt if it so transpires. José Moya, a former general in Castro's army and a terrorist renegade, is purported to be mounting an offensive against Valles and the duly constituted government of Cuba. Whether the Russians are truly involved is unclear at this moment, but, regardless of the source of Moya's backing, if his attempt comes to fruition, I've agreed to give military support to Valles. For democracy's sake, we must keep Valles in power."

A horrified Grant sloshed coffee into his saucer. No, he thought, his body icy. American troops couldn't be committed in Cuba!

Before he had time to question the startling announcement, the President's personal aide informed the guests that they needed to return to their seats for final approach. Grant tried to push past the aide toward the President but found himself herded out with the others.

As his guests walked out of the room, the President stopped Senator Westlake.

"We're pleased your man, Edmund Miller, will be coming over to the National Security Council. I know you'll miss him."

Westlake was dumbfounded. How could Miller have done this to him? he fumed. And how long had it been in the works?

"Well, sir, obviously I don't want to lose him," he said, controlling both his anger and his surprise. "He's been an asset to my office. But I know this move is in the best interest of the country." He walked slowly to the midsection of the plane and dropped into his seat.

In the row behind him, Grant stared sightlessly out the window. The United States committed militarily to supporting Valles—how could this have happened? All was now in the hands of Moya and Rojas. Two more hours.

9:35 A.M.
El Palacio de la Revolución
Havana, Cuba

Valles had finally left. From her position cleaning the hallway, María heard Gomez suggest they survey preparations for the ceremonies from the front steps. If only Valles would stay there long enough for her to get the tapes to Alejandro!

She dragged her equipment into the office and began dusting near the cabinet that held the tapes. The eyes of the soldiers in the hall burned a fire into her back through the open doorway. She despaired of their ever looking away.

Finally she heard them whispering among themselves. A minute more and she'd try to get the tapes.

Still dusting, she moved closer to the door of the cabinet, her racing heart choking her. Now. Now was the time while the soldiers were relaxed and before Valles had time to return.

She moved her body between the cabinet and the open door, the fullness of her skirt concealing the cabinet door. Almost without allowing herself time to think, she slid her hand behind the door until she felt the top shelf. She ran her fingers along the spines of the tapes. Where was the rubber band? She felt back along the row more slowly. There.

With one motion, she brought out the tapes and slid them into her dustcloth. At the same time, she pushed the door closed with her knee. It clicked loudly into place. Her eyes grew wide. Had anyone heard?

No sounds behind her. No shouts. No footsteps.

Slowly, her heart steadied, and slowly she turned and walked to the wastebasket, her legs stiff with tension.

As she dropped the tapes into the basket, Valles walked through the door. After a second of shocked immobility, she pulled trash over the tapes, picked up the basket and moved toward the door.

"Stay where you are." María blanched at the venom in his voice. "Arrange the furniture. Now. I want it done right."

She put down the basket, not daring to check if the tapes were completely covered.

Valles sat down at his desk and watched her speculatively for a moment before he began thumbing through the papers in front of him.

Thank goodness she'd resisted the temptation to search the desk. But when would he allow her to leave? In time to meet Alejandro?

She began straightening and dusting, rearranging furniture as she worked. Her mind seethed, one thought predominant: would Valles realize the tapes were missing?

His voice shattered the silence. "Put those chairs closer together."

María jumped and took a calming breath. She reached for a chair. Then her heart stopped. Valles was leaving his desk and walking toward the cabinet!

She forced herself to begin moving the chair even as she watched him, horrified. He opened the cabinet door. Her body became absolutely still.

The phone rang. Both turned toward it. Valles hesitated, then walked to the desk.

"Yes," he said impatiently. "Hold on." He covered the receiver with his hand and looked at María. "Leave now. Come back as soon as I'm gone. I'm warning you—this room had better be perfect."

María nodded numbly. She bent down and picked up the wastebasket with trembling hands. Her pulse began to race madly. One corner of the tapes was uncovered! She glanced at Valles. He was watching her. Slowly, she turned her back and began walking to the door.

His chair creaked. Her heart heaved, but she kept walking. She vowed to run if she had to.

"Close the door after you."

Without a backward glance, she closed the door.

She had to get outside, now, before Valles finished his phone call.

She walked down the hall, looking straight ahead. Her body was clammy, her breath ragged. Just a few more meters. Once again, the door screeched when she opened it, sending a spasm of fear down her spine.

9:45 A.M.
José Martí Airport
Outside Havana

The touchdown of *Air Force One* marked a historic moment. No President of the United States had visited Cuba in more than thirty years.

The Cuban dignitaries waiting on the runway regarded the plane warily, aware that their actions might be crucial to repairing relations between the two countries and equally aware that they didn't know what was expected of them. Too much had changed in the last few days.

Slowly the plane taxied to the waiting Cuban delegation and stopped. Steps were pushed up to it. Secret Service agents hurried down the front steps and took up positions on the tarmac. Agents already on the ground joined them, all alertly surveying the crowd.

Journalists, their number filling all the seats at the back of *Air Force One*, hurried down the rear steps to a roped-off area where international journalists had been waiting for hours. These reporters had been joined moments before by those on the press plane that had followed *Air Force One* to Cuba but had landed first.

The majority of the journalists would form their own military-escorted motorcade, riding in buses provided by the Cuban government. A press pool made up of a select group of print, electronic and wire-service journalists would stay with the presidential party.

Finally the President and First Lady appeared, framed in the doorway of *Air Force One*. A warm breeze barely ruffled their clothes. They stepped forward and waved, posing on the top step, aware of the import of the event and equally aware of the hundreds of cameras zooming in on them.

On the left side of a long red carpet, the Foreign Minister of Cuba, his wife, the Chief of Protocol and a host of other dignitaries were nervously lined up to greet them. The President and his wife walked down the carpet, shaking hands and listening to introductions, some through interpreters.

After a suitable pause, the senior members of the official party emerged from the plane and descended the steps. They, too, smiled toward the cameras.

Grant, one of the last off the plane, scanned the crowd. He couldn't see Victor Rojas, but then the crowd was huge. He walked down the steps, a strained smile on his face.

The President met the American delegation at the bottom and led them through the receiving line, introducing them to the waiting Cubans.

The cameras continued to whir; the politicians continued to smile.

The President and the Cuban Foreign Minister walked a short distance across the tarmac and stood at attention as a small military band played the national anthems of both countries. American and Cuban flags fluttered in the breeze.

When the last note had faded, the President walked back to his wife; and, followed by Chief of Staff Corforth, they walked the short distance to a waiting limousine, flown over for the Secret Service the day before from Andrews Air Force Base. The others in the official party rushed to their assigned vehicles. For security reasons, the limousine carrying the President wouldn't delay its departure for anyone.

The presidential motorcade roared out of the airport, heading for the Residence of the American representative in Cuba, where a quick country-team briefing would be held.

The Cubans formed their own motorcade and followed the Americans out through the gates. The press motorcade fell in behind. Both would travel immediately to La Plaza de la Revolución.

9:55 A.M.
El Palacio de la Revolución
Havana, Cuba

César Valles walked over to the cabinet. He wanted to replay his conversation with the American President, make sure he remembered exactly what had been said. Wouldn't do to confuse his lies, he thought, laughing to himself.

His hand paused above the shelf. No rubber band held together two tapes. Where were the tapes? Frantically, he searched through the ones remaining. Both tapes were gone!

Valles ran into the hall.

"Who's been in my office?" he demanded, his face pinched with rage and fear.

"Only you, sir, General Gomez and, of course, the maid."

"The maid! Where is she? Where has she gone?"

"She just left to take out the trash," a guard answered, pointing to the door which only minutes before had closed behind María.

"Stop her," Valles screamed. "She's taken my tapes. Whatever you do, get my tapes!"

9:56 A.M.
El Palacio de la Revolución
Havana, Cuba

"Alej," María whispered breathlessly. "Here are the tapes." She slipped them through a gap in the boards. Their fingers touched momentarily.

As he took the tapes, María glanced back toward El Palacio. Her eyes widened with fear. Soldiers were bursting through the door. She threw the wastebasket from her.

"Run, Alej. Run!" she whispered fiercely even as she whirled to her right and began running toward the street.

The guards had stopped momentarily as their eyes adjusted to the bright sunlight.

"There she is! Don't let her get away!"

A shot blasted the air. María leaned over and sprinted toward the corner of the building, her breath already coming in gasps. She had to give Alejandro time.

Another shot ricocheted off the wall over her head, a sliver of brick piercing her arm. She raced across the street, dodging through the crowd, unaware of the trickle of blood showing in a thin red line on her blouse.

She mustn't be caught. They mustn't discover she no longer had the tapes. And she must lead them away from Alejandro.

El Cerro. She'd go to El Cerro. Surely she could lose them in that labyrinth of ruins.

She could hear the soldiers shouting behind her, their boots pounding on the pavement.

10:00 A.M.
Near La Plaza
Havana, Cuba

Alejandro froze where he was. A shot. María! Oh, God, he couldn't go back to help her! Desolation deadened his features even as he resumed his dash to La Plaza. Another shot! María was back there, and he could do nothing.

The hard edges of the tapes he clutched in his hand finally penetrated his despair. The tapes! They were more powerful than any weapon could be. If he couldn't help María—his breath caught in a sob—he at least could help Cuba.

The thought of María gave purpose to his feet. He turned the corner and saw La Plaza spread out before him. Blotting out all thought, all consideration for those things beyond his control, he pushed into the crowd. He had thousands of people to fight through before he could give General Gomez the tapes, thousands of people and none of them María.

10:20 A.M.
The streets of Havana
Cuba

María glanced over her shoulder, her breath coming in short, agonized bursts. The soldiers were so close. Their curses rang in her ears.

Stop them, someone, she prayed. Just for a moment. Slow them down.

Alejandro. Oh, Alejandro. He had to have gotten away. She had to give him time. They mustn't find that she didn't have the tapes.

The House of the Lambs was just ahead. Just a few more steps. She could lose herself in the ruins behind it.

A bullet moved the air at the side of her head.

"No," she screamed. Not now.

The lambs, Alejandro's lambs, were almost in front of her. If she could just make it to the lambs, to the doorway behind the lambs . . .

266

Her legs felt like lead; her head, like a shriek-filled cave. And her breath, her breath was an agonized burn scorching her whole body.

She stumbled slightly, her hip slamming into a lamb. She put one hand on its back, ready to vault over and disappear into the darkness behind.

"She's getting away!"

Their curses filled her mind as she leaped into the air, one hand on the lamb's back, her foot almost on the sidewalk beyond. Her clothes clung to her, molding her body to the sun.

María hung suspended between the lamb's iron back and the blue of the sky. One more second and she'd be free.

The guard who had hounded her for so long didn't hesitate. The AK-47 jerked in his hands, leaving its own unique staccato in the air.

"No-o-o . . ."

María's body spun in midair, hung for an instant as more bullets slammed into it, and then dropped beside the lamb. Her blood formed a halo around her, seeping into the ground which was Cuba.

The guards rushed up, ripping her clothes in their frenzy.

"Nothing. She has nothing! The tapes aren't here!"

The one who'd shot her kicked the twisted wreckage of her body.

His growled "Bitch!" was her only epitaph.

10:20 A.M.
Havana, Cuba

"How much farther?" Rojas asked the driver.

"One mile."

One mile, Rojas thought, staring anxiously out the window. A trip that should have taken minutes had already lasted almost two hours. The streets were clogged with people.

"Hurry," he said, just as he had every five minutes since he'd gotten in the cab. He had to let the Senator know about the tapes.

He turned to stare out the window.

10:20 A.M.
The tower
La Plaza de la Revolución
Havana, Cuba

Fighting through the crowds surrounding La Plaza, shamelessly flaunting the fear induced by his bogus uniform, Gregorio Luzan arrived at the door to the tower. It was ten-twenty.

Four armed soldiers guarded the entrance. One stepped in front of Luzan, an AK-47 helping him bar entry. He demanded identification.

Luzan scowled, his mouth dry with fear.

"I suppose you'll tell me that you're only doing your duty," Luzan said with a sneer, "but General Gomez will hear of this. He's sent me to personally oversee the sound system. Your incompetence has wasted precious time."

Insolently, even as his heart hammered, Luzan thrust forward the forged identification papers and genuine orders. His hand was steady.

As the guard thumbed through the papers and realized their import, apprehension slowly replaced arrogance.

"I apologize for the delay, Colonel, but General Gomez ordered us to refuse entry to anyone. We weren't told you'd be coming, sir."

"Of course you weren't told," Luzan snapped, taking back his papers. "The problem just arose. General Gomez assumed you would have wit enough to recognize the urgency. Hurry, soldier. Don't waste any more of my time."

He followed his escort into the dark stairwell of the tower. They began climbing.

Luzan was dazzled by the spectacle that unfolded as they rounded the last turn. Sunlight streamed through the tall windows covering all sides of the room. Far in the distance, the myriad blues of Havana Harbor sparkled and danced like fiery points in the sunlight. Even the prison at the mouth of the harbor looked clean, benign, Luzan noted with wonder. He marveled at the hundreds of thousands of Cubans filling the streets for miles in all directions, the faded reds, blues and yellows of their clothes reflected like a modernistic mosaic by the sun.

The blazing sun, the blues of the sky meeting the deeper blues of the water, the mass of people, the awesome power of it all momentarily overwhelmed Luzan. Yesterday, he had been in prison; today, he was literally on top of the world. If only the success of the next hour could be assured!

Collecting himself, his breathing finally regular after the long climb, Luzan turned to the others. They'd been staring curiously, unaware that anyone would be joining them, but too used to such changes and to their own unimportance to venture any comment.

Luzan's deep voice boomed in the small space. "I'm Colonel Luchese. Who is in charge?"

Only four people, he counted. He hoped he could handle them all if they questioned his authority.

A tall, thin soldier standing by the far window cleared his throat noisily. "I am, sir. Can I help you?"

"I certainly hope so. I've been sent as the personal emissary of General Gomez. I'll be in charge here and will be making all decisions and announcements. Do you understand?"

Luzan surveyed them, daring anyone to challenge him. Finally, he turned to his soldier escort. "You may leave. Allow no one access to this room without my permission."

10:25 A.M.
United States Residency
Havana, Cuba

The drive from José Martí Airport to the American Residency was a revelation for the President. The shabby buildings, either peeling huge sheets of paint or totally bare of paint; the sere, weed-strewn earth; the ragged Cubans—he hadn't expected to see such overt signs of decay. Although the President didn't realize it, he was following a route specially devised years before by Castro to highlight the nicer sections of Havana, but even here the miasma of disintegration clung tenaciously.

The highway was filled with Cubans, most on foot, all hoping to reach La Plaza de la Revolución in time for the funeral. Many of them stopped to stare at the motorcade, shading their eyes against the sun. When they realized one of the cars bore the President of the United States, they cheered and waved wildly.

Turning away from the scene, the President leaned forward to speak to M. Eugene Corforth, who was sitting on the jump seat.

"What a great photo op, Eugene. Let's take advantage of it on our way back to the airport. 'The leader of the greatest democracy in the world meeting people of the newest.' "

"Of course, Mr. President," Corforth said, writing in his omnipresent notebook. "We'll be sure to set the scene."

"Don't forget to include some children in the shots and no glamorous Latins," the First Lady remarked. "We wouldn't want the world wondering just what kind of freedom the President had in mind."

The two men smiled, then dismissed her. Estelle returned to staring out the window.

The American Residency, with its carefully tended grounds and impressive quarters, came as a relief. At least the United States was keeping up its image, the President thought as they drove through the heavily guarded gates and stopped before the ornate front entrance of the main residence. The lush green lawn and tropical plants were a welcome change from the barren winter landscape of D.C.

Stepping into the balmy air, the President smiled involuntarily, feeling a renewed surge of optimism. He had been right to come.

The country-team briefing at the Residency was short. The President wouldn't give a speech at the ceremonies, which would last several hours, but would have a fifteen-minute courtesy call and photo opportunity afterward with Valles in El Palacio de la Revolución. A press availability would be allowed both before and after the meeting. He'd leave from there to go directly to the airport, stopping for the requested photo op on the way, and arrive back at Andrews at six-thirty in the evening so that their arrival could be covered live.

It sounded good, the President told them.

10:30 A.M.
United States Residency
Havana, Cuba

Where was Victor Rojas? Grant wondered as he paced near the buffet table that had been set up for members of the presidential party. Moya wouldn't have a chance if the President didn't call off the military.

"Is there a telephone I can use?" he asked one of the household staff. He received directions and hurried to it.

"Buenos días, Habana Libre," answered the desk attendant at the hotel.

"Tengo que hablar con Señor Victor Rojas."

"El señor no esta aqui."

Not there, thought Grant, leaning tiredly against the wall. Did that mean he was on the trail of something? Whatever he was doing, he had better hurry.

10:30 A.M.
La Plaza de la Revolución
Havana, Cuba

Ana Aguirre, a student at the University of Havana and Vincente's daughter, worked her way through the crowd to her brother's side. Ana and Enrique had been recruited by Ines Moya to organize the university students in La Plaza.

"Is everyone ready?" Ana asked, scanning the crowd for familiar faces.

Enrique patted her arm. "You needn't worry. Not only have they all come, but they're in good positions, places where the media will be forced to take notice."

"This is exciting, isn't it?" Ana asked, suddenly caught up in the mood of the crowd. "So much is about to happen."

"Yes. For good or ill, Cuba will never be the same."

10:37 A.M.
United States Residency
Havana, Cuba

Grant walked back to the reception room so deep in thought that he didn't see Rojas until the latter grasped his arm.

"Senator, Moya's sent a message. He has the proof and will get it to you before the funeral."

"Where? How?"

"He didn't say, just that you'd need a tape recorder and a Russian translator."

"No problem with that," Grant said. "There's a recorder in the President's limousine, and Corforth's fluent in Russian."

"Thank God. I tried to find a recorder this morning, but Cuba . . ."

"The problem," Grant said, "will be getting to the President in time. Did Moya say what kind of proof—obviously a tape—but what's on it?"

"No, but it's supposed to be incontrovertible evidence."

A sea of Secret Service agents filled the vestibule. "Everyone into his assigned vehicle. We'll leave in two minutes."

"Moya's people have your itinerary," Rojas said, walking with Grant out of the room, "so they know where to find you."

Grant looked at his friend with compassion, understanding how much freedom for his homeland must mean to him. "I'm sorry, Victor," he said, putting a hand on his arm. "I'll watch for them, but it doesn't look good. Time has about run out."

10:40 A.M.
Gregorio Luzan's apartment
Havana, Cuba

"It's time to leave," Moya said.

"Yes, General," Aguirre told him. "The jeeps are out front."

Moya took Ines's hand, and they walked outside together.

10:45 A.M.
La Plaza de la Revolución
Havana, Cuba

Surrounded by the honor guard supplied by General Gomez, President César Valles left El Palacio for the short walk to the platform in front of the José Martí statue. The crowd, eager for excitement, cheered his arrival. Most had no idea for whom they were cheering; but wasn't it enough to be alive, to be free from work if only for a short while? Besides, this man had to be important, surrounded as he was by such an impressive guard.

Valles acknowledged the accolade with a pleased smile, holding both hands over his head as he walked. Graciously he made his way past the rows of lesser dignitaries, shaking hands.

As he came to the steps leading to the platform, he felt a hand on his arm. Colonel Campos pulled him aside.

"The maid has been killed," he whispered.

"The tapes, Campos," Valles said, his voice a growl. "What about the tapes?" He forced a smile back on his face.

"She didn't have them. She was in their sight the whole time so the guards are sure she didn't pass them to anyone. She must have dropped them during the chase. Soldiers are searching for them now. They're sure to find them."

Valles wiped a hand across his forehead. "As long as no one has them, that's all that matters. Make sure they're returned to me personally."

He turned toward the steps. So, the woman was dead. Good.

He walked across the platform, welcoming his august guests and charming each by recounting a shared experience or an event favorable to the other. Finally, he turned to face the crowd. Once again raising his arms, he stood motionless, buffeted by their uninhibited cheering.

As the cheering escalated, Valles's heart seemed to stop. That first meeting with the ministers in El Palacio—could it have been only two days before?—had been a gratifying demonstration of his power, but this, this was immeasurably better. It was like comparing a machine gun to a nuclear warhead. The power. All these people, these hundreds of thousands of people, cheering for him, supporting him, controlled by him.

Everything was going to be all right. Not Moya, not the Americans, not the Russians, not anyone could touch him now. The moment was his. The power was his.

Valles turned and walked to his seat. His gaze held on Basilov. So much for your condescension, my friend, he thought as he sat down.

For a moment, he felt a frightening disquiet. What if the tapes had somehow reached the wrong person?

Impossible, he thought. Impossible. Nothing could stop him now. Everything was under control, his control. God bless the U.S.A., Valles chuckled to himself, smiling at the crowd.

10:45 A.M.
La Plaza de la Revolución
Havana, Cuba

The crowd was jubilant, their spirits bolstered by the unfolding drama. For the most part, they grinned as they moved aside for Alejandro, making way for his uniform but for once unintimidated by it.

He moved as quickly as he could, heading in the direction of the statue of José Martí, which was visible above the crowd. The casket holding Castro loomed above it all like a malevolent bird of prey. Alejandro tried not to think about María. He'd wait for her by the statue as they'd planned.

A little farther now and he would reach the soldiers ringing the section reserved for the dignitaries.

He could hear the sirens of the motorcade in the distance. He hadn't much time. With a final shove he broke through the last line of Cubans pressing against the rope. A row of soldiers faced him, obviously ordered to let no one pass.

Alejandro searched the area. No Gomez. "General Gomez," he said to the soldiers in front of him. "I have an urgent message for General Gomez."

Most of the soldiers had seen Gomez at some time that morning, but not recently.

Alejandro could hear the sirens of the American motorcade getting louder. Should he try to find a way to reach the Senator himself?

A movement to his right caught his eye. Holding the tapes tightly in one hand, he waved his arms above his head. Gomez hurried toward him.

"The tapes?" he asked.

Alejandro handed them over.

Gomez turned and walked rapidly toward the arrival area. The first cars were just turning into La Plaza. The crowd began to cheer.

11:00 A.M.
La Plaza de la Revolución
Havana, Cuba

As the motorcade made its way slowly through the crowd filling La Plaza, Grant stared out the window. These people, he thought, their faces hungry for any excitement, did they understand the state of their country? How many of them realized the hope riding on the next hour?

For what must have been the hundredth time, Grant looked at his watch. Half an hour, really less if they hoped to stop the American military from interfering. He looked back out the window. These poor people, would they have their chance at freedom? How many of those he passed were members of La Causa, ready to endure any sacrifice to make freedom a reality? He had to help them. He had to!

Impatiently he sat on the edge of the seat, poised to get out the moment the car stopped.

11:00 A.M.
Cristobol Army Base
Outside Havana

Ruiz was zipping up his flight suit when the telephone call came from Colonel Sacasa. A smile formed on his face as he listened.

They were going to go through with it! He was about to place his mark on Cuban history. And what a mark it would be!

But first, this was one pilot who needed to make a stop at the head. He might be the best fighter jockey in all of Cuba, but he was damn nervous as well.

Four minutes later, Ruiz walked out of the building and across the runway to his waiting plane. Almost fatalistically, he strapped himself into the cockpit and pulled down the canopy. He flipped a salute to the men below as he taxied slowly to the end of the runway.

On other military bases in Cuba, seven other specially chosen pilots boarded their planes. One of them was Emil Guerrero. His Backfire bomber was his baby. The Russian technology, especially the look-down/shoot-down capability, was awesome. Guerrero felt chills every time he strapped in. But today, today was far more thrilling. Today, the Russians were going to get a taste of their own technology.

At eleven-twenty the four MiG 29s and four Backfire bombers would meet high in the sky southeast of Havana. These pilots faced the most profound challenge of their careers, and all gloried in it.

In thirty minutes, no one in the world would have reason to doubt either their courage or their skill.

11:00 A.M.
Camagüey Army Base
Eastern Cuba

It was time to leave. Lieutenant Paco Camancho, an officer recruited by Gomez, tugged at his uniform, feeling the tools stowed safely in his pocket. Juarez had better be there, Camancho thought as he walked out of the barracks into the glaring sun. He refused even to consider what would happen if he and others like him failed. Taking a steadying breath, he opened the door to the base's operations center.

"Lieutenant Camancho, reporting as ordered," he announced to the bored guard inside. His voice was overloud with tension.

The guard frowned, studying the roster. "Nothing about you here, Lieutenant."

"Look again," Camancho said, his body suddenly cold. Had his allies forgotten him? Or was this a trap, and he'd walked right into it? "General Gomez himself ordered me to make some changes in our equipment. You don't want to stand in the way of the new government, do you?"

"Why didn't you explain that in the first place," the guard exclaimed good-naturedly. "General Gomez's orders are different. Here you are. Captain Juarez is already waiting for you."

"Thank you, Private," Camancho replied. He walked upstairs.

"Ah, Paco," Captain Juarez greeted him. "We've no time to lose. We'll have this place to ourselves for three more minutes. You know what to do."

Juarez's calm voice, his self-assurance, helped soothe Camancho. His hands had to stop shaking if he hoped to accomplish anything.

Extracting a small screwdriver and crude pair of pliers from his pocket, he walked to the console connected to the telephone system. Juarez continued working on the radio transmitters.

Camancho wiped his brow with his shirtsleeve before reaching once again for an elusive wire. Time seemed to speed up as his fingers inexplicably became clumsy.

Finally finished, he glanced at the clock on the wall. He blinked in amazement. Less than three minutes had passed.

When the duty soldiers reported back two minutes later, they found Camancho and Juarez leaning against a wall, talking idly.

"We seem to have encountered some trouble with the system," Juarez said. "We can't decide what to do."

"No need to hurry," one of the newcomers replied.

Camancho and Juarez looked at the clock on the wall, watching the slow revolution of the second hand. Forty-five minutes before communications could be resumed. So much had to happen in that time. Had the communication stations on the other bases been disabled? If even one base was left functioning . . .

11:05 A.M.
La Plaza de la Revolución
Havana, Cuba

The crowd waiting in La Plaza drew back to allow the limousine and backup vehicles to reach the platform. Secret Service agents walked beside the car and studied the crowd, the tops of nearby buildings, the platform. Other watchful agents stood nearby.

The President and First Lady would wait in the safety of their bulletproof limousine until all members of their party were seated. At the optimum moment, they would make their entrance.

Grant and the rest of the presidential party were escorted from their cars toward the front of the amphitheater. Only minutes remained, Grant thought as he scanned the crowd.

11:05 A.M.
Outside Luzan's apartment
Havana, Cuba

Two jeeps were parked at the curb. Moya looked at Aguirre with approval.

"My friend, you've outdone yourself. We'll assuredly make an impressive entrance. I won't even ask how you managed to find two."

Aguirre laughed. "It would be better if you didn't know."

Four soldiers were in the first jeep, two of them holding stolen machine guns in their laps. Aguirre helped Ines into the back of the second jeep, and Moya climbed in beside her.

Dressed proudly in a colonel's uniform, Aguirre sat in the front next to the driver. He surveyed the street and motioned the jeeps to move out. They would travel down Avenido de los Presidentes, a symbolic beginning for their journey, Aguirre thought, and then turn onto Avenido Rancho Boyeros. From there they'd turn onto Avenido Paseo, finally driving directly onto La Plaza. The jeeps advanced slowly, waiting for the Cubans who filled the street to part so they could pass.

Dr. Llada and Ines had done their job well. The crowd began cheering Moya almost immediately, following the lead of the few members of La Causa interspersed among them.

Moya sat in the back of the jeep, the immensity of his responsibility revealed as he gazed at the faces of the Cubans filling the street. Were they right in trusting him? So much power was at stake. Would such omnipotence prove too much of a burden for him? Would it corrupt his values, rob him of his vision and courage?

Impulsively, Moya squeezed Ines's hand, smiling reassuringly at her startled response. Ines would keep him from being seduced by the power. She wouldn't allow him to become overly fond of either himself or his position.

11:07 A.M.
La Plaza de la Revolución
Havana, Cuba

"Senator Grant. Welcome to Cuba." A man dressed in the uniform of a general in the Cuban army took Grant's arm and moved him away from the rest of his delegation. "We are honored you would come."

As he spoke, he handed Grant a program, positioning himself so no one could overhear his next words. "The proof you need is in your program. A tape of your President speaking with Valles, another of the Russian President and Valles. The fate of Cuba rests in your hands."

The proof. Grant opened his program. Two cassettes, neatly labeled, rested between its pages.

11:08 A.M.
Avenido de los Presidentes
Havana, Cuba

More people recognized the General. The enthusiasm of the first few supporters had been contagious, just as they'd hoped, giving courage to others. People seemed to awaken, not just to the obvious excitement of the day, but to the unfamiliar stirrings of hope.

"Moya! Moya! *Viva* Moya!"

Excited Cubans began walking beside the jeeps. The closer Moya got to La Plaza, the larger the crowd swelled until the whole street seemed to move alongside, a river of support flowing with him.

11:09 A.M.
La Plaza de la Revolución
Havana, Cuba

Trusting that this truly was the proof he needed—he let out his breath at the presumption of it all—Grant strode toward the presidential limousine. Chief of Staff Corforth, who was standing on the periphery waiting for the President, stared at him in surprise.

"Eugene, I must speak to the President. Immediately. I have irrefutable proof that Valles is controlled not only by the Russians but also by an international terrorist group."

"Don't be a fool, Senator," Corforth said impatiently. "I'm not about to jeopardize the President's prestige in such a public forum by allowing you a major breach of protocol."

"Damn protocol and prestige," Grant replied, his voice a growl. "The President will have neither if I'm right. He'll be the laughingstock of the whole world." Grant hoped this last consideration might sway Corforth in a way that policy considerations never could. "If I'm wrong, all you'll lose is three minutes from your precious schedule. If I'm right, the President loses everything. Let me talk to him. He promised me that consideration."

Corforth looked at Grant speculatively. Turning, he whispered something to a Secret Service agent standing nearby. The agent lifted his wrist to his lips and spoke into the microphone of the two-way radio hidden in his sleeve.

Grant watched this interplay with growing anxiety. Come on. *Come on.*

He and Corforth stared at the limousine intently.

The thumbs-up sign from the President was barely visible through the darkened glass.

Another agent came over to Grant.

"This had better be good," Corforth whispered as the agent led Grant to the car. Silently Grant agreed.

"Stand by, Corforth," he said over his shoulder. "We're going to need you."

An agent opened the limousine door. Grant climbed in and sat on the jump seat.

"Mr. President, we have no time to lose. You told me that you needed irrefutable proof that César Valles is being controlled by the Russians. Here is that proof." Grant held up the tapes. "May I use your player?" he asked even as he slipped a cassette into the tape machine in the door.

So this was the man Cynthia admired so highly, the First Lady thought. She'd met him, of course, but only casually. Today, for the first time, she could feel his impact.

"Senator, I don't know what you're up to," the President said, "but this had better be important. I'm sure the press is wondering why you're causing this holdup."

"Sir, just listen."

The President's voice came through the speaker, followed by Valles's.

"My phone conversation with Valles," the President said. "What *is* this?"

Grant ejected that tape and put in the next. "That one was to prove the validity of this tape," he explained, blessing Moya for having had the foresight to send them both.

The President heard the unmistakable voice of Valles speaking in Russian. Not too unusual, that; many Cubans had trained there. Then he recognized the answering voice, one he'd heard often, that of his counterpart, the Russian President.

"Just a minute." The President punched the Stop button. "Have Mr. Corforth come to the car," the President ordered. The agent in the front seat spoke into his walkie-talkie.

Grant looked at his watch. Four minutes, five at the most. The military had to be taken off alert. He pulled out his handkerchief and wiped his brow.

The door opened to admit Corforth.

"Eugene, you know Russian," the President said as he pushed the On button. "Tell me what's being said."

" 'Such an easily remedied gesture will have broad appeal.' "

"That's Valles," the President told Corforth.

Come on, Valles, Grant thought, wiping his brow again. Say something that'll help.

" 'That combined with the announcement yesterday that I'm halting all Cuban involvement in worldwide drug activity should persuade the Americans of the good intentions of my government.' "

" 'Still . . .' "

"The Russian President!" Corforth interrupted himself in surprise. "Let's see. 'Still, as long as Moya's free, you're in jeopardy. Remember, support for you hasn't come cheaply. Our mutual alliance with IBTC is important and must be protected. Their support is crucial to both of our economies. You must succeed in controlling Cuba.' "

Thank God! The perfect spot! He reached for the button to stop the tape. Both men looked at him in shock.

"We haven't time to listen to it all," Grant said. "This is a plan for Valles dictated by the Russian President with both countries under the control of IBTC. IBTC, as you know, was formed by wealthy Arabs. Their immediate intent is to control Cuba. You can tell that much. Can't you see that the worst course for the United States is to interfere in Cuba? If we do nothing, Moya will have a chance to come to power. If he's the choice of the people, he'll succeed. If not, we'll have lost nothing. Please, have our troops stand down."

The President regarded Grant through half-closed eyes. "Do you have any proof other than the tape?"

Grant started to open the folder he held in his lap. It contained the satellite photos, an account of his conversation with Dashev plus copies of the intelligence reports he and Cynthia had found. The President put out his hand.

"Give it to me. I'll examine it later. This gentleman will be leaving," he told the agent in the front seat, indicating Grant. "As you reminded me, Senator, we're running out of time."

Grant climbed out. The President signaled for his military aide and his National Security Advisor. He had the car phone in his hand before the door closed.

11:19 A.M.
Avenido de los Presidentes
Havana, Cuba

Many Cubans threw flowers into Moya's jeep, the bright blossoms clinging randomly to the dull brown vehicle. Ines gathered up several, smiling at these tokens of support.

She understood the caprice of human feelings. Today her husband was the choice of the people, loved and respected. In months, even weeks, this affection might well change, caused by a worsening economy, a natural disaster or some imagined wrong on her husband's part; who could predict? Man's affections were easily won and even more easily lost.

But wasn't today glorious, she marveled. This adulation might not last, probably wouldn't, but for now she'd savor it.

Moya stood now in the back of the jeep, waving and shouting encouragement to the crowd. He was both touched and relieved to be remembered and welcomed. These people at least had ignored the careful lies spawned by Valles.

To think that the future of Cuba was tied to something as fragile as a tape. There was no way of knowing if María had succeeded or if Alejandro and General Gomez had had enough time. Even now, no amount of shouting or planning or good intentions could make a difference. Only a small tape in the hands of the right man.

11:20 A.M.
Las Villas Army Base
Outside Havana, Cuba

The plane rose smoothly, its exhaust cutting the sky. Ruiz relaxed, enjoying the thrust of power beneath him. In another minute, three Backfires would rendezvous with his plane and four MiGs in the sky southeast of Havana.

Ah, Ruiz smiled, spying the other planes approaching over the horizon. The eight planes would group here, flying in a double formation over La Plaza de la Revolución at exactly eleven-thirty.

Adrenaline surged through him. Almost imperceptibly, the planes closed ranks, two rows of planes, each formation moving as a single unit. Within moments Ruiz had become a part of a moving spear.

Gradually he felt tension replacing his exhilaration. This might be a grand adventure—it assuredly was—but it was deadly serious as well. After this mission, his life would be forfeit if Valles remained in power. Nothing could hide his part in the takeover.

"Fulcrum One speaking. We'll complete our formation and head into Havana. Let's show them how this should be done. Over."

11:20 A.M.
La Plaza de la Revolución
Havana, Cuba

From his seat on the platform, Basilov had watched the arrival of the limousine of his ally, the American President. His ally for the moment, Basilov thought, smiling to himself, whether the American realized it or not.

A few minutes later he had seen Senator Grant—he'd recognized him from pictures they had on file—climb into the car. Then the Chief of Staff had entered as well. What was going on? Basilov wondered. This last-minute conference was an unexpected move.

And now the President had called for a military aide to bring the "football," a black case containing the President's supersecret access codes to all United States military forces and hardware around the world.

Why would the President need to contact the military? Basilov stood abruptly. Something was wrong. He needed to alert his own military. They might not be able to depend on the Americans for protection against Moya's people after all.

11:21 A.M.
La Plaza de la Revolución
Havana, Cuba

Grant, too, saw the military aide with the black case approach the limousine. His body sagged with relief.

The President was ordering the military to stand down. Thank God. If only he weren't too late. Orders took time to countermand, especially when so many different military units were involved. And every one of them had to be informed. Moya couldn't afford to lose a single asset if he hoped to succeed.

Grant scanned the horizon but could tell nothing. Blue sky. Only blue sky.

11:26 A.M.
USS Yorktown
Off the shore of Cuba, not far from Havana Harbor

Admiral James Lawrence stood on the bridge of the *Yorktown*, binoculars at his eyes. A cup of cold coffee waited untasted in front of him. For the last fifteen minutes, he had been studying the horizon. Buildings in Havana were easily visible. He couldn't see those in San Antonio de los Baños or in Lourdes, but he had those areas under constant radio and radar surveillance. He didn't know what else he could do. Except wait, he reminded himself, the most difficult duty of all.

He wondered what Grant was doing. Damnable to have had to cut him off, but presidential commands couldn't be ignored. And his orders were clear. He must destroy any aircraft which posed a threat to Cuba. Other American ships and planes had been given similar orders.

A push of a button would send his ship's missiles over Cuba; their targets would be destroyed less than a minute later. Lawrence might not want to give that order, but he would. That was what he'd pledged to do when he'd joined the military—support his Commander in Chief.

11:26 A.M.
La Plaza de la Revolución
Havana, Cuba

Basilov slipped off the stage, making his way with difficulty to one of several Russian agents stationed nearby. Only a few were at La Plaza and no uniformed soldiers. In keeping with the directive from his superiors, Russian support of Valles wasn't apparent.

"Contact Lourdes and San Antonio," Basilov commanded the aide. "Tell them to stand on alert. The Americans may have canceled their military support of Valles. We must be prepared to act."

The agent had his transmitter out before Basilov finished speaking.

11:26 A.M.
La Plaza de la Revolución
Havana, Cuba

The Secret Service agent in the front seat of the limousine got out; then, as other agents surrounded the car, still others simultaneously opened the rear doors.

The President and First Lady smiled and waved as they stepped out of the car. Normally he basked in such prolonged cheering. Today he hardly heard it. Had he made the right decision? If so, had he acted in time?

Valles smiled his greeting. The President smiled gravely in return. Did this man belong to the Russians? Or to some Middle East terrorist group? His cosmopolitan air and friendly good looks belied the thought.

The cheering of the crowd crescendoed as the two men shook hands. Television commentators explained the profound significance of that gesture.

Both Valles and the President were aware of the positive impression they were making. Both were equally aware of the cameras recording this momentous meeting, a meeting fraught with so many possibilities. Their words, actually a banal discussion of the size of the crowd, would never be heard, but each hoped the footage of their meeting would be broadcast to every television in the world.

Only the President wondered how significant the moment really was, the President and a few others. He spotted Senator Grant sitting at the front of the amphitheater. Peter Evans was several seats farther down, holding court with those nearby.

The First Lady stood quietly back, momentarily forgotten. She felt no more noticed than a potted plant. She forced her mouth into a dazzling smile. Who said pictures never lied? she thought cynically, turning to face the scaffold of cameras.

She turned back to look at her husband, and her heart softened. Extraordinary what he'd just done, putting his reputation on the line. And for a principle. Maybe he wasn't as self-centered as she'd supposed. Maybe. By tomorrow, would he be back in the same mold, consideration for his image taking priority? she wondered, the protective scab of cynicism once more in place.

Escorted by President Valles, surrounded loosely by Secret Service agents, the President walked back to his wife and then on toward their seats. They paused with well-modulated pleasure to greet and shake hands with the other dignitaries.

11:27 A.M.
La Plaza de la Revolución
Havana, Cuba

A row of Cuban soldiers stood at attention in front of the platform. Their mere presence inhibited the nearby crowd, ensuring an empty area around the platform.

At eleven twenty-seven they moved quietly to the steps leading to the main stage.

Grant watched with racing pulse. Whose were they, Moya's or Valles's?

11:28 A.M.
La Plaza de la Revolución
Havana, Cuba

Four soldiers, members of La Causa, had been assigned by Colonel Sacasa to watch General Basilov. When the Russian general reached his agent, the Cuban soldiers were close behind, close enough to hear Basilov's orders.

"Please hand over your transmitter," Captain Arevalo, one of the soldiers, commanded the Russian agent. "Now," he demanded when the agent hesitated.

"Do as he says," Basilov said wearily, feeling the pistol in his side. So the talk about Moya and a traitor in Valles's inner circle had been correct. He'd warned Valles.

"I'll return to the stage," Basilov stated flatly, his tone brooking no opposition.

"You are, of course, free to do so," Captian Arevalo agreed. "Talk to no one, however. We will be close by."

Wheeling, Basilov mounted the steps. A Cuban on either side, the Russian agent was taken behind the platform.

Basilov knew he wouldn't be allowed near Valles. Not that talk between them would do any good. Time for talk was long past.

San Antonio and Lourdes would have to receive warning from another source. Warning of what, he wasn't sure.

11:29 A.M.
La Plaza de la Revolución
Havana, Cuba

Valles conversed with the President with obvious enjoyment. Seeing them together, perfectly matched, no one could doubt his right to be the new leader of Cuba. One more minute, he exulted, one short minute until the whole world would recognize the legitimacy of his presidency.

11:29 A.M.
Russian intelligence-collection facility
Lourdes, Cuba

In another part of the Russian complex at Lourdes, a soldier sat at his console, his mind puzzling over the strange situation he'd uncovered.

He didn't like bothering an officer unnecessarily, but surely this was important. He approached his superior nervously.

"Something strange has happened, Captain."

"Yes, Corporal?"

"In the last two minutes, all communication on all Cuban military bases has stopped. Almost like three days ago, except only on military bases this time."

The captain sat motionless. "All bases have been affected?"

"Yes, sir. I noticed Camagüey first and checked the others. Within minutes they were all silent. Could this be a tribute to El Presidente, do you think?"

"I think not, Corporal."

Turning, he reached for the phone.

11:30 A.M.
Corner of Avenido Rancho Boyeros and Avenido Paseo
Havana, Cuba

For the last minute, Moya had been staring intently at the horizon.

Rigid with anticipation, he watched as two tight formations of planes appeared and grew larger in the blue, heat-induced haze. What a glorious sight, he marveled, swallowing hard. His relief and awe were reflected on his wife's face as the eight planes shrieked overhead.

11:30 A.M.
The tower
La Plaza de la Revolución
Havana, Cuba

Gregorio Luzan watched the planes crest the horizon, thrilled by their power and beauty. Eleven-thirty exactly. He glanced behind him at the audio system. All was ready. In another three minutes Moya would be in position.

Luzan's breathing quickened. He rubbed his hands together nervously.

So far they had succeeded. So far. As the backwash from the planes shook the tower, the noise of their engines temporarily blotting out every other sound, Luzan prayed.

11:30 A.M.
La Plaza de la Revolución
Havana, Cuba

Valles, as well, watched the planes approach. The round, camouflaged bellies loomed overhead, seemingly only feet above him, before disappearing over the opposite side of La Plaza. A wild cheering ushered them out of sight.

Bombs, Valles thought. The planes were fully loaded. Gomez hadn't mentioned that, had he?

"A nice show," the President told Valles. "Most impressive. But where is the Russian President?"

"He called yesterday with his regrets. The Foreign Minister came instead."

So the Russian President was the one who'd initiated the call, the President thought, regarding Valles speculatively. Would the Russian have called personally if he hadn't felt it worth his while? He wasn't known for courting the unattainable.

The President of the United States turned in the direction the planes had disappeared.

Thank God he'd recognized the enemy in time!

11:31 A.M.
In the skies over Cuba

Six planes continued southwest from Havana, the two that had already broken away continuing their separate flight patterns. In less than a minute those six also separated, each flying toward its designated target.

11:31 A.M.
La Plaza de la Revolución
Havana, Cuba

Where was Gomez? Valles thought, scanning the crowd. He could see Peter Evans watching him. But Gomez. Where was Gomez? Valles wanted to know about the bombs.

He called for an aide, who, after a hurried consultation, rushed off the stage, only to be detained by one of Sacasa's soldiers. Caught up in the drama in the skies, no one paid any attention. Intent on wooing the American President, Valles, too, remained unaware.

11:32 A.M.
The tower
La Plaza de la Revolución
Havana, Cuba

Forty-five seconds after the last plane vanished in the west, Luzan signaled the soldier manning the turntable.

"Now. Full volume."

The soldier placed the needle onto the already spinning record.

The sound of the Cuban national anthem, "La Bayamesa," blared from the many loudspeakers that had been crucial to Fidel Castro's speeches. Luzan let out his breath in relief. At least the ancient sound system was working.

Cubans for more than a mile stood at attention. They loved their country. Communism might have robbed them of much that was good, but it had failed to conquer their native pride. This song spoke to that heritage.

On the platform, soldiers unfurled Cuban flags, the five broad blue and white bands bright against the sky, the crimson triangle a vibrant splash of color.

Ana and Enrique Aguirre tensed at the first notes of the anthem, checking one last time to see if their people were in place. By now the crowd was too great and too volatile for them to be sure. A few minutes more and they'd know; the whole world would know.

11:32 A.M.
Avenido Paseo
Havana, Cuba

By the time General Moya and Ines were within two blocks of La Plaza, the crowd of cheering Cubans surrounding them had increased manyfold. Despite the crowds, their progress was smooth, the people in front moving aside quickly as they approached, then closing ranks behind them.

Moya could see La Plaza.

His heart lurched, seemed about to burst. A free Cuba, was it finally to be realized? Had María and Alejandro succeeded? Had the American threat been neutralized?

He continued waving and smiling, but his mind was on events yet to unfold.

11:32 A.M.
La Plaza de la Revolución
Havana, Cuba

While the anthem played, Grant stood motionless, looking toward Havana Harbor. If the countermand order hadn't been received, missiles would be visible from American ships in just seconds. Unconsciously, he held his breath.

11:34 A.M.
Guantánamo, Cuba

Only the *Yorktown* remained to be contacted, Admiral DePaul was told by his men monitoring the progress of the President's countermand order.

DePaul stared at the radar screen in front of him, watching as the eight Cuban planes veered farther apart.

11:34 A.M.
USS Yorktown
International waters off the shore of Havana, Cuba

The planes had abandoned their prescribed flight plan!

"Battle stations," Admiral Lawrence ordered his men.

They moved into position, silent players in a deadly game.

Hell! One plane was turning to the north, invading their airspace.

"When you get it locked in, launch." Lawrence bit his underlip. Now!

"Fire!"

The missile streaked from the launcher. In less than a minute, the Cuban plane would be destroyed. Lawrence hoped his Commander in Chief knew what he was doing.

The phone rang on the bridge.

"Stop! Stop!" the XO screamed. "The order's been rescinded!"

Lawrence threw himself at the missile launch console, his finger seeking the self-destruct button.

11:35 A.M.
La Plaza de la Revolución
Havana, Cuba

A missile! Grant jumped from his chair. A ship, probably an American ship, had launched a missile!

As he watched, his face a motionless study in horror, the missile exploded, fragmenting in the sky. Pieces of flaming shrapnel plunged into the water of the bay far below.

Grant sank into his chair, wiping sweat from his eyes. Thank God! Thank God!

He stood again, scanning the sky. Would there be others?

11:35 A.M.
La Plaza de la Revolución
Havana, Cuba

As soon as the missile exploded, a phalanx of Secret Service agents swarmed around the President. One grabbed the President's belt and, with his other hand on the President's shoulder, hurried him off the platform. A dozen other agents clustered around, hiding him from view.

He and the First Lady were pushed into the limousine, and the door was slammed behind them.

The President leaned toward the agent in the front seat. "Hold on a minute," he said. "I realize a missile exploded, but where's the danger? Wasn't that one of our own missiles self-destructing? Check to see what's going on. I need to get back on that stage."

The agent began speaking into his walkie-talkie.

"And get Grant over here," the President added. Grant was the only one who seemed to understand what was happening.

11:35 A.M.
La Plaza de la Revolución
Havana, Cuba

The President was leaving! Valles stumbled backward in the rush of Secret Service agents. What was happening? What should he do? He scanned the crowd again for General Gomez.

Gomez! He was the only one who had heard the tapes, Valles realized, the blood draining from his face. Was Gomez the traitor?

he wondered, momentarily forgetting that Gomez hadn't been in the conference room at El Palacio.

He saw Gomez moving toward the American delegation. Valles looked around frantically for some way to stop him.

11:35 A.M.
USS Yorktown
International waters off the shore of Havana, Cuba

"All's clear, but remain on alert."

Admiral Lawrence blew out his breath in an exhausted sigh. Tremors still shook his hands. He'd almost lived the military man's worst nightmare: destroying a friendly target.

Now, if the Russians would only show some sense. He was frighteningly aware of their ships even now lurking at the mouth of the harbor.

11:38 A.M.
La Plaza de la Revolución
Havana, Cuba

Moya's jeeps stopped at the entrance to La Plaza. Several American soldiers stepped in front of them, scanning the vehicles.

"General Moya?" one asked.

"That is correct," Aguirre replied, stepping out of the second jeep and indicating the General. The soldiers in the jeeps moved their weapons into position.

Aguirre waited tensely while the Americans conferred.

"You may go ahead," they finally told him. They had been ordered by Admiral DePaul to allow General Moya access to the amphitheater unless notified otherwise by the American military or the Secret Service.

The first jeep pulled to the side, allowed the other to pass, then pulled in behind.

Moya had ignored the American soldiers and focused instead on the events of the next few minutes. As always, he felt confident. They had come so far. Already, they had surmounted seemingly insurmountable odds.

He looked at the excited faces around him, realizing the trust they felt in him. He smiled down at Ines.

The moment of victory had arrived. The moment of freedom.

11:35 A.M.
La Plaza de la Revolución
Havana, Cuba

"Senator Grant," a Secret Service agent said, "you're to report to the presidential limousine immediately."

Grant left his seat and hurried toward the holding area.

11:35 A.M.
Russian military base
San Antonio de los Baños, Cuba

A few miles to the north, Ruiz led three planes in low over the only Russian military base in Cuba. The planes separated immediately, each heading for its target. Their orders had been succinct: incapacitate the installation so that no retaliatory action could be taken against the new government of Cuba.

The two airstrips were the primary targets, but the communications building and ordnance storage area were targeted as well. Each plane carried four bombs. After destroying his primary target, each pilot was given discretion in dropping any other bombs, remembering that the goal was to incapacitate, not destroy.

Ruiz saw the runway in front of him, a Russian fighter plane sitting in position for takeoff. He could detect no unusual activity on the base. The Russians seemed totally unsuspecting.

Banking to the left, he closed in on the runway, his thumb on the red button.

Two seconds, one second. He pressed the button.

Nothing.

The air rocked with other explosions, but no explosion had sounded under his own plane. The bomb hadn't dropped. Or hadn't exploded.

No! he thought frantically, banking steeply to return.

He saw the other planes flying away, their targets destroyed.

The runway *had* to be taken out.

11:35 A.M.
Hart Senate Office Building
Washington, D.C.

Cynthia stood in Senator Grant's office, mesmerized by the scene on the television screen. Events were unfolding almost too quickly to comprehend.

The President had just been hustled off the stage, the cameras zeroing in on his flurried departure. Was he in danger? None of the commentators had any idea.

And what about the Senator? He'd been visible a minute before in a crowd shot but had been passed over too quickly for her to deduce anything from his face.

She stared at the screen, chewing on the inside of her lower lip, suddenly aware of a background sound growing louder behind the agitated commentary of the television reporter.

" 'Moya.' I think they're saying 'Moya,' " Cynthia whispered to herself.

11:35 A.M.
La Plaza de la Revolución
Havana, Cuba

Grant felt a hand on his arm.

"Senator Grant."

It was the Cuban who had given him the tapes. Gomez fell into step with him. The Secret Service agent, recognizing the head of the Cuban military, didn't intervene.

"You must tell your President," Gomez said, "that the bombs he hears in the distance are ours. We're destroying Lourdes and the Russian military base in Cuba. We're fighting to free our country from outside control. Your President is safe as is everyone here. Please—assure him of our sincerity and friendship."

Grant nodded toward Gomez. "I'll do what I can."

Reaching the cleared security area, Grant ran toward the limousine. An agent opened the door.

11:35 A.M.
Lourdes, Cuba

Sumorov stood motionless by his desk, a newly lit cigarette unnoticed in a plate overflowing with butts. A bomb had exploded nearby, gently shaking their building. A shower of dust drifted down from the ceiling.

Sumorov began dialing, clumsy in his haste. He must warn the security section. The phone went dead in his hand even as he realized the idiocy of his actions.

The building began a demonic shudder.

The stunned Russians in the room grabbed at the desks in front of them, their horror-filled eyes transfixed by the ceiling, as if seeking an answer there.

Another explosion shattered the air nearby, followed by the groans of collapsing buildings. Muted screams filtered through the walls, echoing in the smothered air of the room.

The building shook and swayed again and again, as explosion followed explosion, the whole lasting only a few demented seconds.

Suddenly the tension broke. Chairs banged against the floor as, screaming curses, every soldier bolted for the doors. Before they could move more than a few feet, they, too, were part of the rubble, a blackened crater the only sign that their room had ever existed. Sumorov, Sebanik, the state-of-the-art equipment—all had vanished.

11:36 A.M.
Russian military base
San Antonio de los Baños, Cuba

Ruiz zeroed in on the airstrip, noting exhaust coming from the Russian plane on the ground. Preparing to take off, was it? Frantic crews pushed other planes out of partially destroyed hangars.

The runway had to be destroyed! If he failed, who could guess the devastation which might ensue.

Bullets from Russian soldiers on the ground strafed his windshield, shards of glass grazing his forehead and arm. Blood dripped into his eyes. He ignored it, concentrating on the target.

Two seconds, one second.

He pressed the red button, pressing it again immediately.

Explode, damn you! Explode!

Silence.

"No!" he screamed impotently.

As he flew away, he could see the first Russian plane slowly beginning its run, several others ready to follow. Despairingly, he wiped the blood from his eyes with his hand, smearing his forehead.

A movement to his left caught his eye. Emil Guerrero had returned, Ruiz exulted, sharply banking his plane once more. Even if he couldn't drop a bomb, he could fly protection for his friend.

Once again the airfield came into view. This would be their last chance. He'd crash his plane on the runway, he decided, if he had no other choice. The bombs would surely explode then.

Intently, Ruiz watched Guerrero's plane in front of him, ignoring the bullets pummeling his own plane even as he sprayed shell fire randomly toward the ground.

Guerrero's plane had reached the airstrip.

Come on, Ruiz pleaded, his eyes aching.

Yes! Yes! A billow of dust outlined a huge crater in the center of the runway.

"Viva La Revolución!" Ruiz screamed.

Almost before the words were out of his mouth, his heart lurched in alarm. The Russian fighter plane had reached the end of the runway and was soaring into the air. The bomb had exploded one second too late.

Ruiz turned in pursuit. The Russian plane carried a full complement of bombs!

He hit his forward gun. Nothing. Jammed. The plane was a flying junk heap, Ruiz swore.

And there was Guerrero, dropping out of the clouds right in front of the Russian plane. The Russian had him in his sights, had to.

Ruiz's stomach knotted. If the Russian plane survived, La Causa would be lost.

Full throttle. His plane lurched beneath him.

The Russian bomber loomed ahead. The Russian, recognizing the danger, pulled back on the stick.

Too late, Ruiz thought, his last thought. *Viva La—*

The sky exploded. Pieces of Cuban and Russian planes splintered the clouds.

11:37 A.M.
Hart Senate Office Building
Washington, D.C.

In his office in the Hart building, Bonfire, or Edmund Miller as he was known to most of Washington, stared at the television. What imbecility had allowed this? he raged, anger corroding his belly.

He paced the office, his agitation evident in every jerky movement. His eyes never left the screen.

There was still time, he thought. If the United States decided to attack to protect the President, then success could still be pulled from disaster. The Russians would have their Caribbean base, IBTC would have a sphere of influence in this hemisphere and he would have two secure sources of income. Valles might even be interested in buying some of his inside information, especially when he had a direct line to the Oval Office.

Miller stopped pacing and threw himself into his chair. Even if Valles failed, Moya's Cuba wouldn't last long. His own posting on the National Security Council would place him in just the right position to undermine the new government. His expression became more speculative. That type of engineering might prove even more lucrative for him in the long run.

He reached for the phone.

11:37 A.M.
La Plaza de la Revolución
Havana, Cuba

Just when Valles thought the bombing was surely over, the earth shook once more. What was happening? Now that the President had left, did it matter?

He looked back at Basilov. The Russian ignored him.

11:37 A.M.
La Plaza de la Revolución
Havana, Cuba

Too long an interval had separated the last two faint explosions from the succeeding ones, Grant thought as he stepped into the limousine. Moya's plan had to have been to attack quickly and completely. Were the Russians counterattacking?

"Senator, what's going on?" the President asked.

"General Moya's people are destroying the Russian base on the island as well as Lourdes. The head of the Cuban military just assured me that no one here is in danger."

"And you believe him?"

"Everything Moya's people have said so far has proven true."

"What have you heard?" the President asked the agent in the front seat.

"We've been assured that you're in no danger. However, we have no means of verification. We can either take you directly to the airport or you can stay here. The ceremony is to continue. We strongly recommend you leave."

The President looked at Grant. "I'm going on that stage," he said grimly. "You stay here, Estelle. I don't want you in any danger."

The agent spoke into his transmitter.

"I hope to hell you know what you're talking about," the President said to Grant as he stepped out of the car. "This Moya had better be good."

11:38 A.M.
The tower
La Plaza de la Revolución
Havana, Cuba

The moment had arrived, Luzan thought, picking up the microphone. He looked once again toward the back of La Plaza.

Moya's jeep had entered; Luzan had been watching its progress intently.

He switched on the microphone.

Thirty more seconds.

11:39 A.M.
La Plaza de la Revolución
Havana, Cuba

The crackle of the loudspeakers excited the crowd. Expectantly they waited, turning with interest toward the cheering in back of them.

The members of La Causa heard the crackle as well. They, too, craned toward the back of the amphitheater.

"Moya! Moya! Moya!"

The cheering reached the amphitheater, became a chant.

Understanding overwhelmed Valles. His face turned ashen. Moya. Moya was behind this!

Could something yet be done? Seeing the rapt looks on the faces of the cheering crowd, looking at the back of the American President so blatantly placed toward him, turning to see the stony face of Basilov, Valles felt his last hope die. Blindly he reached backward for his chair, dropping onto it heavily.

It was over, he thought numbly. It was really over.

11:39 A.M.
La Plaza de la Revolución
Havana, Cuba

From his position near the statue of José Martí, Alejandro watched the unfolding drama. They had won. Cuba would be free.

He searched the tumultuous crowd for María, knowing she couldn't have come yet, wondering if she would. The shots at El Palacio echoed in his mind.

11:40 A.M.
La Plaza de la Revolución
Havana, Cuba

Luzan's resonant voice rang through the amphitheater and out through the streets.

"*Señoras y señores*, citizens of a free Cuba . . ."

A hush fell on the crowd. The moment of suspense lengthened.

". . . the President of Cuba . . ."

Television cameras filmed inexorably, catching the expectant looks of the people, the stoic calm of the Russian Foreign Minister, the brittle smile of César Valles, the thoughtful gaze of the American President.

". . . José Moya, the choice of the Cuban people."

In La Plaza, a silent second passed, a stunned second. Then pandemonium erupted. The supporters of Moya led the ecstatic ovation. Signs and banners were pulled from under shirts, the name *Moya* and the word *Freedom* emblazoned on each. Some were almost professional, but most were crude, wrinkled but easily readable. The signs were raised proudly, those bringing them helped by those around.

"Moya! Moya! Moya!" The chant increased, became an almost tangible presence.

Television cameras zoomed in on it all. Ana Aguirre was singled out, her face glowing, her dark hair billowing around her as she cheered and waved her bright banner.

Slowly the two jeeps inched their way toward the front of the amphitheater. Excited Cubans thumped the sides of Moya's jeep, their benedictions urging it forward.

The farther José Moya came, the greater the ovation, until all of Havana seemed to have joined in the rejoicing.

An honor guard led by Colonel Sacasa came to attention as the jeep halted and General and Mrs. Moya stepped out. Flags of Cuba were raised high, forming a passageway for them onto the stage.

As they reached the steps, the General noticed a lone man by the side of the platform. Grant smiled at him. Moya paused, took Ines's hand and walked to him.

"My friend," he said, Grant's hand clasped in both of his. His eyes glistened as he searched for words. "My country owes you much. We can never repay you, but I promise that we'll work to justify your faith in us."

"Cuba is free," Grant said. "Nothing else is necessary."

"Yes, Cuba is free."

With a last look, Moya turned and, with Ines, walked back toward the stage. Up the steps, Cuban flags held high over them, José and Ines Moya walked proudly, humbly. The music of "La Bayamesa" once again swelled through the air, mingling with the joyous ovation of the sea of Cubans filling Havana.

The new President and First Lady of Cuba crossed the stage to the podium.

11:44 A.M.
La Plaza de la Revolución
Havana, Cuba

The American President watched their progress thoughtfully. Moya. Who was this Moya, he wondered, the freedom-loving patriot Bob

Grant contended, the terrorist-supported, Russian-aligned puppet so many claimed or someone somewhere between?

Whoever he was, he would obviously be the new leader of Cuba. The President joined the applause.

He missed seeing Colonel Sacasa's soldiers walk onto the stage and escort Valles away. However, the cameras captured it all. Commentators sputtered their opinions, nonplussed by events. Valles was the perfect leader, they reiterated. Why was he being removed? Moya was a Russian puppet, wasn't he? Why did the President seem to be endorsing him?

From his seat in the first row facing the stage, Peter Evans watched in disbelief as Valles was led away. This couldn't be happening! he thought. Not Valles! Valles was exactly the leader Cuba needed.

He wouldn't allow such injustice to go unreported! He'd fight for Valles, make sure the world knew the infamy of this Moya against a man of Valles's humanity. When he was finished with him, Moya's credibility would be destroyed.

And Grant. What had Grant been doing with the President? No good, obviously. Grant would pay as well.

11:45 A.M.
Hong Kong

"Valles has been defeated and Moya proclaimed President."

"Can Moya be bought?"

"We will try, but we'll have to approach him carefully. He's a patriot."

"We can't wait. Increase our work in Mexico. Their economy continues to falter. They're ripe for manipulation."

"Key on Panama as well. The canal is important."

"I want Cuba!"

"You needn't fear—Cuba will soon be ours."

"The world will be ours."

"Allah be praised!"

11:45 A.M.
La Plaza de la Revolución
Havana, Cuba

"The President of Cuba, José Moya," Luzan announced over the loudspeaker once again, his voice choked with emotion.

Grant watched the people on the stage with interest, these people who had had as much at stake as he. He could see the resignation in Basilov's face, feel sympathy with his predicament. Basilov's masters would not deal kindly with failure, especially failure of this magnitude. He could visualize the panic in Moscow as they realized they'd borrowed heavily from a source that would be sure to exact its payment, a payment they couldn't meet now that they had lost a major source of revenue. Tomorrow, Grant would further explain that interesting alliance to the President. Whether he would listen . . .

For now, the President was obviously plotting his own version of events, one that would reflect well on himself. So be it, Grant thought. The President could say what he wished now that the threat against the United States had been defused.

And Moya. Grant looked at him with admiration, feeling a welling of compassion for his friend. The General had aged appreciably since their only meeting, and not just from the passing of years or the abuses of prison life. He understood, Grant realized, the high price of this moment. He might not yet realize the names of the men and women who had died, who had made that final sacrifice, but he would know that toll had been exacted. Freedom was not without cost. Those patriots who had willingly paid the ultimate price might never enjoy the fruits of their sacrifice, but their legacy would live, gaining expression from the daily joys that could only find voice in the sanctuary of freedom.

Smiling gravely, José Moya stood before his people. This day had brought victory. He rejoiced in that victory. But today was merely a beginning, a shining moment before the real work could begin. So much must be done for his country; so many changes must be made, difficult ones and grindingly slow.

Moya surveyed the multitude before him. These people had suffered so much, deserved so much, expected so little.

Raising his hands more in thanksgiving than triumph, President José Moya addressed the people, his people.

It was over.

It was truly over.

And it had just begun.